DAWN TREADER PRESS

This book is a work of fiction. Names, characters, places, and incidents either are products of the author's imagination or are used fictiously. Any resemblance to actual locales, events or persons living or dead is entirely coincidental.

TITLES BY
Joshua Graham

Coming May 1, 2012
Darkroom
Howard Books/Simon & Schuster

Award Winning Titles

Beyond Justice

Suspense Magazine Best of 2010
Barnes & Noble #1 bestseller
Amazon Kindle bestseller
2008 Amazon Breakout Novel Award Competition Semi-Finalist

The Door's Open

2010 Authonomy Christmas Story Competition

The Accidental Series

The Accidental Existentialist
The Accidental Exorcist
The Accidental Acquittal (Death and Taxes)
The Accidental Healer
The Accidental Hero
The Accidental Rebel
The Accidental Poltergeist

Historical and Fantasy

Once We Were Kings (Ian Alexander)
Four Gifts for Aria
Legend of the Tiger's Throne (Ian Alexander)

Praise for
BEYOND JUSTICE

"...A riveting legal thriller.... breaking new ground with a vengeance... demonically entertaining and surprisingly inspiring."
~PUBLISHERS WEEKLY

"...hits the ground running...handled by a deft hand."
~Adrian Phoenix, IN THE BLOOD (Pocket Books)

"This tense, fast-paced story of outrageous injustice, insidious evil, and looming disaster has everything the savvy reader should expect, and more. [Graham] belongs to a new, emerging wave of writers who dare to color outside conventional lines. And he does so with style!"
~Glen Scorgie, THE JOURNEY BACK TO EDEN (Zondervan)

"...a genuine page-turner with a twist that makes it stand out from most thrillers and legal dramas."
"...What sets this thriller apart is the deft handling of religion."
"...When Graham turns to courtroom drama, the writing is tense; when he's inside Sam's mind, the emotions are wringing."
~Author Magazine

"This book was so much more than a mystery novel; it was an exercise in faith, understanding, joy and mercy in their purest forms."
"...twists, turns and surprises to be found here."
"...filled with so much in the way of emotion."

"...Take the time to read this book. You will not be disappointed."
~Suspense Magazine

...A MASTERFUL LEGAL THRILLER
...A book worthy of a feature length Hollywood movie...
...Graham has intricately woven together these elements of cyberspace and our criminal justice system in a way that keeps avid mystery readers spellbound.
...Graham's BEYOND JUSTICE is the best mystery novel that I have ever read.
...a plot worthy of Hollywood, told by a fantastic author with a deft touch and feel for intrigue!
...a fitting climax in true John Grisham form.
...a powerful testament to faith and religion, woven into a masterful murder mystery.
~East County Magazine

"This is not a tame Christian book, it's full of heart wrenching scenes that will make you shudder.
There's one surprise after another and it's a "can't put down" thriller...the ending was brilliant!
"This is Joshua Graham's first book and it is a doozy!!
I can't wait to read more from this very talented author."
~**ReadingAtTheBeach.com**

"...a riveting legal thriller that has heart and a fabulous message."
"...really intense suspense!"
" I was...balled up with emotions and intense suspense from start to finish."
"...a great legal thriller..."

"... great drama and romance as well.
"...tied together with a fabulous message of love and redemption."

~**A Life in Review**
"...Superbly done!"
"...a legal suspense thriller beyond any other."
"...Filled with page turning, edge of your seat twists."
"...most definitely a 5 star novel by an incredible author"
"... this suspense novel will pick you up in one place, carry you through thrilling turns and emotional rides, and will set you down at an unexpected place, all the while leaving you with a powerful message that will set your mind to thinking. About life. About loss. About justice. About everything."
...Joshua Graham has become an author who I will be collecting books by for a long time to come and has made me anxious for his next book!
~**Reviews by Molly D. Edwards**

Connect with Joshua Graham at:

http://www.joshua-graham.com
http://www.facebook/J0shuaGraham
http://www.twitter/J0shuaGraham

BEYOND JUSTICE

Joshua Graham

PART I

The descent into Hell is not always vertical.

Bishop Frank Morgan

CHAPTER ONE

The question most people ask when they first meet me is: How does an attorney from a reputable law firm in La Jolla end up on death row? When they hear my story, it becomes clear that the greater question is not how, but why.

I have found it difficult at times to forgive myself for what happened. But a significant part of the answer involves forgiveness, something I never truly understood until I could see in hindsight.

Orpheus went through hell and back to rescue his wife Eurydice from death in the underworld. Through his music, he moved the hearts of Hades and Persephone and they agreed to allow Eurydice to return with him to Earth on one condition: He must walk before her and not look back until they reached the upper world. On seeing the Sun, Orpheus turned to share his delight with Eurydice, and she disappeared. He had broken his promise and she was gone forever. This failure and guilt was a hell far worse than the original.

My own personal hell began one night almost four years ago. Like images carved into flesh, the memories of that night would forever be etched into my mind. The work day had been tense enough—my position at the firm was in jeopardy because of the inexplicable appearance of lewd internet images in my folder on the main file server.

Later that night, as I scrambled to get out the door on time for a critical meeting with a high profile client, my son Aaron began throwing a screaming fit. Hell hath no fury like a boy who has lost his Thomas Train toy. In my own frenzied state, I lost my temper with him. Amazing how much guilt a four-year-old can pile on you with puppy-dog eyes while clinging to his mother's legs. His sister Bethie, in all her seventh grade sagacity, proclaimed that I had issues, then marched up to her room, slammed the door and took out her frustration with me by tearing through a Paganini Caprice on her violin. All this apocalypse just minutes before leaving for my meeting, which was to be held over a posh dinner at George's At The Cove, which I would consequently have no stomach for.

I couldn't wait to get home. The clock's amber LED read 11:28 when I pulled my Lexus into the cul-de-sac. Pale beams from a pregnant moon cut through the palm trees that lined our street. The October breeze rushed into the open window and through my hair, a cool comfort after a miserable evening.

If I was lucky, Jenn would be up and at the computer, working on her latest novel. She'd shooed me out the door lest I ran late for the meeting, before I could make any more of a domestic mess for her to clean up.

The garage door came down. I walked over to the security system control box and found it unarmed. On more than one occasion, I had asked Jenn to arm it whenever I was out. She agreed, but complained that the instructions were too complicated. It came with a pretty lame manual, I had to admit.

The system beeped as I entered the house, greeted by the sweet scent of Lilac—her favorite candles for those special occasions. So much more than I deserved, but that was my Jenn. Never judging, never condemning, she understood how much stress I'd been under and always prescribed the best remedy for such situations.

From the foot of the stairs I saw dimmed light leaking out of the bedroom. It wasn't even date night, but I had a pretty good idea what she was thinking. So before going up, I stopped by the kitchen, filled a pair of glasses with Merlot and set out a little box of chocolates on a breakfast tray—my secret weapon.

As I climbed the stairs I smiled. The closer I got, the more I could smell the fragrant candles. From the crack in the door classical music flowed out: *Pie Jesu* from Faure's *Requiem.* Must've been writing a love scene. She always used my classical CDs to set her in the right mood.

A beam of amber light reached through the crack in the doorway into the hallway. The alarm system beeped. She must have shut a window. It had just started to rain and Jenn hated when the curtains got wet.

Kathleen Battle's angelic voice soared.

Pie Jesu Domine,
Dona eis requiem,
Requiem sempiternam.

Jenn didn't know a word of Latin. She just liked the pretty tunes.

I nudged the door open with my foot.

"Honey?" Caught a glimpse of a silky leg on the bed. Oh, yes. I pushed the door open.

Shock ignited every nerve ending in my body like napalm. The tray fell from my hands. Crashed to the ground. Glasses shattered and the red wine bled darkly onto the carpet.

Jenn lay partially naked, face-down, the sheets around her soaked crimson. Stab wounds scored her entire body. Blood. Blood everywhere!

"Jenn!"

I ran to her, turned her over.

She gasped, trying to speak. Coughed. Red spittle dripped from the corner of her mouth. "The kids..."

I took her into my arms. But her eyes begged me to go check on them.

"You hang on, honey. With all you've got, hang on!" I reached for my cell phone but it fell out of my belt clip and bounced under the bed.

On my knees now, I groped wildly until I found the cell phone. Dialed 9-1-1. Barely remembered what I said, but they were sending someone right away.

Jenn groaned. Her breaths grew shorter and shorter.

"Bethie... Aaron."

Her eyes rolled back.

"I'm going. Hang on, baby. Please! You gotta hang on!" I started for the door. Felt her hand squeeze mine twice: Love-you.

No.

Tears streamed down my face. As I began to pull away, she gripped my hand urgently. For that split second, I knew. This was the end. I stumbled back to her. Gathered her ragdoll body into my arms.

"Jenn, oh God, Jenn. Please don't!"

"Whatever it takes," she said. Again, she squeezed my hand twice. "Mercy, not...sacrifice." One last gasp. She sighed and then fell limp in my arms, her eyes still open.

Holding her tight to my chest, I let out an anguished cry.

All time stopped. Who would do this? Why? Her blood stained my shirt. Her dying words resonated in my mind. Then I remembered. *The kids.* I bolted up and ran straight to Bethie's room.

Bethie's door was ajar. If my horror hadn't been complete, it was now. I found her exactly like Jenn—face down, blood and gashes covering her body.

Though I tried to cry out, nothing escaped the vice-grip on my throat. When I turned her over, I felt her arm. Still warm, but only slightly. Her eyes were shut, her face wet with blood.

"Bethie! Oh, sweetie, no!" I whispered, as I wrapped the blanket around her.

I kissed her head. Held her hand. Rocked her back and forth. "Come on, baby girl. Help's on its way, you hold on," I said, voice and hands trembling. She lay there unconscious but breathing.

Aaron.

Gently, I lay Bethie back down then got up and flew across the hall. To Aaron's door. His night light was still on and I saw his outline in the bed.

Oh God, please.

I flipped the switch.

Nothing.

I dashed over to the lamp on his nightstand, nearly slipping on one of his Thomas Train toys on the carpet. Broken glass crackled under my shoes.

I switched on the lamp on his nightstand. When I looked down to his bed, my legs nearly gave out. Aaron was still under his covers, but blood drenched his pillow. His aluminum baseball bat lay on the floor, dented and bloodied.

Dropping to my knees, I called his name. Over and over, I called, but he didn't stir. This can't be happening. It's got to be a nightmare. I put my face down into Aaron's blue Thomas Train blanket and gently rested my ear on his chest.

I felt movement under the blanket. Breathing. But slowly—irregular and shallow.

Don't move his body. Dammit, where are the paramedics?

I heard something from Bethie's room and dashed out the door. Stopping in the middle of the hallway, I clutched the handrail over the stairs. Thought I heard Aaron crying now. Or maybe it was the wind.

My eyes darted from one side of the hallway to the other. Which room?

Faure's Requiem continued to play, now the *In Paradisum* movement.

Aeternam habeas requiem.

Something out in front of the house caught my attention. The police, the paramedics! Propelled by adrenaline, I crashed through the front door and ran out into the middle of my lawn which was slick with rain. I slipped and fell on my side.

Nobody. Where were they!

Like a madman, I began screaming at the top of my lungs. My words echoed emptily into the night.

"Help! Somebody, please!"

A dog started barking.

"Please, ANYBODY! HELP!"

Lights flickered on in the surrounding houses.

Eyes peeked through miniblinds.

No one came out.

I don't know if I was intelligible at this point. I was just screaming, collapsed onto the ground, on my hands and knees getting drenched in the oily rain.

Just as the crimson beacons of an ambulance flashed around the corner, I buried my face into the grass. All sound, light, and consciousness imploded into my mind as if it were a black hole.

CHAPTER TWO

It's never been clear to me when my neighbor, Pastor Dave Pendelton scraped me off the lawn and brought me back into my house. Outside, neighbors all gawking through the blinds in their windows, not one of them had come out.

Except Dave, of all people. Pastor Dave of City on a Hill, Jenn's church. He seemed nice enough, but I never completely trusted him. This was due in no small part to my absolute distaste for organized religion. Ironically, Jenn had become born again soon after we got married and began attending not only Sunday services at Dave's church, but their weekly small group Bible study as well.

I sat on my sofa in a chilled stupor, a blanket draped over my shoulders while paramedics worked feverishly around both of my children upstairs. According to Dave, they had arrived just as he came out to get me. I was so shell-shocked that I didn't recall their arrival.

Another team had gone to the master bedroom.

"Jenn?" I bolted up. "Jenn!" They carried her down in a gurney, a white sheet over her face. The anguish within couldn't crack through the frozen wall of shock around my mind.

Next came my kids, but they were not covered. The paramedics worked on them as they brought them down and wheeled them to the ambulance. "Bethie! Aaron!" I shouted and tried to run over. Dave held me back.

"Let them, Sam."

I was trembling, shaking my head, as they raced off. Jenn couldn't be gone. It couldn't be my kids in that ambulance. It was like watching a movie. Flashing lights, sirens.

"Let's go." Dave grabbed my arm and rushed me into his car. We chased the ambulances, leaving behind a pair of squad cars, their red and blues groping out into the rain like a lighthouse in a hurricane.

My home had become a crime scene.

As soon as we arrived at Children's Hospital's Trauma Care Center, a medical team rushed Bethie into one room and Aaron into another. Frozen, I stood, chest rising and falling, eyes darting between the two rooms.

"Bethany's a lot worse," Dave said.

I nodded and went for the door to Trauma One. He caught me and turned me around to the correct room. Dave went into Aaron's room just as I entered Bethie's.

The next thirty minutes were torturous. About a dozen doctors and nurses crowded around Bethie, two of them squeezing a plastic bag to assist with her breathing. Instruments rattled in the crash cart as the trauma surgeons surrounded her. IVs webbed around her, into her arms.

Speaking in rapid succession, overlapping each others' words, yet somehow maintaining some form of intelligible communication, the team's dialogue all meshed together.

"Epi's in."

"She's bradying down."

"Atropine in."

"We're losing her!"

They began CPR. Then the whine and snap of defibrillator shocks. Jolted me as well. One of the nurses announced that they'd gotten a pulse back, but a very weak one. Bethie just had to pull through.

Doctor Yang, one of the doctors not completely engrossed in the code, came over, pulled down her face mask. "She's lost a lot of blood. We're doing everything we can, but you should prepare yourself."

"For what?"

"Is there anyone you'd like to call?"

I wanted to scream that her mother had been murdered, less than half an hour ago. I could not accept the fact that my little girl was within moments of death..."Please, you have to save her!"

Doctor Yang nodded and returned to the team. Seconds later an alarm from the EKG blared again. Bethie's pulse was gone.

The lead doctor called out something about joules. "Clear!"

Again, with the defibrillator. Bethie's torso arched up and fell. The EKG blipped, but the line remained flat, the tone static. The lead doctor was now performing chest compressions with both hands. Gently! I wanted to cry out. But I knew they had to do this to help her. This went on for a while, but it was clear that her pulse continued only because of the doctor's efforts.

"Bethie?" I managed to whisper. It was starting to hit me. Not even an hour after Jenn's death, I was about to lose my daughter.

"Mr. Hudson," Doctor Yang said as she approached. "Do you want to be with her now?"

Tears stung my eyes like acid. Gradually, the cacophony of voices died down. I could now discern something that I had vaguely heard earlier through all the commotion—one of the doctors in the background announcing each elapsed minute since Bethie's heart had stopped.

"Thirty-seven minutes since arrest." The chest compressions continued.

"Mister Hudson?" Doctor Yang said, again, her tone sympathetic, but a bit more urgent. Less and less of the team were looking at Bethie now. They kept eyeing the clock.

The lead doctor had been doing chest compressions for some time now. He looked to his team. "Shall we?"

"He just lost his wife," one of the nurses replied. "Can we try a little longer?"

He nodded and continued the compressions. After a while, they tried the defibrillator again. No response. A solid green line slithered across the screen. The nurses looked up at the other doctor. He stood still for a second, glanced at the wall-clock and shook his head. "Time of death..."

"We did all we could, Mr. Hudson," Doctor Yang said. "I'm so sorry."

"NO! Save her, dammit!" I rushed for the table on which Bethie lay as still as silence. "Don't let her go!" I reached for the defibrillator paddles. A large orderly grabbed and pulled me away. I shouted at the top my lungs. He didn't release me until I stopped thrashing. The nurses stepped back.

When I calmed myself, the lead doctor approached me.

"We did everything possible, but her injuries were too severe. I'm sorry."

I couldn't speak. First Jenn, now Bethie. Anger ebbed, giving way to despair. I walked over to my little girl.

"Sweetie..." I held her lifeless hand, brushed the hair out of her face and kissed her forehead. "I'm sorry. Daddy's so sorry." Before I knew it, I was curled up on the floor and sobbing, still reaching up and holding her hand. The orderly tried to help me to my feet but I couldn't do it. Eventually, they managed to get me up and pour me into a chair.

"Sir, do you need a moment?"

I nodded.

They drew a curtain and left me alone with my daughter. That's when I lost it. I don't think I'd ever cried so hard, or pounded my fist so many times into a wall, or screamed so loud in my entire life.

Aside from the wounds and blood, Bethie looked like she could have been sleeping. How could she be gone? How could Jenn? I felt disembodied.

The activity outside the trauma room increased. Walkie-talkies, intercom pages, hurried footsteps, gurneys rolling.

The doctor emerged from the curtain.

"I'm sorry, but there's someone outside you need to speak to." Outside the room, an officer from the Sherriff's department tipped his hat.

"My condolences on your loss, sir. But I need to ask you a few—"

"This isn't the best time."

Dave Pendelton arrived.

I gripped his sleeve. "Aaron?"

"He's still in surgery. Trauma One."

Behind him was one of the TCC doctors.

"Is he going to make it?" I asked.

"Too soon to say. He's suffered severe trauma to the head and internal organs."

"Can I see him?"

"Not yet."

I spent the next hour answering the deputy's incessant questions.

What was my name, date of birth, social security number, place of employment, phone numbers? He asked for identification.

"Do we really have to do this now!" I huffed, fumbling with my wallet.

Dave helped take it from my shaking hands and gave the deputy my driver's license and social security card.

The officer asked for the same type of information for Jenn, Bethany and Aaron—the victims. My mouth became bitter. Dryness impeded my words. The deputy was sympathetic and seemed genuinely sorry to put me through this. I couldn't concentrate.

Dr. Salzedo, the trauma surgeon arrived.

"How is he?" I asked.

"We've stabilized him. He's been moved to the Pediatric ICU."

I exhaled in relief.

"PICU's on the third floor."

I got up immediately and turned to Deputy Schaeffer. "If you'll excuse me." If there was anything to hold onto amidst the devastation, it was the hope that Aaron had survived.

I wasn't prepared for what I saw when I got to his room.

For some delusional reason, I had expected to find my son sitting up, with a few bandages and other dressings, but smiling at me. He would call out, "Daddy!" and we'd embrace, holding on to each other as the last surviving remnants of our family. When I entered, however, I found him unconscious. Tubes of all sorts invaded his body. A ventilator assisted his breathing and all I could hear was hissing, buzzing and beeping medical equipment.

"The next twenty-four hours are crucial," Dr. Salzedo said. "We'll know better with time."

Aaron was in a coma with injuries to his head, spine, and internal organs. Internal hemorrhaging had been controlled, for now. But things could get better or much worse, unexpectedly. Everything was still iffy.

I stood by his bed and held his hand. Warm. Thank god. He would have appeared peaceful and simply asleep, but for all the equipment he was hooked up to. It seemed grotesquely uncomfortable.

Dave stood over Aaron, laid his hand on his bandaged head and mouthed a silent prayer. I didn't like him imposing his religion, even if Aaron had attended his church with Jenn and Bethie since his birth. But I was too exhausted and beyond objecting.

"You're welcome to stay with Aaron as long as you wish," said Dr. Salzedo. "But there's nothing to be done now but wait and monitor his progress. You've been through hell and really should get some rest. We'll call you if anything changes."

"No, I'm staying."

"Sam," Dave said, his hand on my shoulder. "Maybe you should—"

"I said, I'm staying."

He leaned over and said something to the doctor, who nodded in turn.

"I'll stay too, then," Dave said. "We can take shifts."

"Thanks, really. But..." I couldn't think of a good enough excuse besides the fact that he was starting to creep me out with all his kindness. "If you don't mind, I'd like to be alone with my boy."

"I understand." He pulled a business card from his pocket and handed it to me. "If you need a ride home, give me a call."

I thanked him again and he left. The Sheriff's office was good enough to post an officer outside the room. "You hang tough, buddy," I whispered into Aaron's ear and kissed him. "When you wake up, I'll take you to McDonald's for a happy meal." My voice broke. I had to believe he would get better. It was the only shred of hope left.

CHAPTER THREE

The yellow tape had been removed. A squad car idled on the sidewalk in front of my house as the neighborhood awoke to a new day. At the wheel sat Chris, the young partner of Lieutenant Jim O'Brien. Chris glanced my way then turned away. I couldn't tell if it was intentional, his sunglasses obscured any hint. O'Brien was talking to one of the investigators at my door. Good to see a familiar face. When he saw me get out of the taxi, he came over and removed his hat.

O'Brien and I first met under tense circumstances—with his rifle pointed into my chest. It was during a shooting and hostage crisis at Coyote Creek Middle School, where Bethie attended. Along with all the other parents, I stood for hours in the parking lot not knowing what was happening inside.

I grew tired of waiting around not getting any answers. So I marched right up to the police line. My cell phone started buzzing and I reached for it. He thought I was reaching for a weapon and he drew his rifle. Pissed and defiant, I pressed my chest right into the barrel. He wasn't going to shoot me. The other parents might have, though. On that, the longest afternoon of my life, two girls were killed. One of the stray bullets grazed Bethie's arm.

Afterwards, Jim and Chris came over to question Bethie. Chris, who couldn't have been more than twenty-five years old, seemed not only to enjoy Bethie's starry-eyed attention, he almost encouraged it. I was never completely comfortable around him since.

As I walked up the very lawn, on which I'd slipped last night, Jim removed his hat. "My God, Sam. I'm so sorry about Jenn. And Bethie? Dammit. You dodge a bullet, only to—" he stopped himself and scowled. "How's Aaron?"

"He's hanging on."

"You should get some rest."

"I spent the night at Children's." From the corner of my eye, I noticed his partner looking our way. I turned my head and again he averted his gaze. "What's with Chris?"

Jim drew a deep breath. "Dunno. He's been in a mood since he found out. He really liked your family. 'Specially the kids." Suddenly, I felt the need for Zantac. Jim pulled his hat from under his arm, placed it on his head and nodded. "Don't hesitate."

"Thanks."

"Oh, by the way," he stopped and handed me my cell phone. "Found this under your bed. It's already been dusted and checked, so I guess you can have it back." With a strong pat on the back, he said good-bye and got in the car with his partner, who for some reason hadn't looked my way once since I arrived.

Just then, a news van pulled into the cul-de-sac.

"Oh jeez, not again." My rifle-in-the-chest standoff had been captured by a photographer and the picture appeared in the North County Times. Made me look like freakin' Tank Man of Tiananmen Square. One thing led to another and the next thing I know, I'm doing a taping in my house for Channel Seven news. A couple of days later, Brent Stringer, best-selling writer and op-ed writer for the *Union Tribune* did an interview feature. The media, in all its wisdom, spun me up as San Diego's Superdad. The subsequent fame was about as welcome as a tax auditor in mid-April. I'd just gotten out of the limelight.

O'Brien stepped out again and intercepted the reporters and paparazzi.

"Thanks, Jim," I said silently. A young woman stood in my open door. I hadn't noticed her until I padded halfway across the lawn. She wore black slacks, a black blazer and black sunglasses. I figured it was her black BMW parked in my driveway. Had to wonder what her favorite color was. Silently counting the steps to the second floor, she dabbed the air with her index finger repeatedly.

I cleared my throat, extended my hand.

"Mister Hudson?" Her hand felt like a dead fish. "I'm detective Pearson, County Sheriff's Department. Do you have any form of identification?"

"Do *you*?" I reached for my wallet.

"Driver's license, social?" Pearson flashed her badge quickly then examined my driver's license. She looked back up at me, scrutinizing my face. "Hmm." She handed it back. "Let's go over a few questions, shall we?"

"Would you like to come inside?"

"No." She proceeded to ask the same questions the deputy had asked last night at Children's.

"I've already answered these questions."

She looked up from the PDA. "It's routine. You're probably thinking clearer after resting."

"Doubt it."

Again, Pearson tapped her PDA with a thin, black stylus. She fired off the rest of her questions with chilling detachment. "What time did you come home?"

"About eleven o'clock." A thousand cockroaches skittered up my back as she studied my face. Thankfully, she returned to her PDA.

"What room did you go into first?"

"My daughter's"

"When did you first realize something was wrong?"

"No wait. I first went into the master bedroom, where I found Jenn." My knees grew weak. I braced myself against the door frame.

"So, you first went into your own bedroom, not your daughter's."

"That's right. I was thinking of which child's room—"

"Once again, Mister Hudson," she said, enunciating. "When did you first realize something was wrong?"

"I didn't think anything was wrong until I found Jenn, stabbed and bleeding to death."

"Let's not jump to conclusions. Exact cause of death has not yet been officially determined."

"Excuse me?"

"Why don't you leave that to the coroner and stick with the facts."

"Fine."

"Are you aware that we came here to speak with you last night about the pornographic materials found on your work computer?"

Taken aback, I gasped. "No, but that stuff wasn't mine. What the hell's that got to do with anything?"

"Where were you around 7:30 PM last night?"

"On my way to a client meeting in La Jolla. Is that when you came?"

"Can anyone vouch for your whereabouts around 11:00 last night?"

"I was on the 52 freeway, driving home. Alone. Oh my god, did you say anything to my wife about the porn?"

"No, sir."

"It wasn't mine!"

"As I said, we didn't mention it. That's still under investigation." More tapping. "Mister Hudson, relax. I'm sure you'll want to do everything to help us move this investigation along. Right?"

"Of course."

"Then you won't mind going to the crime lab to provide samples."

"Samples?" The hair on the back of my neck became thistles.

"DNA swabs, blood, fingerprints."

"What for? Am I a suspect?"

Her dark brown eyes glazed. "We routinely take samples to exclude you as a potential suspect. The longer you wait, the colder the trail gets. Refuse, and you'll raise the question as to why, and then—"

"Of course I'll do it. It's just that...it feels like you're treating me as a suspect."

"Unless you've got something to hide—"

"What is your problem?"

She scribbled something on a business card and handed it to me. "County Sheriff Crime Lab. That's the case number. You don't need an appointment. If I were you, I'd get to it this morning before eleven, or things might start to appear unfavorable."

"Are you threatening me?"

"I would never do that, sir."

"Yeah, well..." Before I could say another word, she was halfway to her BMW. She got in, lifted her wrist, tapped on her watch, then pointed at me.

My head spun as her Beamer roared out of the cul-de-sac, leaving me standing in the doorway. Dread coursed through my veins like Freon.

CHAPTER FOUR

When I arrived at the San Diego County Sheriff Crime Lab I presented the case number, verified my identity and for the next half hour had various samples of my bodily essence collected. Cotton swabs in my mouth, strands of hair from various parts of my body, some more private than others, blood, and saliva.

Took less than an hour, but it was something I wouldn't soon forget. I left the lab with a sense of relief, glad that I had finally done something to move the investigation forward.

Aaron was still in the Pediatric ICU when I returned to see him. Dr. Conway was a young man, probably a new resident on rotations. Looked like he'd done a few too many. Dark rings under his eyes betrayed fatigue. He held a clipboard under his arm as he spoke. "It's a miracle that your son survived."

I failed to see anything miraculous about a four year old boy, comatose, with oxygen lines in his nose, IV drips and other wires and tubes enshrouding his tiny frame. "When will he wake up?"

The Doctor rubbed his neck, failed to suppress a yawn and consulted his clipboard.

"Well?"

"There's thoracic damage as well as cervical spinal damage which is causing neurological problems with breathing and circulation."

"Spinal? Is he going to be paralyzed?"

A cleaning lady entered with a broom and started spraying disinfectant in the back of the room. "Not now," Doctor Conway told her and sent her off. Industrial Lysol. The smell made me queasy.

"I hate to put it this way," Conway said, "but we can't be certain he will even survive another day. The fact that he's alive is astounding, given the extent of his injuries. But even if he comes out of the coma, there are quality of life concerns."

I pulled up a chair and sat by my son. His breathing was irregular and shallow, his hand warm but stiff. It twitched every now and then.

The image of Aaron, lying in a casket smaller than should ever exist arrested my breath. But the thought of him growing up as a paraplegic, sentenced to life in a wheelchair, unable to run and jump and play—that made my heart sink. He was always such a happy boy, not a care in the world. To rob him of life this way was almost as bad as taking it away from him completely.

"The initial hemorrhaging seems to have subsided," Conway continued, "But there's swelling now, putting pressure on the brain. We can't tell just yet the extent of the damage, or how much more might be caused if the swelling continues."

"What are his chances?" I would have given anything to trade places with him.

"If Aaron was an adult, I'd say close to none. But children are amazingly resilient because their bodies are still growing and developing."

"Please. What are his chances?"

"If there are some unforeseen complications, such as hemorrhaging or severe cerebral edema, he could suddenly take a fatal turn. On the other hand, I'm surprised he's survived at all, so who knows? We'll just have to wait and see."

"Basically, you don't know."

"I wish I could tell you more."

Aaron's chest rose suddenly, as if he was finally able to take in a full breath. I waited for him to open his eyes. *Come on, kiddo, come on.* I squeezed his hand twice, gently—*love-you.* But alas, no change. "What's the plan, any kind of treatment?"

"The plan for now is to keep the swelling down, keep draining fluids, prevent infection, and make it to tomorrow."

"Can he hear me?"

"I wouldn't talk to him much right now, don't want to stimulate him until the pressure comes down."

"What *can* I do, then?"

The doctor bent over Aaron, lifted his eyelid and shone a light into his eye.

"Be with him."

CHAPTER FIVE

Nothing can prepare you for the violent deaths of loved ones. Arranging for their funerals was more than I could handle alone. The passing of seven days did little to numb the pain. Thankfully, Dave Pendelton and some the members of his church helped me through the process.

The funeral was a quiet event. I had Jim O'Brien to thank for keeping the media away. He stood at a distance, in uniform. His partner Chris sent his regrets but was not able to attend.

A few members of Jenn's church had asked if they could attend. I was surprised that only twelve had asked to come. Jenn would probably have wanted the entire congregation there.

Jenn's agent flew in from New York. It was the first time we met in person. While singing her praises, Barb mentioned the figure on Jenn's book advance. Had it been any other time, I would have been impressed. Six figures never seemed so insignificant.

Pastor Dave gave a short sermon and read some of Jenn's favorite verses from the book of Proverbs:

> *Trust in the LORD with all your heart and lean not on your own understanding; in all your ways acknowledge him, and he will make your paths straight.*

One of the congregants played a guitar while a young lady sang *You Are My Hiding Place.* A tear rolled down my cheek and I struggled to hold it together. Jenn's parents sat with me. Maggie put her arm around me and we held each other.

Several eulogies were given, mostly for Jenn, a couple for Bethie. Oscar, Jenn's father, stood to give his eulogy, though at times his voice cracked. "I've buried more buddies after the war than I can remember. You'd think I'd be used to it. But burying my daughter and granddaughter is something I never—" He pulled a handkerchief from his breast pocket, wiped his eyes and nose. Maggie squeezed my hand.

"As a child," Oscar continued, "Jenny was shy, but strong-willed. Didn't know the meaning of giving up. I still remember driving her to the pet shop to get that puppy she wanted. She worked all summer scooping ice cream at Baskin & Robbins and saved every penny until there was enough for the puppy, the shots and supplies. She took care of Jimbo until he died at the ripe age of seventeen, three years after she got married.

"That was my Jenny. Stubborn as a mule, taking care of those she loved, no matter what it took." Oscar stepped away from the podium and returned to his seat.

I finally worked up the strength to say a few words. Gazing out at the crowd, I realized that aside from Jenn's parents, we had no living relatives. Neither of us had siblings, were never close to our few cousins, and any uncles or aunts were either dead, or in a mental institution. Members from her church, City on a Hill, were the closest thing Jenn had to an extended family. But I had no family other than my wife and children. For the most part, I was addressing strangers.

"I wish I had an anecdote or two..." It felt like a tumor had just developed in my throat. "Anyone who knew Jenn..." I caught a glimpse of their caskets and lost it. Several others wept with me. Finally I got a grip. "I'm sorry. I don't know what to say except that... the world is a darker, colder place now."

When it came time for the burial, eight men from the church served as pall-bearers. I followed the procession to the burial site, which was thankfully within walking distance of the memorial hall.

The caskets were lined up next to each other. I requested that they remain open during the prayers so that Jenn and Bethie would have one last moment in the warm San Diego sun they loved so much.

In a soulful baritone, Dave led everyone in a hymn—*When the Roll Is Called Up Yonder.* This would be the last time I'd see Jenn and Bethie's beautiful faces. Ever.

He sang the last verse solo:

Let us labor for the Master from the dawn till setting sun,
Let us talk of all His wondrous love and care;
Then when all of life is over, and our work on earth is done,
And the roll is called up yonder, I'll be there.

As they all repeated the chorus, I placed Bethie's violin and bow under her hand, which was cold and stiff like wood. I touched her face, her silky brown hair. My little girl. Such a wonderful life taken from her. So much she'd never experience, touch, taste.

And to think, barely three weeks ago, I had almost lost her in the shooting at her school. Nothing worse could possibly happen, I had thought. "Goodbye, baby girl," I whispered. "Daddy loves you." I was reluctant to pull myself away, but Jenn was also waiting.

Not even death could diminish her beauty. Jenn's countenance beamed with peace, contentment and a hint of a smile—that playful grin she wore when she knew something I didn't. Beneath her hand I placed the wallet photos she always carried of her children—Bethie and Aaron as two-year-olds. I also put the picture frame that she kept on her nightstand—the one with a white jasmine blossom she had picked on our honeymoon and taken home to preserve and pressed. One of the happiest times in our life.

The casket lids descended. *Just one more look, please.* Then they were lowered into the ground. Dave said a final prayer as each person dropped a long stemmed rose into the graves. Poor Aaron. He didn't get to say good-bye to his mommy or sister.

Then it was over.

Tearful hugs and handshakes, mostly from people I hardly knew, and I found myself seated alone on a mint-green, metal folding chair. An unceremonious front loader roared by bringing sand to drop into the graves. I decided to say my final good-byes. I couldn't bear the sight of that huge monstrosity dropping sand on top of them, had no idea the very end would be so mechanical.

Part of me—perhaps the best part—would be buried with them as well, forever.

The front loader's hydraulics hissed.

I walked away, not looking back.

The sun had just begun to set. Amber light infused the family room. I opened a bottle of Robert Mondavi and brought it with me as I walked upstairs to see if I could settle into my bedroom. I wasn't ready. The wine stain was still there, along with some of the blood stains which I hadn't yet cleaned. We never had that last drink together.

I retreated to the guest room and turned a chair towards the window facing Black Mountain. Across an amber canvas, the sun expired and gave way to a purple veil just over the horizon. Hot air balloons rose up taking people on romantic excursions. Flames from the burners illuminated the evening sky. I'd spend my evening with my Merlot, which I planned to drain directly from the bottle.

Intent on anesthetizing myself, I took a pillow from the guest bed, wrapped myself in a comforter, and sat in an armchair, staring out at the hills. My eyes, my entire body and spirit began to shut down before taking my first pull. Perhaps I'd just sleep until morning. Not a bad plan.

But it was quickly thwarted when my cell phone buzzed.

The caller ID showed "restricted." Perhaps it was Children's Hospital, calling to inform me that Aaron had come out of his coma.

"Mister Hudson, this is Detective Pearson."

"I gave at the office last week."

"I need to speak with you again."

"Why?"

She cleared her throat. "To update you on the investigation. Let's meet tonight."

"What?"

"Your house. Twenty minutes." She hung up before I could tell her what to do with herself.

CHAPTER SIX

With a bottle in one hand and a pair of wine glasses in the other, I opened the door. For all I knew or cared, Anita Pearson could have been an android. Her partner, Detective Batey, stood behind her hugging his arms as a dry gust swayed the palm trees outside.

Without a thought for my bare feet, disheveled hair, and shirt tails hanging over my pants, I held out the bottle and empty glasses. "Care to join me?"

"We're on duty," she said.

"Suit yourself." I gestured to the living room. A chill ran up my spine as an unseasonably cold breeze blew through the doorway. "Have a seat."

Batey smiled and began to sit in my black leather recliner.

"I'll stand," Pearson said.

Batey backed up and stepped away from the chair.

"Fine. You stand, I'll sit." I set the bottle and glasses on the glass coffee table.

She pulled out her PDA and started tapping again. "How was the funeral?"

"Just lovely, thanks."

"Mmm-hmm." Her eyes were glued to the PDA. When they weren't, she didn't even attempt to meet mine. Instead she scanned the room, the windows, the furniture.

Human looking enough, Detective Batey, seemed nothing more than a bodyguard. He shrugged as if to say, "Don't look at me, she's in charge."

"You were going to update me on the case?" I said to Pearson.

"We'll have the crime scene DNA results any day now. A comparison with CODIS should lead us to some important conclusions. The samples you gave, however, might not be processed for a while."

"The purpose being, of course, to exclude me as a suspect."

"Right." Her eyes narrowed, her gaze, the rusted point of a spear. More incessant tapping on her PDA. "How would you characterize your marriage?"

"Things were great. We had a new lease on life, you know, after my daughter survived the shooting."

"Any problems, disagreements?"

"No."

"You sure?"

"I told you. No problems."

"You didn't have any arguments on the night of the murder? One of your neighbors heard you shouting."

"I wasn't shouting at her."

"At who, then?"

"My son."

Back to the PDA.

"No, wait. You see, Aaron"

"How old was your son, Mister Hudson."

"Is. He *is* four. You see, he misplaced his—"

"Four years old." *Tap, tap, tap.* My brow became moist. A drop of stinging perspiration rolled into the corner of my eye. I wiped it quickly, hoping she wouldn't notice.

She did.

Took more notes.

"Shouldn't I have an attorney present?"

"You're not under arrest."

"Then why this interrogation?"

"Just taking a statement."

I slammed my fist on the coffee table. "This is the third one!"

Pearson flipped the leather cover of her PDA shut and shoved the stylus in. She stood, her face devoid of expression, and arched an eyebrow. "It's in your best interest to stay calm, Mister Hudson."

"Calm? You show up a few hours after I bury my wife and daughter and all but accuse me of—!" Maybe it was the stress, the fatigue. I couldn't help myself from shouting. "Have you no decency!"

She lifted her index finger. "We'll be leaving now."

As Pearson and her partner started for the door, Batey whispered, "Very sorry for your loss, sir." I couldn't get myself up to see them to the door. I gripped the arms of my recliner and nodded half-heartedly.

"Come on, Randy," Pearson droned and shooed him out the door. She was about to close it behind her when she peeked back in. "You might be hearing from the District Attorney's office. Try not to be so defensive."

CHAPTER SEVEN

The initial forensic reports from the crime lab arrived. Anita Pearson had her killer. She knew it in her gut, which in her five years as detective, had never been wrong. Almost never. Yesterday's visit to Sam Hudson confirmed it.

Victim number one—Jennifer Hudson—died of multiple stab wounds. There were signs of blunt force trauma to the head.

Victim number two—Bethany Hudson—died of multiple stab wounds. Traces of semen found on her along with pubic hairs from the attacker. This was all it took for Anita to charge like a rhino into the D.A.'s office.

"We've got the right guy," she said to Thomas Walden. "I knew it the moment I laid eyes on him."

"Hudson? Come on, how's it going to look going after the husband? He just lost his family."

"How's it going to look if you don't get a conviction? Hudson did it. I need a search warrant."

"Anita, there's this little thing called due process."

"He knows we're on to him. If we don't hurry, he might just take a flight to Buenos Aires and fall off the radar."

"You closed the crime scene already."

"It happened in the man's home, for Chrissakes. We searched what we could inside and around the house. But I need to see his personal computer, his file cabinets."

"You want a warrant based on what, a hunch?" The D.A. scribbled something onto his desk blotter-calendar. Probably writing down a reminder to take his poodle to the groomer. *Pig.*

Without taking his eyes from his calendar he muttered, "You're risking a Probable Cause hearing." He finished scribbling and looked back up. "Come back when you have something more solid."

"You want solid? Go ahead and authorize the crime lab to expedite Hudson's DNA samples—top of the list." She fixed an icy gaze. "And I'll bring you probable cause on a silver platter."

"Oh, really?"

"But delay things, and this guy vanishes before we match him? I'll be serving you pie, your choice: humble or crow, either way it'll be all over your face."

Three ridges creased Walden's forehead. He reclined in his leather chair, put his hands behind his head, leaned back, then smiled. "Everything legit with the sample collection?"

"Voluntary... more or less."

He lowered his reading glasses and cast her a doubtful look, exasperation rising like steam from a cow pie.

"It *was.*"

"Oh, all right. I'll get the warrant, but I won't expedite the tests."

She stood up, rapped her knuckles on his desk. "This'll be a slam-dunk."

"I'll have Larry draw it up."

"Oh, great." Why'd it have to be weasely, ex-boyfriend Larry?

As she walked towards the door, Walden said, "Anita..."

"What?"

"I want this conviction as much as you do. Same sides, right?"

Pearson turned around, opened the door and muttered, "Right."

"Don't you forget it."

She was already gone.

CHAPTER EIGHT

For the next few days, paperwork and drudgery dominated my life. Death certificates, insurance forms, fending off reporters. The mere act of getting out of bed seemed insurmountable. Each day the sun rose and intruded through the window of the guest room. I still could not bring myself to sleep in my own bed. Though I had it cleaned, the chill of death still lingered.

Nearly two weeks passed. Despite the fact I was living off of pizza, Chinese take-out, and all manner of high-calorie junk, I lost ten pounds. Dave dropped by now and then to see if I was okay and to offer help in any way I might need. Initially I declined, but by the third week, I was so overwhelmed that I tossed my pride and accepted.

"I'm not sure what I need," I said, letting him into my house, which looked like the bachelor pad from hell. Boxes of stale pizza strewn everywhere, black garbage bags that should have been thrown out a week ago, and dirty laundry obscured the floor. "I just don't know."

"I think I might have a clue."

Later that day, Dave showed up with four people from Jenn's Bible study group. They arrived with brooms, mops, and other supplies to clean the house and dig me out.

"Oh, I couldn't—"

"You should go and see Aaron. Take all the time you need." Dave picked my car keys and jacket off the floor and handed them to me.

A white haired lady, holding a mop said, "Go on, Mister Hudson." She patted my cheek with a maternal hand. "We'll just tidy up a bit while you're out."

It was hard to say no to a person that reminded me of Aunt Susan. Even harder to refuse an offer to have my landfill cleaned. Suddenly, words began to fail. "I just—I don't know what to…"

"It's okay, Sam." Dave turned my shoulders, facing me towards the garage. "Go ahead and be with your son."

Aaron was stable, though still comatose. The doctors had nothing new to report. About all I could do was hold his hand, speak to him and just be there. For about an hour I stayed with him, just holding his hand, talking to him, now that it was okay to do so.

"Remember that trip to Wild Animal Park we were talking about?" I brushed a hand through his hair. "Well, I'm taking you there. We'll see rhinos, lions, you can chase the ducks all you want this time." The words caught in my throat. "You just need to wake up soon. Okay Aaron?" Tears filled my eyes. "I miss you."

The nurse came in, apologized and turned away.

Wiping my face with my arm, I waved her back. "It's okay. Just about ready to go."

Without aim, I drove on the freeway until I arrived at La Jolla cove. There, I sat on a warm rock, watching the tide-pooling kids holding hands with their parents. Soon, as the waves began to roll in, churning white froth in the rocky crags, the families vanished. Even the seals left the protected shore, leaving me alone with thoughts that were fast becoming unwelcome residents in my mind.

Two hours later, when I came home, the house looked as clean as it had ever been. The carpet had been vacuumed and shampooed. All my papers were neatly arranged. Decorations were set back in place. On top of that, for the first time since Jenn's death, the scent of home-cooked food floated sweetly in the air.

As I entered, haunting echoes filled my mind—the kids running to me, assaulting me with hugs and giggles as they did every night when I came home from work. Bethie would put her violin down and jump into my arms, even though she knew she was getting too big for that.

"Daddy, daddy," Aaron would shout. "Fly me!" I'd pick him up, hold him horizontal and run all the way down the hall, the two of us shouting, *To the sky, past the moon and into the heavens. To infinity and beyond!*

What I wouldn't give now to look into the kitchen and catch a glimpse of Jenn, with that knowing smile she had on our Wednesday "date" nights.

In the foyer, Dave and the others were putting on their sweaters and jackets. Lorraine, the elderly lady who reminded me of Aunt Susan smiled and patted my cheek. "There's a casserole in the oven, dear. Just heat it at 350 for ten minutes."

"I'm speechless." The house almost looked like my home again. "Thank you. Thank you all."

Dave smiled. "Jenn was a sister to us."

Since Jenn started attending City on a Hill, I had stiff armed them, cast them with the rest of the religious hypocrites. These people, however, were unlike any of the other religious people I'd known.

So moved was I by their kindness that I did something I never dreamed I'd do. I invited them to join me for dinner.

The unexpected food shortage crisis was quickly averted when Lorraine sent Alan to Vons to get more chicken and vegetables. The aroma of buttered rolls, roasted rotisserie chicken, sweet white corn on the cob, and sautéed vegetables made my mouth water.

I sat at the table with my guests, certain that by the end of the night I'd be preached at, pressured—albeit politely—to confess my sins and give my life to Jesus, Hallelujah! But the closest it came to that was Dave asking if he could give thanks before we ate. Of course he could. Were she here, Jenn would have had it no other way.

For the rest of the evening, we recalled things about Jenn and Bethie, some of which I would never have otherwise known, because their religious life was something I never took part in.

By the meal's end, we retired to the living room with coffee and happily distended bellies. Alan, who had come with his wife Samantha, leaned forward and drew a slow breath.

"Mister Hudson," Alan said.

"Please, everyone just call me Sam, okay?"

Alan's wife Samantha grinned. "Might get confusing."

"I'm wondering, Sam," Alan continued. "Would it be okay if we prayed for you tonight?"

"I don't know." I shifted in my chair. "I'm not all that comfortable with it."

"Honey," his wife said. "He's not—"

"Really," I said. "It's all right. I appreciate it, but it's not necessary."

"Don't be shy, Sam," Alan said. "Anything at all, just say the word."

"Honey, please," Samantha's brow wrinkled. "He said he's not comfortable."

An awkward silence fell.

"Well," I said, to break the ice and bail poor Alan out, "My son could use all the prayers he can get." Right away I regretted it. I began to imagine some kind of snake-handling, holy roller, voodoo session. But it was too late to rescind now.

Dave nodded and came forward. Alan took hold of his wife's hand, who in turn took Lorraine's, and so on until the entire group encircled me.

Here goes.

Again, there was silence. But it was an expectant silence. Like something truly remarkable was about to happen.

And it did.

It started with a low-pitched rumble under our feet. Then came the creaking of the house's wood frame. Windows rattled. Before long, the entire house was shuddering. Reminded me of my childhood subway rides on the D-Train into Manhattan. A light side to side rocking.

Lorraine let out a gasp.

The group began to pray simultaneously.

Though everyone else's eyes were squeezed shut, mine remained wide open. A warm, tingling sensation trickled from the top of my head down my spine and spread through my body. Another fifteen seconds and it was over—the prayers and the tremors.

Lorraine was the first to speak. "You'd think after thirty years in California, I'd be used to these earthquakes."

"Sure you didn't plan this with the Man?" I smiled at her and pointed heavenward. "Because it wouldn't be the first time someone tried to scare me into religion."

She shook her head. "I've been jumpy ever since Northridge. Don't you get scared?"

"Not really. Just another little San Diego tremor. We're pretty far from any major fault lines." Lorraine blushed and laughed. "Thank you for the prayers. I can honestly say it was earth-shaking."

Whether it had been a true spiritual experience or an emotional high, their prayers helped. I no longer felt isolated. Someone knew my pain, someone cared.

And they didn't even ask me to say the Sinner's Prayer.

CHAPTER NINE

The morning after, I called George, my supervisor at the office but he didn't pick up. Probably saw my number on his caller ID and let it roll over to voicemail. I needed to come in and copy a couple of files from my work computer which contained life insurance contact information. The very idea of getting paid for Jenn and Bethie's deaths repulsed me, but the funeral and the burial had cost thousands. We'd depleted our cash reserves on our new house. Reserves were something I had to seriously consider now as Aaron's insurance deductibles were beginning to pile up. What would happen if, God forbid, I should lose my job and benefits?

I called Human Resources to discuss issues of insurance claims. Amanda answered. She seemed startled and abruptly put me on hold. A cheesy popcorn version of *We've Only Just Begun* played while I waited.

"Sorry to keep you, Sam," she finally said. "How are you doing?"

"I'd be lying if I said fine."

"I'm so sorry."

"Amanda, I need to talk to you about my life insurance benefits."

"Of course."

The next few words were difficult to utter. "How do I go about making a claim?"

A pause. She muffled the receiver with her hand and I vaguely heard her murmuring. Then she was back. "You're going to need to come into the office."

"Can I bring a copy of the death certificates or do you need the originals?"

"Either is fine. You've got to come in right away. Okay?"

"I suppose." Why so urgent?

"Like today?"

"I can be there in an hour."

"Good. We'll see you then."

The first stop was my cubicle. I hoped to avoid all the sympathetic wishes and concerned faces. To my surprise, no one in my department approached me. Instead, they turned their heads and pretended they hadn't seen me. That worked just fine for me.

I was stunned to find my cubicle completely empty, save for a cardboard box and a sheet of paper on my desk where my computer and monitor used to sit. It was a memo on the firm's letterhead and simply said:

Samuel Hudson,
Please report to Human Resources for your exit interview.
Fred Chase,
Director, Human Resources.

"What the hell is this?"

"Sam, please. Have a seat." Fred sat stone faced at his desk, hands folded. He seemed calm, but I could see the apprehension in his eyes.

"I will not have a seat! Tell me why I'm being canned."

He sighed, glanced around the room. "This isn't really open for discuss—"

"Dammit, Fred. I just lost my wife, my daughter. My son's in a coma. I need the medical insurance."

"You're an at-will employee in the state of Califor—"

"Cut the crap!"

"Do you have all your personal effects?"

I answered by stabbing my index finger down at the cardboard moving box. "It was George, wasn't it?"

"His decision, yes."

I always knew George was looking for the perfect opportunity to get rid of me. I never imagined he would sink this low. "Look at my record, Fred. I've performed on par—no, above par, won bigger settlements than any of my peers, never took time off without authorization. I was up for partner. Sure, I took more than my allotted bereavement days, but I had tons of vacation and sick days banked."

He held his hands up. "It wasn't that either."

I kicked his desk. The sound echoed down the hall and into the main lobby from Fred's door, which I only then remembered was open. We remained silent for a moment. He lowered his voice and motioned for me to shut the door.

"Listen to me, Sam. What you do on your own time is none of our business. But what you do with the firm's computer on the firm's time, is."

"What, paying bills online? Updating my Netflix queue? iTunes? For that, I'm getting the ax?"

"Come on, Sam," he hissed and leaned forward. "You know what I'm talking about. Your *private* hobbies."

"No way. None of that was mine."

"We have regulations about that sort of thing."

"I came forward with it!"

He shifted in his chair, tugged on his collar as if it had suddenly shrunk. "Do you have any idea what kind of liability you've exposed the firm to? Child pornography on a company computer? What if a client saw that? This is automatic grounds for termination."

Anger boiled within me, threatened to blow like Mount St. Helen's. I'm not a violent man, but I became keenly aware of my potential. "Okay Fred, Listen" I said, curbing my temper. "Go ahead and investigate all you want, but I need to make those insurance claims."

"The investigation's concluded. And I'm sorry, but your benefits have been terminated as well."

"No, wait. You don't understand—"

"I think we're done, now," Fred said, shutting a folder on his desk with a polyurethane smile. He handed me a slip and a pen. "Need you to sign this exit form. Section Two states that the reason for your termination has been explained to you."

I snatched it out of his hands, threw it aside. "This is insane. I have never—!"

"It's final. Nothing I can do about it. Anything you'd like to say for the record before we conclude?"

Only two words. Which I shouted repeatedly as I leapt over his desk, tackled him to the floor and grabbed his throat, shaking his head like a rattle.

Until someone called security.

Shock is too mild a word to describe my state as I walked back to my car, escorted by a pair of security guards. I didn't particularly love this job, but it had always been a stable part of my life. I slammed the trunk shut and when I looked up, I saw my best friend standing there.

"Mike, listen," I said, hoping to find my old buddy and only ally rushing to my side.

He only shook his head. "What the hell, Sam? What the bleeding hell?" The look on his face, disappointment and disgust. If this was one of his damned pranks, I'd have to thoroughly kick his ass.

"How could I what, get fired?" I said. "Does everyone know why?"

The side of his mouth began to twitch. His eyes were molten lava. "All this time, you pretend to be my friend, a decent guy."

"I never downloaded any of that stuff! What kind of sick—?"

"All this time, you made me believe that I was the screw-up, that I was morally bankrupt, while you, the almighty, the self-righteous, can't-do-wrong, Samuel Hudson..."

"Just stop for a sec—"

"You sick sonofabitch!" This was no prank. Mike got right into my face, his voice hissing. "They're investigating me too. Because I *was* your friend."

"Come on, Man! You know I wouldn't download that stuff!" With open hands, I stepped forward. But he recoiled, as if I carried the Hantavirus.

"Wouldn't you? Man, I don't even know you anymore."

"Don't be saying that, Mike. All these years, you've known me. Do you—"

"Keep the hell away from me and my family!"

"No. No, Wait. Just listen to me."

"To think, I let you stay under my roof. With my wife, my kids!"

"Mike!"

But he was off. And for good measure, he turned and flipped me the bird. A gust of Santa Anna put a bitter taste in my open mouth, causing me to choke on the dryness.

I leaned back against my car, let out a long breath, shut my eyes and waited for the jackhammer in my chest to slow down.

Then it was quiet.

Nothing but the wind blowing, dry leaves scraping against the asphalt, and a car rumbling through the parking deck.

My neck ached. Best if I went home and slept it off. Then I realized, My God! I'm losing all my medical benefits along with my salary. Things couldn't possibly get worse.

But they did.

"Mister Hudson?"

I opened my eyes. Before me stood Detectives Pearson and Batey. Pearson's hand rested on her hip, right above her gun. I groaned and rubbed my neck. "You've got to be kidding."

"You need to come down to the station with us, now."

"Why?"

Batey turned me around, directed my hands up against my car and began patting me down. A crowd had gathered by the balcony. George stood amongst them with his arms folded over his chest, watching the whole thing.

Pearson's words echoed in my head, becoming more distant as she spoke. "Samuel Hudson, you're under arrest for the murder of Bethany M. Hudson and Jennifer Lawrence Hudson..."

CHAPTER TEN

I sat alone in an interrogation room at the Sherriff's station in Poway and remained silent. How could this have happened? Had to be a mistake.

After twenty minutes in a creaky wooden chair, staring at the wall clock and the one-way mirror, I breathed a sigh of relief when Detective Pearson finally entered the room. I gave her a reluctant smile. "The cuffs really aren't necessary."

Instead of a PDA, she held a yellow legal pad and pen in hand. She sat at the opposite side of the table, scribbling notes. "There's one question that stands out."

I didn't answer.

"Why your own family?"

It took all my self control not to react the way I felt: violent. I took a deep breath and stared into her glassy eyes. "Shouldn't I have an attorney present?"

"You *are* an attorney."

"I mean, a *criminal* defense lawyer."

"I can't advise you on that," she said. "You're certainly entitled as per your rights, but that's up to you."

I thought of calling someone from criminal back at work, but they all watched me get arrested. No way would the senior partners allow anyone to represent me. First the child pornography, now murder charges. They'd do best to distance themselves from me as much as possible.

"Do *you* think I should have a lawyer?" I was testing her. Criminal wasn't my field, but anyone who watched *Law & Order* knew this much.

"I can't give you legal advice. You want to talk to us with or without a lawyer, that's your choice. But your resistance won't reflect well."

"I need to make a phone call."

"You're certainly entitled to that as well. Meanwhile, you're looking at two counts of Murder One at the very least. Rape of a minor, aggravated assault, we're talking special circumstances—"

"This is insane."

"This is a capital. But with a confession I might be able to talk with the D.A. and get you a deal. Get it down to life without parole. Without a full trial, you'd save the tax payers of San Diego County a lot—"

"What are you, on crack?" An ironic laugh escaped my lips.

Pearson tossed her paper and pen on the desk and leaned forward with her hands pressed firmly into the gray Formica. "Something amusing?"

"Only this joke you call law enforcement."

"I'm just trying to make things easier." Our eyes locked. She sat down again, tying to look unperturbed. "For everyone." She wouldn't look at me now.

"So is this the part where you smash a wine bottle and stick the jagged edge into my face and say, 'Don't be foolish, vee have vays of making you schpeak?"

"Scumbag."

"I'd like to make that phone call now."

"You'll get that, when I say so." She continued to write. A minute passed with no sound save for the scratching of her pen.

"You *know* this is wrong. Why are you doing this?"

"You don't get to ask the questions here," she said, her eyes never leaving the form.

"Ms. Pearson."

She didn't look up.

"Detective."

That approach didn't bear fruit either.

Slamming my bound fists onto the table I shouted, "Dammit, young lady, you look at me when I'm talking to you!"

That worked. Two seconds from Chernobyl, she lowered her pen and stood up slowly. "I will look at you when and if it suits me, you low-life, bottom-feeding—"

"All right, you're crazy."

"I know your type. I've known you all my life."

"Get me that phone."

"That'll only happen when—"

"Now!"

She squinted with her left eye. I thought for sure she would pistol whip me. Instead, she gathered her things, turned around and stepped outside. The door swung shut. The mini-blinds rattled. I sat alone for another forty minutes, watching the clock's minute hands blaze like a snail towards 11:30 AM. My stomach rumbled, but I was too upset to even think about food.

As the day crawled on, I found myself wondering why Pearson was so determined to pin the murders on me. Maybe she was psychotic. Perhaps George had framed me—but how? Why?

Or could it be I was actually criminally insane, with no recollection?

I shrugged off that thought with a shudder.

Around noon, a slim, twenty-something man entered the room. His khakis hung loose on his lanky frame. His white short-sleeved shirt and tie with little palm trees screamed freshman. Sandy hair kept falling over his freckled face, as he set his briefcase on the table and removed his sunglasses. When he extended his hand, I was sure he'd say, *Dude...this arrest is like, totally bogus.* But instead he said, "Kenny Dodd. I'm an attorney."

"You'll excuse me if I don't shake your hand." I held up my cuffed wrists.

"Oh...yeah. Sorry, man." Slow and laid back, his eyes never quite fully opened. He pulled out a legal pad and fumbled with a stack of paper. "Let's see," he said, flipping his head back in a vain attempt to get his bangs out of his eyes. Looked more like a sheepdog than an attorney. "You've been arrested for murder—"

"Are you court appointed? I haven't made my phone call yet."

"They'll get you a phone soon, if you want. I just want to help you out here, before they try to squeeze a confession out of you."

"But—"

"Sir, it's okay. Now, you've been read your rights?"

"Back in the parking lot, when they cuffed me."

"You were aware of your right to having an attorney present?"

"Yes."

"Can we talk about it now?" He scratched the back of his head.

"I suppose. Are you court appointed?"

"As I said, I'm an attorney." Something wasn't right. I chewed my lip and squinted at him. I sniffed the air for the scent of pot. "Mister Hudson, I'm here to help. So I'm going to have to ask you some questions."

"Let me see your business card."

He looked as if I had asked him to strip naked in the middle of a Sunday ladies' church luncheon for a full body cavity search. "Dude, it's all good. I'm just trying to help."

"Show me some identification, *Dude*!" For the first time, his eyes opened wide, his face became pale. Dude started packing his things. "Hey, wait!" I said.

As he stepped to the door, he spoke in a sober tone. "You're only making it harder for yourself, man."

The restraints kept me from moving more than a couple of inches from my chair. I began to shout, hoping someone outside would hear. "I want my phone call! Do you hear me? I'm being denied my rights! Somebody get—!"

The door slammed shut. Though it was less than six feet from me and unlocked, I was stuck. Imprisoned already.

Finally, at about 3:00 PM, Detective Batey entered the room with a phone, one of those gray Polycom conference room speaker phones. He plugged it in, tested for a dial tone and sat on the opposite edge of the Formica table. He also brought a paper sack from In-N-Out Burgers with a sweating cup of Coke. One whiff of the fries made my mouth water. He set the food down, just out of my reach, took out one of the fries, tasted it and made some "mmm" sounds. My stomach growled, protesting the torture.

My head felt light, my hands trembled slightly. The air condition vent blew right down on me. But I refused to let him know he was having any effect on me.

"Ready for your call?" he asked.

I nodded and told him that all my contacts were on my cell phone—which had been confiscated, along with all my other things I had to sign for when I arrived. He stepped outside and later returned with it.

My first instinct was to call home and tell my wife. A sharp pang abruptly reminded me why that wasn't possible. Apart from Aaron, I had no living relatives. Forget calling Mike or anyone at the firm. The thought of calling Jenn's parents even crossed my mind. It left as quickly as it had come. What would I say? 'Ma, Oscar, can you help me out? I've been arrested for the murder of your daughter.'

Finally, I asked Batey to look through my cellphone contacts for my neighbor, Dave Pendelton, an emergency number Jenn had insisted I keep. Good thing I did.

Batey dialed the number on the Polycom. After five rings Dave's answering machine picked up, instructing to leave a message. I shook my head at Batey and he terminated the call. "Want to try another number?"

"Same name, try his cell."

Again, the phone rang.

"Hello?"

"Dave?" I gestured to Batey for privacy. He stepped outside.

"Speaking. Who's this?"

"It's me. Sam."

"Sam? How are you?" He was in his office at church, giving premarital counseling to a young couple. He couldn't believe that I'd been arrested. He asked me to hold the line while he excused himself from the session, then he returned.

Did I have an attorney? No.

Did I want him to get me one? Yes.

Did I need him to come to the station? If possible.

"Sit tight, Sam. I'll see you soon."

CHAPTER ELEVEN

Anita Pearson didn't believe in luck. She was good at her job. Damned good. She could always spot a domestic within the first hour of investigation. One problem this time: No murder weapon. Sure as hell wasn't going to hold her back, though.

As for motive? Something would rise to the surface. Always did, given enough time. Hudson had no known history of conflict in his marriage, no fights, previous violence, or abuse. Not on record, anyway. He appeared to be a loving husband who'd never laid a hand on his wife or children. Didn't matter. They all looked like that in the beginning. This case was all but closed.

But solving the case was one thing. Getting a conviction and adequate sentence was another, thanks to those snakes known as defense attorneys. Almost as annoying were those rookie uniforms, District Attorney Investigators, (DAI's, they liked to call themselves), and anyone else who might misstep, causing a crucial piece of evidence to be suppressed during trial. Worse still was having all her hard work undone by a probable cause hearing because of that kind of sloppy work on someone else's part.

Thanks to crap like that, three murderers and two rapists had been released back into the very feeding grounds from which she'd yanked them. All in the past two years. Hence, her hatred for slimeballs who preyed on innocent women and children. Hence her need to shut down emotionally and become as cunning as the very psychopaths she hunted.

No way Sam Hudson would slip through her net. Sonofabitch repeatedly stabbed his wife, raped his daughter, and bludgeoned his four year old son. He needed to be exterminated like the vermin he was. And if Anita had her way, as slowly and painfully as possible.

When Kenny Dodd left the station without so much as a word from Hudson, she threw her hands up in the air and got Thomas Walden on the phone. "Three hundred DDA's and you send Kenny Dodd? The hell were you thinking?"

"It's worked before."

"It was stupid. You're gonna get this whole thing kicked. What'd you do? Go to Pacific Beach, pick up a stoned surfer and stick a briefcase under his arm?"

"Did Hudson confess?"

"Take a guess." Anita exhaled and waited for her blood pressure to go down. "I can't believe you tried that. Good thing he didn't talk, because it'd all be inadmissible."

"Then relax."

"I need that search warrant. Now."

"What's your probable cause?"

"A tip from Hudson's former employer, George Schmall. He was instrumental. So how about that search warrant?" She waited for him to answer, though she knew what he would say next.

"What have you—"

"A buttload of evidence."

"Statements? Potential witnesses?" Walden asked.

"Kiddy porn. On his work computer. In a law firm! Freakin' deviant."

"Child pornography, eh?"

"Listen, Tom. I can only hold him here for so long. I need to search his car, his home computer."

Walden grunted. A good sign. "All right, you got it."

"Call you soon as I get back."

"Anita," Walden said, his voice guarding from enthusiasm. "This could be a high profile case, as big as Matt Kingsley."

It hadn't even been two months since the Hollywood action hero was convicted of murdering his wife in their Rancho Santa Fe mansion. Anita wished that she could have been the one to take the bastard down. "I understand." But she didn't give a piss about Walden's political agenda.

"Don't misstep," he said.

"Same to you."

CHAPTER TWELVE

At 4:35, Dave and a slender woman came to see me. Her complexion made you wonder if she had actually worked on her tan or if she was just one of those naturally blessed Asians. Her navy trousers matched her jacket. She was attractive, but didn't dress in a way that drew undue attention to her figure, as so many Southern Californian women do.

"You okay?" Dave asked me.

"I don't think so."

"This is Rachel Cheng," he said. "She's a defense attorney and a member of our church." When I stood, I realized just how tall she was. I'm no giant, but at six-one, I didn't have to look down very far to meet her gaze. She reached out to shake my hand. My fingers were still greasy after wolfing down the burger and fries from Detective Batey. I wiped my cuffed hands on my shirt before shaking hers. "Sorry, didn't have a chance to freshen up."

She smiled. "That's quite all right."

"Listen," I said. "I really appreciate your coming down here, but I don't know if I can afford anything."

Dave patted my shoulder. "Don't worry about that for now, okay?"

"Please," Ms. Cheng said. "Have a seat." She spoke with stately gentleness, carried herself with a confidence that suggested a savvy person with whom you'd best not get into a debate. "Do you feel that your rights have been violated in any way?" she asked, her smile quickly fading as she opened her portfolio and started to take notes.

"They sent someone in who tried to pass himself off as a defense attorney. At first, I thought he was court appointed. Criminal's not my field, but I'm no fool."

Rachel's eyes widened. "You're an attorney yourself, aren't you?"

"Lewis, Garfield & Brown, Tax Controversy and Litigation." I huffed. "That kid was no lawyer."

"That was Deputy District Attorney, Kenneth Dodd."

"Oh."

"A stunt like that? I wouldn't put it past Walden. Did you tell him anything?"

"That I wanted to make a phone call, that's all."

"Good," she said. "Wouldn't have been admissible anyway." She reached over and squeezed my hand. "Now, let's start from the beginning."

I recounted the entire ordeal from the moment I stepped into my cubicle and found that I'd been canned. So many unanswered questions. Not the least of which, the child pornography in my network folder. I felt embarrassed to mention it and vehemently denied culpability.

"Don't worry," she said. "We'll get to the bottom of this." When I finished she stood up and I noticed her... violet eyes? Colored contact lenses. I tried not to stare.

"Did you know that they searched your house?" she asked.

"No, when?"

She regarded Dave and scribbled some more.

"Around noon today," Dave said. "That female detective and some uniformed officers. They broke your door down."

I wanted to speak my mind, but thought better of swearing in front of the Reverend and the lady who was now my attorney.

"I'm going to the Magistrate's," Rachel said. "We'll get you out. First things first."

"What's the plan?" I asked.

"I'm going to try to get this whole thing tossed. You were denied access to a defense attorney, though you asked."

"They never said I couldn't have one."

"I know, but they didn't let you make a phone call until hours later. And look how long they've kept you here—they haven't booked you yet. In the meantime, they tried to trick a confession out of you." She had a secret weapon up her sleeve. I sensed it. As they were about to leave, I stood and cleared my throat.

"Ms. Cheng?"

"Rachel."

"All right, Rachel." I hesitated. But I had to know. "Mind if I ask you a question or two, as you *are* going to be my attorney."

"Sure."

"I know this may sound incredibly rude, but—how old are you?"

Her smile faded slightly. "I'll be twenty-nine this January."

"How long have you been practicing?"

"Got my bachelors at Berkeley, Masters at UCLA Law. Passed the bar shortly after." If I weren't looking straight into her confident gaze, I might have imagined a hint of defensiveness. But you wouldn't know it from her violet eyes.

"My question was, how long have you been practicing?"

"About four years."

"What firm are you with?

"Actually," she said. "I'm a solo operation."

Our eyes locked. Neither of us blinked.

"I'm sorry, but...how many criminal cases have you actually won?"

"One hundred percent of them." Rachel stood tall, her lips glistened, reflecting fluorescent overheads.

"How about a number instead of a percentage?"

She and Dave looked at each other. Dave spoke close to my ear. "She's really good, Sam. Trust me."

"How many?" I tried to keep my voice down.

"One."

The smile fell from my face.

"And it was one heck of a trial," Dave said.

"One!" I nearly missed my chair as I sat back down. I didn't want to appear ungrateful, but the thought of my future resting in the hands of someone with practically no experience gave me pause.

"Mister Hudson," she said, in a calm voice. "If I can get you released on bail or O.R., will you trust me? You can always fire me if you're dissatisfied."

I blew out a long breath and thought about it. "All right. Let's do it." As if I had a bevy of attorney's to choose from.

CHAPTER THIRTEEN

During the search of Sam Hudson's house and car, Anita Pearson seized a personal laptop along with documents from his file cabinet. His car was impounded for evidence. Analysis would take some time. Just as she thought, she found a CD in his briefcase with copies of the same kiddy porn images found in his network folder. This sicko was going down.

When she got back to the station, Detective Batey approached her like a boy who had stolen loose change from his mother's coat pocket.

"You what?"

"Come on, Anita. The guy's been in there all day. Letting him eat wasn't going to hurt the case."

"He's scum! And you treat him like some kind of VIP?"

"Keep this up and we're all going to be in trouble." Technically Batey was right. But that didn't excuse him undermining her.

"All right, go on, get outta here." Sitting at her desk, fiddling with the coiled phone cord as she waited for Larry at the District Attorney's office to pick up, Anita kept her eyes on the clock. 6:25 PM. Uniformed officers were now escorting Hudson from the interrogation room to the squad car. Maybe a night in San Diego

Central would make him more willing to confess. She glowered at Batey and he cringed in his chair.

"Pick up, dammit," she muttered at the phone. Again she glared at the clock. Finally the call connected. "Larry Finkel, DDA."

"Where is it?"

"On its way. Hello to you too, Ani—."

"You said you'd have it here before noon."

"No. You demanded it by noon. I said I'd do my best."

"I called you this morning to remind you. Again!"

Larry stayed silent for a while, probably thinking up some lame excuses. Finally, in a hushed tone, he said. "In case you've forgotten, I'm up to my ears in paperwork for the Walker trial."

"How could I forget? You cry about that every chance you get." Granted, the infamous Coyote Creek Middle School shooter case was important. And the irony of his connection to Hudson was not lost on her. Leonard Walker shoots two students, nearly kills Hudson's daughter. Hudson finishes the job. Anita started to chew on a pencil eraser.

"On top of that," Larry said, "I'm managing a caseload the size of Montana and my calendar's busting at the seams."

"Made your bed. Not my problem."

"Why're you always busting my balls like that?"

"You owe me, that's why."

Silence. He hated when she called him on that. After they broke up last year, when she caught the little prick cheating on her, he'd promised to always use his position at the D.A.'s office to help her. Anita hung that over his head like a fetid salmon. And she would likely do so for the rest of his natural life.

"Come on, Anita. It's on its way." Even as they spoke, the warrant arrived, hand delivered via courier.

"It's here. Bye."

As she read the warrant a low-pitch growl emerged from her throat, threatened to break out into a scream. She crumpled the warrant and threw it into the wastepaper basket, kicked the door and sat down at her computer, typing up all possible justifications for what she had done. None of them had strong enough legs on which to stand. She had gotten too eager to put Hudson away, too arrogant, and too careless.

Detective Batey fished the wadded-up search warrant, smoothed it out on Anita's desk and whistled. Now he knew why she was so upset.

CHAPTER FOURTEEN

The next morning, Rachel and Dave brought me a clean change of clothes—black slacks, white dress shirt, and a red tie for my arraignment. Deodorant would've been nice, as I wasn't given the luxury of a shower down at the San Diego Central Jail.

Tax attorneys typically don't get to see the seedy side of the criminal court system. My wrists chafed under the white plastic tie-wraps. Ankle chains scraped the floor. When I entered the courtroom, my ears and cheeks burned. The gaze of every person in the courtroom drilled into my skin. I felt like a pig led to the slaughterhouse.

Behind a wooden table, I stood next to Rachel. Dave sat right behind me in the gallery. The honorable Judge Matthew Crawford awaited the reading of the docket number.

His Honor was a short man with a balding pate, delineated by two white strips of hair on each side of his head. Every now and then he wiped his glasses with the sleeve of his robe. The scowl permanently etched into his features testified to the fact he was not as impatient as he looked.

He was much *more* so.

Across from Rachel was Thomas Walden, the District Attorney. He stood at least a head taller than her. A robust man in his fifties, he wore a dark suit, a bright yellow tie and spoke with a haughty New England accent.

When the case number was announced, my attorney stepped forward. "Rachel Cheng for the defendant. Waive reading and enter a plea of not guilty. I'm requesting that the charges be dropped."

"Thomas Walden for the State, your honor, and is counsel joking? The State would request that the defendant be held without bail."

"My client is innocent."

"All right, Ms...Ms..." Crawford narrowed his eyes at Rachel and glanced down at his notes.

"Cheng, your honor. Rachel Cheng."

"Right." He cleared his throat. Let's continue." My heart pounded. Where was the real killer? *He* needed to be here, standing before this judge, not me.

"My client is not a flight risk."

Walden scoffed. "You think he'll sit around waiting for his conviction?"

"His four year old son is lying in a coma at Children's hospital right now."

Crawford's shoulders slowly rose, then fell.

"Your honor," Rachel said, "I respectfully request O.R."

"Are we even talking about the same case?" Walden said, with a sneer. "You know the severity of the charges, and you want him released on his own recognizance?"

"Do I even get a chance to make an argument, your honor?"

"All right, all right, fine," Crawford said, barely interested. "Does the defendant have strong ties to the community? Relatives, extended family?"

"His in-laws."

A grunt and the judge scribbled something, no longer looking at Rachel. "And how long has he resided in his community?"

"He's lived in Rancho Carmelita for four months."

"Not very long."

"But he's lived in San Diego for about five years."

"Current employment?"

"Unemployed. But he was a tax attorney for a reputable law firm—"

"From which he was recently fired for possession of child pornography," Walden interrupted.

"Alleged possession," Rachel said.

Walden huffed. "Your honor, seriously. This man should be held without bail. God forbid he kills again, before the trial. The child pornography alone—"

Unable to contain myself, I bolted up from my chair and said, "It wasn't mine!" The chair fell back and hit the floor.

"Bailiff," Crawford said. The deputy leaned in my direction with his hand conspicuously resting on his gun. I sat back down in my chair after Dave propped it back up.

"Sam, please. Keep calm," he whispered.

Rachel glanced over to me. Then back to Crawford. "Your honor. My client denies the allegations. There's no definitive proof that the downloaded images are actually his."

Walden smiled. "It was in his own network directory."

"Sticking to the case at hand," she said, "my client has no priors."

"One out of four," Walden said, containing the chuckle. "Not bad."

"All right," said Crawford. "Bail is set at three point five million dollars." He lifted his gavel and just before he rapped it down, Rachel interrupted.

"Your honor, the Eighth Amendment requires that the bail not be excessive."

"Excuse me?" His left eyebrow cocked upwards.

"Bail should not be used to punish a person for being *suspected* of committing—"

"Believe it or not, Counsel, I am familiar with the Eighth Amendment," Crawford said, his pitch rising.

Walden stood there, resting his chin in the sling between his thumb and index finger, his elbow on his other hand. He was smiling as Rachel rolled out more and more rope to hang herself with.

Rachel went on. "But the purpose of bail is to afford an arrested person freedom until actually convicted of a crime, and the bail amount must be no more than is reasonably necessary to keep him from fleeing, before a case is over."

Crawford, leaned forward, lowered his bifocals and glared. "You're obviously a little wet behind the ears, Ms. Cheng, and that's all right..." No, it's not, I thought. I'm dead. "But let me give you a bit of advice—would that be okay?"

Rachel nodded.

"Do not lecture the court on the Constitution!"

She kept her head up with a hint of defiance. Swallowed. "I apologize, your honor. But it seems to me that you're setting bail as preventive detention?"

Walden struggled to keep a straight face.

Eyes widened again, the judge glared at her with incredulity. "Keep this up and I'll bump it to four million." Crawford raised his gavel.

"At this time," Rachel said, wincing as though the gavel was about to land on her head, "I would like to move for a probable cause hearing."

Both Walden and Crawford threw their hands up, rolling their eyes. "Oh for the love of—"

"Ms. Cheng," Crawford growled and then drew a long breath. "I am not known for my patience."

"Oh my God," I murmured. The void in my chest was matched only by the sinking feeling in my gut. I put my head down into my arms on the table, but Dave reached over the rail and yanked me back up by the elbow.

"Keep your head up," he said, releasing me before the bailiff noticed.

I plastered on my 'dignified' face.

"Prosecutorial misconduct, your honor," said Rachel. "My client's Fourth and Fifth Amendment rights were violated."

"You have evidence?" Crawford said.

"Yes."

Walden turned around and looked at Detective Pearson, who sat expressionless.

"Go on, then," Crawford said.

Rachel came back to the desk and pulled some papers from her briefcase. "Trust me?" she whispered.

Did I have a choice? I nodded, tentatively.

She patted my arm and approached the bench. Walden rolled his eyes again. I wondered if they might roll right out of his head.

Rachel took a deep breath, then began. "Though my client was read his Miranda rights, he was not given access to a phone or an attorney for several hours. At least two attempts at interrogations were made, despite the fact that my client had in fact stated that he wanted an attorney. The District Attorney's office sent Kenneth Dodd, DDA, in an attempt to extract a statement by knowingly and willfully misrepresenting himself as a State appointed *defense* attorney."

Walden cleared his throat. "A simple misunderstanding, Your Hon—"

Rachel clicked her tongue. "Give me a break." As she fired off her list of improprieties, the D.A. could barely get a word in edgewise. With each item, the smugness on his face faded. The judge's scrutinizing glower gradually shifted to Walden.

"My client was detained for over eight hours before he was booked in the San Diego Central Jail."

Arms crossed over her chest, Detective Pearson tugged on her earlobe.

"And finally," Rachel said. "I have eyewitness testimony that puts the Detective Anita Pearson at my client's residence, conducting an illegal search."

Walden pressed forward. "We had a warrant!"

"Would you care to show it to the court?" Rachel said, placing her hands on her hips.

Walden started turning back to Pearson, but stopped. He looked to the judge, smiling like he had a perfectly reasonable explanation. "I can produce a copy if you just—"

"Here." Rachel pulled a sheet of paper from her jacket and slapped it down under His Honor's nose. Judge Crawford lowered his glasses and peered over the rims, held the sheet up closer. "That's a copy of the search warrant which I got from the D.A.'s clerk." Rachel said.

"What's the problem, Counsel?" Crawford asked.

"If Your Honor will kindly look closely at the clerk's stamp, it will show that this warrant was issued yesterday at 4:55 PM. More than four hours *after* the search was actually conducted. Yesterday, at 12:15 PM, Detective Pearson broke down the door and conducted a warrant-less search of my client's premises."

Leaning back in his chair, Crawford rumbled and shot Pearson a withering glare. "Anything else, counsel?"

Brushing back a strand of hair, Rachel met his gaze. "Given the gross improprieties in my client's incarceration, I once again request he be released on his own recognizance."

"This is ridiculous," Anita Pearson said, unable to remain seated. "The time discrepancy is immaterial. We *had* probable cause and found more evidence—"

"Which is now fruit of a poisonous tree," Rachel said. "Let's have that P.C. hearing now, shall we?"

With his indignation now aimed at the detective, Crawford said, "Immaterial?"

Walden tugged his collar. You could almost see the steam rise out.

"Detective," the judge said. "The court does not condone what you've done. Nor am I interested turning the focus of this case towards constitutional rights." He turned to Walden. "If you want a Probable Cause hearing..."

Walden frowned and shook his head tightly.

With a bit more respect, Crawford said, "Nevertheless Ms. Cheng, I agree with the State about the severity of the charges. I cannot simply grant the O.R."

"Presumption of innocence until proven—"

"Request denied."

"But Your Honor—"

"Ms. Cheng!"

My heart plummeted. I could almost hear it splashing into the digestive acids which had already eroded the lining of my stomach. I would be spending God knows how many months in jail, just waiting for my trial. Unable to see Aaron, or be there for him.

"Bail is set to fifty thousand dollars." Crawford rapped the gavel.

The transformation on Rachel's face was so drastic, her smile so wide, that it wouldn't have surprised me if she ran up to the bench and gave Crawford a hug, planting a big, wet kiss on his shiny bald head.

His Honor lifted a cautionary finger. "On the condition that he agrees to wear a GPS tracking device on his ankle until the trial."

I nodded my consent.

"My client agrees," said Rachel.

The gavel hit the sound block again, and it was settled. Dave and I both exhaled. He thumped me in the back. "Yes!"

With her back turned to the judge, Rachel gave me a thumbs up and a broad smile. She returned to the desk with a triumphant lilt in her step. "Congratulations," she said, shaking my hand.

"Rachel, thank you."

The deputy unlocked my wrists and ankles. I was free to go.

For now.

CHAPTER FIFTEEN

The accused shall enjoy the right to a speedy and public trial. This part of the Sixth Amendment, derived from the Magna Carta, was a right I gladly exercised. The sooner we proved my innocence, the better.

The trial was set for late December, less than two months away. When Walden announced he was going to seek the death penalty, I felt so ill I couldn't eat for the entire day.

Time passed too quickly in some ways, too slow in others. In addition to preparing for the trial, we had to find the killer and prove my innocence, all in a matter of weeks. As far as the D.A.'s office was concerned, the case had been solved. The trial was just a formality.

Rachel started looking for a private investigator.

With an anklet that tracked my location and movement anywhere on the planet, I couldn't leave my house without the sheriffs' watchful eye. My father-in-law was quite vocal in his protests against my visiting Aaron. Any visit by me had to be supervised by the hospital security staff. In Oscar's mind, I was guilty and therefore dangerous. He never liked me much from the start and I suppose finding me guilty would make it easier for him to cope with his daughter's death. Who better to blame?

The doctors said Aaron seemed to be out of the woods now, though complications always threatened. Visiting him was always the highlight of the day. And at the same time, the most heart-rending.

I'd been terminated from my firm without severance. My life plummeted into a quagmire of anxiety, despair, and financial hemorrhaging. Bad enough I could no longer pay the mortgage, but the most painful blow was losing the medical benefits. Without Blue Cross, I had no way of paying for Aaron's medical bills.

The fifty thousand dollar bail was posted with a five thousand dollar bond. But it didn't take long before I completely depleted my reserves—exercised my options, sold my stocks, and maxed out my credit cards with cash advances.

MetroLife would not process my claims because I was the defendant in my wife and daughter's slaying. At best, they'd wait until I was proven innocent. How would it look if they paid out 2.5 million dollars to a convicted murderer?

As for Rachel's retainer, she had not yet brought it up, so I didn't ask, which went against my nature. But I was so desperate, I swallowed my pride and accepted her services not knowing how I would pay.

I began interviewing for jobs all over San Diego, and eventually as far as Orange County. But it was fruitless. No one wanted to hire a murder suspect.

Brent Stringer wrote an editorial in the Union Tribune about my arrest. He expressed regret for having just a month ago written an article that made me out to be a modest hero—Superdad.

To correct that mistake, he tarred and feathered me as a psycho who had fooled and shocked the community. In three scathing paragraphs I went from Superdad, national hero, to Super creep, a "sick deviant and a danger to society." He held nothing back. Like Matt Kingsley, I deserved to be put down like a rabid dog. It was too bad the State of California didn't castrate animals like me.

Thank you very much, Brent.

Good to see that journalistic responsibility was not dead.

After a month of failed job hunting, I admitted to myself that my legal career was over. My checking account dwindled to triple digits and charge cards went over their credit limits. I had to look elsewhere. Not even Carl's Junior, Walmart, or the Chevron station would hire me.

The best I could do to keep from going insane was to spend my time going over the case with Rachel, combing through the prosecution's so-called evidence. I had forgotten to mention the CD of the pornographic images in my briefcase to Rachel. I had decided to keep that copy for my own evidence, in case anything happened to my network directory. A stupid thing to do, in retrospect. Thankfully, it was deemed inadmissible due to the illegal search.

Walden, however, entered the original child pornography found in my network directory at the firm as evidence. He planned to profile me as sexual deviant who raped and killed his own daughter. The murder and assault weapons—a Henckels International classic 8-inch stainless-steel chef's knife, Aaron's aluminum baseball bat—both with my fingerprints, had been found in my garbage containers out at the side of my garage.

I had no alibi. Though there were dozens of cars driving on the I-52 that night, who could possibly ID me in a moving vehicle—in the dark?

There was, however, one ace in the hole that could make all the difference between execution and exoneration: my DNA results. Unfortunately, the report wouldn't be back until well into the trial. And having what they considered enough physical evidence plus witnesses to testify against my character, the prosecution was certain they would get a big fat G.

With each day more heart-breaking than the last, I had to limit my visits with Aaron to once every three days. I simply couldn't afford the gas or parking. And time was running out. I had to work with Rachel on the case.

By Thanksgiving, I received the first of my medical bills since the insurance ran out. There was no way I could pay it. Even if I liquidated everything, sold the car, the house, there was barely enough for another month. At current market value, the profit margin looked anemic. We had taken a home equity loan and spent the money on that stupid home theater system I'd always wanted, and the swimming pool. Now, the water company and SDG&E were threatening to shut off service.

With a heavy heart, I put the house on the market—Jenn's beautiful dream house which she had made our home. I nearly wept when I signed the listing agreement with my agent.

For days on end, I racked my brain, trying to work up theories on who the killer might be, and why he'd chosen my family. But I always came up empty.

All the while, I kept Dave and the Bible study group at arm's length. The day after they'd kindly offered to pray for Aaron, I got arrested. My one little venture into religion had left a bitter aftertaste. Despite my appreciation for all they had done, I would never let my guard down like that again. At this point, I simply couldn't deal with a bunch of religious people.

A month later, however, out of a job, money, and hope, I had come to the end of my rope, the end of myself. On Thanksgiving day, a knock came at the door. It was Dave.

"Hope I'm not bothering you."

I invited him in, offered him a drink. We sat and bantered at the breakfast nook table.

"How's Aaron doing?" Dave asked.

I shook my head and studied the days-old crumbs on the table. "He's still in the primary stage of his coma. The doctor says his GCS is 3." The Glasgow Coma Score consists of three components—eye, verbal and motor response, each rated from 1 to 5, five being the best. Aaron was basically non-responsive. With a GCS of 3, he was categorized as severely disabled—dependent on daily support.

"There may be damage to the cervical spine, which means—" I felt a huge weight on my chest. "It means he might suffer respiratory paralysis or permanent quadriplegia." Right away, I pictured Aaron, alert and awake, lying in the hospital bed, confused and scared. "*Daddy, I can't move...*" There lay a boy I used to chase around the house and scold for jumping on the furniture. Paralysis from the neck down seemed as cruel as death. I then recalled the image of

Aaron trying valiantly to hold back the two big tears from running down his face, the last time I saw him conscious, the night I yelled at him in frustration. Impaled with regret, I rubbed my temples. Would that be his last memory? Would he ever know how much I really loved him?

The last thing I wanted to do was break down in front of Pastor Dave, but that is exactly what I did. I didn't have enough fight left in me to hold back. I held my head in my in hands and just let it all out.

"Sam, I know that the doctors can't do much for him now. But I have seen people healed of incurable diseases and conditions." I didn't answer. Just let him talk while I regained my composure. At the same time I felt a rising curiosity. "I've seen people healed through faith and prayer."

"The last time you all prayed for me, I got arrested."

"True."

"Look Dave. No offense, but I don't think anyone can know how trivialized 'religious encouragement' feels unless they've lost someone close."

"You're right," Dave said. "But I *do* know."

"How's that?"

"Didn't Jenn ever mention it?"

"What?"

"About ten years ago, I lost my wife and son to a drunk driver."

Sometimes you just don't see it coming, when you're about to be proven wrong. All this time, I thought no one could possibly understand my pain. And Pastor Dave, great a guy as he was, could only spout quaint platitudes. I realized that there were many more lessons to learn in life. "I'm really sorry, Dave."

He let out a long breath. "It's all right. Long time ago."

After a short silence, I stood up and asked him if he wouldn't mind coming with me to the backyard. Jenn's flower bed had become overgrown and I thought if we worked on something—

anything, like pulling weeds—it would take the edge off the awkwardness.

"Blue Wonders are some of the heartiest plants," Dave said.

"Grow like these," I said, pulling a scraggy weed from within the patch. It never stood a chance against the Blue Wonders.

Quietly, we continued to work until finally he spoke again. "The guy actually accelerated past the stop sign after hitting Lisa and the baby. He crashed into a street lamp, killing himself."

All I could do was shake my head. Not only had he walked this same road, he was miles ahead of me.

"I was a mess," Dave said, his features darkened. "Of course I was devastated, but I was angry too. Angry at that idiot driver, angry at myself. I was even angry with God."

I straightened up, wiped the sweat from my brow. November afternoons in San Diego can be pretty hot. "You? Angry at God?"

"Yeah. I had just retired from the Corps. Just dedicated my life to ministry." He too stopped and wiped his brow. "After the burial, I tore up my seminary application and shook my fist at God. But I was told that it was okay to be angry with Him. He can take it. And there's no use trying to hide anything from Him anyway."

"So what did you do?"

"I stayed away for a while. Couldn't understand why God would allow this to happen to his children. Why didn't He protect my family?" He caught a particularly tough weed and yanked twice before it came out at the root. Rubbing the back of his neck, he walked over to the fence that separated our properties. He reached for a garden shovel in his yard and started digging up more weeds from Jenn's Red Riding Hoods.

"After all that," I said, "how could you return to your faith, much less become a pastor?"

"Well, that's a story that could take all night to tell."

"I might just ask you about it one day."

"Sure thing," he said and glanced at his watch. "But I have to get going now." I stood up, removed my gloves, put them back in a supply box and stood at the back door. Dave put his shovel back over the fence and came to my side. "Hey, this is your first holiday without them. I know how empty that feels. Why don't you come over for dinner? The group would love to see you again."

"No proselytizing?"

Dave smiled and patted my back. "Just dinner and company." They'd never really done that, but I just wanted to make sure. Old habits.

CHAPTER SIXTEEN

When I arrived next door, the first thing I noticed was how warm and inviting Dave's home was. He'd lived alone for years, but nothing about his house suggested solitude. Things were tidy, books lined handsome cases, paintings of idyllic scenery adorned the walls. Photos of his late wife and son hung prominently over the fireplace.

One particular photo caught my eye: Dave and his wife Lisa holding their son. Dave came over and said, "Adam, he was six months old." The younger Dave stood proudly in full dress uniform next to his lovely wife outside their house in Sabre Springs. I could see the street corner over to the side in the background, where the street lamp stood. Where they were killed. Just a few paces from their home.

"Beautiful family."

"Thanks." Dave invited me to take a seat in his living room. I sat in a comfortable chair, which I quickly learned was a recliner, as he pulled the lever on the side. "I'm going to check on the Turkey."

Ten minutes later, the rest of them arrived. Dave asked me to get the door. Lorraine, the motherly casserole woman greeted me with a warm kiss on the cheek. Alan and Samantha gave me hugs and Jerry, who hardly said a word the last time we met, simply smiled and presented me with a bag of pistachios, one of which he snatched for himself. Then, to my surprise, another guest came in from behind him— not one of Jenn's Bible study group, but certainly one I was glad to see.

"Hey there!" Rachel said, shaking my hand. "Oh, this is silly!" she said, and pulled me down to give me a hug and a kiss me on the cheek. My face heated up. I had not felt the touch of a woman since Jenn died. It was a bit odd because of our attorney-client relationship. Awkwardly, I returned the kiss and took her jacket, as Dave herded everyone to the dining room.

The sweet aroma of corn slathered in butter, Turkey with stuffing and gravy, along with creamy mashed potatoes, tickled my nose as we gathered around the table. I tried my best to smile as everyone held hands and Lorraine said a blessing for the meal. It had been less than two months, but it felt as if I'd been without my wife and kids for years.

I can't remember the exact words Lorraine prayed, but she inspired me to think of things for which to be thankful. After she finished, we partook of the food, hot apple cider and pleasant conversation.

Alan and Samantha announced that they were going to have a baby. A sudden hush came upon the room. They quickly turned to me apologetically. Samantha covered he mouth with her hand and looked like a Doe before a Peterbilt. "I didn't mean to be insensitive."

"Don't be silly," I said. "I'm happy for you both. There's not enough good news these days, anyway." I proposed a toast to the expectant couple and allowed myself to enjoy this temporary sense of belonging. My surrogate family. They were all I had now.

Turkey has something in it called tryptophan, which makes you feel relaxed, even sleepy. I hadn't experienced much of either recently, but this combined with a glass of red wine and good company, was just what the doctor ordered.

Lorraine came back from the kitchen with an apple pie she had baked. Jerry stood next to her grinning and holding a tub of French vanilla ice cream and an ice cream scooper. Far be it from me to turn down homemade apple pie a la mode, that would just be plain rude. We all made room in our distended bellies for dessert.

Afterwards, we dragged ourselves to the living room where some of us men loosened a belt notch or two and reclined around the coffee table. Lorraine served hot tea.

Rachel told a story of how she met a cute gondolier last summer on a trip to Venice with two girlfriends from church. She bemoaned the fact that, though they'd promised to correspond, she lost his email address. It was then, for the first time, that I noticed: the way she smiled, just slightly crooked, how her jet black hair fell half over her face, how she brushed it aside with elegant, porcelain fingers, her silly soprano laugh. I caught myself staring at her, her smile suspended, waiting.

"What?" she said.

Snapping myself back to reality, I said, "Didn't you give him your contact information?"

"Of course not. I just met him. What if he turned out to be some kind of psycho cyberstalker?"

"You live oceans apart."

Rachel picked up her teacup, her violet eyes looking up at me as she sipped. She licked her lips and said, "Don't you think it's important to be careful on the internet?"

"Of course I do. I just don't believe in paranoia." I shrugged. "A little common sense is all you need."

"Cyberstalkers," Samantha said with a shudder. "That's why I never, ever use any instant messenger programs."

Instant messenger.

This brought back something I hadn't thought of since it happened. One evening, just a few days after the Coyote Creek shooting, Bethie had left the computer on, logged into her AOL Instant Messenger. I was about to sign out for her when one of her buddies popped up and asked if she wanted to play a game he'd written.

Curious, I decided to impersonate Bethie.

AnyBeth818: what kind of game is it?

Huliboy: it's like checkers. I'll show you. click the link.

I clicked it. Something installed in the background and a game window appeared. It was full of colorful game pieces—unicorns, mermaids, kittens. All on a bright pink game board. Looked cute and designed for children a bit younger than my twelve year old. I wanted to ask Huliboy his or her real name, but that might tip Bethie's friend off that it was her father chatting. I'd have to get more information in a clandestine fashion. I typed:

AnyBeth818: anyway, my homeroom teacher, mr. bennett said I need to be on time during attendance or he'll mark me absent

Huliboy: OMG! what are you on? ur homeroom teacher is ms fischer!!pls, you're always on time! tryin 2 confuse me or something?

With Bethie's real teacher's name confirmed, I decided Huliboy was really a classmate after all. I continued to play the game for a couple of minutes with its childish music in the background and cute little squeaks and animal sounds the game pieces made every time you moved them.

After two games, both of which I lost, I told Huliboy that I (Bethany) had to go to bed because I had an exam the next morning—which was true.

Huliboy typed, "See you tomorrow." And I did the same. I would explain to Bethie in the morning that I'd met one of her internet buddies, played a cute game, and to tell this classmate that it was all in good fun. We'd all have a good chuckle about my losing a children's game to a middle-schooler. But with all the busyness of life, and stress from work, I had never gotten around to telling Bethie about it.

Talking and laughing all at once, Allen, Samantha, Rachel and Lorraine continued to discuss the perils of the internet. "The filth kids have access to these days," Alan said, gently placing a hand on Samantha's belly. "I'll tell you this, no internet for my kid until he's twenty-one." I thought about the porn that found its way into network directory and my cheeks grew hot.

"Well, when it comes to computers," Samantha said, "I can't help but be paranoid. We have this guy at church—Neil Matthews. He was a victim of identity theft. Some hacker stole his information and charged over ten thousand dollars with three of his credit cards. They caught the guy, but Neil still had to pay for some of it. Investigators said that if he'd used some firewall software, none of it would have happened."

My back ached from pulling weeds with Dave earlier. The tea's aroma soothed my mind. Tendrils of steam floated into my face and warmed me as I took another sip. We each took turns recalling some of our more memorable Thanksgivings and laughed at stories of disastrous family dinners.

"Like the time Bruno, my eighteen pound calico, climbed up on the table," Lorraine recalled, "jumped and landed spread eagle on the turkey and claimed it for himself.

"That's not as bad as when my uncle Henry had too much mashed potatoes and sneezed," Alan said.

"Oh, hon!" Samantha said, shoving him with her elbow. "Not the Uncle Henry story. Please!"

Before long, Jerry whispered to Lorraine who reported to us that it was getting past his bedtime and she had to drive him home. Everyone else took it as a signal that they too should leave, despite Dave's urging to the contrary. Lorraine held onto Jerry's arm as they walked to her car.

Rachel, Alan and Samantha were putting their jackets and sweaters on when my cell phone buzzed.

It was Children's Hospital.

The smiles around me dissolved as I listened to the nurse on the other end deliver the news. When I hung up, Dave came over. "What's the matter?"

I could barely bring myself to speak.

"Sam, what's the matter?"

Finally, I drew a stuttering breath. "It's Aaron."

CHAPTER SEVENTEEN

Rachel, Dave, and I arrived at Children's hospital in less than fifteen minutes, partly because of non-existent traffic on Thanksgiving day, partly because he had driven in excess of 80 miles per hour. A stern security guard met us at the entrance. He glanced at a photo in his hand and instructed us to stay in place. "Samuel Hudson?"

"That's me. I'm here to see my son. They said it was urgent."

"I'm sorry, but you're going to have to wait here."

"What?"

"There's been a temporary restraining order filed against you."

Rachel came to my side. "When? By whom? He hasn't been served."

The guard pointed to the entrance. I turned around and saw Lieutenant Jim O'Brien walking towards us, his black and white squad car parked just outside the glass doors. A different partner, a female officer, remained inside the car.

"Jim," I said, sighing with relief. "There's been a misunderstanding here."

"Afraid not." He handed me an envelope. "Consider yourself served." The TRO was filed by Oscar and Maggie Lawrence's attorney.

"Unbelievable," I muttered and showed it to Rachel.

"I'm sorry," Jim said, thumbs in his belt. "Seems like the grandparents are suing for legal custody as well."

Dave joined the huddle. "I'm going up to speak with Aaron's doctor." The security guard got Jim's approval and permitted Dave to go. "I'll be back."

"I can't believe this," I said, taking the paper back from Rachel. "They've hired Chatham, Young & Bauer."

"Oh dear," Rachel said. "Them."

Jim scribbled his signature on a Proof of Service document. "Do I need to stick around to enforce this?"

"No."

"I'll be on my way, then."

Before he got to the exit, I called out, "Just one question, Jim." He turned to face me. "How did you know?"

He pointed down to the GPS tracker on my anklet. "The Lawrences' wanted to make sure you didn't get within a thousand feet. I would've preferred to wait at least until the morning to serve you, but when we saw you were approaching the hospital..."

"You really think I would hurt my son?"

"You're a suspect. I was assigned to serve you the TRO. I have a duty to uphold."

"You didn't answer my question."

"Yes. I did." And with that, he tipped his hat to Rachel and left. I stood there stunned. How could they do this? *He's my son.*

Rachel and I sat side by side, on blue, vinyl-padded chairs in the general waiting area for what seemed an eternity. I spent most of the time with my head in my hands, fretting, unable to speak. There were moments that I forgot Rachel was there, she was so quiet.

At one point, I picked my head up. She appeared to be asleep, sitting back in her chair, her eyes shut. But her lips were moving. Her brow knitted while this was happening. I thought she might be having a bad dream.

"Rachel?" I whispered, gently nudging her with my elbow. "You okay?"

She opened her eyes. Sharp and lucid.

"Bad dream?" I asked.

"I was praying."

"Yeah, well. The way things are looking, prayer might not help." She patted my knee and smiled. "Know something I don't?"

"In a way."

"Care to let me in on it?"

She turned to me, glowing like the dawn of a new day. "You might not appreciate it the way I do."

"What?" How could she possibly look so positive, so excited?

"I'm going to be completely open with you, all right?" I nodded, having no idea of where this was going. But I was determined to find out. "I just got a word."

"A word?"

"Yes. From God. Sometimes it's referred to as a word of knowledge or a prophetic word."

"So, what did God say?"

She grasped both of my hands, and took a deep breath. "Okay. It's really five words." She just smiled.

"Would you please?"

"All right, here goes." She paused—I wasn't sure if it was for drama, or to further torment me. Then she said the words. "It's going to be fine." A subtle, smile stretched across her face. "Isn't that wonderful?"

My mouth remained slightly agape until I spoke. "Is that it?"

"What do you mean, is that it?"

"Can't God be a little more—I don't know—specific?"

"It was like a sense of assurance. I don't know specifically what He meant, but I know the word was for you. Have faith. God loves you. He loves Aaron. It's going to be fine."

Rachel was intelligent, hadn't an ounce of deceit in her, nor was she insane. What motive could she possibly have to lie? And, I wondered, when God spoke, shouldn't there be thunder, lightning bolts, writing on the wall, a burning bush, like Charleton Heston in *The Ten Commandments*?

The next ten minutes might as well have been ten years. I paced around until Rachel asked me to stop. It was making her anxious. Finally, Dave returned. We ran up to meet him.

"How is he?" I asked.

"He had an infection from fluid build up in his lungs and a high fever. He stopped breathing. But the Motrin got him down to 101 and he's on a ventilator now."

"He made it," I said, so relieved I almost laughed.

"He's still non-responsive, but alive."

I sighed, "Thank God."

Rachel and Dave smiled at each other.

"Amen," Dave said.

CHAPTER EIGHTEEN

The trial was set for December 19. Rachel spent the days leading up to it interviewing just about everyone I knew in search of witnesses who might prove helpful to my case. She ran herself ragged, sometimes working eighteen hours a day and on weekends.

She secured a private detective by the name of Richard Mackey, a friend of Alan and Samantha. He liked to be called "Mack." With my innocence as his starting point, he was investigating every angle, every lead, in search of the killer.

Mack was an ex-cop from Poway who had retired early, after winning seven million dollars in the California Super lotto—his share in a 31 million dollar jackpot that he and others from his softball team had claimed. The money hadn't spoiled Mack, though. Aside from retiring at the ripe age of forty-one and moving to a slightly larger, slightly newer house, he and his family lived pretty much the same as always. He took on only the most interesting cases and charged only a nominal fee. He took my case *pro bono.*

Oscar and Maggie secured a Domestic Violence Restraining Order with relative ease, doing away with the temporary one. My only contact with Aaron came vicariously through Dave, Rachel, and some of the other Bible study group members.

Now Oscar and Maggie were suing for legal custody. They got it. Painful as it was, the ruling neither shocked nor hindered us from plowing headlong into the murder case. One oblique benefit to

Oscar and Maggie taking guardianship was that they could claim Aaron under their medical insurance.

Pastor Dave offered me a position at his church cleaning the sanctuary, offices, bathrooms. The pay wasn't great, but it was better than nothing. "I would have offered it to you from the start," Dave said, "But I knew you had to try to make it on your own first." He was right. I would have been insulted, too prideful to have considered a janitor's job just a few weeks ago. Now, I was happy with whatever I could get. I have a feeling Dave knew I'd get really depressed or go crazy, without something to do every day.

My house sold within a day of listing. The San Diego real estate market was still strong back then. Houses stayed on the market for less than a week before they got snatched up by hungry buyers. A seller's market. Escrow was to close just one week before my trial.

The time came for me to pack up and move out. Anything I had not already sold, I packed away into a total of twenty cardboard boxes. These were the last physical remnants of my home. All the furniture was sold along with the house—the buyer loved Jenn's taste in home decor and that gained me an extra ten thousand dollars in the selling price. I would actually come out a couple of thousand dollars in the black.

Three days before the close of escrow, I walked through the house, packing items of sentimental value. Rachel came over to help me decide what to keep and what to let go. She knew it would be too difficult for me to do alone.

We started in the master bedroom. All the furniture had been covered with pale sheets. The bed hadn't been slept in since the night of the murders. I packed away photos, a large framed wedding picture, some of Jenn's favorite books, her unfinished manuscripts.

Packing Jenn's clothes away in boxes proved more difficult than I could have imagined. As Rachel and I stood in the closet, taking things down from hangers, something caught my eye. It was that silly necklace of seashells I made for her on our first date. As a girl, she had always dreamed of going to Hawaii. With that necklace, I made a promise to take her there one day.

"Why do you keep that old thing," I would ask, years later.

"It's a reminder. Of your love, of how you always keep your promises." She wore it on our honeymoon in Maui, and every time we went to the beach.

Gazing at the necklace in my fingers, I recalled Jenn's perfume, her silken auburn hair that draped over my arm as we walked the La Jolla shores on brisk moonlit evenings, enjoying our time off and trying to ignore our guilt for leaving the kids with a baby sitter.

Some of the necklace's shells were broken, their color faded. But holding it, I still sensed her presence. Her smile, her goofy laugh.

"That one special?" Rachel asked.

"Yeah."

"You should save it," she said, giving my hand a warm touch. The necklace went into a single container which I'd labeled 'Keepers.' A small box that held only the most precious of mementos.

In Bethie's room, there were too many things to consider. I picked out the keepers—one of her baby pictures, her first violin, a 1/16th size, concert recordings and programs. I couldn't watch as Rachel packed the rest away for long term storage or donations.

Aaron's room proved equally difficult. Because he was not actually gone, it seemed wrong to be putting his things away. The Thomas train table, his most prized earthly possession, was too large to be put in storage. I refused to sell it, rationalizing that it would be difficult to explain why I had gotten rid of it when he awakens.

For the first time in a long while, I sat by the train table as I'd done with Aaron many times after work. Every night when I came home, he'd run up to me and make me "fly" him around the house. I'd pick him up, hold him horizontally and together we'd say, "Up into the sky! Past the moon and into the heavens!" Then we'd race down the hallway with his wings spread, and we'd shout, "to infinity and beyond!"

The warmth of Rachel's shoulder against mine reminded me of her presence. She pushed little green Percy around the wooden tracks and said, "My nephew has the same table."

"His pride and joy, right?"

"Yeah."

What I wouldn't give to fly Aaron again. Or to sit there playing trains with him, making up stories and acting them out—just one more time. "God, I miss him," I said, my voice cracking as I held the blue Thomas engine in my hand. "I miss them all." I bit my lower lip to keep from breaking down.

"Oh, Sam." She put her arms around me as I wept, still clutching the train engine in my fist. I didn't want her to see me this way—empty, broken, weak. But there was no use hiding it. "It's okay," she said, whispering warmth into my ear. "You're entitled to a good cry." She tightened her arms around me, pressed her cheek to mine and stroked my back. "Just let it all out."

Her breaths punctuated her own muffled sobs. A tiny whimper confirmed what I had suspected all along. After all the stories she'd heard, all the pictures, she'd grown to love Jenn and my kids like her own family.

I don't remember now how long we stayed in each other's arms. But it occurred to me that besides Jenn, my mother, and Maggie, I had never held another woman this close since I got married. Pulling back, I wiped Rachel's tears. She studied the floor.

With all the negative publicity that comes with being a defendant in a murder trial, I had become a pariah in San Diego. Most of the time it made me angry. But deep down, the worst part of it was the loneliness. Rachel touched a part of my soul that so desperately needed to be known. With her eyes still shut, she lifted her head with glistening lips parted.

I leaned in towards her, placed my fingertips on her face, let them rest there. My breath grew short. It felt so natural. I brought my lips so close to hers that I could feel her breathing.

I wanted this.

So did she.

Just as our lips were about to touch, we both pulled back. She turned her head and I pushed myself back to a respectable distance. "I'm sorry, Jenn— Rachel!" *Dammit.* As if I wasn't already mortified enough.

She smiled demurely and shook her head. "No. *I'm* sorry. Should have known better." Neither of us wished to dwell on what might have proven a mistake. We stood up and acted as if it never happened.

"Thank you for all your help," I said. "Not just for today, but for everything."

"Come on. Let's finish up."

After Rachel left, I spent the rest of the evening preparing for my evacuation. The next day, Dave helped me move the boxes into a self-storage unit. A couple of boxes went next door into his garage. I'd be staying in his house until I found a place of my own, which, on a church janitor's salary, could well have turned out to be a homeless shelter. Dave welcomed me to stay as long as I liked.

On the day escrow closed and with great reluctance, I handed the keys over to the real estate agent. The house was far from empty, though. My children's laughter, the warmth and aroma of home cooked meatloaf, bread and corn, the soft padding of Jenn's feet, trying not to wake the kids, at 6:30 every morning as she went downstairs to prepare breakfast—it was all still there. Even as the door swung shut for the last time.

CHAPTER NINETEEN

The offer stood at murder one, life without parole, which according to the D.A. was extremely generous. He didn't think we'd prevail in a capital murder trial. "It's a gift," he told Rachel. "And why waste time and taxpayer dollars to proceed with a trial you know you'll lose?" This came the day before opening arguments.

Rachel's office, if it could be called an office, hid between an insurance broker's and a travel agency in Clairemont Mesa. Cubicle would better describe it. We sat at a second-hand desk donated by friends from church.

"You need to consider it, Sam. If we lose—"

"No." Watching my wife and daughter die, seeing my boy beaten within a sliver of his life, was bad enough. But to lie and say I did it? At times I would actually welcome the death penalty, if for no other reason than to put an end to it all. But in my heart, I kept hearing Jenn say, "*Aaron needs you.*"

I am ashamed to admit there were even days when I doubted he'd ever pull through. Sustaining hope was exhausting, especially when forbidden to visit. Still, Aaron became my sole reason to go on. That, and the furious determination to find the bastard who did this to my family and bring him to justice. And I didn't mean the California Criminal Justice System. If I ever got a hold of him, I would try, convict, and execute him in the court of Sam Hudson. No punishment was too cruel or unusual for that animal.

Mack had worked long hours chasing down every potential lead and witness, interviewing every expert—pathologists, criminalists, computer forensics. Refusing to concede that he'd exhausted all possible avenues, he remained optimistic.

When I pressed Rachel about my chances, however, she was not nearly as positive. "We really needed the DNA test results," she said. "It's our best piece of exculpatory evidence."

"What's the hold up?"

"I'm not sure." She exhaled forcefully. "Their case is highly circumstantial, but I have to tell you, it's going to be tough. Juries in murder cases like these want blood." She came over, sat in a chair next to me and put her hand on my shoulder. "You might want to consider the deal."

"And lie to the whole world, saying I raped Bethie, killed her and her mother, beat my son into a coma with a baseball bat?"

"I'm not saying that."

"Then what are you saying? Because that's exactly what it'll sound like."

"You're facing the death penalty, Sam. I'm not certain we can win this."

"I can't believe you're even suggesting it."

She took a deep breath, held still for a long pause. Then stood up and rubbed her eyebrows. "I'm just—! I'm just trying to keep you alive."

"At what cost? Dammit Rachel, you're starting to sound like those TV-show lawyers."

She stepped over and jabbed her finger at me. "You're letting pride get in the way of what's most important, and trust me, it's not your reputation or your good name!"

"Oh really?" I stood too.

"Yes, really. What good will you be to Aaron if you're dead?"

"I won't be much good to him if I'm put away for life."

"At least you'll *be* alive!"

"And he wakes up only to find his father pled guilty to killing his mother and sister!" We stood face to face, her arms crossed tightly across her chest, my fists clenched. If anger and frustration had been flames, the entire building would have burned to the ground. Neither of us had slept more than a couple of hours a day for the past few weeks. It was taking its toll.

Blowing out a long breath and running my hand through my hair, I went over to her. "Rachel, tell me. Are you still willing to go in there and fight?"

"Of course. It's just..." She turned her back to me.

"What? What is it?"

"I...I just can't..."

I went over stood behind her. "You can't what?"

She turned around and with anguished eyes, said, "I can't imagine the thought of you laying there, strapped to a table with tubes in your arms. I can't imagine them injecting you with— I just can't..."

I didn't know what to say. She was embarrassed and clearly hadn't meant to make this about her feelings. But there they were. And they mattered to me a great deal.

"We have to fight this," I whispered, wanting to but afraid to reach out and give her a reassuring touch.

"I know. To plead, that would be lying." She turned to me, her composure regained.

"Is your God a just God?" I asked.

"Yes, but…"

I lifted her chin. "Then we have to believe that truth and justice will prevail." She nodded and sniffled. "Didn't you get a word or five back in Children's hospital, that night?"

"Yeah. *It's going to be fine.*"

"That's right. Now, we might not have evidence on our side but we have the truth. That's got to count for something."

With a valiant smile, she said, "I wish I had your faith."

"At least you have someone to place yours in."

"I've been praying for you every night."

"I'll take whatever help I can get."

"Not just for the trial," she said, twisting a lock of hair in her fingers. "I pray that you'll find a home for your faith." Her words resonated within me, made me feel cared for in a way I hadn't since losing Jenn.

I looked her in the eyes and thanked her. Rachel started to gather her things. When she was ready to go, she turned to me.

"Walden'll pull it from the table once we go to trial. You sure?"

"No deal."

CHAPTER TWENTY

If your impression of a judicial building has been shaped by Hollywood, then the San Diego Superior Court building will not be what you'd expect for something as dramatic as a capital murder trial. No grand cupolas, no towering marble columns. Just flat concrete and glass.

When you first walk inside, you're not greeted by breathtaking views of vaulted ceilings with gold-etched frescoes, depicting the ideals of American jurisprudence. You're walking into a government building—drab, cold, air as stale as the daily grind of the hundreds of the people who work there.

People stand in line, placing their briefcases and purses onto conveyor belts, running them through x-ray machines, before walking through metal detectors. You'd think you were about to board a 747 during a code red terrorist alert.

When I entered the courtroom, I sensed the people seated behind the waist high partition in the gallery glaring with scornful eyes. I didn't realize my head was drooping until I saw Dave Pendelton. He pushed his thumb under his chin, silently reminding me: *keep your head up*.

I met Rachel at the defense table and we took a seat. An armed deputy stood in plain view with a clear shot.

"You ready?" Rachel asked.

"Not really."

"Good. Keep that tension, but hold it together."

"All rise," the bailiff announced. "The honorable Judge Jonathan Hodges." My best interview suit hung loose on my shoulders. In less than three months, I had lost thirteen pounds. According to Rachel, Hodges was the worst possible judge we could have gotten. When it came to capital cases, he was an irate hard-liner.

Hodges took a seat on a black leather executive chair; a wall of law books neatly lined the shelves behind him. He thumbed through a couple of pages of a legal brief, an expensive pen in hand, then motioned to the prosecution to begin.

Second chairing, Deputy District Attorney Kenny Dodd stood and pitched the opening statement to the jury. This was not the same "dude" at the interrogation room in the Poway sheriff's station. He'd cut his hair, looked all business, his tone crisp and professional—nothing like that California beach bum I'd met a couple of months ago.

"We're here today because of a crime so horrible, so brutal, most people would find it hard to even imagine. This is the stuff you read in fiction, couldn't happen in real life. But, members of the jury, the evidence will show that truth is indeed stranger than fiction. And more brutal." Dodd walked closer to the jury box and pointed to three blown up photos—Jenn, Bethie and Aaron.

"Jennifer and Bethany Hudson were attacked in their own homes. Raped and stabbed repeatedly. Little Aaron Hudson, while asleep in his bed, was struck in the head repeatedly with a baseball bat and now lies in a coma, even as we sit here now. This all happened in the supposed safety of their own home. Couldn't happen, you might think, not in a quiet, well-to-do neighborhood like Rancho Carmelita.

"But that's not the biggest shocker. The man who did this wasn't some random burglar, some unknown killer. He was the husband and father of this beautiful family." He pointed right at me. I wanted to shrink into my seat until I remembered Dave's strong arm, behind me, ready to yank me up.

"The evidence will prove Samuel Hudson, a pedophile, with financial motive, did in fact murder his family. He did so by taking full advantage of their trust. A sacred trust given to the one person they depended on to provide for and to protect them.

"When the trial is over, justice will be in your hands. You'll see no other choice but to find him guilty." He gazed at the photos on the easels, shaking his head sadly. "Jennifer, Bethany, and Aaron are depending on you to do the right thing." Dodd thanked the jury and returned to his seat.

Without hesitation, Rachel stood up, fastened the top button of her navy blazer and walked quietly to the jurors. "Seeing is not believing. Not always, anyway. The prosecution will attempt to place before your eyes what they consider evidence, in order to pin the blame on the easiest scapegoat they could find. They want a quick conviction, not the truth. But their entire case is circumstantial. There are no eyewitnesses to this crime, nothing that can be proven to an absolute certainty.

"Mister Dodd used that tired, old cliché, truth is stranger than fiction. And he's right." She leaned closer to the jury box. "Imagine this. You come home and find your wife stabbed, dying in a pool of blood. With her dying breath, she compels you to go, check on your children. What do you find? The most horrible thing possible. They've been attacked as well. You spend the night watching your daughter die in the ER and the only comfort you have is that your four year old son has survived. But he's in a coma, from which the doctors doubt he'll ever recover.

"Ladies and gentlemen of the jury, this is every man's nightmare. But it gets even worse. Now imagine that you've just buried your wife and daughter, you're trying to pick up the pieces of your life, and suddenly you're arrested and charged with their murder.

"You've lost your job, you're slapped with a restraining order so you can't even visit your son in the hospital, and you've lost legal guardianship. Your son. Your only family left, who may never come out of his coma, who may very well, at this moment, be dying." She turned to me. "All this while you're forced to stand here, accused of these horrific crimes you couldn't possibly have committed."

She turned to the photos.

"Jenn, Bethie, and Aaron weren't the only victims," she said, emotion filling her words. "My client is a victim too. He's a victim of the real killer, a victim of an irresponsible media, a victim of the district attorney's office, and the police. The police, who aren't bothering to look for the real killer, who is out there now, waiting to strike again.

"Sam Hudson is innocent. Start with that assumption. It's not only your moral duty, it's your legal duty. By law he is presumed innocent. And in truth, he is."

When Rachel finished, she seemed to stand ten feet tall. Never had I seen her speak with such authority and conviction. Why did I ever doubt her? The jurors kept their eyes on her as if she were Moses holding the sacred tablets in her hands.

And this was just her opening statement.

The first witness Dodd called was Detective Anita Pearson, clearly a seasoned pro on the stand. Words rolled off her tongue like greased ball-bearings, giving the impression of one who was never mistaken. With detached simplicity, she responded to the questions pointing at diagrams of my house, its exterior, the interior floor plans, and a table with various items such as the murder weapons, laid out and tagged. She detailed a step-by-step re-creation of the events based on the crime scene investigation.

"The defendant came home while the victim and her children were asleep. The victim may or may not have awoken to find herself being repeatedly stabbed with a knife."

"Can you identify the murder weapon used on Mrs. Hudson?" Dodd asked.

"Yes. It was an eight-inch Henckel's chef knife." She pointed to the knife. Dodd stepped over to the table. He picked it up and walked it by the jury before entering it as evidence.

"Please continue, Detective."

"With the wife fatally wounded, the defendant proceeded to the second victim's room."

"The second victim being?"

"His daughter, Bethany Hudson." Gasps and murmurs floated throughout the courtroom, as though these horrific details were new and had happened only yesterday. "The defendant stabbed her several times."

"How many times, Detective?"

She turned to the jury. "Eleven."

"And then what happened?"

"The defendant then proceeded to rape and sodomize his *daughter*—"

Someone sprang up from the gallery, a man about my age. His eyes flashed with rage as he rushed over to me screaming, "You sick sonofabitch! You're gonna burn in hell after we pump you full of poison and watch you die!"

A few jurors let out frightened cries. Several people in the audience pulled back, making plenty of room for the crazed man. Out of sheer instinct, I slid my chair away from the oncoming attack. Just before he reached the rail, an armed deputy blocked his way.

There was such a commotion that Judge Hodges could barely be heard, pounding his gavel and shouting for order. When the dust settled, I found Dave Pendelton and the armed bailiff standing in front of me, ready to take the deranged man on hand-to-hand, if necessary. The bailiff escorted the man outside.

Hodges' face burned crimson as he addressed the courtroom. "If anyone else thinks they may be unable to conduct themselves as civilized human beings, save me the trouble and leave the courtroom now. From this point on, I promise to hold in contempt the perpetrator of the next such outburst. That's something you can contemplate in a jail cell just a few blocks from here."

You could have heard a mouse breathing. No one dared so much as twitch. Their eyes fixed upon the judge like children staring at a wooden spoon in the hands of an angry mother.

Shaken, I slid my chair back to the table.

"You okay?" Rachel asked. I could tell she was unnerved.

"Yeah."

Dodd continued to question Detective Pearson. With each response, she painted a bloody picture of what she was convinced I had done. I kept my nerve as best I could, clutching the armrest of my chair.

"Then the defendant went to his son's room," said Pearson.

Dodd held up a glossy eight by ten. "Aaron Hudson."

"Yes."

"How old is Aaron?"

"Four." One glance at the jury and I knew Dodd had them rapt.

"The defendant entered the room while the boy was asleep," Pearson continued. He took that aluminum baseball bat." She pointed at it on the table. Dodd entered it as State's evidence. "And at that point he struck the sleeping child at least three times in the back of his head."

She faced me. "What kind of man...what kind of *animal* does this to his own child?"

"Objection," Rachel said, unimpressed. How she remained so calm, I had no idea. I wanted to pound the desk, pound Kenny's face.

"Sustained," Hodges said. "Detective Pearson, you will refrain from commentary and please do not address the defendant."

"Don't fall for it," Rachel leaned over and whispered. "They're trying to rile you up in front of the jury. Just stay calm." I nodded and simmered while the prosecutorial tag-team continued

"Regarding the murder weapons..." Dodd held the knife in his right hand, the bat in his left. "Were there any latent fingerprints found?"

Pearson glared at me again before turning back. "On the knife, there were two identifiable sets. The victim's and the defendant's."

"Were the stab wounds on both the mother and daughter consistent with said knife?"

"Yes."

"And were Mr. Hudson's prints found on the bat?"

"Yes."

"Where were the murder weapons found?"

"In the defendants' garbage container, on the side of his garage."

I whispered to Rachel, "Can't we say anything?"

"Not now."

I stole a glance at the jury, most of them were transfixed with Pearson's testimony. One or two jurors glowered in my direction. I averted my eyes.

Next, Dodd set up two easels with white poster boards on which he fastened large, color photos taken at the crime scene. The blood on the sheets of my bed were difficult enough to behold. But when he displayed the pictures of Bethie's four-poster canopy princess bed, and Aaron's Thomas Train sheets, all covered in blood, I had to force myself not to look away.

The final stake in the heart came in the form of coroners' photos. I had to turn my head and cover my mouth. They were close ups of the stab wounds on Jenn and Bethie's abdomens, backs, arms, hands. But the worst of the lot were the images of their faces. Pale and lifeless. I had tried my best to erase the memory of their faces when they died, but these photos, brought them all back. After about twelve photos, I was certain that the case was closed and that the rest of the trial would be an exercise in futility.

CHAPTER TWENTY-ONE

Rachel approached the witness stand like a mongoose confronting a cobra—Rachel being the mongoose, of course. Her questions were terse.

How long have you worked for the County Sheriff's Department? How many times did you question the defendant? These along with a few basic questions laid the groundwork for her cross-examination.

Now to the evidence.

"You say my client's fingerprints were found on the murder weapons."

"That's right," Pearson replied, with all the charm of a corpse.

"Was that knife from a set in their house?"

"Yes, it was missing from the block in the kitchen until we found it."

"Is it possible that Mr. Hudson, the owner of the house, may have used that knife in the kitchen earlier that day and left his fingerprints on it?" In fact, I had.

"It's not the only evidence we have."

"Please answer the question."

"Of course it's possible, but—"

"Thank you." Rachel held her index finger up, preventing her from saying more. "And the same could be said for the baseball bat?"

"Again, it's not our key piece of evidence. But when you—"

"Perhaps I should simplify the question for you. Is it possible that my client might have left fingerprints by handling the bat, say, to show his son how to hit a ball?"

"Yes, it is possible, but as I said—"

"Thank you." Another abrupt cut-off. "Now regarding the search and seizure of my client's property. Isn't it true that you conducted an illegal—?"

"We had a warrant."

Rachel held up a copy of the document and entered it as evidence, then handed it to the judge. "In fact, you had no valid warrant at the time of the search. This warrant was stamped by the clerk hours *after* you'd conducted it. I have eyewitnesses who place you and a uniformed officer at property hours before it was issued."

"None of the evidence presented today is from the group of items seized during that search. You made certain of that."

"What I did, Lieutenant, was hold you accountable to the law."

"Oh please!"

"Did you conduct an illegal search: yes or no?"

Pearson glowered at Rachel. Her face twitched. "Yes."

Rachel nodded. Let it sink in. The mongoose cautiously paced around the cobra, then struck in a way that surprised everyone. "Lieutenant Pearson, isn't it true that you are up for a promotion?"

"Objection," Walden said, annoyed. "Relevance?"

Hodges regarded Rachel.

"Goes to the witness's bias and history of ambition, which clouded her judgment in favor of ensuring a swift arrest and conviction despite—"

"Objection! Lacks foundation. She's grasping."

"Sustained. Ms. Cheng, move on."

"Yes, your honor." Nice try. The jury wasn't impressed.

"Detective Pearson, as you interrogated my client, did you ever consider, even for a moment, that he might be innocent? That maybe he really did come home and find his family attacked, the way he consistently told you in multiple statements?

"No. I could see it in his body language, his demeanor during all his interviews. He was nervous. According to my experience—and I haven't been wrong to date—guilt was written all over his face."

"You concluded he was guilty before you had any physical evidence?"

"I didn't conclude anything at that point, but I did trust my instincts."

Rachel lowered her gaze. The mongoose was poised to strike. "You've got a pretty good track record don't you?" she stated, more than she asked.

"Yes, I do."

"You've closed just about every case you've worked on, right?"

"Yes."

There was a marked accelerando in Rachel's questions. "You'd love to put a bullet in my client's head if the law permitted you, wouldn't you?" My heart raced like a thoroughbred in the homestretch.

"Objection!" cried Walden.

"You would, wouldn't you? If you could find a legal loophole, you'd shoot him!" The entire courtroom bristled. Like most of the jurors I was at the edge of my seat.

Pearson turned to the jury. "If some animal came and violated your sister, wouldn't you?"

With a smile, Rachel took a deep breath. "I have to confess, I might," she said. "But I'm curious. You mentioned ... your sister."

Pearson remained silent, her hands now planted firmly on the arms of her chair.

"Do you have a sister, Ms. Pearson?"

Walden objected. Hodges overruled.

"No," Pearson said.

"Let me remind you ," Rachel said, "you're under oath."

"I do *not* have a sister."

"Quite true. You do not *have* a sister. Because she died over twenty years ago. Isn't that true, Ms. Pearson?" Again Walden raised an objection. But Rachel was so locked into a groove that Hodges didn't hear it. Or he was ignoring it.

"Yes," Pearson replied. "She died when I was ten."

"And how did she die?"

"Objection. Request that the court instruct counsel to stick with this case," Walden said.

"She opened this up," Rachel said, "by mention of her sister."

"Overruled. I'll see where this is going." Hodges turned to Rachel. "I'm giving you a short leash, Counsel."

"Ms. Pearson, isn't it true that your sister committed suicide at the age of twelve?"

Her eyes narrowed. "Yes."

"Isn't it true that prior to her suicide, she suffered depression after becoming pregnant?"

"Yes." The rest of the answers were 'yes,' as the mongoose sunk her teeth in and thrashed the cobra.

"Didn't she get pregnant as a result of a rape?"

"Yes."

"Wasn't the rapist in fact, your father?"

The crowd stirred. Hodges gaveled for order. Pearson kept silent, but you could almost hear the embers crackling from the fire in her eyes.

"Anita," Rachel said, now sounding sympathetic. "The police reports from 1983 indicate that your father was convicted of repeatedly molesting your older sister back when you were only ten years old. According to the transcripts, during his sentencing, you shouted threats." She read from her notes. "You said, "I'll kill you, you son of a bitch! I don't care how long it takes, I'll kill you! True or false?"

The courtroom fell silent.

"He's still alive," she replied, frosty disdain dripping from her lips.

"Isn't it true that you have a personal vendetta against all rapists? Especially those who attack young girls?" Pearson opened her mouth to reply but Rachel cut her off. "Isn't it true that you've been eager to convict rape suspects based on your gut—so much so that you're willing to break protocol... even the law? Isn't it true that this; all of this—is about revenge?"

"No, no, and no!"

Then something truly unexpected happened.

Detective Anita Pearson, the deadly cobra, the Ice Princess, began to melt into tears.

"Thank you, Ms. Pearson. You've been most helpful." Rachel returned to the desk and took her seat beside me. But before she sat, she turned around again. "And Ms. Pearson. I am truly sorry for your pain."

Giving her a moment to recompose herself, Walden handed her a Kleenex.

"First of all, on behalf of the State of California, Ms. Pearson, I would like to express my appreciation for the excellent work you've done in bringing some of the most violent criminals to justice. You've done a great deal to keep the citizens of San Diego safe."

She nodded, sniffed and held her head high again.

"I only have one question for you, detective. Have you ever allowed your personal feelings and/or your background to influence your judgment in an investigation."

"Never."

"Did you do so with Mister Hudson?"

"No, sir."

"Nothing further."

CHAPTER TWENTY-TWO

During a short recess, Judge Hodges called both counsels into his chambers, the trial resumed. I would later learn that His Honor denied Rachel's motion to suppress the child pornography found in my network directory. She argued that the contents of that folder are considered "work product."

Walden laughed aloud. "Company computers enjoy no privacy." His honor would indeed allow it as evidence.

Next, Walden called my former supervisor, George Small, to the stand. Brillo and Clorox couldn't wipe the smugness from his face. He testified that I had been terminated for using the firm's computers to purchase and store child pornography.

On cross, Rachel tried to establish the possibility that someone else could have planted it. She also tried to make George admit that I had always been a valued member of the firm, he kept bringing it back to the porn and how that brought serious liability to the firm's reputation. How at first, he expected their investigations would clear me. But when it pointed to me, he had a legal obligation to fire me and turn me in.

Unshaken, Rachel placed her arm on the rail by George and looked right at him. "Now, Mr. Small."

"Schmall."

"Right. Schmall." She leaned into him. "You've never liked my client, have you?"

"Objection!" Walden was on his feet.

"Goes to bias."

"Overruled." Hodges rubbed his eyes. "Mr. Schmall, answer the question."

"He's not winning any popularity contests with me. Or anyone else for that matter," George said.

"Is that a yes or a no?" asked Rachel.

"I guess that's a no."

"Isn't it true that the two of you were colleagues a year ago, before you were promoted to partner?"

"Yes."

"And when you became his supervisor, did you ever tell him that you would see him fired before you ever recommended him for a promotion?"

"Not in those words exactly."

From her papers Rachel pulled out a printout. "I have here an instant message transcript from February this year in which you wrote to my client: You think you're better than me, just because they gave you the Franklin case? Well, six months later, I'm your freakin' boss! And you are never going to make partner while I'm here. Better start looking for another job."

"We just had an argument," George tried to explain. "Heated words, that's all."

"This goes on for another page or so," Rachel said. "And the only words my client says in response are: 'sure, George', and 'whatever.'"

Rising from his chair, Walden said, "Move to strike. This is work product."

Hodges shook his head. "Go on, Ms. Cheng. But not much longer without bringing it home."

"Thank you," she replied. With a deep breath, she stepped back from the witness stand and began her attack run. "So, once again, Mr. Schmall. You don't like my client, do you?"

"Asked and answered," Walden said.

"How can anyone like a child molesting murderer?" George said.

"You've wanted to get rid of him since he reported you for legal misconduct and the firm reassigned the Franklin case to him, isn't that so?"

"In the end, I got the promotion, not him!"

"He was a constant reminder of your shame, so you'd do anything to get him fired, wouldn't you?"

"I didn't say—"

"You'd even go as far as getting the help of some computer expert to plant pornography on his computer, wouldn't you?"

"Objection, argumentative!"

"What else have you done to frame my client?"

"Your Honor!" Walden cried. The entire courtroom filled with chatter. Hodges started banging his gavel, calling for order.

"I asked you a question, Mister Small!" Rachel said.

"Schmall," George shouted. "Schmall, you stupid Asian bitch!"

With an arctic gaze that rivaled Anita Pearson's, Rachel stepped back, gave the jury a look and said, "I've no further use for this witness."

CHAPTER TWENTY-THREE

When Fred Chase took the witness chair, I experienced a profound hollowing sensation in my innards. Walden methodically walked him through the debacle in his office. Now everyone knew that I attacked my human resources director in a rage. That did wonders for my character portrayal.

Even with Rachel's cross examination, in which she managed to convey that my rage was understandable, under the circumstances, I felt the jury's sympathy draining away.

I left the courthouse uncertain. Rachel had thoroughly trashed Anita Pearson on cross. Casting doubt in George's direction was a stretch, though. And Fred Chase? She did her best. It was only the first day of the trial and already I was drained.

Most of the credit for digging up the dirt on Anita Pearson, went to Mack, Rachel's private investigator. It didn't thrill Rachel particularly, having to expose the detective's past. A necessary measure, however, and Rachel didn't regret it if it helped my case.

Completely ensconced behind Black Mountain, the sun lay to rest in an amber crested bed. Night fell like an ominous curtain. Dave drove us home on the I-15. How many times had I taken this same route with my kids sound asleep in the back and Jenn by my side, after a concert downtown, or a trip to the zoo, or a day at Sea World?

As usual, dinner was simple. We ordered Chinese from Szechuan Palace and sat around the house like college roomies. I wanted to avoid televised coverage or commentary about my trial, but after an exciting episode of 24, previews for the 10 o'clock news rolled around.

A small video clip of Walden waving his arms around dramatically. The caption read: HUDSON MURDER/RAPE TRIAL BEGINS, STORY AT TEN. No matter what channel we switched to, the coverage was rampant. Finally, Dave and I agreed we'd had enough television for the night. He went to the kitchen to grab another couple of Amstels when the phone rang.

It was Rachel. After a few exchanges, Dave stepped over and handed me the phone.

"I hope you're not watching TV," Rachel said.

"Why? We're famous."

"I'm serious."

"That bad, huh?"

"Lots of talk on both sides."

Although I was dying to hear what everyone was saying, I had promised not to pay much attention to the media. The stress wouldn't help me in court. "How do *you* think we're doing?"

"I'd be a lot more worried if they had some direct evidence."

"We need to get that DNA test back from the crime lab."

"Mack's working on that. Should get an ETA in a couple of weeks."

Provided I wasn't convicted by then. "That'll be our trump card, right?"

"A double-edged sword. For you, the DNA results would be both direct and exculpatory."

As for witnesses, Mack had interviewed just about everyone who'd known me, Jenn, or the kids. Nothing useful turned up, but he was still optimistic. By the end of our talk, Rachel encouraged me to get plenty of rest—I'd need my strength for court. Just before she hung up I said, "Rachel, wait."

"Yes?"

"You did great today. I really appreciate it."

"Thanks, Sam."

"I mean it. Not just today. I appreciate everything you've done. You don't know how much it means."

"My brother died in prison while serving a life sentence for a crime he didn't commit. I know." Somehow, when she said 'she knew', I felt a connection with her. Not sure exactly what it was. I was vulnerable, she'd been compassionate. That was all.

No. I couldn't allow feelings to develop. We said good-bye cordially and I hoped she wasn't thinking about this as well.

All was quiet for the rest of the night. Through the window, pale moonlight bathed my house next door. Only, it wasn't my house anymore. I was an exile.

Dave went to take a shower while I remained in the living room with the television off. I looked for something to read, anything that happened to be lying around. Anything but the *Union Tribune.*

Though my eyes were starting to feel like sandbags, my mind still ran with all kinds of thoughts about the trial. On the far side of the coffee table sat a burgundy, leather bound Bible, its pages open with a satin bookmark in the center of the spine. Curiosity got the better of me and I picked it up. It was open to a random passage.

At first, I found nothing terribly enlightening— just thoughts on living a moral life and a bit of theology. But then I came to a paragraph that stood out to me.

I read it again:

> *He committed no sin, and no deceit was found in his mouth. When they hurled their insults at him, he did not retaliate; when he suffered, he made no threats. Instead, he entrusted himself to him who judges justly.*

A warm, tingling sensation coursed through my body, from my head down to my feet. Various fragments of the passage kept repeating in my mind:

He committed no sin.

Then I heard Jenn's voice, her last words— "*Mercy, not sacrifice.*"

Rachel's "prophetic" word came to mind—*it's going to be fine.* Aaron had been in this coma for two months now. *It's going to be fine.*

All the words swirled around in my head. The Bible passage. Jenn's words. Rachel's. I could swear some of them were audible.

My breath grew short. A bead of perspiration rolled down my face. Inexplicable warmth infused my entire body. For a moment, it felt as if the floor underneath had vanished. But I didn't fall. The room spun. I shut my eyes, unable to breathe until I opened my eyes. The words seemed to glow and rise from the page.

By his wounds you have been healed.

Have been healed?

I didn't realize that I was holding my head between my knees—crash position—until Dave said very quietly, "Sam, you okay?"

"Oh...Yeah...I'm fine."

"You sure?" he asked.

"Just a bit overwhelmed."

"Can I get you anything? Coffee, warm milk, Tylenol?"

"I'm okay, thanks. Just need some rest." Grabbing his proffered hand, I pulled myself up and smoothed out the wrinkles out of my perspiration-dotted shirt. "Tomorrow's another round of testimonies."

"You're in good hands."

"Yeah."

As I started up the stairs, the phone rang. Dave answered it in the kitchen. "Hello?"

I stopped to listen.

"Who is this?" Dave said. I peered over the rail, into the kitchen. "I know you can hear me, so listen carefully. Do not mess with me!" He stabbed the END button.

It didn't take much to figure that the call came from someone upset with Dave, a local pastor, for hosting a killer and rapist in his home. I wanted to grab something, pummel it. Harassment was the last thing I needed from life.

It was just warming up.

CHAPTER TWENTY-FOUR

It seemed like the trial would go on forever. The D.A.'s first expert witness, a computer forensics expert, showed evidence that I had indeed purchased and downloaded child pornography over the internet. He traced credit card transactions to me. Couldn't they see this was blatant identity theft?

Somehow, the hacker stole my credit card information and switched my settings to online statement delivery two weeks prior. Rachel argued that identity theft was common and got the forensics expert to concede to the possibility. On redirect, Walden poked holes in this argument.

The prosecution brought in all kinds of character witnesses, many of them my former co-workers. Amazing how much they wanted to see me convicted. None of the testimonies hurt as much as Mike Seiffert's. My best friend. "You had us fooled, you sick bastard!" he said, pointing straight at me with an entirely alien expression. Thirteen years of friendship. Gone.

My entire social context collapsed. It had been doing so for some time now, but Mike's testimony hammered it home. I contemplated this as I rubbed my ankle where my GPS tracker chaffed.

After another bruising week in court, something occurred to me. Dave, the Bible study group, and of course, Rachel, my attorney, all "religious fanatics" whom I had once despised, were now my only friends.

As long as I'd known him, I'd always been curt to Pastor Dave. But he never even hinted at it. Not even once. Now, facing him every day, hat in hand, living in his home made it more difficult.

Each time I approached the subject, he would deflect it. "We don't need to revisit it," he said one Sunday morning over breakfast.

"Actually, I do."

"I don't hold any of it against you."

"Thanks, but I need to just say it once and for all. Come on, Dave. You of all people know the value of confession."

He set his mug down, wiped his mouth and sat back. "If it's that important to you, go ahead."

"Since we met, I've been less than kind to you. Rude, to be more precise."

"Sam, really—"

"No, let me finish. You've shown me nothing but kindness. Considering how I've treated you... I owe you an apology," I said, now aware of his earnest gaze.

"You owe me nothing."

"You deserve an explanation." A boulder had been lifted from my chest. "You, Rachel, the Bible study group, you're not like any Christians I've known. I thought you were like the rest, judgmental, intolerant, out of touch, I just figured that Jenn had met some decent people who'd eventually disappoint her, given enough time."

"Glad we didn't."

"Me too. But don't expect me to convert, okay?"

Dave let out a hearty laugh. "Sam, have any of us ever tried to push our beliefs on you?"

"No."

"Have we ever made you feel less accepted because of our differences?"

"No. That's just it. What kind of religion is it if you don't go around preaching fire and brimstone, and guilting everyone?"

"You really want to know?"

"I'm curious, that's all."

"Got any plans this afternoon?"

"Other than sitting around?"

"Then why not come and see for yourself?"
"I'm not going to your church."
"Neither am I."

CHAPTER TWENTY-FIVE

Today's service was not held within stained glass and hallowed walls. For Dave, church wasn't in the actual building, it was where ever its people gathered with a common purpose.

Along with the members of his church, Dave took me to the Seabreeze projects near Rancho Penasquitos, where single parent families struggled to raise their children, while working two or three jobs just to make ends meet. Virtually orphaned, many children here saw their parents for only a couple of hours a day. On weekends, this meant lots of kids, lots of time, and very little in the way of guidance, or just good clean fun.

A sunny winter day in San Diego feels like spring in New York. Freshly mowed lawns exude a sweet aroma, flowers bloom and sunlight warms your back, giving you a deceptive sense of hope. But the constant woosh of cars behind Seabreeze Apartments made me think of life passing by these kids at freeway speeds. In the front, however, a wide grassy area, bordered with white-barked camphor trees, stretched across the common area like a park without playground equipment.

Members of City on a Hill, visited often and had been adopted into this community, often helping families by donating supplies, providing baby-sitting, grocery shopping, homework assistance, and tutoring. They also supported local schools by donating much needed supplies, volunteering to repaint and refurnish dilapidated classrooms, and even providing counseling for troubled kids.

On the open lawn, a picnic table covered with red gingham housed a veritable feast. A generator hummed as it powered the air pump for an inflatable monster truck jumpy. It swayed as kids bounced around inside, laughing with delight, a luxury they'd never otherwise enjoy. All this, courtesy of City on a Hill.

Fried chicken, vegetables, potato salad, cole slaw, apple pies, and one of Lorraine's famous casseroles enticed the residents. I licked my lips at the scent of it all. I saw the top of Lorraine's silver head as she sat in a lawn chair surrounded by half a dozen young women. She was handing out care packages—toiletries, soap, toothpaste and brushes, and even some luxury items like bath oils and makeup like the mother hen she was.

Lorraine smiled and waved me over. I turned to Dave who simply nodded and went over to talk to Alan and Samantha, who was not quite showing yet, but glowed the way first-time mom's do when they're with child.

As I approached the circle of ladies, their smiles faded. It took me a moment to understand.

"Ladies, this is Sam," said Lorraine.

"Sam?" one woman in the group said, her face pale. "Sam Hudson?" Quiet gasps floated into the air. They looked like a bunch of cats, too spooked to run.

"Now, ladies," Lorraine said. "Sam is innocent. It's just a matter of time before he's acquitted."

"I...I have to go," a young mom said, her words barely leaving her mouth. "Think I left something on the stove."

"Me too," another said, nearly tripping over the lawn chair.

Lorraine sighed and threw her hands up. "Ladies, please. There's no need—"

Another one: "Thanks Lorraine, gotta run."

My stomach clenched. From their wide-eyed sweeps, scanning the area for their children and an escape route, it was clear what they thought and how they felt about me. They all got up and slinked away, tails tucked.

"Whatever happened to *innocent* until proven guilty?" Lorraine called out. None of them so much as turned their head as they plucked their children from the picnic tables and pulled them back behind closed doors.

"I'm sorry, Sam." Lorraine opened her arms, wiggled her fingers inviting me into a grandmotherly embrace. "I'm so embarrassed."

I had been following Rachel's advice—not paying attention to the media and was unprepared for this. For all those mothers knew, a child-molesting murderer was on the loose. "Didn't mean to break up your little meeting."

"Never mind those girls. I'll straighten them out."

"Don't be too hard on them."

She smiled, touched my face. "Make sure you have some of my casserole before it's all gone."

I thanked her and went in search of Dave. When I found him, he gestured for me to follow him to the table where lunch was being served. "Did you meet Lorraine's group?"

"Uh, well," I frowned.

"Oh, don't tell me."

"Yeah."

"Man, I'm sorry. I don't know what to say."

Over lunch, I couldn't help but notice the sidelong glances, the whispering parents huddled together. When they realized who I was, many of them left with their children in tow. Despite my discomfort, I kept a cheerful demeanor and pretended not to be bothered.

This seemed to be working fine until a scowling man walked over. His tight, black tee shirt revealed taut muscles. He glared at me with volatile eyes. Dave put himself between us.

The guy said, "I ain't got no quarrel with you, Pastor Dave." Trying to muscle his way through, he stabbed a finger at me. "It's this murdering pervert I got a problem with!"

"Settle down Charlie," Dave said, with a grip on his shoulder. Charlie pulled away, a cigarette dangled from the corner of his mouth as he spoke through his teeth.

"Get the hell out of my neighborhood, Hudson. You wanna rape your daughter, kill your whole family? That's your problem. Just keep the hell away from mine."

I tossed my empty plate onto the table and started walking back to the car. As I passed Charlie, he grunted an obscenity and shoved me.

"You really don't want to do this," I said, turning slowly to face him, my fist so tight it trembled.

"Oh, you gonna kill me too?" He sneered, his eyes flared.

"Go to hell." I started off again.

"After you!" Charlie pushed past Dave and came right at me, fist coiled. I turned around just as Charlie took a swing at my face. Before I could react, Dave grabbed Charlie by the wrist, twisted his arm behind his back, sending him to his knees. Charlie gritted his teeth and moaned.

"Time for you to go home, Charlie Fayne, " Dave said. "Think things over, okay?"

Charlie couldn't answer intelligibly, he was too busy straining. His only reply came in the form of a pathetic series of nods.

"You don't know a thing about Sam," Dave said.

More nods. Charlie's face turned red. Then Dave released him. Charlie let out a grunt, fell on his ass and fumbled back to his feet.

"Okay Pastor Dave, I'm going."

Dave grabbed his forearm again. Charlie winced. "You forgetting something, man?"

"What?"

"You weren't particularly courteous to my friend, were you?" Dave shoved him over to me. I took a step back.

"Look man," Charlie said. "I'm sorry, okay?"

"Forget about it." Despite the calm in my voice, my heart was pounding. Charlie spat on the ground then trudged back to his apartment, muttering all the way.

Dave shrugged an apology in my direction. "He really is a nice guy, when he remembers to take his meds."

"That boy's just not right," an old man at the table said, then shoveled a spoonful of Lorraine's casserole in his mouth.

Dave encouraged me to stick around for the next community project—visiting recovering addicts in a rehab center. But I just wanted to go home and rest. That was enough stress for one day.

CHAPTER TWENTY-SIX

Each day the trial went on, I found myself inching closer and closer to a conviction. After a month of the prosecution's case, it finally hit me. I might actually be found guilty.

Walden had established the elements. Which were, of course, preposterous. But tell that to the jury.

Based on the Medical Examiner's report, the attack had to have taken place while I was supposedly driving home from the Padres game. If I'd even been there. No alibi. *Opportunity.*

Of course the murder weapons had my prints on them, I'd used the knife earlier that night to help Jenn cut vegetables while she helped avert Aaron's meltdown and find his Thomas Train toy. The baseball bat used in his assault only had his own fingerprints, and mine. Because I held it often to demonstrate a proper swing. But the prosecution called this proof. *Means.*

The final element was by far the most imaginative. And the most damaging. Walden had concocted quite the story with George. I knew he was going to block my promotion to partnership. And later, my employment at the firm fell into jeopardy because of the porn.

But Walden's theory got even more fantastic: I had recently moved into a fairly expensive house in Rancho Carmelita, where the mortgage pushed the limits of my budget. The insurance money I'd collect from the deaths of my entire family would total two and a half million dollars. Plenty to pay off my house, invest and live off the interest. Add to that the fact that I'd probably been molesting my daughter and it was just a matter of time before she told someone—like her mother. I'd be ruined. *Motive.*

Like a dead fish tethered to a rock, my approval ratings sank. Not since Hollywood wife-killer, Matt Kingsley, had there been anyone so infamous, so reviled by the media and the public alike.

Now came the defense phase. "Your honor," Rachel began. "In light of the State's failure to adequately meet their burden, the defense moves for summary judgment, at this time."

"Motion denied."

It didn't phase her at all. Rachel called Dave Pendelton as her first witness. By his testimony, he took me into his own home, offered me employment at his church when no one else would even look at my resume.

"Do you believe that Mr. Hudson is capable of the crimes of which he is accused?" Rachel asked.

"Absolutely not. I've known him to be a loving father and husband. Protective and caring towards his family."

Rachel thanked him and yielded him to the prosecution for cross examination.

Kenny Dodd did the cross. To my surprise, he emerged from his laid-back surfer persona like a shark. "Reverend," Dodd said. "Isn't it true that prior to the murders, the defendant had barely said a word to you, though you were next door neighbors?"

"Yes. He wasn't comfortable—"

"Thank you. So, is it your testimony that prior to the murders, prior to his moving in with you, that you didn't really know him well?"

"His wife was a member of my church and our Bible study group, she—"

"I wasn't asking about the victim, I was asking about your acquaintance with the defendant."

Dave pulled his lips into a tight line. "Prior? No, I didn't know him that well."

"So when you say that you absolutely do not believe he could have committed these crimes, when you say that you've known him to be a loving father and husband, you really don't know what you're talking about, do you?"

"Objection," Rachel called out.

"Overruled." Judge Hodges instructed Dave to answer.

"As far as I know," Dave said, "Based on everything his wife said, and my own observations, I *do* know what I'm talking about. He could not have committed these crimes."

"As far as you know." A brief pause to let the damage sink in and Dodd fell back for another attack run. "Let's go back to the night of the murders. According to the statement you gave the county sheriff, the first indication of trouble was when you heard the defendant calling for help in the street of your neighborhood, is that right?"

"That's correct."

"A bit theatrical, don't you think? And according to the same statement, you went inside and found the victims in the following state, and I quote: The wife was already dead, the daughter bleeding badly from multiple stab wounds and the son unconscious with blood all over his head and pillow."

I swallowed hard as the memories returned. Dodd read the statement with all the sensitivity of Novocaine.

Dave acknowledged the statement.

"Did you notice anyone breaking and entering the house that evening?" Dodd asked.

"No."

"You're aware that the investigation found no signs of forced entry?

"Yes."

"Did you see or hear anyone fleeing the scene?"

"No."

"The defendant had an alarm installed, did you know that?"

"Yes."

"Did you hear it go off?"

"No, I—"

"That's because-according to the alarm logs— it had not been armed. Did you know that?"

"How would I?"

"Indeed, how would you?" Dodd leaned an elbow on the rail. "And how would you know if the defendant hadn't actually committed the murders, the rape?"

"I just know he didn't."

"Can you say—and I remind you you are under oath—that beyond the shadow of a doubt, you know for a fact that Mr. Hudson did not actually commit those murders and then come outside acting as if someone else had done it?"

"I—"

"Under oath, Reverend. So help you God." I didn't think it possible, but my opinion of Kenny D. dropped a few notches lower.

"I don't believe he did it—"

"But can you say to an absolute certainty?"

Dave didn't blink. He took a deep breath and said, "No."

"Nothing further." Dodd returned to the prosecution table. I expected Walden to give him a high-five, but he simply sat down with a smirk and fixed his cuffs.

His Honor looked to Rachel. "Redirect?"

Come on, Rachel.

With shoulders sagged, she shook her head.

For the next couple of days, it was more of the same—testimonies by character witnesses. Rachel managed to coax Maggie Lawrence to the stand and say under oath that she'd always liked me since I started dating her daughter, that I was a wonderful son-in-law. But Maggie kept glancing over to Oscar, who didn't share her opinion.

Walden proved merciful in his cross examination. Wouldn't win him any points with the jury going after an old woman. Maggie was too gentle, too frail. Her testimony barely made a dent anyway.

CHAPTER TWENTY-SEVEN

On the weekends, I swept the halls and vacuumed the sanctuary of the church. Decent wages, given the job description. Aaron's condition remained unchanged. It killed me to think that at any given moment, he could wake up, at any given moment, he could pass on. And I wouldn't be there for him.

Dave and some of the church members visited him regularly. They prayed over him, sang hymns to him, read to him. Lorraine always came back with a smile and told me how strong little Aaron was.

"That's my boy," I would say, trying to conceal my heartache.

Rachel often reminded me of the word of knowledge she had been given: "*It's going to be fine.*" I still didn't know what to make of that. Nevertheless, I clung to hope. The alternative was not something I could consider.

Despite her faith, however, a weariness began to etch into her features. Over time, she smiled less, her hair sometimes appeared disheveled, and her eyes were often bloodshot. I would later learn that she'd been so focused on my case that she had not been taking care of her health, her personal life, or her finances.

Once in a while, a potential client would approach her with an injury case here, a wrongful death case there. Take them, I'd tell her. She didn't. As a result, her mortgage fell into default and she was about to be evicted from her office space. Creditors hounded her with threatening phone calls and letters via certified mail.

Rachel found herself caught in a catch twenty-two. Had she the financial means, she could hire the best investigators—forensic and otherwise. But she simply couldn't afford it. It was just her, Mack and one computer forensics consultant for expert testimony.

We needed more time. Even with my DNA results subpoenaed, Judge Hodges refused to grant a continuance. To buy time, Rachel scared up as many witnesses out of the woodwork as possible. Just about every member of the Bible study group was called to testify. She even called on Mrs. Holden, one of my neighbors who agreed to testify to my good nature

Instead, Mrs. Holden turned coat and became a hostile witness. According to her, I was a disgusting, incestuous, child-molesting murderer who should be shot right there on the spot. Her entire testimony was struck from the record, but the damage was done.

Undaunted, it was Rachel's intention to drag out the case until the day that my DNA results were ready. Which would be tomorrow. Relief was finally in sight.

Rachel set her translucent, cup of purple Taro Iced Boba with a girthy straw down on her desk as she spoke with Walden over the phone wedged between her left shoulder and ear.

"You've got to be kidding!" she said, now pacing around her desk. "We've waited all this time, and now this?" Rachel spoke with her hands, her features were flushed. To no avail, I tried to hear what the tiny voice coming from her phone was saying.

"What basis have you—? No. No! I'll fight this motion. You know I'll win...Yeah. All right, 8:30 AM... Yeah. Don't *you* be late!" With that, she stabbed a button on her cordless phone and looked as if she might throw it against the wall.

"What now?" I asked, my head spinning from her incessant pacing.

"This is unheard of."

"The lab results?"

"Walden's filing a motion to suppress."

"No way!" Now I was standing, tempted to join her pacing.

"He'll never get away with it," Rachel said, finally stopping and sitting on the edge of her desk. "DNA is much too important. Hodges won't pass over the results. Motion to suppress—give me a break!"

"Suppress on what grounds?"

"He wouldn't say. Guess we'll find out tomorrow."

Walden had to be scared. When—not if—my samples excluded me from those on Bethie, it would smash a gaping hole through his case. He was sweating now and desperately scrambling to bury the one piece of exculpatory evidence that would acquit me.

His Honor's chambers were as cozy as a mausoleum. Thick layers of dust lined the antediluvian bookshelves. The shades were drawn shut as though they'd been so for years. Judge Hodges sat behind a large cherrywood desk adorned with photos of his grandchildren, who, by now were probably about Rachel's age. He listened callously to Walden and her arguments.

Hodges' best efforts went to negotiating an onion bagel with copious amounts of cream cheese, trying to keep the crumbs off his robe sleeves.

"Your honor, this is completely inappropriate," Rachel said. "Counsel is trying to suppress evidence that clearly has the potential to acquit my client." She glared directly at the District Attorney. "What kind of stunt is this, anyway?"

Hodges wiped a smudge of cream cheese from his bagel off the corner of his mouth and got some on his sleeve. It left a white stain which surprised and frustrated him. He wet a paper towel with water from his Arrowhead bottle and tried to clean it off as he spoke. "Tom, this is thin."

Walden straightened up. "The motion is based on the fact that the defendant was coerced by detective Pearson into giving his DNA, blood, and hair samples to the crime lab."

"Give me a break!" Rachel said.

"Nevertheless, we feel that the defendant was intimidated by the detective, who has been known for heavy-handedness. It could reflect badly on my office. The DNA tests should be deemed inadmissible. I will not allow this to open up grounds for a mistrial."

"Your Honor," Rachel said, doing some suppressing of her own. "It's clear that counsel is hiding—"

"I resent that," Walden said.

"Then why are you afraid of disclosing the results? Your Honor, though it's not a huge surprise coming from Mister Walden, this is prosecutorial misconduct."

Locking their gazes, silence ensued between the attorneys. Hodges, who was making even more of a mess on his robe, finally tore himself from his battle with the errant cream cheese and spoke out.

"I have to agree with Ms. Cheng. I want to know whether or not the defendant's DNA matches that found on the girl's body. The motion to suppress is denied."

Walden sputtered. "But your honor—"

"Provide the defense with the lab results by 10 AM."

Walden exhaled. His shoulders drooped. "Fine. I'll have the crime lab to fetch the results this morning, Your Honor." Walden turned to Rachel. "I assume you'll want to introduce the evidence in court this afternoon, Ms. Cheng?"

She nodded, trying to contain a look of triumph on her face. After the judge dismissed them, Walden gave Rachel a sheepish smile and said, "I had to try, you know."

"Whatever."

CHAPTER TWENTY-EIGHT

Having pushed my way through the hallways crowded with reporters and photographers, I was flustered by the time I entered the courtroom.

Rachel wore glasses today. Her eyes were webbed with red and dark circles attested to a sleepless night. And while her eyes were slightly hidden behind stylish tortoise shell spectacles, it was the first time I saw them without the artificial purple tint. Tired as she was, she greeted me with a smile brighter than I'd seen for months. I could see it in how she carried herself—her chin up, stride confident—Rachel was feeling good. She wore a black business suit—pants, not the usual knee-length skirt. Her confidence osmosed to me as well.

Rachel's first witness of the day was Ashok Kumar, an identity theft specialist from NetSecure in Oceanside. Upon examination, he testified and demonstrated how it was possible for someone to have pulled up a credit inquiry—Experian, FICO, etc.—and gotten a hold of all my credit card account numbers, active or not.

"It happens all the time, you know," Kumar said.

"Makes you wonder what other things can be done to frame an unsuspecting victim." Rachel turned and looked over to George Schmall in the gallery. "Is it your expert opinion, Mr. Kumar, that someone could plant evidence in this way?"

"Objection," Walden said from his seat. "She's tacitly accusing the State's witness."

"Overruled."

She peeled her gaze from George. If she got the jury to wonder about him, it might go to reasonable doubt. She reiterated the question, this time facing her witness.

"Let's put it this way," said Kumar. "If someone had the knowledge and skill, they could easily frame anyone they wanted this way."

"Thank you. Nothing further."

Walden approached the witness slowly. With a condescending smirk he said, "Mister Kumar, is it true that you work in a two man firm?"

"Yes."

"How many times have you been called by defense attorneys to testify in identity theft cases?"

"I don't know exactly."

"Come on, now. Ballpark."

"Maybe about ten or—"

"Try twenty-eight."

Kumar shrugged.

"And in all those cases, how many of the defendants were found guilty."

"Again, I'm not—"

"Try zero."

Leaning forward in his chair, Kumar frowned and said, "Those verdicts weren't based primarily on my testimony, you know."

"In fact, we can't tell just how competent you are, if we go by the conviction rate can we?"

Kumar's jaw muscles rippled. "My work is to identify evidence of identity theft. It's your job to draw conclusions."

"Seems to me you've got a bigger career as a professional witness than—"

"Objection," Rachel said, controlling her tone.

Kumar slapped the rail with an open palm. "I take exception to that, sir!"

"You're done, thank you," said Walden with his back turned to the witness. He was already wrapping up his notes, already walking back to the prosecution's table.

The redirect was nothing more than putting out the fire Walden had lit under Kumar's chair. If Walden's cross had brought Rachel down even a notch, it wasn't showing. Kumar was the last of our witnesses, unless of course, I was to take the stand, which by law, I was not required to do.

But doing so would afford me the opportunity to present myself to the jury, my first-hand account of that fateful night, present myself as sympathetic and hopefully make it difficult for them to believe that I was capable of crimes. But at the same time, I would surely fall prey to a vicious and manipulative cross-examination by a D.A. with a high conviction rate and low ethical standard.

It would all be moot after my DNA test results excluded me, however. If ever there was a case-buster, DNA was it. Through these tests, death row convicts are exonerated. DNA is the linchpin of dramatic acquittals. This along with the fact that I had no criminal record at all—not even a moving violation—would surely cinch it.

I was confident.

The jury had been sent to lunch half an hour early because the test results had arrived, hand delivered by a paralegal from the D.A.'s office who had probably been sitting on the report longer than they'd let on.

Back in His Honor's catacombs, Rachel paced around like a caged panther while Walden stood behind one of Judge Hodges' dusty wingback chairs, shifting from foot to foot.

Hodges opened the envelope and started thumbing through the pages from the crime lab. If the perpetual frown etched in face had grown more or less severe, Rachel couldn't tell. Leaning against a window sill, she tapped her fingers incessantly until the judge's eyes emerged from the report. "Would you mind? I'm trying to read."

"Sorry," Rachel sighed.

"Your honor," Walden said, tugging on his necktie. "Once again, I would like to ask the court to reconsider my motion to suppress this—"

"Will you give it a rest?" Rachel hissed.

Two minutes later Hodges stood up and held the pages out. To whom, Rachel wasn't certain. But when the judge nodded to her, she knew. Triumphantly, she stepped over to his desk.

As she read the report, however, her stomach twisted into a fisherman's bend. Her hands began to tremble and she dropped the pages on the desk. Her throat was so dry that barely a pathetic squeak came out when she spoke. "What...? How's this poss—?"

Walden came over, looked over her shoulder and made tsk-ing sounds. "Counsel, you should have agreed to the motion to suppress."

She was too stunned to make a coherent response. "But this report—"

"Proves that your client's semen was found on his daughter's body," Walden said, exhaling with self-satisfaction. At that point, Rachel wanted nothing more than to kick Walden's ass and impale his privates with the point of her heels. She'd fallen straight into his trap. Walden had in effect eliminated the possibility of suppressing the evidence, robbing her of a mistrial. The judge had ruled that the evidence was admissible. Rachel had all but demanded it.

"Your Honor?" she said, but didn't know what to ask him. He wouldn't make direct eye contact with her. "Your honor, please. This is unfair surprise. I'd like to request a continuance."

"No freakin' way," Walden said.

"You keep quiet, Tom," Hodges said, jabbing a finger. "I've known you to troll the depths, but this...this is low. Even for you."

"All perfectly legal," he said, palms open, his face beaming with a toothy grin.

"Ms. Cheng," Hodges said softly. "While I sympathize with your position, proper investigation on your part may have prevented this."

How? Rachel didn't command the resources that the District Attorney's office did. She was behind on her office rent and falling behind on her mortgage of which she was already three months behind and in redemption. Another two months and, according to California's non-judicial foreclosure laws, her home could simply be put on the market and sold by the bank.

Still shaken, Rachel's lip quivered. She fought to keep her eyes from welling up. "Please, your honor. I need some time to prepare a response. Counsel has misled me—"

"You can't prove that," Walden said. "And besides, it's perfectly legitimate for my rebuttal."

"—to believe that the evidence would be exculpatory. I'm not prepared."

"Regardless, this is direct evidence. Damning too." Letting out a slow breath laced with a grumble, His Honor shut his eyes, removed his glasses and rubbed his temples. "All right. I'm giving you one day. That's all."

"But—"

"Do not test the court's generosity, Ms. Cheng."

She nodded, gathered her papers and retreated from his chambers. Then flew down the hallway and holed herself up in a ladies room stall. She'd been bearing the weight of a tremendous burden for several months with a splintered match stick.

Rachel dropped her briefcase, stood there, one hand pressed against the wall, one over her mouth. All her work and worries were collapsing around her. She sobbed for a good fifteen minutes.

CHAPTER TWENTY-NINE

Rachel's eyes were still red when she broke the news. Mike Tyson might as well have nailed me with an uppercut. "That's impossible!" I said, gripping the edge of the worn table in the witness room. I dropped into a chair. "There's no way—"

"Level with me, Sam." Rachel's voice trembled. "They matched your DNA to the semen found on Bethie."

"No way in hell! It's got to be another setup."

"Chain of custody is air-tight. It's yours."

If I weren't so perplexed, so utterly shocked, I might have been able to think more clearly and speak calmly. But I couldn't. I found myself raising my voice, pounding the table. "They planted it!"

"Who, Sam? Who?"

"I don't know. Maybe Pearson, one of the CSI's?"

"No, they got samples from the crime scene before you gave yours."

"Hell, a clerical error?" This was so impossibly surreal I could barely think.

"They've got a fool-proof accountability system. It's no mistake. Your semen was found on Bethie." An entirely alien expression descended upon her pale countenance. "I have to ask..."

"What?"

"I'm sorry, I have to—"

"Ask me what!"

"Did you do it? Sam, did you rape your daughter?"

"No."

"Did you kill her?"

"No."

"What about Jennifer—"

"No!"

"Aaron?"

"NO, DAMMIT, NO!" Before I knew it, a chair flew across the room, smashed into the wall with a loud crash. It had flown from my hand. Rachel winced, tears flowing down her cheeks, breathing with a quiver, but eyes fixed with determination. The door opened and an armed officer stuck his head inside. "Problem, ma'am?"

She shook her head. "We're okay. Thanks."

He gave her a doubtful once-over and said, "You sure?"

"Yes. My client just got some very disturbing news and was...upset."

He looked at me doubtingly and said to Rachel, "I'll be right out here." The door clicked shut.

"It's all over." I sat down and buried my face in my hands. As for how my semen ended up on the crime scene—I couldn't bring myself to say "on Bethie"—I couldn't think clearly enough to speculate.

"I'm sorry, Sam."

"You think I'm actually capable?"

"As your attorney, what I believe is irrelevant. I have an ethical duty to zealously defend you to the best—"

"Yes or No, Rachel."

She stared at me for a moment longer than I would have preferred, then answered. "No. I don't believe you did it. Nor do I believe you could."

"Good." The tension ebbed as we held each other's gaze. I could breathe again.

"But I can't get this evidence suppressed." She went on to explain how the DA had tricked her.

"So we're doomed. What'll we do?"

Rachel sat down across the table, reached out and took my hands in hers. "With your permission, I'd like to ask Walden to reconsider the deal."

"We've been through this already."

"Not this close to verdict."

I tore my hands away. "What makes you even imagine I'd change my mind!"

Gathering her papers and stuffing them into her briefcase, she stood and said, "All right. We have a twenty-four hour continuance so I can study the reports and prepare some kind of a response. You'd better get some rest and start thinking about..." I knew what she meant to say, but the words were too fatalistic for her to utter.

"I know." Besides Aaron, there really wasn't anyone I felt compelled to see one last time, before... well, just before the final phase.

"If you need to contact me, call my cell," she said on her way out. "My land line's been shut off along with my hot water. I think electricity goes next week."

I stood up to see her to the door, but she didn't so much as look back. As she stepped through the doorway, I grabbed her hand. "Wait."

She looked up to the ceiling, shut her eyes as if my words were barbed. "I have to go."

"Look, I'm sorry," I whispered.

"It's okay, I understand." She started off again, but I gently pulled her back to me. It wasn't my intention, but she ended up in my arms. Before I could put some distance between us, she relaxed and leaned the back of her head into my chest.

My heart hammering, my head spinning, I couldn't sort things out. I backed away and turned her around to face me. "I just wanted to say, thank you. No matter what the verdict."

A tear escaped her eye. "It's going to be fine."

CHAPTER THIRTY

Standing on the corner of Broadway and Front, waiting for Dave to pick me up, I almost felt like a free man. Deputy Amarillas stood with me but didn't say much, just kept his eye on me. Shaded by the visor of a Padres baseball cap and dark sunglasses, I buried my face in the Union Tribune. The last thing I wanted was to be recognized by my adoring fans.

The midday sun stretched high above the buildings. My navy suit absorbed so much heat that I had to take the jacket off. I kept shuffling my pant cuffs, self-conscious of the GPS anklet peeking out.

I looked at my watch, then to the deputy and shrugged. "He's running late. Maybe traffic." The poor officer kept eyeing the hot dog vendor on the curb. Each time the stainless steel lid opened for a customer, steam from within lifted out carrying the savory aroma of Hebrew Nationals, sweet onions, and sauerkraut.

Amarillas stood ramrod straight, eyes hidden behind mirrored shades, hands on his hips. He might have looked cool if he wasn't licking his lips like a puppy in a butcher's window. It was, after all, lunch time.

I appreciated the State's concern for my safety, but I was standing in broad daylight outside of the San Diego Superior Court. Nothing was going to happen to me.

"You know what? I'll be okay," I told him. "My ride's just a little late."

"You sure, sir?"

"Go on, I'll be fine."

He tipped his hat and nodded. "I'll be on the steps where I can keep an eye on you." I thanked him and was tempted to buy a frank for myself, but I had lunch plans with Lorraine and Dave. If they'd ever show up.

Just as I started to search for his number on my cell phone, I saw someone familiar, just across the street with a finger pressed into one ear, a cell phone into the other. When I realized who it was, something ignited in my chest. I couldn't have been thinking straight, because a second later I was storming across Front Street. Nearly got hit by a taxi cab, but I went forward and stood right over him as he spoke into his cell.

He looked up at me, clearly perturbed at my proximity. "Can I help you?"

It was Brent Stringer. I hadn't seen him since he interviewed me for the "Superdad" article.

"I think you've done plenty, already," I said and removed my sunglasses. I was expecting him to cower. Instead, he shook his head and held up a finger.

"Call you back, okay? Bye." He flipped his cell phone shut and slipped it into his pocket.

"I just want to know one thing," I said, seriously trying to keep from smashing in the guy's face. "Why?"

"I just write the truth, okay? The public has a right to know."

"I haven't done anything."

"We'll see if the jury sees it that way, won't we?"

"I thought you'd gotten to know me, my family. Made me out into some kind of national hero. You know I couldn't have done it. But now, you've convicted me in the press."

"Nothing I wrote was libelous, our legal department vetted that last article. It was just an op-ed piece, my own opinions."

"This must be great material for your novels."

"I strive for authenticity." A dark smile eased onto his face. "Tell me, Sam. How did it feel doing your daughter, just before she—"

I caught him by the throat. Thrust forward with such force that his back smacked against the plate-glass window of a coffee shop. I clamped down around his throat. "You sick bastard!"

He tried to speak, but my grip choked off his words. But even as he tried to pull my fingers off his throat, he managed to keep a smug demeanor. With his eyes, he mocked me. When they rolled back and he began to lose consciousness I decided to let go. The writer gasped like a trout on the dry ground.

"You... are such... a...a freak!" he said, holding his neck. He touched the back of his head then held up his blood-stained fingers for me to see.

The Deputy Amarillas took hold of my shoulder. I pulled Brent to his feet and shoved him back against the window.

"Problem here?" Amarillas said.

No words. For a moment I actually thought, since I was about to get convicted of first degree murder, they would only have to add another count to my charges. Might as well get my pound of flesh.

Brent waved Amarillas off. "It's okay. Sam was just showing me a move from his Tae Kwan Do class. Just got a little carried away. Didn't we, Sam?"

With his hand conspicuously near his gun, the deputy looked to me but I didn't answer. The anger hadn't yet subsided, but I was ashamed. What had I become? A small crowd pretending not to be looking dispersed. Might as well have made a public confession to the crimes I'd been charged with.

I glared at Brent then started back to the corner where I was supposed to be waiting for Dave. Where was he anyway? I crossed the street while the deputy asked Brent if he was all right. Brent nodded, smiled and smoothed out his shirt. He shot me a look, grinned, shook his head and flagged down a cab. Amarillas decided to stay with me until Dave arrived.

After calling one or two more times, I only got Dave's voicemail. I didn't have Lorraine's cell phone number and no one was picking up at the church. He was almost an hour late now and I was starving.

So I bought a hot dog and sat on the court steps waiting.

A half hour later, Dave called.

"Where are you? "

"Five minutes from you. Sam, I'm really sorry... about the delay." His voice was shaking.

"What's wrong?" He didn't answer. "Dave?"

"Something's happened."

CHAPTER THIRTY-ONE

Whatever had happened, it must have been serious. Dave stared over the steering wheel and out into space.

"Want me to drive?" I said. He nodded and started to climb over to the passenger seat. The car started to roll forward when he took his foot off the brakes. "Dave!"

Startled, he jerked his head up and pulled up the parking brake.

"*Definitely* better let me drive," I said.

Another vacuous nod.

Five minutes later we were heading back north on the 163.

"What's happened, Dave? Are you all right?" At first, barely a sound came out when he moved his lips. He cleared his throat and tried again. "There was a fire."

"Fire? Where?"

"Church."

"Andy called around Ten O'clock. Said the church had been vandalized. Last night someone scrawled in red, on the doors, *"Their blood is on your hands too*!" Windows were smashed. They trashed the sanctuary."

"Oh my God."

He continued. "When I got there today, I was expecting to find broken glass, overturned chairs. Instead, there were fire fighters trying to put out a huge blaze. Andy had gone back to get something from his car. He heard an explosion. Turned around and the entire building was up in flames."

"Anyone hurt?"

Dave choked back tears and nodded. "They couldn't get to her in time. She was in the kitchen preparing sandwiches for the homeless shelter."

"Who?"

"All her life, all she wanted was to serve people. To show them God's love."

"Dave, who was it?"

He squeezed his eyes shut, shook his head tersely. "She never hurt anyone. Never an unkind word." I wanted to pull over onto the shoulder as we merged with the I-15, but the traffic was moving too quickly.

"Who was it?" I asked, again.

He buried his face in his hand, took a deep, tearful breath. "Lorraine."

As long as I'd known him, I never saw Dave like this. He was always the model of strength and resolve. With hardly a word since entering his house, he went straight to the living room, kicked a vase over and fell into the sofa, his head in his hands.

Not knowing what to say, I sat across from him and kept silent. In the short time that Lorraine and I got acquainted, she treated me like a son. I never ate enough, was getting too skinny, never wore enough. A casserole awaited me in Dave's kitchen, whenever she came over for Thursday night Bible studies.

I sank into the cold leather and remembered her warm smile, fair hair, and eyes wrinkled by years of smiling. If she had no other influence on me, it was her joy—indefatigable joy. And that, she had in spades. Though her life had not been an easy one, she always counted her blessings. "Joy, my dear Samuel," she once said, straightening my collar, "is not the absence of pain, but the presence of the almighty."

I missed her already. Didn't realize it until I noticed her Bible resting on the coffee table. Its faded cover must have been black, years ago. She often left it behind after Bible study and came back for it the next day. Only this time, she wouldn't.

For what felt like an hour, Dave and I sat there, the only sounds, our breathing, the ticking of an old wall clock, and eventually, children returning from school and playing and laughing out in the cul de sac.

"Is there anything I can do?"

He shook his head.

"Dave," I said, unable to form my thoughts. "Why?"

"Who knows?" he sighed. "We've asked this since Cain killed Abel."

"Why God lets bad things happen to good people?"

"Yeah."

"And?"

"We can't know exactly what God has in mind when he allows the wicked deeds of evil people to ravage the lives of the innocent." His words were strong, but a look of anger kept at bay loomed behind his eyes. "But I keep hanging on to the belief that if we knew the future, we'd likely take the same road God set before us, if we had to do it all over again."

"Even with the death of loved ones? You take a lot on faith."

"My entire life is based on faith. That, and the knowledge that death is not the end. Everything changes when you see that."

"So you think God allowed all this tragedy for a greater purpose?"

Dave's eyes fell to the floor. *Please, don't spout some inane platitude.* Finally he said, "Right now, I can't see it. Can't make any sense of it. It doesn't seem fair. To Lorraine, to our church. All we did was what Christ taught— serve and show love to the needy, the downtrodden. Why did God allow this to happen? Honestly? I don't feel it's right."

"How *do* you feel then?" As if I had to ask.

"Angry! Angry at the thugs who torched the church. Angry at the criminal justice system that isn't lifting a finger to find Jenn and Bethie's killer—now that they have you." He punctuated the thought with a fist on the arm of the sofa.

Settling down, Dave sank into the upholstery, rubbing the back of his neck. Calmer now, he said, "I have to admit, I'm angry at God too."

"Aren't you afraid He'll strike you down with lightning or something?"

He shook his head. "We've been here before. God can certainly take *my* anger. He understands what I've been through. And despite all the pain, He's been faithful."

"That's not the image of God I grew up with." To me, God was this monolithic, celestial kill-joy that sat in a judge's robe with a powdered wig. Lightning bolts shot out of his gavel and he was basically ready to condemn the slightest hint of wrong-doing. The whole world was doomed because of this harsh and angry, all powerful being." This was the god of my father, Ian Hudson—a lying, cheating wife beater who only invoked God's name to control and abuse people.

Dave picked up a picture from the end table—his young wife, holding their baby. He touched the photo with tenderness, then covered his eyes.

I stared out the window, giving him some time to recompose. Dave set the picture back down. He glanced over at the wall clock, wiped his eye and stood up. "I have to go to the sheriff's office to answer some questions."

"Want me to come with you?"

"Thanks, but no. Lots of people to talk to. I won't be back till late."

"You okay?" I asked.

Letting out a slow breath, Dave finally looked me square in the eyes.

"Yeah. It's going to be fine."

A chill bolted up my spine.

After he left for the sheriff's, I sat in the kitchen and brought myself to eat a long overdue lunch—Lorraine's potato casserole, left over from last night. I slid the pan into the microwave with reverence and wondered if I should say a silent prayer for the old girl. Her death had all but eclipsed the blade of the guillotine that still loomed over my neck.

CHAPTER THIRTY-TWO

The decision to take the stand came after hours of pacing, hand-wringing and mental volleyball. With the damning DNA test results coming in the rebuttal, there wasn't much we could do but cast a wide net of reasonable doubt and hope that I appear sympathetic before the jury.

But would they believe me? What possible explanation could there be for the DNA match? My case was being charged as a Special Circumstances murder—aggravated assault, rape, rape of a minor—and the state was seeking death by lethal injection`.

Wearing her savvy glasses today, Rachel's hair was tied back and she sported a sharp navy business suit. She warned me not to get overly emotional nor detached while testifying. "Just be yourself." The problem was, over the past few months I'd forgotten who that was.

She leaned against the rail of the jury box such that when I answered her questions, the jurors would get a good look at my face. I told the whole story from the moment I left for my client meeting until when I ran out into the street, covered in blood and screaming for help. By the time I was done, I thought for sure there would be at least one juror dabbing her eyes.

Nothing but impassive stares.

Under oath, I had spoken the truth, poured out my heart, and they weren't buying it. I was the last of Rachel's witnesses. She had called criminalists, EMS, doctors, members of the Bible study group.

On cross examination, some of our key witnesses were casually impeached by Kenny Dodd, others torn to shreds by Walden on cross. Several of them stepped down from the stand in tears.

Now it was my turn.

Walden waited a few seconds after Rachel took her seat. Then he stood up, buttoned his jacket and approached me. "You stabbed your wife twelve times, then raped your daughter and stabbed her ten times, didn't you?"

Rachel objected immediately. He acted as if he didn't hear.

"Then you went to your son's room and beat him with his own baseball bat, didn't you?"

"Objection."

"Sustained." The judge shook his head but was alarmingly tolerant.

"Isn't it true that you'd recently moved to Rancho Carmelita, even though the cost of living was a lot higher than expected, that you had reservations about being able to afford it, but your wife believed you could manage?"

"Objection," Rachel said. "Irrelevant."

"Goes to motive."

"Overruled."

I answered in the affirmative.

"You were having trouble making your monthly bills weren't you?"

"We managed," I replied.

"In fact, according to an Experian credit report, you have two 30 days on your mortgage and HELOCs, two 30 days on your American Express Card, and a 60 day on the Visa card which you used to buy the kiddy porn."

"Objection!"

"Allegedly...." Walden smoothed his necktie. "Allow me to restate the question. You were experiencing financial hardship, weren't you?"

I explained that with the recent move, I hadn't gotten to changing the mailing addresses for my bills and amidst all the commotion of unpacking and settling into a new home, I had forgotten all about them until the lenders contacted me. "I made my payments the same day they called."

"But on paper, one could argue that it looks like financial hardship. Wouldn't you agree?"

"One might, if he wasn't interested in the truth."

"And you're just honest Abe, aren't you?"

Rachel bolted from her chair. "Your honor!"

"All right, Counsel," Hodges said to Walden. I glared at the D.A., but there was no way I'd take the bait. "Mister Hudson, let's just say—for arguments sake—you were feeling financially pressured, but for some reason you didn't want to upset your wife, who wanted a new house. So you agree to buy a home in Rancho Carmelita that costs..." he flipped through his papers and said, "...nine hundred and fifty-thousand dollars..." He took a deep breath and exhaled as the figure sank into the minds of the jury.

Without a pause, I said, "We were in complete agreement about—"

"Please wait until I've asked a question. Now, you're hurting financially, you resent being pressured into this situation..."

"Objection."

"Again, goes to motive, Your Honor," he countered.

"You're reaching," Hodges replied. "Speed it up."

He thanked the judge and continued.

"Were you happily married, Mister Hudson?"

"Yes."

"Really?" Was I supposed to answer that? I hesitated and instantly regretted it.

"Asked and answered," Rachel said.

"Let me ask you another question," he turned to Hodges with open hands. "And, begging the court's indulgence, I promise it's related." The judge consented. "Did your wife, daughter, and son have life insurance policies?"

"Yes."

"For how much?"

Was Rachel going to object? Sure, it was relevant to motive, but shouldn't she object? She was writing on a legal pad and reading a pile of notes. "It was a standard policy," I finally said. "The policy was based on assets, liabilities, potential loss of income—"

"Please just answer the question. How much?"

"Two and a half million."

It was clear that Walden was a shrewd prosecutor, but now, by the way he arched his eyebrow, puffed his chest as if aghast—or at least conveying a silent, "aha!" with his eyes, it was becoming apparent what a masterful thespian he was. He turned slowly to the jury. "Two-point-five million." Walden whistled. "That's a lot of money. "Well, *that* would certainly solve your financial problems, wouldn't it?"

Now Rachel objected. But I couldn't sit on that one. "Look! I didn't—!"

"You didn't answer my question, Mister Hudson. But you know what? Don't bother." He walked to the evidence sitting on the table and picked up the knife that had been used that night.

"Does this look familiar to you, Mister Hudson?"

"Yes, it's from my kitchen."

"In fact, it's the murder weapon, isn't it?"

"That's what the police say."

"Can you explain how your fingerprints got on it?"

"It's simple. I'd been cutting vegetables earlier that evening."

"Yes, so you've told us. But isn't it true that your fingerprints were on it, because you used it to stab your—"

"OBJECTION!" Rachel's voice filled the courtroom.

"Mr. Walden," Hodges said. "I'm warning you."

He smiled, nodded a fake apology—bastard knew he was crossing the line.

"Fine," Walden said. "I have the same questions about the baseball bat, but everyone knows what I'm getting at. The question, Mister Hudson, is this: Besides those of the victims, why were your prints the only ones found on the murder weapon and the bat?"

"Because the killer was wearing gloves."

"The killer was wearing gloves," he repeated, with a twisted smirk. I was ready to grab Court Exhibits 5 and 7 and demonstrate on Walden. "Do you really expect us to believe that excuse? You're not about to pull a Johnny Cochran on us here now, are you?

"It's the truth!"

"You *would* deny, if in fact you killed them, wouldn't you?"

I wasn't going to answer that. I just tried my best to keep my poker face on.

"You're a southpaw, aren't you?" he asked.

"Yes."

"Did you know that the Sherriff's department criminalists have determined by the knife wounds that the attacker was also left-handed?" Acting surprised is fairly simple, especially when you're not acting. Pretending not to be surprised—therein lies the challenge.

How had we missed that? Not that the answer really mattered. Walden had kicked me in the crotch and my reaction was all he was really after. He got it in flying colors. "I repeat. Did you know that the attacker was left-handed?"

"No."

"My, my. What a coincidence," said Walden with a vinyl smile. He pointed at the horrific, blown up, photos of my wife and daughter. "So you just came home and just...*found* them that way."

"No, I already said that—"

"Right, right. You claim they were still alive when you first got to them."

"That's exactly what happened."

"Right. So, let's review: You killed your wife."

Rachel objected.

"No," I replied.

"Raped your daughter."

"No."

Again, Rachel objected. The judge pounded his gavel, but Walden was on a roll. He was in my face now, making a violent stabbing motion. "Stabbed her, over and over and over and over."

Rachel was shouting her objections.

I couldn't restrain myself. "No!"

The audience's murmuring crescendoed and Hodges rapped his gavel one last time. "Mister Walden!"

"Then you took a bat—!"

I leapt to my feet. "No dammit! I didn't do any of that!" Fists clenched, I don't know how close I came, but I wanted to grab Walden by the throat.

He stared at me, feigning surprise. "Do you want to hurt me, as well?"

"MOVE TO STRIKE!" Rachel leapt to her feet now.

"Too late, counsel," Walden sneered. "Your client's already done that. And his family paid the price." And with *that* fatal blow, he went back to the prosecution's table. "Nothing further."

Rachel's redirect should have caused the jury to at least doubt Walden's assertions. If it did, they gave no such impression. While the court recessed for lunch, I asked Rachel what the deal with Walden was—his cross examination was pretty lame. "How can he be so thick?" The anxiety in Rachel's eyes answered more clearly than her words.

"He's just warming up for the presentation of the DNA evidence."

CHAPTER THIRTY-THREE

When determining guilt or innocence, DNA evidence is for the most part an absolute. The presentation of this "new evidence" came as no great surprise to us. To the jury and the public though, it was a land mine. That made it much easier now for them to convict and sentence me with a clear conscience.

My stomach wrenched tight as the prosecution's expert witness from the lab took the stand. I kept wiping my palms on my pants. Rachel had only a few questions for the DNA expert, most of them a weak effort to impeach. How much were you paid to testify? How much do you make each year testifying for the D.A.'s office? Has your testimony *ever* contradicted the prosecution's case? You wouldn't want to risk a lucrative career by admitting it, if you'd fudged the test results to make my client appear guilty, would you? The desperation was lost on none.

Finally, Kenny Dodd called out his objection, which the judge sustained. But Rachel was done. Had she sufficiently damaged the witness' credibility? Difficult to tell because he didn't flinch even at the most inflammatory questions. Walden had more than enough time to coach him on the admission of the DNA test results—State's Exhibit 24. We knew this was coming.

There was no defense rejoinder. It would have been nice to have a few surprise witnesses of our own like perhaps, Mack testifying that there had been evidence found at the crime scene indicating an intruder. But the killer was so meticulous that he left nothing. Not a trace. It was basically my word against the State's.

Both the defense and the prosecution rested.

I never realized just how manipulative and tasteless a lawyer could be until Walden began his summation. He clicked a button on a portable CD player and a recording of Bethie playing the slow movement of *Spring* from Vivaldi's *Four Seasons* filled the courtroom. All the while, he held up a photo of the most precious, angelic little face I'd ever known.

"Bethany Hudson. Twelve years old. So much ahead of her. So much promise. But now, she will never experience the joys of life—her unique and beautiful life: a Carnegie Hall debut, a first kiss, marriage, children of her own." The poster-sized photo was taken by the Union Tribune photographer for the feature Brent Stringer had done on me, just weeks before the murders.

The music added just the right blend of beauty and melancholy. Juror number five wept openly. Juror number six put her arm around her and patted her shoulder.

Next, pictures of Jenn. Walden had gotten a hold of our photo album and had seized some of my most prized memories. He held up a photo of Jenn in her wedding gown. Her smile lit up the room even through her mere likeness. I missed her so much.

"Jennifer Lawrence-Hudson. In the prime of her life. A budding writer poised for a successful literary career, a devoted wife and mother, faithful member of her church and community. Betrayed and killed by a deviant, pedophile of a husband who cared only about the insurance money.

"Ladies and gentlemen of the jury, from the testimony of our witnesses and the blood that drips from the defendant's own hands, the evidence is beyond compelling. The fingerprints, the credit card records, the child pornography, the semen found on his own daughter. What else does anyone need to conclude that he is guilty? Guilty beyond a reasonable doubt.

"This was a premeditated crime of greed and sexual perversion. And let's not forget the attempted murder of his own son, Aaron Hudson, who now lies in a coma with practically no chance of recovery. He was only four years old when his father took a baseball bat to his head.

"To be clear, these were first degree murders with special circumstances. In the name of justice, of truth, I implore you. You must find the defendant guilty on all counts. Show him the same mercy as he's shown his victims—his own family—he deserves as much. Anything less would not only be unjust, it would be immoral." He finished by holding up a photo of the three of them. "These beautiful children and their mother never had a chance to express their shock at such a betrayal. They no longer have a voice." He set the pictures down on prosecution's table and returned only to jab a finger at the jurors. "You must be their voice, for they have none but yours." He held their gaze like Svengali then returned to his table.

After a few seconds, the entire courtroom fell silent.

Rachel got up to approach the jury box. She hesitated. For the first time in the entire trial, she spoke with open and empty hands. "Ladies and gentlemen of the jury, the State has proven nothing. From the initial investigation by a severely prejudiced, and I daresay, disturbed detective, to the possibly tainted DNA samples and report by a biased career witness, their handling of this case could possibly be one of the worst miscarriages of justice in the history of the United

States.

"The court will remind you of the burden of reasonable doubt. Unlike a civil trial, criminal cases demand much higher levels of proof. Certainly much higher than what the prosecution has tried to pass off.

"Samuel Hudson was framed. Based on that truth, it is clear that the prosecution's evidence could have been planted by any number of people, none of which, by the way, have been examined or even brought under suspicion. Anyone capable of independent thought can see that there's plenty of reasonable doubt to go around a few times and back.

"Every bit of evidence is circumstantial and the prosecution has twisted it to fit their theories. And, ladies and gentleman, that's all they are, theories. Hypotheticals which can be reasonably and credibly explained. The real killer wore gloves. Of course my client's fingerprints would be found on household items found in his own house. The DNA test results could have been falsified. It would take a very thorough investigation to scrutinize the State's chain of custody over the evidence. They're counting on you not to question this. Don't let them dupe you like that. You cannot be a hundred percent certain—and I mean absolutely certain—that my client committed these heinous crimes. Therefore, by law, you must return a verdict of not guilty. It's not just your legal duty, it's your moral duty, to uphold a system designed to protect the rights of the innocent, designed to prevent this country from becoming a police state.

"Members of the jury, you are about to arrive at a verdict that can mean life or death to an innocent man who has already suffered unimaginable loss. Would you join hands with the real killer, wherever he may be right now, and help him finish off his last victim?" Tears had been dried. All eyes in the jury box remained fast on Rachel. "Or would you quickly end this unjust ordeal for my client and urge the state to investigate and find the real killer? It's all up to you."

CHAPTER THIRTY-FOUR

Rachel paced around the witness room, her eyes sometimes squeezed shut.

To break the monotony, I asked, "What do you think?"

"It's really hard to tell." She leaned back against the wall and studied the drop-ceiling panels. I lowered my head, trying to shut it all out: the low-pitched droning of the overhead fluorescents, Rachel's soles rubbing against the linoleum, and the ding of the elevator down the hall filled my mind, followed by images of Jenn and Bethie. And then there was Aaron.

"We're going to lose, aren't we?" I said, rubbing my eyes.

"Honestly? It'd take a miracle—"

"You still believe in them, don't you?"

She let out a tired breath, deflating before my very eyes. "I thought I did."

"Aren't you going to pray about this?"

Taking a seat next to me, she held her forehead in her hand and said, "That's all I've been doing since... Anyway, it might be all we have now."

"Yeah."

"Do you mind?"

"Nothing to lose," I said with a shrug.

After a pause and a deep breath, she began. Just as she was about to finish her prayer in Jesus' name, the clerk rapped on the door.

"Jury's back." Quicker than we'd anticipated.

It was time.

No matter what, I would face the verdict with my head held high. Judge Hodges turned to the jury box and welcomed them back. "Juror number ten, it is my understanding that the panel has made a decision. Is that correct?"

"Yes, Your Honor." Juror number ten, the foreman, was a stern looking man about my age with absolutely no trace of emotion, no hint of their decision to be discerned from his face.

Folding his hands, Hodges said, "Would you kindly hand the verdict forms to my bailiff?" I struggled to keep from shaking. Couldn't breathe, my stomach cramped, but I kept my head up. I clenched my jaw to prevent my face from twitching as the bailiff walked over and took the verdict forms, then went over and handed them to the Judge.

Hodges lowered his reading glasses and stared at it for much too long. Finally, he handed the forms back to the bailiff and said, "each of the forms has been properly executed. Please recite the verdict for the records."

Rachel held my hand tight. She was trembling as well. While the bailiff read from the papers, I held my breath.

"The people of the State of California, plaintiff, versus Samuel

Ian Hudson, defendant. Case number SCD 164989. Verdict: We, the jury in the above-entitled case, the crime of murder, in violation of penal code section 187(a), find the defendant Samuel Ian Hudson guilty as charged in count one of the information, and fix the degree thereof as murder in the first degree."

That thin filament on which I hung my hopes, snapped. The entire courtroom stirred with gasps and cries of relief. I had to brace myself against the table when the bailiff read the subsequent charges. Another murder one, special circumstances of rape, battery. It all spun around my head as the din of the crowd crescendoed.

More words exchanged between the judge and the D.A. and Rachel, but I was gone. The next thing I knew, Hodges rapped his gavel, sending a jolt through my body. The bailiff cuffed me and led me to the side exit. With reddened eyes, Rachel said something about an appeal. All I heard was the cacophony of every voice in the courtroom blurring together.

Oscar Lawrence glared at me while Maggie covered her face and wept. Towards the back of the room, young men high-fived each other. I caught Mike Siefert's eyes and he quickly turned away.

"Watch your step," the bailiff said as we left the courtroom and met a pair of armed guards. There would be a hearing for my sentence later, but it didn't take Nostradamus to predict the outcome.

I was headed for death row.

PART II

The gates of Hell are open night and day;
Smooth the descent, and easy is the way;
But, to return, and view the cheerful skies;
In this, the task and mighty labor lies.

— John Dryden

CHAPTER THIRTY-FIVE

Salton Sea State Penitentiary is California's newest Supermax prison. With the constant threat of overcrowding at San Quentin and Pelican Bay—the prototype on which Salton Sea is based—the logical choice was to build yet another facility. Like its predecessor, it houses some of the state's most violent offenders.

Situated in the desert between Imperial and Riverside Counties, Salton Sea is an inland saline lake, located in the Colorado Desert. The supermax that bears its name lies miles from civilization, completely severed from the outside world by razor wire, concrete, and armed guards.

I was kept in the Security Housing Unit or the SHU, as the inmates call it, and spent twenty-two and a half hours a day solitary, in my cell, a cramped eight-by-eight. Separated by three locked doors from an armed control booth office I could see no other prisoners. Nor could I see the light of day.

Everything about my cell was concrete: a concrete stool, concrete walls, concrete writing table. About the only thing that wasn't concrete was the toilet and sink. Those were stainless steel. White, heavy gauge perforated metal covered my door. No one in our pod could see outside their cells. I was allowed to shower three times a week, which seemed to effectively slow the rotting process. Unlike the other prisoners, SHU inmates are fed like animals twice a day. Meals are placed on trays and slid through slots in the cell doors.

I was afforded the opportunity to exercise unshackled outside for a maximum of ninety minutes per day in an area known as the dog-walk, a twenty-eight by twelve foot exercise yard enclosed claustrophobically between a set of twenty-foot walls. Any other time I left my cell, they kept me in waist restraints and handcuffs with an armed double escort. Before and after "exercise," I had to stand naked before the control booth for a visual strip search. In full view for all to see. Beyond humiliating, but you get used to it.

In the dog walk, several inmates were separated into different exercise boxes, if you could call it exercise. We'd pace around and around the edge of these concrete yards like caged tigers. I felt more like a forsaken lab rat. Forsaken by time, by society. About the only person I saw on a daily basis was Butch Hurley. And the one constant with him was that stinking toothpick he always chewed on in the corner of his mouth. I wondered if it was the same one from day to day. Never saw him spit it out, never saw him put a new one in. If ever there was a redneck, it was Butch.

Butch was my correctional officer.

He stood about five foot eight. Not huge, but what he lacked in height, he made up for with intimidation. Butch had the magnetism of an armored tank. You see him coming, you get the hell out of the way. The day I arrived at Salton Sea he said, "While you're here, *I* am God." It wasn't far from truth.

Life at Salton was on a different plane of reality. The culture, the tacit laws, none of it resembled that of the outside world. One rule, however, quickly leapt to the forefront: stay alive at all costs. Much of that depended on the whims of your C.O.

At meal times, a tray full of half-warmed food slid into the slot under my cell door and if Butch was in a good mood, I might even get a spoonful of Jello. *If* he was in a good mood. And that was difficult to determine, much less predict.

One morning while in the dog walk, something terrifying happened. The doors of our individual exercise boxes remained open with none of the guards present beyond the locked main gate. A hulk of an inmate stepped out into the open area. Gritting his teeth, muscles about to burst out of his sweat-stained tank top, he looked like Schwarzenegger...on steroids.

Out of the second cage, a tough looking black guy, not quite as muscular but every bit as belligerent, stepped out, snarling and beating his fist into his palm. The two approached each other with caution.

I noticed Butch leaning against the chainlink fence with a shotgun in hand and the ever-present toothpick in his mouth. Watching it all. And from the glint of his teeth you could see he was going to enjoy this.

The other cons stepped back against the wall—blacks on one side, whites on the other. What was going on? I figured it'd be safer to stay with my own kind, meaning the whites.

"Yo, Dog!" one of the black inmates called out. "Kick that cracker's ass!" The inmates in my row shouted just as wildly.

"Rip him a new one, Russo!" The fighters lunged, grabbed at each others' necks. Dog gripped Russo in a choke hold. Russo rammed his fist into Dog's stomach but Dog kept punching his face.

Forget about the C.O. breaking it up, he was in on it. Standing next to Butch now were two other guards, laughing and cheering. Probably betting on who would win. I had heard about prison violence, but never expected this. My palms became slick. I wiped them on my shirt. *Oh god, let me out of here.*

Heavy thuds of body blows resounded. Fists and faces full of blood now. Russo finally pinned Dog down with his knee. Wrapped his hands around Dog's throat and you could barely hear the black guy gurgling. My own fingers ached from gripping the chain link fence. *That's going to be me one of these days.*

Russo laughed, while Dog's limbs flailed about. The black guy's eyes bulged, his tongue hung out of his mouth. Russo growled, and thrust his arms down to tighten his grip. "Huh? Ya like that, nigger? Want some more, ya say?" Butch cackled as he collected money from the other two guards. Dog must've been their man. They'd just about seen enough.

But then, Dog reached behind his back, down into his pants, as if he were scratching his rear. That same hand flew right back out and caught Russo in the throat.

Blood splattered down onto Dog's face and onto the floor. Russo let go, sputtered and grabbed his own neck. Blood dripped from his hand. With an abrupt kick, Dog freed himself from under his opponent, who was now writhing on the floor with his throat slashed open.

"Hey!" Butch swore as he opened the gate and cocked his gun. Dog held his bloody hands up, fingers spread. A shiv clinked against the concrete. A stupid grin stretched across his face as the C.O. approached. The two other guards stood back, guns ready.

"You ought to thank me, B," Dog said. I would soon learn that Russo had been the head honcho for Salton Sea's white supremacists gang, The Fourth Reich. Not anymore.

With the butt of his rifle, Butch smacked Dog to the ground. "You have any idea how much paperwork I'm going to have to file because of that shiv?"

"You just mad cuz you lost the pool," he said, smiling at the other two guards. Their own grins vanished when Butch turned around and barked, "Call the infirmary!"

"Too late, B," said Dog. "He dead already. I better be getting my crank for winning, you hear?"

"Shut up!" Dog seemed to know better than to try to get up. He just let Butch cuff his hands and ankles before being yanked up to his feet. When it was my turn to get shackled, I was trembling. This was the first time I actually saw someone get his throat slashed.

I'm not supposed to be here, I thought

Over and over, in my head.

I can't be here. Can't be.

My cuffs started rattling and I realized just how scared I was. I willed myself to stop. Couldn't let the other inmates see. They were already giving me dirty looks.

Later that evening, Butch came by my cell. "So, enjoy your first SHU brawl?"

I didn't answer.

"Happens all the time, don't worry about it." He then went around from cell to cell, banging on the doors with his rifle. When he came back to me his tone was more stern. "Look Hudson, you ain't said a word to me since you arrived. You got a problem?"

I just huffed.

He slammed his rifle against my door again. This time much louder. "Think you're better than me? You ain't nothing. And nobody out there knows or cares about what I can do to you. So you'd best start showing me some respect!"

I went right up to the mesh and slammed it with the heel of my hand. "All right," I said. "I've got something to say."

"Yeah? What?"

"I want to talk to the warden!" Howls went up and echoed throughout the pod. Butch was laughing too. "Oh, so you want to see the warden, huh? What, you want an upgrade to the presidential suite?"

More laughter.

"I'm going to tell him about the prisoner abuse down here," I said. "About the cock-fighting racket you're running."

"Oh, right. That. Yeah. He'll believe *you* over a decorated C.O. of fifteen years."

"You can't do this!"

"Right." Another smack against the door and he walked away, spat his toothpick on the ground. "Liked you a whole lot better when you weren't talking." He swaggered away, footfalls slow and fading. "Might just have to fix that."

CHAPTER THIRTY-SIX

By the time the beating stopped, I found myself alone on the floor of the shower stall, cold water still spraying my back. Because they jumped me while I had shampoo in my eyes, I never saw my attackers. But judging by the way I was held face down while simultaneously punched and kicked on all sides, there must've been at least three of them. Felt more like twenty.

My last conscious recollection was a crimson stream gathering and spiraling down the drain. I suffered a mild concussion and spent the night in the infirmary with three broken ribs. The message was clear. Don't cross your C.O. That, and keep your big, stupid mouth shut. The stitches and scars would serve as a constant reminder.

Each week, the gladiator fights continued, though Butch made it clear that no one was to be shanked. Try telling the nation's most violent criminals to use restraint. Eventually, the paper work must have become too much of a nuisance. The fighters were now instructed to fight to the death. The winner would sometimes be shot—no doubt the official result of attacking another inmate and disregarding warnings from the C.O. to stop. If anyone outside ever heard of our gladiator matches, they simply would not believe it possible.

Somehow, I managed to avoid becoming one of the contestants. They probably figured someone as soft as me would've been disappointing to watch. No fun watching a guy get wiped out in less than a minute. I earned the nickname "Silkworm."

For safe measure, though, I started working out again. I was up to seventy five pushups a set, even twenty, one-handed. Some of the inmates liked to flaunt their musculature by wearing cutoffs and tanks. I kept it to myself, always wearing a loose fitting California Department of Corrections shirt over my undershirt to hide my progress. The element of surprise might come in handy one day.

Butch and I seemed to have settled into an understanding where we didn't cross each other's paths. But this wouldn't last forever. Simply ignoring me didn't suffice. Eventually, he had to gain the upper hand.

"Here's the deal," Butch said, after I finished showering.

"Do you have to talk to me only when I'm naked?"

He wagged his eyebrows. "I'm going to give you a paper bag. Leave it under the bench in Cage-D tomorrow, during exercise time. That's all there is to it."

I toweled off and wrapped myself. "You want me to smuggle contraband for you?"

"You got a point?"

"Just what side of the law are you on, anyway?"

Butch leaned against the doorframe and chortled. Then he looked me up and down. I didn't like the way he was leering, it made me feel filthy. "Within these walls, Silk, I *am* the law. Gonna do it or not?"

"Not."

He stuffed the bag back into his jacket. "I'm disappointed."

"You'll get over it." Why did he need me to do this when he could easily have slipped the contraband into whatever cell he wanted to? There had to be something more to it.

"You're looking pretty buff these days, buddy." He pulled out the toothpick and admired its badly mangled end. He put it back between his lips and puckered, making a sick, kissing noise. If Dog or any of the other inmates had made the pass at me, I might only have been repulsed, not surprised. But the thought of Butch...I was going to be sick.

He came closer and yanked the towel off my waist, leaving me more vulnerable than I'd ever felt in my entire life. The gust sent a shiver up my spine.

"Back off!" I was up against a wall, completely naked.

Butch reached over and began to touch my face. "Why can't you just get with the program like the others?"

I smacked his hand away and slid out of his reach. "I'd rather die."

"Careful what you wish for," he said and let out a sigh. Acquiescing with his bushy unibrow, Butch stepped away and dropped my towel on the floor. "One of these days, you'll look back and wish you'd been more... open to possibilities."

Back in my cell, I tossed and turned uncertain if it was because of Butch's thinly veiled threats or the images of the past that continued to haunt me, first in my sleep, and now preventing it.

God, I missed my family. Sometimes I thought of them all together, sometimes individually. Every now and then, I'd hear door hinges sing a high-pitched tone. The sound would remind me of a delicate solo violin line and make me think of Bethie. At twelve years old, she was already a virtuoso violinist, soloed with the Los Angeles Philharmonic at Eleven. Our pride and joy. How could this be?

The sound of my cell door sliding open jolted me from my nightmarish sleep. It must have been four in the morning. "Get up!" C.O. Cummings barked. He bound my wrists behind my back and shackled my feet, while Butch stood with his gun aimed straight at me. They checked me for shanks and then shoved me out the door.

"Let's go! Move it!" Cummings said.

"Where?" My eyes hadn't yet adjusted to the light. I could barely open them.

"Get going!" Butch shouted. "I told you that I was the law. You break it, I break you."

All the way on the ride in the truck to wherever we were going, Butch kept talking to me about how lucky I had been in the SHU, especially with him as my C.O. "I didn't ask too much. Never made you fight. Didn't want to get your pretty face messed up."

"You tried to set me up."

"Yeah, that contraband was just a test.

"Your bitch test?"

"You failed." With a perverse grin he said, "Come on. It was just a couple of nickel bags and a cell phone." He put his arm around me and played with his toothpick. "Would've made you my own special connie. With all the benefits."

I tried to struggle free but I was completely shackled. If I tried to jump out of the truck, Butch and his men wouldn't hesitate to shoot. He pulled out his toothpick and put his mouth right next to my ear. His hot breath made my stomach turn.

"You might reconsider—if you live long enough." His lip brushed my earlobe. Fed up, I thrust my head into his face and hit it hard. Butch let out a grunt. His lip was bleeding. But he remained cool and gave me a menacing smile. "Oh, you're a feisty bitch." He rubbed his busted lip, looked at his bloody fingertips, then started sucking them. Sick. "You'll be begging for me to take you back, trust me."

"Whatever." Where were they taking me, anyway?

The answer came as we stopped and they brought me into another building. A much larger one. The guards buzzed me in, checked me head to toe, and led me to a cavernous area with countless cells lined up over two tiers.

Anxiety lodged in my chest as Butch began to chuckle and snort. "Silk, you may already be famous. But ain't it nice to be somewhere where everybody knows your name?"

"What are you doing?" I said.

"The good news is—your time in the SHU is over. But the bad news is, so is your protective custody."

"No, wait! You can't do this!"

"Already done, pretty-boy," he said, brushing my face with the back of his hand. "Welcome to Gen-Pop."

CHAPTER THIRTY-SEVEN

Lying awake in sheets soaked with cold sweat, I felt grateful the upper bunk of my new cell remained unoccupied. Butch left me in there, promising that I wouldn't be alone for long. Was that supposed to be good?

From what I knew about life in Gen-Pop, I'd be afforded a great deal more freedom: outdoor open yard time, access to the law library, the canteen, even phone calls and religious services. One might almost think that Butch had done me a favor.

But when a rude buzzer announced the start of a new day, I knew he had a plan for me. If I didn't get shanked the moment I came in contact with the other inmates, I'd surely be tortured by the suspense of not knowing exactly when and how it would go down. I never thought it possible to miss solitary.

My first day in B-Yard was strangely reminiscent of my first day of Junior High School. The sun began its frenzied ascent into the desert sky. Cloud shadows crept across the verdant lawns and concrete basketball courts. Three discernable groups dominated the scene—the blacks, the whites and the Mexicans. Everyone seemed to know their place. I stood alone in a corner.

A couple of skin-heads did pullups on a steel bar, their muscular arms covered with tattooed swastikas. On the other side of the yard, a black guy did dips while two brothers stood by his side, talking and gesticulating aggressively. Not daring to make eye contact, I kept my head down.

Every time an inmate walked past me or looked my way, my blood pressure kicked up a few notches. Did they know who I was, what I was in for? What I wouldn't give to be invisible. On the other hand, I was grateful for the fresh air. It had been months since I'd been in an open, outdoor area larger than the Dog Walk.

I shut my eyes, faced the sky and let the warmth of the sun bathe my face. I couldn't help but smile. If only for that short moment, it felt almost as if I'd been released. Until I caught a hard blow between the shoulder blades and fell to the grass.

Dull but excruciating pain shot up my spine. I saw nothing but several pairs of legs passing by. From the laughs and insults in Spanish, I could tell that I'd just been welcomed by Northern Mexicans. I didn't want to get up too quickly, lest they take it as a sign I wanted to fight back. But if I stayed down too long, someone would notice and from now on, I'd be marked easy prey. Great first impression.

I got up, dusted myself off and watched the backs of their heads as they strutted away. One of them turned back and glared at me. I frowned and nodded at him with my chin. He pointed his chin at me. If I wasn't mistaken, he just told me to watch my back. Either that, or I was *carne muerto.*

Reaching around my back, I felt where I'd been hit and then examined my fingers. No blood. I exhaled in relief but kept looking over my shoulder as I started to walk. The last time I looked there wasn't a wall in my path, but that's exactly what it felt I had walked into when I turned around. My head recoiled and I nearly lost balance again.

"Watch it!" said the wall, a bald Caucasian man with a scar across the side of his face. He towered over me. I'd seen some big guys before, but this guy made them look like midgets. He grabbed me by the shirt and slammed me against a concrete wall, squinting tightly at me.

I tried to apologize, but the wind had been knocked from me. My mouth opened and shut like that of a dying fish. Aside from his formidable stature, he seemed unremarkable. The only thing that stood out in my mind was the tattoo on his arm. A crucifix with the bleeding Christ hanging on it.

I shook my head, *Please don't kill me.* He let me down and shoved me back. Nearly falling on my hindquarters, I braced myself against the wall.

"You stupid or something?" he said, glaring at me. "Keep gawking at the sky like some kind of idiot and someone'll get the idea to kill you—just for the fun of it."

My chest heaving, I tried to speak. "Sorry...I didn't—"

"Stay out of my way!" Anything I might say would have sounded stupid. Thanks for the advice—oh, and by the way, thanks for not squashing me like a cockroach. I just nodded and watched him leave. He strode directly into a mass of white inmates who quickly spread out and made a path.

But what puzzled me was when he walked right into a group of black cons and they did the same, though with some furtive taunting. Behind his back. You could tell they respected him. Or feared him, anyway. Something told me it wasn't just because of his size.

That I survived my first day in the yard, that no one appeared to have recognized me as Sam Hudson, was highly suspect. Butch was definitely up to something. An inmate convicted of my crimes would be targeted right away. But having me shanked right away would rob him of the fun of watching me wander like a kitten in a junkyard full of rabid dogs. I would give him no such satisfaction.

That afternoon I had a visitor. My heart skipped a beat when Rachel Cheng, came to visit. As my defense attorney she had been filing for an appeal while Mack, the private investigator she hired continued looking for the real killer.

Unfortunately, the appeal had been denied.

"Maybe it's time you moved on," I said.

Rachel looked up at me through the protective glass. Her eyes—today violet, courtesy of those whimsical colored contact lenses—shimmered and she pushed a stray lock of raven hair behind her ear. "Sam..." I could tell she had been at least considering it.

"You've done your best," I said. "It's time to get your own life back on track."

"If I'd tried harder," Rachel said into the handset, her eyes welling up. "If only I'd found something, anything." She studied the polished chrome around the Plexiglas window and ran a finger along its edge.

"No. Rachel, don't blame yourself."

"You were framed."

"Say that in here and I'll get more than a couple of laughs and snorts."

"Do you have any idea who could have... who would have wanted to do it?"

I'd only been thinking about that for the past year. "Lots of people had access the days before the murders," I said. "The killer got past the security system."

"Logs show that it was disarmed, with the manufacturer's default passcode at 10:30 PM. A half hour before you came home."

I was the only person in the house who even knew the manufacturer's passcode, used to reset the unit. I turned my palms upwards and shrugged. "There are only two possibilities," I said, so weary at this point that I wondered if death by lethal injection might be more merciful. "One: someone committed the perfect crime, or two—" She blinked with a puzzled look. "Two: I did it."

"Come on, Sam. Don't even think that."

"Hell, the whole world believes it. The evidence points to me. Maybe I did it and just can't remember. Maybe I went crazy and blocked it out."

Rachel rose from her chair, leaned in close to the window. Her eyes swept around and she whispered. "Do *not* repeat what you just said. Not ever, not to anyone. Someone in here could twist it into a confession and—-"

"And what, send me to jail? To death row?" I snorted.

"Sam, listen to me! If there's ever going to be a chance for another appeal, you cannot, I repeat, can *not* be going around saying things that a paid snitch can use against you."

"You're assuming there's hope."

For a moment, not a word came out of her lips. Her poignant eyes glistened. "So that's it, you've given up?"

"I don't think... I just can't go through it again. Raising my hopes, only to have them crushed." Rachel had done an amazing job during the trial. At several points, I really thought the jury would turn an N.G. I was wrong.

"We've got to keep fighting," she said.

"What's the point?"

"Aaron."

What I said next, I'd regret for years to come. I was so rapt in self-pity that I hadn't realized just how low I'd sunk. "For all we know, he's not going to make it."

Rachel's eyes widened. It was as if someone had told her that a nuclear warhead had detonated less than a mile away. "How—? Sam, of all people. How could you?" Defensiveness would have been my default reaction—shifting the blame to her for goading me into it with her incessant exhortations of hope since we first met.

But it was all me. I knew it. "I....I didn't mean that."

"No, I don't believe you did." I couldn't face her."I have to go," she said. "Anything develops, I'll let you know."

I nodded, still avoiding her eyes. She tapped the window. "Sam."

"What?"

"We're all still praying."

"Thanks." It was the furthest thing from my mind. If there even was a God, he'd let me down, big time.

Rachel left and I felt like I'd just handed my son over to an executioner. How could I even think that he wasn't going to make it? Self-contempt prompted a decision. From that moment on, I would never entertain the thought that Aaron might not make it. Never mind what the doctors said, I would not live my final years resigned to the death of my son.

From that moment on, I'd be a fighter.

CHAPTER THIRTY-EIGHT

I returned to my cell and found it now occupied by another inmate. When he saw me at the door, he leapt to his feet and hit his head on the metal bed frame.

"This your bunk?" He rubbed his fuzzy head, eyes shifting from side to side like some kind of rodent. His considerable front teeth and pointy nose, which wiggled like he was sniffing around for something, did little to counter that image.

"It's okay," I said, reaching out to shake hands and introduce myself.

"NO!" He cringed, covered his face and fell onto the floor in a fetal position.

"What —?" A loud buzzer sounded and all the doors in our block slammed shut. My cellmate was now lying in a foul-smelling puddle he'd just made. I let out a sigh and stood away from him, leaning against the wall until he seemed ready to get up.

"You okay down there?" He finally looked up and decided I wasn't about to kill him. I grinned at him with a, "what is your problem?" look.

He beheld his urine soaked pants and groaned. "Aw, man!" He got up and smoothed out his pants, realized he just got his hands wet and sighed.

"What's your name?"

"Artie," he said. "Pleased to meet you." He extended his hand but I graciously declined to shake it.

"Yeah, well. I'm—"

"I *know* who you are," said Artie, his beady eyes swiping around the cell. I straightened up. Right away, he cringed and covered his head. "No, please!"

"Would you stop that! I'm not going to hurt you." That only made him cower again. It took another ten minutes before he stopped knee-jerking at my slightest move. So rather than talk, I threw down a used towel and with my foot, mopped up the yellow puddle. When I was done I kicked it under the bars of our cell. "You can have the bottom bunk if you like," I said.

"You sure?"

"Yeah."

"In exchange for what?"

"Nothing, what are you talking about?"

"Nothing."

Artie was the last person you'd expect to find in Salton. He'd pass out if he saw a mouse. I sat on a stool on the opposite side of our cell and waiting for him to stop pacing.

A female C.O. stopped outside the cell and tapped on the bars. Artie whooped with a start. *Great he's going to wet himself again.*

"Hey Possum," she said, peering through golden bangs that peeked through the rim of her cap. "Welcome to B-block." she kicked the soiled towel away".

I regarded my cell mate with an ironic smirk. "Possum?"

"Yeah."

"Why do they call you that?" I asked.

His eyes were shiny ball-bearings, his ears stuck out of the sides of his head. "No idea." Regarding the officer, he said, "Hey Gracie, thanks for giving me a celebrity cellie." At once, I noticed her unusually kind demeanor. Unusual for a C.O., anyway.

"Celebrity?" I said to Possum.

"Everyone knows you. Superdad turned—"

"You're Sam Hudson, aren't you?" she said, lifting her eyes to meet mine. There was a melancholy look in those sapphire eyes, the corners of which wrinkled as she smiled. Though she must not have been much more than thirty-five, it made her appear a decade older.

"I'm afraid you have me at a considerable disadvantage."

"Sergeant Sonja Grace," she said. "I'm one of the C.O.'s here in B-Block."

"Yeah, well. Nice to meet—"

"I read about you in the papers."

With a deep breath in, a sharp one out, I said, "Who hasn't?"

"No, I mean I remember your picture out in front of the School Yard during the hostage crisis. You know, the one with you facing off with the officer, with his rifle in your chest?"

"Oh, Coyote Creek Middle School." Seemed like ages ago, and certainly eclipsed by the tragic events of that fateful night, only weeks later.

"Bubba's got some *cajones, muy grandes,*" Possum said. "He was a real hero."

"Hero," I scoffed. "Right."

"Until your conviction, anyway," Possum said.

"And your boy?" Sergeant Grace said, completely catching me off guard. Her smile dissolved.

"Excuse me?"

"Your son. Did you get to see him before....?"

"No, I didn't."

A pained expression filled her eyes. "Sorry to hear it." What was it to her? She stared down the tier and sighed. "Anyway, like I told Possum, welcome to B-Block. Keep your nose clean, your cell clean and we'll get along just fine. Got it?"

"Yeah."

"I'll be seeing you." Sergeant Grace tapped on the bars of our cell with her nightstick and left.

"Seems nice," I said to Artie.

"Absolute doll."

"So," I said, "What's your story?"

He crinkled his nose, examined our cell. "I ain't got one."

"Everyone's got a story," I said. I would learn later, that Artie "Possum" Castigliano had been an accountant for a large seafood import corporation. He was doing time for participating in a State tax scandal. Could his company have been a client of my firm—that is, former firm, Lewis, Garfield & Brown?

Of course, he was innocent and had been set up. But no one in Salton was stupid enough to belly ache about stuff like that. Most of the cons saw Salton as a promotion, a place to hone their criminal skills. Complaining of a wrongful conviction was not just showing weakness, it was a disgrace. Then again, Artie the Possum had just peed in his pants a few minutes ago.

"Okay, so what are *you*?" Possum asked. "Psychopath? Sociopath? Plain old nasty guy?"

"What?"

"Everyone knows what you're in here for. You got issues, man."

"That's what I was convicted of," I said. "We've all been convicted. Whether we did it or not is besides the point." This Possum might actually be a rat. No way I'd say anything snitch-worthy.

"True. True-true," he said, bobbing his little round head and looking around the cell.

"So, how much?" I said.

Possum's eyes zipped around the cell. He answered in a hissing whisper. "Nine-point-two-five." Nearly ten million dollars in evaded state taxes was plenty motive. And he made an easy scapegoat. Poor guy.

"How long've you been in?" I asked.

"Five years."

I'd have figured five days, maybe. "How'd you manage to—?"

"Killed my cellie."

"You?" An unintentional laugh erupted from my belly. "Good thing I wasn't eating, I might have choked."

"All right, all right, all right. Show a little respect, will ya?"

"Sorry."

"It was an accident," he whispered, looking over my shoulder. "My cellie in A-block was trying to shank me. I ducked, he slipped on one of my Accounting Times magazine covers, fell and landed with the shank in his neck. Sliced himself in the jugular."

"So how'd you convince everyone that you did it?"

"Before anyone saw anything, I jumped on his body, grabbed his shiv and started slashing him, shouting all kinds of crap. They were all too surprised to question whether I'd actually done it." Possum explained that it had been the most horrible thing he'd ever done, but it probably saved his life. He now had a reputation for being unpredictable and a surprisingly skillful killer.

He couldn't kill a germ with Lysol.

But I wouldn't betray his secret. The prevailing wisdom in Gen-Pop was that, despite his appearance, Artie the Possum was dangerous. And because his dead cell mate had been a lieutenant in *La Fraternidad,* Salton Sea's most violent prison gang of Northern Mexicans—whose tendrils of crime reached far beyond the confines of the supermax—there were no charges brought upon Artie. It had been recorded as self-defense.

"Five years and still kicking," Artie said as he spread out his belongings. He stopped at a photo of an attractive young woman holding up a baby. "That's Jack," he said, handing me the picture. "He'll be five in November."

Right away, my thoughts went to Aaron who was about the same age. It had been such a long time. I missed him terribly and wondered if I'd ever see him again. "Lovely family," I said, returning his picture.

Possum stared at me and swallowed. "Don't worry, I ain't telling anyone," he said, softly. "Promise."

"Telling anyone what?"

"Look, that columnist—what was his name, Brent Stringer...?"

My stomach clenched. "Yeah."

"He wrote some pretty nasty crap about you in the Tribune that biased the jury. And I don't care if he's a bestselling author, he screwed you."

"The jury agreed with him. So what are you *not* going to tell anyone about me?"

"That you're innocent."

My brow tightened. "Far as you know, I'm not."

"Oh, you're innocent all right. I see it in your eyes. Couldn'ta done it."

I didn't like the fact that I was so transparent to a person I'd known for less than ten minutes. "Doesn't matter," I said. "I'm a condemned man, in case you've forgotten."

"Eh. You make do. Just look at that Tookie Williams guy up in San Quentin. He's been on the row since '81." Possum spread his arms wide with open palms as if he were about to offer a benediction. "Twenty-one years later, they haven't even set an execution date."

"The appeals system might keep me alive just as long, eh?"

"Unless the cons or the C.O's get you first." With his formidable front teeth, Possum nibbled on his lower lip and wagged his eyebrows. "Me? I plan on living forever."

CHAPTER THIRTY-NINE

For the next several months I had just about forgotten about C.O. Butch Hurley. Aside from the occasional scrape with a couple of Crips and a *La Fraternidad* freshman, I managed to keep to myself without serious injury. Of course I'd engaged in the occasional fist fight, that was a matter of survival. To lay down and take a beating was inviting much more and much worse. For good measure, I always landed a few good punches before getting taken down.

Now in my second year at Salton, everyone knew who Sam "Silk" Hudson was, and what he was in for. Playing into that image was distasteful. But again, a matter of survival.

Visiting privileges for Gen-Pop inmates were far better than for those in the SHU. The only people who came to see me were Rachel, Pastor Dave and on the rare occasion, Alan and Samantha, from Jenn's Bible Study group. Just a few months back, their baby girl entered the world via emergency C-section. With my blessings, they named her Elizabeth, though I'm not sure they'll ever call her Bethie. They never failed to show up with albums full of photos. Beautiful little thing.

Rachel continued her monthly visits and updated me on all the appeals motions and filings, a couple of possible leads by Mack, who I met a couple of times behind the glass wall. More than the updates, I looked forward to the company. Rachel, Dave and the others were my only connection to life outside. Every now and then, they would ask my permission to pray for me. Sometimes I agreed, other times I declined. Thankfully, in all the times since I'd met them, they'd never tried to proselytize. By far, the best thing that came of these visits were the personal items which Rachel brought me.

My cell was now lined with exactly fifteen photos of my family. Not one more than regulations allowed. These pictures came along with Jenn's family Bible, which was perhaps the most personal of all her earthly possessions. Within its memory pages, she kept notes of family milestones. Aaron's first spoken word, a program from Bethie's first recital.

With her many scribbled-in notes and highlighted verses, reading her Bible was like discovering a side to Jenn I hadn't previously known. The passages which mattered to her most were underlined as well as highlighted. Seemed like her spirit inhabited the pages.

One crisp January morning, I brought Jenn's Bible with me to B-Yard. There I read it while the sun warmed my shoulders. Whenever we were let out, I tried to keep a distance from Artie the Possum, but he stuck to me like a puppy with a tennis ball.

I turned around. Walking backwards I said, "Quit following me."

"I ain't following you, I'm just going to the same place you are."

"Right."

He was looking at my Bible as our feet touched the soft grass strip that led to the concrete picnic table—my favorite reading spot. The lawn had just been cut. Still walking backwards, I shut my eyes, took in the sweet scent. For a moment I imagined that I was back home, or in Maui. Anywhere but a maximum security prison.

"Uh, Silk?" Possum said. I kept walking backwards, letting the sun warm my face. Wasn't going to let him ruin the moment.

"Silk!" Before I could do anything about it, I backed straight into a cement wall.

Only, it wasn't a wall.

I turned around and there was that hulk I literally bumped into several months ago. His muscular arms were folded over his chest, his bald pate shining in the sun and his eye twitching. I dropped Jenn's Bible. Holding up a hand, I backed up slightly. "Hey, man. Sorry, I wasn't looking."

"What are you, stupid?" He pronounced it *stoo-pid.* There was that unforgettable tattoo on his arm again, a thorn-crowned Christ, with blood dripping down his face.

Not again. My throat went dry. "I didn't see you."

"What's this?" he said, bending down and reaching for the Bible. Great.

He flipped through the pages and scowled. "You believe this stuff?"

"I... well...No, of course—" He looked up and glared at me through the one eye that wasn't twitching and squinting. "I mean, maybe some of it," I said. "Kind of."

For the past year, I'd managed to maintain the air of a dangerous inmate. Tough talk, tough fists. All it took was one look from this guy and my knees turned to jello. "Make up your mind!" He slammed the Bible shut and tossed it back at me. I caught it in my chest and held on as if it might somehow shield me—like garlic from a vampire.

He trudged away, bumped his shoulder into Possum, who fell consequently on his rear. When he was gone, Possum got up and started waving his hands around and cussing. Under his breath of course. The big guy turned around and glowered, Possum gasped and ducked behind me.

Still shaken, my mouth still bitter, I asked Possum, "Any idea who that was?" This was the second time I'd seen this guy and lived to tell.

"You're kidding, right?" he said, still behind me.

"Seriously."

Coming out from hiding, Possum looked to the left, then the right, over my shoulder, behind his back, left and right again. Then he said in a furtive tone, "That was The Bishop."

"Bishop?" Odd tag. "I've run into him before."

"So what'd he break, your nose, your arm?"

"Nothing."

"Yeah, right," Possum said and clicked his tongue. "You ran into him before." He started pacing. If I didn't know him better, I'd think he was nervous. He was just being Possum.

I planted my butt onto the cold concrete bench. "Any idea why he's called Bishop?" I asked. But before he could answer, my Bible slipped out of my hand. It fell open to a random page. I reached for it and the words seemed to leap out at me. Reading the first few verses, a chill crept up my spine. My scalp tingled.

> *The Spirit of the Sovereign Lord is upon me,*
> *Because the Lord has anointed me*
> *to preach good news to the poor.*
> *He has sent me to bind up the brokenhearted,*
> *to proclaim freedom for the captives*
> *And release from darkness for the prisoners,*
> *to proclaim the year of the Lord's favor*
> *and the day of vengeance of our God...*

I slammed the book shut and began to breath rapidly. Possum was too busy standing guard like a meerkat on its hind legs to notice. Since I started reading Jenn's Bible, there had been a few times the scriptures seemed to come alive, as it had once in Dave Pendelton's house. Words appeared to lift right out of the pages. Specific words. The last thing I needed was to have another one of those weird experiences out in B-Yard.

"Yo Silk. What's up?"

I shook my head, tried to get my bearings. "Nothing. I'm feeling a bit light-headed." At that very moment, the ground began to tremble. Another tremor, typical to this part of California.

Possum's agitated shuffling accelerated. But my head was spinning and I didn't want to get up too quickly. "Silk, we gotta go."

"What? Why? It's just a little tremor. It'll pass." This wasn't the first time this had happened since I arrived here at Salton, what was his problem? Sure enough, within seconds it was over.

He grabbed my arm and started pulling. "It's not the quake, trust me," he said, his tone rising in pitch and anxiety. "We need to go. Pronto."

I got to my feet and I saw why. Four white guys wearing dark blue CDC sweats were approaching with purpose. Possum swore in triplicate and whimpered. We were surrounded. These guys were the kind that would slash our throats and walk away laughing.

"Don't mess with Silk!" Possum shouted. From behind my back, helpfully.

The leader of the pack approached, picking breakfast bits from between his teeth with his pinky. The only hair on his buzz-cut skinhead was the goatee on his face. He got right into mine. "Hudson, right?"

"Who wants to know?" I said, affecting a stone cold mien.

"Don't matter who I am," said Buzz-head, with a distinct southern drawl. "What matters is who *you* is...Silk." It was then that I saw the swastika emblazoned on the leader's collarbone. The Fourth Reich.

"You going to stand around yapping all day?" I said. "Get with it!"

"I'll make it simple. It's all going down real soon. We're taking down *La Fraternidad.* It's time for you to declare your allegiance."

"And here, I thought you had something intelligent to say."

The guy who was next to Buzz-head's leaned forward and said, "Where you gonna stand, son?"

"I'm not standing anywhere. I'm just going to sit in my cell while you idiots kill each other."

Buzz grabbed me by the shirt and shoved me against the chain link fence. "Don't be a smartass, motherf—"

"Get it through your thick skull," I said. "I am not going to fight!" He had me pinned, but I was not about to betray even an ounce of fear.

"Oh, you gonna fight all right," Buzz said. "Time comes, you gonna fight or be killed." He let go and rubbed his whiskery chin. The sandpapery sound made my skin crawl.

"What is this, a public service announcement?" I said.

"Call it a warning, call it an inquiry. When them shanks start flyin', I wanna know if you's a friend or foe." A malevolent grin cracked his features. "Wouldn't want to slash the wrong person out there."

"Silk...!" Possum was now trapped between the other Reich members. They were laughing and pushing him around, watching him cower. I took a step towards him, but Buzz blocked my way.

"See them Mexicans over there?" He pointed to the far side of the yard. A row of them were exercising, doing martial arts moves, perfectly synchronized.

"What about them?"

"Every day, lined up there, drilling, working out. Looks like freakin' boot camp. Think they're doing all that to get into some kinda *Feng Shui* zone or something?"

"I don't really care what they're doing."

"You'd better. There gon' be a war."

I looked him straight in the eye. "Over what?"

"Territory, respect, control of the yard—how long you been in here, anyway?"

"It's got nothing to do with me."

"So, you with us or not?"

"We'll see." No way I was going to get involved. I just wanted to get away, and quickly.

"Where's your shank?"

"Like I'd tell you."

Buzz shoved me back, rattling the fence again. My stomach tightened in anticipation of a stab wound. "Watch yourself," he said. "You so much as fart in the wrong direction, I'll gut and filet you myself."

"Great," I said, with a defiant sneer. "I like seafood." His boys started laughing. He fired a warning shot with his eyes. They stopped.

"Let's go," he growled. As they left, I was sweating so profusely my shirt stuck to my back. And yet, at the same time, confidence rose up from within.

"Hey, I've got a question for *you*," I said. Buzz turned around and returned. Possum cringed. "Is Butch Hurley behind this?"

Buzz nodded like a bobble-head dog in the rear window of a pimp's car. He flashed a wide smile, regarded me through the side of his eye. "Butch, eh?"

"Is he?"

The answer came in the form of a right hook to my jaw.

CHAPTER FORTY

I had heard about the prison riots in Pelican Bay, how the fighting continued until inmates were finally shot dead with live rounds. The shadow of such terrifying events hung over me for the following months. Was this part of Butch's plan—to have me shanked during a riot? Or to have me shot by a guard when it all went down?

Every time I saw Buzz, the Fourth Reich leader, who I later learned was called The *Führer* by his followers, I tried to learn more about the impending war. He would only reply with a question of his own, "You with us?"

Neither of us got our answers.

In the bowels of Salton, the sounds of furtive, yet incessant scraping in the gloom of night kept me awake. All around me, inmates sharpened pieces of metal, plastic and wood against the concrete walls. Shanks, shivs—didn't matter what you called them, everyone had them. Except me. Even Possum had a couple which I didn't want to know about.

More disturbing was the sound of heavy breathing, grunting and groaning. Some mutually consensual, others, clearly not. This sent my head under my pillow and made me thankful that my cell mate was timid. And straight.

Every morning, I'd wake up exhausted, lying in sheets soaked with cold perspiration. The only way I felt secure was to get up around 5:00 AM, before anyone else. I would read magazines, legal journals or Jenn's Bible. One of the inmates thought it would be funny to give me a copy of Brent Stringer's recent novel, *Cast The First Stone.* It remained on the bottom of my slush pile.

The more I read the scriptures Jenn had highlighted in bright yellow, the more questions arose about her faith. One verse stated, "*No greater love has this than a man lay down his life for another.*" I figured this referred to Jesus Christ. But what did that mean to a believer? Were they supposed to become a bunch of self-sacrificing martyrs? Perhaps I could ask Dave the next time I saw him. More important matters always came up during the visits and I would forget to ask.

Out of sheer curiosity, and for lack of a better way to find peace and quiet, I began attending religious services. Though the chaplain had worked at Salton for three years, he still seemed anxious around convicts. He never stayed long enough after service to talk to any of us. After delivering his message, he always rushed off and left us to meditate. Under guard, of course.

One September morning, I decided to linger in the chapel to meditate upon the homily he'd just delivered—a quaint message about doing good for no other reason than pleasing God. Easy for him to say—he got to go home to his wife and kids every night. The truth was, I felt depressed, resigned to the idea that my wife and daughter's killer would never be caught and brought to justice, that I would never see Aaron again.

I put my head down, as if I were praying. Actually, I just wanted to rest quietly, away from all the blustering inmates in B-yard. Only one other inmate remained in the chapel. He sat way in the front of the chapel, his head bowed.

There came a sound that at first gave the impression of air hissing out of a punctured tire. *Sssssssssssssss...* Not paying it any mind, I yawned and shut my eyes again.

SSSSamuel.

I opened my eyes wide, noticed the inmate sitting in a chair three rows in front of me—just the back of his head, couldn't make out his features. Something about him seemed familiar, though, as if I already knew him. I walked over to him and cleared my throat.

Without turning around he said, "What do you want?"

"You called me. What do *you* want?"

"Huh?"

"Do I know you?" I said.

He turned to face me and his jaw fell open. "Who—? Holy—!" He slid across the row of chairs, knocking one over. Anger flared up in my chest. I couldn't believe it was him, couldn't believe he was here right before my eyes.

"Walker!"

The Coyote Creek Middle school shooter fell off his chair. "Keep away, all of you!" he cried, shielding his face. I pushed a couple of chairs aside and walked over to him. "No, please," he cried. "Don't!"

Walker had pled insanity to the shootings, and gotten two consecutive life sentences. It shouldn't have come as a complete surprise to see him here, but I had expected him to have ended up in a psychiatric ward.

The hefty black C.O. stepped over. "We got a problem here?

"No sir." In one brisk motion, I pulled Walker to his feet and planted him down in a chair. "Buddy here mistook me for someone else." I patted him on the shoulder and squeezed it firmly. Walker winced, and kept shifting from side to side, peering around my back. "We're just going to have a little talk," I said. "About religion."

"Y'all be cool, hear?" the C.O. said. "And show some respect." He nodded to the cross in the front of the chapel and returned to his post.

Frightened and speaking with a timid voice, Walker stuck out like a sore thumb here in Gen-Pop. It turned out that he'd been recently released from the Psychiatric Services Unit, after treatment for paranoid delusions.

Defensive from the start, he reminded me that while he had

nearly shot Bethie in the classroom in the midst of his spree, the crimes *I* had been convicted of were just as bad. Worse, in fact. "So who are you to judge me?"

"I'm not judging you." I said, and wanted him to believe it.

He craned his neck over my shoulder. "And will you tell your friends to quit staring. They're giving me the creeps!"

"What friends?"

"Those two big guys in white!"

A quick glance behind me revealed no one but the C.O. talking quietly into his walkie-talkie. "Uh...right. Never mind them, just tell me, once and for all: why did you do it? Something just snap?"

Still gazing over my shoulder he said, "I'll talk, just keep those guys away from me."

"What guys!"

"Just tell them to back off, all right?"

"Fine." I said, and turned around. The C.O. raised his eyebrows. I shrugged and subtly spun my index finger around the side of my head—he's whacked. Then playing along with Walker's delusion, I spoke into the air. "You guys chill, okay?" It didn't calm him much. "All right then," I said to him. "Tell me."

"Well, you see. I was on a mission."

"For the secret service, right?"

"Don't mock me, okay? I ain't retarded."

"No. Of course not." I waxed serious. "So, what kind of mission?"

"A mission from God."

Well, that explained it. "Come on."

"I'm not kidding."

"I get it. You actually do want to get back into PSU, right? Safer there—that must be it."

"No, no, no! Hate it there! I only told the doc what he wanted to hear so I could get *out*. They keep pumping you full of drugs in there, to keep you mellow. I'm never going back in there again. Ever!"

"All right, all right." No point arguing. I took a deep breath and waited for him to settle. "How exactly did God tell you to go and shoot those kids?"

He cast a furtive glance around the chapel, then leaned in close to whisper. "God was telling me His will for months. That day, He commanded me to bring a gun to the school."

"Really. What was it, a burning bush? A pillar of fire? Writing on the wall? I mean if God—"

"Oh, now you're taking the good Lord's name in vain?"

"No. Sorry. Go on."

He settled back into his chair, exasperated. "God spoke to me through the internet."

"The internet, eh?" He really seemed to believe it, which made him more pathetic than despicable. Almost.

"I did everything He commanded. I shot the two prettiest girls in the class." Walker wrung his CDC cap. "But God didn't tell me what to do after that. I thought He'd speak to me, I thought he'd protect me, but He didn't. I must have failed Him somewhere down the line!"

"Walker," I said, glancing back to the C.O. who was now talking on his cell phone. "Just calm down okay?" His eyes could not stay still. "Now, was it through email? A chatroom?"

"Instant Messenger."

"Tell me, what made you think it was God?"

"No." He shook his head. "You're just trying to get me back into PSU. I see right through you." Again, he looked over my shoulder. Then with a scowl and a furtive whisper he said, "That's why those guys are here, right?"

"Want me to call them over, now?" Walker shook his head, looked nervously at the guys he believed stood behind me. He really did need to get back into PSU. "So how do you know it was God?" I said.

"I have no friends, okay? No one knows anything about me. But God knows everything. When he IM'ed me, He told me all kinds of things that no one else knows. That only He could know."

"Like?"

"My mother's maiden name, my social security number, what kind of condoms I buy online...everything."

I wanted to give him a brief lecture on how all these things were easy pickings for identity theft, but it would only fall on deaf ears. "So God proves himself to you and then just goes and tells you to kill?"

"What do you think, I'm nuts?"

I declined to answer.

"God loves me," he said, gazing at the stained glass windows. "God has a plan for me—I have to keep believing that. He encouraged me with scriptures when I was lonely. He is the greatest friend I ever had. I have a personal relationship with Him." His eyes went back to the ground. "Or at least, I *had* one."

"How long until he told you to go and kill those girls?"

"Four months, twelve days." Not once did Walker ever mention why God wanted him to kill two innocent children. I was about to ask him about it when another question popped up into my mind. "Did God have a screen name?"

Walker let out a chuckle. "Boy are *you* naive."

"Well?"

"Yeah, how else could he IM me? How else could I put Him on my buddy list?"

"Right. What was it then?"

He thought about it for a moment. "God has to use weird screen names... I mean, come on. Who's going to believe someone who IM's you with the screen name of God, or Jehovah?"

"I hear you. So what was it?"

"It was something like...."

My innards became knotted. "Well?"

"Hold on. I need to think."

"Think faster!"

"Okay, okay. It's coming to me. But I don't think He wants me to tell anyone."

"Hold out on me now and forget about PSU, me and those guys back there will make sure you get to ask Him in person."

"All right, All right! I'm not sure of the exact spelling—"

"Spit it out, dammit!"

Walker took a deep breath. "It was something like... *DrHu* or *Huliboy* something."

My chest felt like it had been crushed by a boulder. Huliboy was the screen name of a person who IM'd Bethie just days before she and Jenn had been murdered.

CHAPTER FORTY-ONE

Friday morning started with shouts from down the pod. Already awake, I heard the commotion, stuck my pocket mirror through the bars of my cell and peered down the row. I barely caught a glimpse of the officers entering the cell.

"We got a hanger!" Sergeant Mancuso shouted. "It's Walker!"

A mere three days after we spoke, Walker hung himself with a bed sheet. Thankfully, not before revealing that screen name, a possible link to my wife and daughter's killer. I stood there stunned, gripping the cold bars.

Possum sat up and rubbed his eyes. "You don't look too good." I kept trying to watch for action in Walker's cell. Nothing. He was gone.

For the rest of the day, rumors buzzed around B-Yard like flies on carrion. Some believed that Walker's cellmate, Luis "Louie" Guzman had strangled him in his sleep, and made it look like a suicide. Other's purported that Walker had read an inbound letter, crumpled it up and went to bed. The next morning he was hanging by a bed sheet.

Over breakfast, I spoke with Sergeant Sonja Grace about Walker but she didn't know much. Instead, as she was about to go off duty, she asked me about Aaron.

"It's been a while since I've seen him," I said. "During the trial, my in-laws, his grandparents slapped a restraining order on me."

Sonja furrowed her brow and turned away. "That bites."

"Worst part is the thought of him dying and my not being there for him."

She quickly wiped her eye before turning to face me. "I know what you mean. I never got to say good-bye to Brandon."

"Your son?"

She nodded. "Died of leukemia last year."

"I'm sorry."

"His father... that damned—!"

I set my fork down and pushed my plate aside. "What happened?"

"Pathological bastard had weekend custody. Took Brandon one Saturday and dropped off the face of the Earth. After two weeks of the FBI hot on his trail, he calls to turn himself in. Brandon died in a hospital three days before he called!" She slapped the table and all the trays rattled. "I didn't even get to say good-bye." Covering her eyes, she said, "I never saw my baby again!" She sobbed quietly and said, "Wanna know the worst part? The last time I saw Brandon, I scolded him for arguing with me about going to visit his dad! He knew something was wrong. He knew."

Uncertain of whether I should hold her hand or not, I thought, *How do you comfort your C.O.?* "Sergeant Grace..."

"It's okay, Sam." She sniffed, recomposed herself. "Call me Sonja."

"I can't imagine how I'd feel if Aaron were to die."

"Believe me, you don't want this regret hanging over your head."

With my elbows on the table, I rested my head in both hands and sighed. "I know."

"I read about your case. The D.A.'s sloppy but lucky." Nice to know not everyone judged me by Brent Stringer's scathing editorials. "You need to work hard with your attorney and get the hell out of here."

"Easier said." Leaning in close, I said, "But that's exactly why I've got to speak with Louie Guzman. I think he might know something about Walker's outside connection. Something he said connected with me, I'm just not sure what. Guzman might know."

She stood up and pointed to the exit. "Walk with me."

Armed with a physical description given by Sonja, I went out to the yard to look for Louie Guzman. The problem was that he stood ensconced between four or five members of *La Fraternidad,* embroiled in a heated discussion. In Spanish. To come within twenty feet of him meant crossing to the west side of B-Yard, past three battalions of Northern Mexicans.

I once saw a recently incarcerated black guy march through the lines to confront one of the *Frat* lieutenants who had looked at him the wrong way while he was playing basketball. The black guy walked right into the middle of the gang. Ten minutes later, he was carried out on a stretcher, a sheet over his face, his throat slashed.

Regardless, I had to know the facts surrounding Walker's death. Louie might hold the only clue to Walker's God-character who contacted him with the same instant messenger screen name as the person who contacted me shortly before my family had been attacked. And though Walker had only spent a few days in Gen-Pop as Guzman's cellmate, Louie must have known something about his suicide. Or murder. It was stupid to confront him, but I was desperate.

Possum had an appointment in the infirmary for chronic irritable bowel syndrome. Had he been there in the yard with me, he would surely have stopped me from entering the lion's den. I almost wished he was.

Swallowing the tumor in my throat, I stood tall and walked across B-yard. At first I passed by members of the Fourth Reich. Some of them called out, asking me when I was going to join them. I ignored them.

The skin heads all turned as I walk right past them and towards the blacks. Some of them swore and clicked their tongues as I marched towards my doom. "Dead man walking."

Within seconds I was surrounded. All around me, all I could see were blue jackets and shirts, some with the letters CDC printed on them. The sun vanished behind the crowd of black inmates surrounding me. I was enveloped in aggression.

"You tired of living, boy?" One of them said.

"I just need to get over there," I said, pointing to the *Frats*.

"He tired 'a livin'," another said and grabbed me by the shirt. I'd rehearsed scenarios like this over and over in my mind. Without giving it a second thought, I grabbed the guy by the wrist, used his resistance to pull myself towards him and smashed my fist right into his nose.

The nauseating crunch might have been my hand. Or his nose, I wasn't sure. He fell back and groaned, blood oozing down his mouth. I flexed my fingers. It was his nose.

In an instant, I found myself surrounded by flaring nostrils, wild eyes and gritting teeth. I was dead. But then, to my surprise, they all started howling with laughter, slapping their thighs and pointing at the guy I nailed.

Nosebleed got up really quick and really hot, made a fist and threw a punch at my face. But a hefty guy caught his arm and pulled him away.

"'Yo! 'Sup with that?" Nosebleed shouted, surprised as I was.

"Respect, my niggah, respect," said the hulking black man, pointing at me. "Silk here earned himself a little just now." Though he was wearing a white tank top, muscles popping at the seams, he carried himself with the air of aristocracy. His voice was profound and commanding. Everyone gave him a wide berth whenever he took a step or turned in their direction. I expected them to start genuflecting.

"This between me and him, Luther," Nosebleed snarled. He

backed away and his lips fluttered when he tried to smile. "Why you all up in my soup?"

Luther grabbed him by the throat and slammed him up against the wall. "Up in yo soup? Niggah, I say kill, you kill. I say back off, you back off. Ain't no soup here but mine!"

Nosebleed's eyes were about to pop out of his head. With whatever slack that remained in his neck, he nodded. When Luther let him go, the poor guy gasped and wheezed.

"I don't gotta explain myself to no one," Luther said and glowered at the crowd. "No one touches Silk. You feel me?"

The crowd grunted.

"Yo Luther," another inmate who was just as big and scary as him said. "I seen him kickin' it with them Nazi's."

Luther turned slowly and said. "He ain't with no Nazi's, a'ight?" A tentative murmur arose from the crowd. It was sliced off when Luther looked up with razor blade eyes.

Nosebleed looked around for support. Then stepped forward. "How do you—?"

"Cuz Bishop said so," Luther proclaimed. From where I was standing, I could see a tiny space between two of the guys on my left. If I ran quickly, I could squeeze through. Not only was I all up in their soup, I was drowning in it.

"Bishop! Nosebleed scoffed. "Man, why you gotta be so tight with that cracker?" An unsettling stillness ensued. It seemed as if the entire gang had taken a step back. Luther glared at Nosebleed. Then he smiled.

Relieved, Nosebleed smiled back, a gold tooth glinting in the sun. "Aw man. Sorry, yo," he said, "I shouldn'ta—"

"Hey, no sweat, son." Luther walked over, leaning from one foot to the other, and draped his arm around his shoulders. Buddy-buddy. "I know how you feel about Bishop."

"Nah, man. He cool. Anyone you—"

"A'ight." The nods and smiles grew wider. Luther laughed.

Nosebleed did too. Still fixed on my escape route, I noticed a change in *La Fraternidad's* formation. They eyed our assembly with suspicion. A handful of them started pointing at us. I quickly wiped the sweat from my brow and looked around.

Luther and Nosebleed were yucking it up now, as if it had all been a big joke. Too weird. One look back over the gang's shoulders and I would ask to be excused.

Then I heard a swift thud-padded, cracking sound. I turned around and saw the entire crowd ebbing like water from the shores of Torrey Pines. Down on the ground lay Nosebleed, hands over his face and groaning. If I hadn't completely broken his nose earlier, Luther surely finished the job.

The last thing I heard Luther say before they all left was, "Respect, my niggah, respect."

My Spanish wasn't good enough to know exactly what they were all saying, as I crossed into the Frat quadrant of B-Yard. The few phrases I did understand went along the lines of "crazy mutha," and "stupid idiot," roughly translated. The list of pejoratives probably ran a lot longer than I realized.

Several shoulder bumps later, I finally reached Guzman. Most of *La Fraternidad* seemed interested in what was going on back on the other side of B-Yard. Talk seemed the last thing on "Louie" Guzman's mind.

"What do you want?" he said, his eyes and attention clearly elsewhere.

"I need to ask you about your cellie."

"He's dead."

"I know. But did you happen to notice anything strange before Walker's death?"

"Before?" Guzman hacked and spat out a clam. "*Coño!* That boy was nuts, man. They should have kept him in PSU."

"Do you know if he had any outside contact, in the days leading up to his death?" I leaned back against the chain link fence, keeping the rest of Louie's buddies in my periphery. They were staring at the blacks.

Louie's eyes kept jumping back and forth from our little deposition to his Frat brothers, who were now huddling. He shifted from foot to foot. Looked like he had to use the bathroom. "You mind? I'm a little busy here."

"Come on, Louie."

Giving me the once over, his brow twisted. He tilted his head and squinted. Then he slapped his hand on my chest, grabbed my shirt, pulled me forward and snarled. "I said, I'm busy."

"Just tell me about Walker, and I'm out of here."

He swore in Spanish, shoved me back, and started walking away. I heaved a defeated sigh. But he turned around, midstride and shouted, "Lenny was getting postcards from God!" Spinning his index finger around the side of his head, Louie added, "Friggin' whacko said that God told him to hang himself!"

"What? Wait!" Just one or two more questions, that's all I wanted. But Louie was already jogging into a large crowd of Frats, who swarmed like sharks and stalked B-yard with malice.

The blacks were busy playing basketball, talking, playing cards, and generally looking tough. On the East side of the yard, The Fourth Reich stared back at the Frats, in my general direction. I tried to swallow but my throat had gone dry. The Frats ignored me as I made my way back to the gate. Rec time was just about over anyway and the safety of my cell beckoned. Only, I never made it back in time to avoid the oncoming storm.

CHAPTER FORTY-TWO

The attack came swiftly. An army of Mexican inmates rushed towards me as I jogged across the yard. For a moment, I thought I was the target. But when I noticed the motion on the East side of B-Yard— Buzz, The *Führer,* and the Fourth Reich converging—I realized that the war he warned me about was about to break out.

Not knowing which way to turn, I stopped dead in my tracks. Along with the blacks, I was caught between two colliding forces. The blacks seemed confused too. A sea of blue, gray and white engulfed me in seconds. To my amazement the Reichs and the Frats attacked the blacks rather than each other.

All around me fists flew. Inmates assaulted each other with punches, kicks, and all manner of shank and shiv. A loud buzzer sounded and over the P.A. the guards shouted, "Get down! Get down!"

Both Nazis and Frats assaulted the blacks who, despite their furious efforts, were outnumbered and taken by surprise. I could hardly breathe and tried in vain to squeeze my way through the melee. All the shouting, the smell of sweat and halitosis threatened to overwhelm me. I was moving, but like a tiny boat without a sail, tossed by waves of murderous inmates.

The guards continued shouting for us to get down. But there were only six of them versus more than a hundred brawling inmates.

Shots fired into the air had little effect. Then came the moment I had dreaded since Butch dumped me in Gen-Pop.

Two Reich members grabbed me by the arms. I thrashed about and kicked but could not make contact. They threw me on the ground. My back smacked against the pavement. Pinned down, there was nothing to do but shut my eyes as the two struck me repeatedly in the face, the gut.

Blood filled my mouth. I nearly choked on it. Butch was finally getting his revenge. It wouldn't have surprised me if he had orchestrated the riot for this very purpose. I finally coughed out words of desperation. "You don't have to do this!"

"Shut up!" Another blow to the face.

"You let Butch call the shots? Run your life?" The Nazi standing over me reached into his waistband and pulled out something sharp. He knelt down and held my throat with his free hand. "Don't do this!" I said.

The edge of a razor sharp shiv pressed into my neck. The Nazi bore down and began to break my skin. *Oh God, help me*! The Nazi tightened his hands around my throat. Pressed the shiv in harder. I shut my eyes. This was the end.

And then, something remarkable happened.

All the weight on my chest, my shoulders, and my neck lifted away. I opened my eyes. My attackers' faces were pale. They'd dropped their shivs and their mouths hung agape. Then they turned and ran.

I sat up and searched for an oncoming threat.

Nothing.

Just a bunch of inmates shouting and killing each other. The riot grew more fierce. Sore from the beating, I stood up and felt my neck. A drop of blood colored my fingertips. I should be dead. Why had they run?

Another verbal warning from the guards burst through the din of klaxons and shouting inmates. Another set of gunshots rang out.

This time everyone in the yard dropped to the floor.

I was still standing in a stupor.

"Live rounds!" Someone reached up, grabbed my arm and pulled me to the ground. It was Louie. Laying on my belly, I saw it. Just twenty feet ahead of me, one of the Führer's lieutenants was sprawled across the concrete, half of his head blown away, the other half lying in a puddle of blood and gray matter.

CHAPTER FORTY-THREE

I never thought I'd live though the riot, nor the informal execution Butch had ordered. But I did, and when all was said and done, I walked away with relatively minor injuries.

The two Nazis that attacked me had been admitted to the PSU. Rumors had it that they claimed they saw something so terrible that they were all too happy to be taken into psychiatric protective custody. They offered no resistance when taken in for questioning. Probably squealed on Butch. They never stood a chance, though, because Butch was full of plan B's. And C's and D's for that matter. Of course, the doctors decided—or were instructed to state, more likely—that the two Nazis should be medicated for their hallucinations.

For the next week, we were on complete lockdown. During that time, the most exciting thing that happened was Nosebleed getting shanked by the Frat boys in the shower, and a fairly large but brief earthquake, which was pretty common around this part of Southern California. Possum tried to squeeze under his bed that night.

Sonja Grace brought me a copy of the *Union Tribune* . She thought I might find the cover story interesting. The headline read: *La Jolla Businessman Charged with Murder of Wife and Child.* It could have easily been written some two years ago when I was on trial. The accused, Charles Boynton, was an upstanding member of the La Jolla community. An investment broker with Henley-Spears, he lived in the cradle of luxury. He was handsome, in the prime of his life with everything going for him—a beautiful wife and high school senior daughter headed for Yale, a two million dollar house with an ocean view, and so much more.

The murder charges stunned everyone. But it was the rape charges that sent chills through my blood the day Rachel brought the paper with her for a visit. Looking at the stitches on my head, and the crimson-stained bandages on my throat, she said, "I heard about the riot. You okay?"

"Been better. How's Dave doing these days?"

"They've finished rebuilding the church. Dedicated the sanctuary to Lorraine's memory."

"Yeah, Dave told me last time he visited." It had been a brief visit and interrupted by an urgent matter that required his prompt return to San Diego.

"Have you been injured?"

"Everyone gets hurt in here at some point." I was too engrossed in the newspaper article to answer with more detail. I should have told her about the whole thing—how Butch had probably set up the riot and ordered the two Reich members to kill me. But that would only have made me appear paranoid. And crazier still, if I told her that the two guys who tried to kill me were now in PSU, claiming to have seen a pair of otherworldly beings, glowing white and wielding flaming swords. "Rachel, this Boynton case. It's eerily familiar."

"What's even more strange is that it's the *second* such murder since—"

I finally met her eyes. Brown, no colored contacts today. "Are they calling them Hudson copy cats?"

"They're calling them all kinds of things."

"Seems to be an epidemic," I said. "Fathers killing their wives, raping their daughters."

"That's not even funny."

"Wasn't trying to be," I said, peaking over the pages. Something was definitely wrong. Today, Rachel hardly smiled, offered no words of hope. I didn't ask. Instead, I mentioned what had happened with Walker, his contact with someone on Instant Messenger who manipulated him into shooting the girls at Coyote Creek, and eventually killing himself in prison.

"The same screen name?" Rachel asked.

"That's got to mean something."

"I'll have Mack look into it." There should have been a lot more discussion about this, but Rachel seemed distracted. She pulled her chair closer to the table. One advantage of being out of the SHU was that visits were permitted in an open common area, well-guarded, of course, and not behind an inch of plexiglass.

"Rachel, what is it you're not telling me?"

She turned away for a moment. When she looked back into my eyes, I could tell something was wrong. "Do you remember that Thanksgiving when Aaron was first put on a ventilator?"

"How could I forget?" I said.

"And you remember that word of knowledge I got while waiting with you in Children's Hospital?" Rachel said.

"Yeah, *It's going to be fine.*" Not exactly what I'd expected a prophetic word from God to sound like. But as an atheist, it didn't matter to me one way or another.

"There's something I have to tell you."

"What is it?" I said, barely breathing.

She glanced around the stark room at other attorneys talking with their clients, girlfriends holding hands with their convict-boyfriends. I hadn't noticed how arched her shoulders had become until they slumped down and she exhaled. "It's Aaron."

I set the paper down. News about Aaron had been pretty static lately. Nothing ever required this dramatic a prelude. "What is it?"

"He's suffered another infection. There's a lot of fluid in his lungs. He's been running a high fever."

I swallowed, opened my mouth to speak, but couldn't.

Gazing out the window, she sniffed, dabbed her eyes and said, "They don't think he'll make it through the night."

CHAPTER FORTY-FOUR

It took a while for the news to sink in. After laying in a coma for two years, my son was going to die. I didn't want to accept it. Even after Rachel left, I paced around my cell, then out in the yard. Screw Butch, if he had another surprise for me.

Standing watch by the concrete picnic table, Possum asked me why I was pacing, why I was so agitated. His words barely registered. Until he grabbed me by the arm. "Cut it out, Silk!"

"What?"

"You're talking to yourself. Freaking the hell out of me."

"Leave me alone."

He stood perfectly still, eyeballed the yard, then drew close and whispered, "You wanna join your Nazi buddies in PSU or something? Knock it off."

I stopped and turned to face him. "It's Aaron."

"Oh no." His features crumpled with an expression which only a parent could fully understand.

"They're saying he won't make it through the night."

"Sucks."

"Yeah," I sighed. Sometimes finding the right words to express yourself is too much of a challenge. I slammed the bed frame. "Dammit!"

Possum put his hand on my back. "Maybe if you talk to the

warden, he'll let you out with a guarded escort to see him. You know, to say good-bye?"

I shook my head. "Even if he agreed, there's still a restraining order." I slammed my hand against the bars so hard it made some of the guards to turn their heads.

"Do you believe in God?" Possum asked.

"I don't know, do you?"

Possum's nose twitched. "Might help to talk to someone."

"Chaplain's too scared. Five minute sermon and he bolts."

"They don't call him Father Speedy for nothing."

"I don't know. I just don't know." Why would I want to talk to anyone about a God who—if he even existed—had been so cruel to my family. As much as I respected Rachel, that word she claimed to have gotten from God—*it's going to be fine*—just wasn't panning out. What kind of God would make a promise like that and renege?

"Well, I ain't all that religious myself," said Possum. "But alls I know is that when we got our backs up against the wall, there's one name we call out, whether we believe or not." He smirked. "You got a better idea?"

I shrugged.

"Whatcha got to lose then?"

"What, you want me to pray?"

"Won't cost you anything but the time it takes."

"Maybe," I said, desperate enough to try anything. "But I don't know the first thing."

"There's one other person you might try." Possum's beady eyes darted around, stopped, then met my gaze once again. "Whatever you do, don't tell him I suggested it."

"All right."

"And don't let his past, or his nickname fool you, okay? He's not someone you want to piss off."

"Don't worry about that."

"You know, maybe this wasn't such a good idea, after all."

"WHO, DAMMIT!" I grabbed his shirt and started to shake

him.

"Him!" Possum stood up pointed down into the corridor, to the one person I would have never guessed. And he was heading our way.

I was going to be ill.

CHAPTER FORTY-FIVE

I learned from Possum why they called Frank Morgan, the most feared inmate at Salton Sea, the Bishop. And I'd have to jump through some frightening hoops just to get close enough to talk to him. If I survived, I would kill Possum for suggesting it.

"Excuse me, Bishop?" I said. Either he didn't hear me, or didn't care to turn around and answer. His massive back was turned and he sat at a concrete table grunting to himself unintelligibly. I tapped his shoulder.

Big mistake.

With a fist ready to strike, he spun around and snarled. "What do you want!" As far as I could tell, Bishop was engrossed in a caveman like conversation with he, himself and Irene.

"Sorry, I just—"

"I don't like being interrupted." He stood up, tilted his head and popped vertebrae in his neck.

"I'm sure you don't. But I need to talk to you." What was I thinking? I didn't even know where to begin. Right off the top of my head, I said, "You were a priest, weren't you?"

He narrowed his eyes with contempt, then he started walking

away. Should I follow him or did I want to keep living? I thought of Aaron. If prayer was his only hope, then it didn't matter if I believed or not, I had to take the chance—on God, on Bishop.

"Hey, wait!" I went after him, determination overtaking good sense. At first I kept a safe distance. "Look, I need your help. It's my son. He's dying."

Bishop stopped. Without turning around to face me, he said, "So what do you want from me?"

It took a moment to finally say it. "I need you to pray for him."

Bishop turned slowly, his lip curled. His clenched teeth barely allowed words to escape. "You think I'm some kind of holy man, a shaman?"

"You were a Jesuit priest."

He pulled on his sweatshirt. "You see a collar somewhere?"

"No, but—"

"Rosary beads?"

"But you—"

"Don't you get it, you idiot? I'm not a priest!" He stormed off again.

Damn. Of course he was no longer a priest. He'd been sent to prison for a violent crime. Dangerous as he appeared, however, I doubted that he was guilty of the crimes of which he'd been convicted. There was just something about him—not tangible. Perhaps it takes an innocent man to discern another—perhaps I was deluding myself.

Before he got too far, I went after him. The thick grass cushioned my footfalls. Bishop ignored me. I called out to him again, but he would not stop. Finally, I caught up and reached for his shoulder. As soon as I gripped it, he swung around.

What happened next came so quick I can hardly recall. In a flash, I was on the ground with what felt like a broken jaw. When my vision cleared, Bishop bore down into my face, huffing. "You do not want to get on my bad side, Hudson!"

I spat salty blood onto the ground. "You might not be a priest anymore, but you must still believe. Please, I need you to pray for my son."

"I don't bother with God anymore. You think He's going to take time out of His busy schedule to listen?" He shoved me back down into the grass. "*You* pray for him!"

CHAPTER FORTY-SIX

That very day, while I lay in my bunk with a cold towel on my bruised jaw, the evening edition of the *San Diego Union Tribune* reported two items of morbid interest. First, another man had been charged with the rape and murder of his wife and daughter. This third murder happened in Poway.

But it was the next report that truly stunned me. An email had been sent to one of the staff writers at the paper. The sender identified himself by a cryptic, mythological name. The text from the email read:

Dear editor,

That your journal likens the recent wave of brilliantly executed dramas to a psychological pandemic is offensive. With each of the recent sublimations, resulting in the spiritual transcendence of mothers and their daughters, I have manifested my glory. You seek swift punishment and of course, you convict as I direct: the fathers, the husbands. I have stood silent about that for my own reasons. But I will no longer permit my glory to be misdirected.

My chosen subjects, I mold for my pleasure. I am incarnate in the lives of my favored creatures as I beatify them. For all intents and purposes, I am God. But that you may conceive of me in your feeble mortal minds, you may call me by a more conventional name.

Kitsune

When Rachel read the article, she felt a disturbing sense of convergence. She called Mack immediately.

"Are you certain?" Mack said.

"It's worth a look." Rachel was already putting on her Nikes, still reading the paper on her coffee table. The glass top reflected the sickle moon through the window of her studio apartment. "Something about that name, *Kitsune*, sounded familiar, so I Googled it. It's the name of a mythical Japanese fox."

"That's interesting but—"

"And that screen name that had contacted Sam," Rachel said, with the phone clamped between her ear and shoulder, as she wrestled her running shoes on. "That was someone called Huliboy."

"You've got a point somewhere in all this, I hope?"

"*Huli!*" She said nearly falling forward as her foot popped into the shoe. "It's Chinese for fox. That much I knew. There are tons of Chinese legends about shape-shifting fox spirits called *Huli Jing*."

"All right, hold on. You got two Asian fox tags, so what?"

"Three screen names, because Walker told Sam that the person who said he was God and told him to kill the girls at Coyote Creek used a screen name too: Dr.Hu, spelled H-U."

"Right, *three* people with fox—"

"No, Mack. Don't you see? When you fill in the blanks it all makes sense."

"Ray, I'm just not follow—"

"One killer, three different screen names. Walker's cellmate claimed to have heard him say that God told him to kill those girls at Coyote Creek Middle School. And then later, "god," who had been sending him post cards in jail, commanded him to kill himself."

"Where's Walker now?"

"Dead!"

"What?" Mack exclaimed. "He actually did it?"

"I'm on my way to see Sam's boy. But first, let's meet at your office. Do you still have Sam's personal laptop?"

"They botched the warrant, remember?"

"Great, we'll look through his IM logs. I'm emailing you a .zip file with evidence we can take to the police. Don't go anywhere, I'll meet you in fifteen minutes."

As she drove her '82 Corolla out of the carport, Rachel hadn't the slightest idea that her laptop, still connected to the internet, was running a hidden piece of spyware which she had unwittingly downloaded upon opening an email link for an e-card greeting. The executable was less than 500 kilobytes, but by harnessing components of the computer's operating system, it tracked every keystroke, every visited webpage, every search engine query. It even tapped into her computer's webcam and microphone, and transmitted her conversations along with other personal movement, and sent it back to its creator—*Kitsune.*

CHAPTER FORTY-SEVEN

"Can you even entertain the possibility that you might be wrong?" Mack said to Detective Anita Pearson, on the phone. She had been that scary officer who arrested Hudson and pushed the legal boundaries to the limit in doing so. Despite her good looks—if you went for the goth-girl type, that is—she must have had Freon for blood.

"Let it go," she said. "The case is closed, the perp is exactly where he deserves to be."

"One: I believe Hudson was framed." And that he'd been the target of some bizarre prejudice, based on the way Pearson went after him—as if he, and all other accused rapist/murderers were responsible for her own personal pain. Mack held his tongue on that one.

"DNA doesn't lie. You've been off the force too long, old friend."

"And two: I think we're onto something."

"What are you talking about?"

"I'm forwarding you something Rachel Cheng put together. Keep an open mind. Check your inbox." As Mack explained the new information about Walker and his divine chat sessions, he glanced down at his watch. Fifteen minutes since Rachel's call.

Should've been here ten minutes ago.

Anita's diatribe went on and on about why the criminal justice system worked, and how slimy defense attorneys only got in the way. But Mack was distracted. Rachel was now half an hour late. She was never late for anything. If she said five minutes, it meant be ready in three. Anita's words became a blur while Mack's eyes jumped back and forth from his watch, to the door, to the window looking out at his driveway. "I'm going to have to call you back," he said and hung up on her, mid-sentence.

He held down the 6 key on his cell phone until it started dialing. He drummed his fingertips on the top of his mahogany secretary. "Come on, come on."

"You've reached the voicemail of Rachel Cheng, please leave a—" Mack swore, punched the END button, and went straight for the coat closet, keys in hand.

The best thing about driving after 8:00 PM on the 163 was that Rachel could do an easy seventy-five, as long as there were no CHP's hiding beneath the underpasses. What she didn't like so much was the fact that there were so few road lamps. She hated driving in the dark.

She turned on her radio to see if there was any news on the so-called *Kitsune*. In his publicized email to the *Tribune*, the writing was so bad she couldn't help but shake her head when she thought of it. She pictured a nerdy, pimply teenager, sending the email from a Public Library terminal, trying to conjure up the image of a mustache-twirling villain. Why they even bothered publishing it was beyond her. But what if this was indeed who she'd suspected?

She turned the dial some more and smirked at her makeshift clothes hanger antenna. All she got was static. "Come on!" she said, slapping the dashboard. For about two seconds, a couple of measures of a Murray Nissan dealership commercial played.

Sappy jingles.

Then a news reporter came on. "In today's news, The *San Diego Union Tribune* published a cryptic email sent by someone who calls himself *Kitsune*..."

Rachel groaned. "Come on now, just hold on for another sixty seconds."

"The email implies that the sender is somehow involved, if not responsible for the latest wave of domestic murders and rapes in San Diego. Officials have been reluctant to comment, but are saying that—-"

Static.

She banged on the dashboard. "Come on, you piece of junk!" The stupid radio never failed to cut out just before something important. She growled and hit the dashboard a couple more times.

Through the rear view mirror she saw a pair of headlights. The car had been following at a fairly close distance. Had been there for a while now, despite the fact that all lanes around her were clear.

Before she could react, the headlights behind her swelled and then vanished behind her bumpers. Her pursuer's car rammed into hers sending it spinning towards the shoulder, tires screeching. Rachel let out a shriek.

At seventy miles-per-hour, the slightest turn easily becomes a deadly swerve. She slammed the brakes and instantly regretted it. The car spun out of control into the dark. Lightning streaks of headlights from the opposite side of the freeway flashed before her eyes. Then the ever growing splash of a white concrete shoulder barrier filled the windshield. She was going to die.

She squeezed her eyes shut.

CHAPTER FORTY-EIGHT

Because Butch had somehow managed to slip me under the radar and throw me out of protective custody and into Gen-Pop, there were times that I wondered if I'd survive long enough to my see my own execution. And yet there I was, still alive. I almost forgot that my days were numbered, forgot that a death sentence hung over my head. Like my son, Aaron, only he was sentenced by a different judge.

So many people I knew and loved were gone. And now, as if my sorrow was not complete enough, Aaron. As I lay in my cell, staring at the paint peeling off the ceiling, cold tears streamed down the side of my face and wet my ears. The realization that my son now faced death, and for all I knew might already be dead in that hospital room, was sobering.

I tried not to let my quivering wake Possum, but I couldn't help but sit up, fold my hands, and whisper in desperation. "God, if you're there, if you are what you're supposed to be, then help my son. He's only six, never hurt anyone. You just can't let him die." I wiped my face. "And if you really are there, then don't you think you should have prevented this in the first place?" Pausing to consider the possibility that I might actually be talking to *The* Almighty, I decided that perhaps a little humility was in order. "I won't ask for anything else. If it's your plan to have me die for crimes I didn't commit, then so be it. Just let Aaron live."

"Oh, so you're praying now?" A voice whispered, mocking me.

I sat up and turned to the sound. "Butch!"

"Miss me?"

"Go away." I turned around and lay back down.

"I heard about your son. What a shame."

At that moment, approaching footfalls stirred his attention. He squinted down the tier into the gloom. "Who's there?"

"Lieutenant Hurley? That you?" It was Sonja.

"That's right," he replied. "What are you doing here, Sergeant?"

"My rounds, sir."

Please stay. Anything, just get Butch out of my sight.

"I'm busy here, Gracie," Butch growled. "Go on break, I'll let you know when I'm done."

"Yessir," she said. The sound of her footsteps made a heart-sinking diminuendo.

When the exit door slammed, Butch spat out his toothpick. It made a soggy sound when it hit the ground. He then inserted the first new toothpick I'd ever seen him with.

"What do you want?"

"Oh nothing," he said and chewed on his new toothpick. "Just wanted to see how you were doing."

"Still alive. Sorry to disappoint."

"Yeah, well. I don't know what you did to freak my boys out like that—"

"I didn't do anything." I said, and lay back down, hoping he'd get bored and leave.

"Anyway,' Butch said. "I just came to let you know that if by the off-chance you was thinking of trying to talk to anyone about my business up in the SHU, don't bother. But hey, if you'd like to, go right on ahead. Be my guest. I can have you join your buddies in PSU. Hell, maybe the drugs'll mellow you out so much you won't have to feel the pain of knowing your little boy is gonna croak all by his little lonesome." He started laughing. Despite my best efforts to block his very existence, I found it impossible to ignore the taunting.

"You done?" I said.

"Why don't you go ahead and say your little prayers? It's the sweetest lil' thang." I thought of calling for a guard, but remembered that Butch outranked them all. "Come on," he said. "Go ahead and pray if it makes you feel better."

"Would you please leave?"

"Probably screwed the little tyke too, didn't you?"

That was it. I leapt down from my bunk and rushed him. And though there was plenty of steel between us, he flinched with surprise as I slammed my hands on the bars. Possum grunted and snorted, but remained asleep.

Then for a brief moment, I saw something I'd never yet seen in Butch's eyes.

Terror.

"What the hell?" he stammered, as a flash of light lit his face. If his eyes opened any wider, they would have popped out of his head. He was staring past me. I looked over my shoulder expecting to see Possum, but he was still snoring in his bunk. Butch rubbed his eyes and backed away until he bumped into the railing. He turned, still gawking into my cell, and stumbled down the tier, cussing himself.

The sudden appearance of my shadow on the ground drew my attention. Not possible. I turned around and found the light source. It was coming from my bed.

Jenn's Bible.

I blinked repeatedly, rubbed my eyes. Still shining. The light filled my cell and warmth radiated with its beams. Why wasn't Possum waking up?

I was drawn like a moth to a fire. By the time I got to the Bible, its warm brilliance enveloped me completely. I reached forward and to this day, I could swear, I felt someone take my hand and lead it to the pages.

I took hold of the book. Then there came what felt like a great wind rushing through the cell. It whirled around inside for a while then blew outside, taking the light with it. My face felt as if it had been baking in the sun for hours, but it didn't hurt. When finally I could see again, I found that I had opened my Bible. A random page, I thought. But when I looked down and read the passage, I felt—rather, I knew it was anything but random.

It was the account of a Roman centurion whose servant was deathly ill. The centurion, not wanting to leave his beloved servant's side, sent a message to Jesus, begging him to heal the servant. When Jesus said that he would come to the house, the messengers were instructed to say,

...say the word, and my servant will be healed."

When Jesus heard this, he was amazed at him, and turning to the crowd following him, he said, "I tell you, I have not found such great faith even in Israel." Then the men who had been sent returned to the house and found the servant well.

A sense of inevitability, of reassurance overwhelmed me, as if God had spoken directly to me. I wanted to wake Possum and tell him, but he'd probably think I was crazy. Two years ago, I'd probably agree. But I wasn't. I knew what was happening. After all I'd seen, I finally got it. My pathetic attempt at prayer which started off as a tiny seed had now grown into a tree of faith.

Without another thought, I turned to a page in the back of the Bible which Jenn had written in notes. Next to that was a printed page. The Sinner's Prayer. I'd been eyeing that page for months and it finally seemed appropriate for me to say it, now that I truly meant it.

"Lord, I come to you in prayer asking for forgiveness. I confess with my mouth and believe with my heart that Jesus is your Son, and that he died on the cross that I might be forgiven and have eternal life in the kingdom of heaven. Father, I believe that Jesus rose from the dead and I ask you right now to come into my life and be my personal Lord and Savior. I repent of my sins and will worship you all the days of my life. Because your word is truth, I confess that I am born again and cleansed by the blood of Christ. In Jesus name, Amen."

At that moment, not only could I see my life, my past, all the wrong I'd done, I could feel its weight, lifted from my heart and mind. And joy. Joy unlike I had ever experienced overflowed. Just like dear old Lorraine used to tell me: Not the absence of pain, but the presence of the Almighty.

Clutching the Bible to my chest, I kept repeating that blessed phrase over and over in my mind. Rachel's word of knowledge, the promise:

It's going to be fine.

I almost forgot to pray for that miracle Aaron needed. But a miracle is exactly what happened next.

CHAPTER FORTY-NINE

"Sam," came the whisper. I got up and turned around. Dim light silhouetted Sonja Grace as she gestured for me to come to the bars. "Hurry!"

"What is it?" I asked.

"What happened to Lieutenant Hurley?"

"Butch?"

"Never seen him run so fast."

"Something spooked him," I said, peering down the tier.

She shook her head and spoke even softer. "Listen, you gotta trust me okay?"

"I already do."

To my amazement, Sonja proceeded to unlock and open my door. From a small duffle bag, she tossed over some clothing. "Change into these."

"Oh, no way," I said. She stood there guarding the door as I stripped to my boxers and put on a C.O.'s uniform.

"Come on, come on. Two minutes and Murphy gets back from the John. He sees you in that and we're both dead."

As soon as I stepped out into the tier, she slid the door gently and locked it. None of the other inmates woke up or said anything, which struck me as odd. "Okay, Sonja, where are we going?"

"To make sure you don't live a life of regret."

CHAPTER FIFTY

Mack had never driven slower than 70 on the freeway. Crawling at 25 was like pulling teeth with a pair of rusty pliers. Must be construction or an accident. With each car that zoomed by, opposite him on the northbound 163, he grew more and more impatient. "Come on, already!"

Rachel would have called, he kept thinking. Something was really wrong.

Two miles past Clairemont Mesa, Mack saw the flashing red and blues of a police car, pulled over to the left shoulder of the freeway. He slowed down and his heart turned cold at the sight of the twisted wreckage. Rachel's Toyota, its frame crumpled like a beer can, had flipped over onto the driver's side.

After he identified himself, they waved him over to the accident scene. He leaned down to look through the rear window. "Where is she?" Mack demanded, marching right up to the young CHP officer.

"I'm sorry sir, EMTs took her ten minutes ago."

"How'd she look?"

He shook his head.

"Where'd they go?"

"Sharp Memorial."

A minute later, Mack was back in his car, flagrantly ignoring speed limits.

CHAPTER FIFTY-ONE

Anita Pearson's idea of a hot date was chatting online. People in "carbon space" were way too complicated and unpredictable. The internet was a lot safer. Carbon-space men were all genetically predisposed to lying, cheating, or screwing up and/or around.

She had many male IM buddies who worshipped her. They'd fallen in love with her avatar, that little square photo which presumably depicts the person behind the IP packets. It was in fact her picture, a full body shot of her in a bikini, but her face pixilated by Photoshop. She enjoyed the cyber attention- and the power trip. They were virtually eating out of the palm of her hands, among other places.

And there was the sex.

Cybersex was way underrated. It was cleaner, it was safer, and she was always in control. And while she had her pick of men to "cyber" with, just for fun on lonely nights like tonight, one man had distinguished himself. He was her favorite.

As a lover, he was gentle, but passionate. And with him, it was so much more than sex. He was her soul mate. And she his. No one knew her like this.

"You had me at LOL," she would say, or type, rather. But the truth was, they'd fallen in love gradually, over the years. He was a prince. First came the birthday emails, then over time, flowers on their online-anniversary. And recently, the thing that sent her heart soaring like nothing else, that made her feel completely feminine—his poetry.

On every conceivable occasion, he wrote her poems and emailed them, singing her praises, extolling her innermost qualities which no one else knew about. She was his lady and he, her troubadour. Far better than any relationship she'd ever had with a carbon-space man.

He never forgot the little things, was always truthful and completely vulnerable towards her. And talk about considerate. Once, she locked herself out of her apartment. She texted him and—despite the fact that he lived in Omaha, Nebraska—he called for a locksmith, who showed up within minutes.

Once and only once, had he brought up the idea of marriage. But as soon as she started to show her hesitation, he backed off quickly. She might actually have found him to be the perfect mate, if not for her intense distrust of men. But that was soon to change. Anita could feel it.

For now, they both contented themselves with the status quo. It worked for her and tonight, after one of their best sessions ever, she was basking in the glow of his affection.

With her blanket draped over her bare thighs, she typed and giggled, tingling with the afterglow. He had made her feel loved, cherished, and completely sexy.

An email alert chimed. Anticipating a little tidbit from her lover, Anita clicked on her inbox. Was it a poem? A sonnet? A limerick? Sure enough, there was a message from him. But directly under that, there was another message that had been sent two hours ago. It was that email from Richard Mackey, that retired cop who turned P.I. She selected Mack's message and put her finger on the delete key. No way she'd let him spoil a perfect night.

Her lover's IM box flashed impatiently. *Getting lonely here.*

Just a sec. I'm going to read your email, but gotta clear out some SPAM.

A tiny portion of her conscience bothered her, like a pebble in a shoe. But she pressed the delete key anyway, and sent Mack's email, attachments and all, into the trash folder.

The next few minutes were spent with a hand over her mouth, suppressing laughter. This was the dirtiest, funniest limerick her lover had ever written, the craziest variation on "There once was a man from Nantucket..."

It put her in such a light-hearted mood that she decided to undelete Mack's email and take a quick peek at it. For the most part, in law enforcement techno-babble it said, "blah-blah-blah." She opened the attachments and gave the information a cursory glance.

Anita's attention was divided between her cyberlover and her half-hearted reading of the documents from Mack—apparently compiled by that wet-behind-the-ears defense attorney, Rachel Cheng.

But gradually, her attention shifted to the reports, the data. The smile on her face faded, she began neglecting her IM window. As if on the furry legs of a tarantula, dread crept up her back and nested in her hair. A shiver coursed through her blood. Jolted her.

It was the realization, the collision of worlds—madness, desperation and reality. She kept glancing back and forth between the report and the IM window.

Anita gasped aloud.

She leapt out of bed, still naked.

Her laptop thumped onto the carpet, the IM window flashing, beeping incessantly. She picked up the laptop like a dead rat and dropped it on her bed.

He was still typing. *What's wrong?*

It was the screen names, her cyber-lover's and the one in the report.

Too close to be a coincidence.

MrFoXxX.

CHAPTER FIFTY-TWO

Not far from Sharp, where Rachel lay in critical condition, a prayer vigil went on at Children's Hospital in Aaron's room. Samantha and Alan led prayers and singing around the boy. His grandparents, Oscar and Maggie were also present, holding his hand, stroking his hair. Dave wanted to be there, but he had been away for the entire month on a relief mission to the Honduras.

Alan noticed that Aaron's breathing had become shallow, his complexion like the sheets in which he lay. A secondary infection had filled his lungs with fluids. He wasn't responding to fever reducers either. In his weakened state, there was just no way for him to fight it. The doctors had already told Oscar and Maggie to start making preparations.

For the past two hours, he and Samantha prayed for Aaron while their daughter Elizabeth reclined in a stroller, asleep and oblivious. Also present was Jerry, who laid a little bag of pistachios on Aaron's pillow.

Alan left several messages on Rachel's voicemail, but was too involved to notice anything was wrong. The entire Bible study group was determined to stay by Aaron's bedside until the end.

At 11:00 PM Oscar and Maggie got up, kissed their grandson and said their tearful good-byes. They thanked Alan, Samantha and the group for their kindness and told them it would be okay if they all decided to go home.

But they didn't. They wouldn't.

By midnight, Jerry had fallen asleep in a green vinyl chair. He hadn't eaten any of the pistachios he'd brought. Samantha took Elizabeth home and Alan remained, the only one still praying.

After he read the Twenty-Third Psalm to Aaron, he realized that Rachel hadn't shown, hadn't even called. He decided to try her at home one more time. After two rings, her answering machine picked up. He tried her cell phone, expecting her voicemail. But to his surprise, the call connected.

"Hello?"

"I'm sorry," Alan said, "I must have the wrong number."

"Wait! Alan? It's me, Richard Mackey."

"Mack? Thought you sounded familiar. What are you doing answering Rachel's—?"

"She's been in an accident."

It hit him like a cinder block. "Is she okay?"

Mack went on to explain what had happened and where she was being treated. Rachel had suffered a concussion and the doctors were reluctant to say much else.

"I can't leave just now," Alan said. "You know about the Hudson boy, don't you?"

"Yeah, well. They're not sure Rachel's going to make it through the night either."

After hanging up, Alan prayed some more. He'd promised to stay until the very end, Sam would have wanted that. But Rachel was a sister to him. He'd never forgive himself if he didn't at least go to see her. Hopefully, he'd be back in time. Running his hand through Aaron's hair, he said, "I'm sorry, but I have to go."

What I wouldn't give, at that moment, to run up to Alan and give him a bear hug, thank him for being such a faithful friend. Instead, from behind a curtain by the room's other door, I watched him say good-bye to Aaron and leave. I couldn't risk making Alan an accessory, if I got caught.

I glanced up at the wall clock. Five minutes was all Sonja could afford, or she'd be late for her second shift back at Salton. She sat waiting for me in her midnight blue Mustang, parked by the Hospital's service entrance. The plan was to return as quietly as we had left.

When the coast seemed clear, I went over to my son. For a moment, my legs wouldn't move. I didn't realize that I'd stopped breathing until my lungs forced me to.

"Aaron?" I whispered. A shadow passed by the window of the door that Alan had left through. Immediately, I pulled the curtain around Aaron's bed.

He lay there, with tubes in his windpipe. The mechanical beeps and hissing sounds indicating the artificial rhythm of his assisted breathing. I couldn't help myself from crying.

It had been about two years since I last saw him. It now felt like twenty. I put my hand on his head, bent down and kissed his face. "My boy. My sweet, boy." How could such joy intertwine so intricately with such sorrow?

I fell to my knees. Having just given my life to God, there was no better opportunity than now to bring my supplications to Him. Placing my hand on Aaron's forehead, I prayed, "God, please. Don't let Aaron die. He's just a little boy, never hurt anyone. You have the power to heal him. Just say the word, Lord. Just say the word and he'll be healed."

I waited for something. A lightning bolt, writing on the wall, anything to show me God was listening. Nothing. Just a quiet recollection of Rachel reciting, "*It's going to be fine.*"

"Lord, I know you were pleased with the faith of that Centurion, so I'm going to go out on a limb here. Just heal him. I promise I'll do whatever you want me to, from now on. Whatever it takes—"

The door opened, jolting me out of my prayer. "Who drew this curtain?" said a male voice. Without even a chance to kiss my son good-bye, I dashed over to the other side of the room, towards the second exit door.

"Hey!" shouted the orderly, as I darted out the door. I vaguely heard him calling for security as I flew down the stairs. At the bottom of the steps stood the back exit door, which led to the back alley where Sonja awaited. The *boom-boom-boom* of my frantic feet alerted a security guard who had just entered through it.

Back up the stairs I went before he got a good look at me.

One level up, I found an exit and ran down the hall, passing rooms full of sleeping patients. In my haste, I nearly tripped over an IV drip stand. I found an empty corridor and ducked inside, plastering my back against the wall. Chest heaving, I stuck my head out just enough to get a look at the clock above the receptionist's desk. I was to meet Sonja in two minutes. But I couldn't have her face criminal charges on my account, though that is exactly what she'd risked from the moment she helped me get out.

Certain that I'd been seen in my CDC Corrections Officer uniform, I shed the beige shirt and brown hat. Now wearing a blue T-shirt and green pants, I walked out into the open, looking like I was supposed to be there.

"Evening ma'am," I said to the receptionist, who never lifted her eyes from the computer.

"Hi there."

With the service exit blocked, I would have to exit through the main entrance and sneak around to the back. I hit the down button and waited for the elevator doors to open. The LED arrows indicated that one of the cars was going up, the other down. Sweat rolled into the corner of my eye and stung. I stood as close to the elevator as possible.

DING!

Wrong car. The up elevator door slid open. Subtly, I turned my back so that I faced the down elevator, which for some reason, was taking its sweet time in arriving.

The people exiting the up elevator came out and stopped talking.

Where was my elevator?

"Excuse me," one of them said. From the corner of my eye, I could see that he was with the Sheriff's department.

Pretending to have a headache, I held my hand over my eyes and groaned, "Yeah?" I turned to face them with half of my face covered.

"We got a report of an unauthorized person in—" What? Why did he stop? "Sir, you okay?"

"I'm fine. Migraine." *Where's that stupid elevator?*

"Hey, you CDC or something?"

"I, uh..."

"You're out of uniform," he said. I wondered if Sherlock here noticed I was sweating like a hog before an ax and a tree stump.

"Yeah, well..." Sherlock's partner whispered something to him. The next thing I knew, he grabbed my wrist and pulled my hand away from my face.

"Let me get a look at you," he said.

Just then my elevator dinged, the doors slid open. "There he goes!" I shouted, pointing over their shoulders. In the second it took for them to turn their heads, I jumped back into the elevator, hit the close button and shoved him back as forcefully as I could. Sherlock lost his balance and fell on top of Watson, his much smaller partner. Before they could pick themselves up the doors began to slide shut.

However, Sherlock reached his arm between the doors to stop them from closing. "Stop!" The doors jammed, beeped, and slid open.

I grabbed his arm with two hands, and this time, with my foot I heaved Sherlock with enough force to send him back even further than the first time.

But he held onto my wrists and pulled me out of the elevator.

"Get off of me!" I shouted and swung myself around him. Watson got behind Sherlock just as I pried his hands off, hooked my foot under his legs and rammed him with my shoulder. They both grunted and fell back into the elevator, just as the doors slid shut.

As I ran down the hall and turned the corner to another staircase, I heard the elevator ding once more. Sherlock and his partner were speaking on their walkie-talkies, giving my description. "No, didn't get a good look," he said. "I think he's headed for the south stairwell. No, wait, maybe its..."

I shut the door quietly and padded down the east staircase, which led to the first floor by the Trauma Care Center entrance. A quick glance down the hall revealed a pair of officers standing outside the doors.

What was I thinking coming here?

Just then, a flurry of activity crowded the entrance doors. An EMS team rushed in with an injured girl. Talk about deja vu. Doctors and nurses rushed to the door, crowded around the girl coming in on a gurney.

Just two yards before me, in a chair, rested a doctor's lab coat. Before anyone saw me, I ran over, slipped it on and rushed to join the team.

The entire chorus went on reporting the patient's status, what measures they'd taken. I stood close enough to learn that the girl had been in a car accident, her parents died in the crash.

The two police officers looked my way and approached. Had they gotten Sherlock's description and did they recognize me? Before either of them opened their mouths, I said, "Thank goodness you're here. Security's alerted us of an unauthorized visitor, last seen on the third floor."

"Yeah," the officer said. "Anyone here seen him?"

I pointed to the staircase I'd just come down. "I think he might have gone through that stairwell. If you hurry—"

"Thanks Doc."

I walked casually out the doors and turned another corner. Letting out a huge breath, I thanked God for helping me not get caught. When I reached the back lot, my heart sank.

Sonja's Mustang was gone.

What was I supposed to do, turn myself in? Begin a new career as The Fugitive?

"Pssst!"

I swung around, but didn't see anyone.

"Sam! Back here!" Behind the trunk of a Palm tree, Sonja waved me over. She hadn't abandoned me.

"You're nuts!" I said, as I walked over to her. "How are we ever going to—"

Before I could say another word, she slapped my face really hard.

"You bastard!"

"What?"

"My sister! How could you sleep with my sister!" Immediately, I realized what she was doing and went along with it.

A security guard shone a flashlight on us and called out. "You two!"

Obscuring my face behind her head, Sonja, said, "Sir, you a cop? 'cause if you are, I want you to arrest this pig! For sleeping around with every woman in San Diego," she glared at me, "and her sister!"

"Get outta here before I do call the cops!"

"Come on, honey" I said, "Let's go."

"Don't you ever call me that again!" She marched back to into the thick of the trees. My back still facing the security guard, I went after her. "Wait, sweetheart!" Just behind us, on the street, her Mustang waited under a yellow street lamp.

"We gotta get back, now." She unlocked the doors and got in.

"Yeah." I too stepped inside, rubbing my face.

"Sorry about that. Did you get to see him?" Sonja asked.

"I did."

"Say good-bye?"

"Yeah," I lied.

"At least you got to say good-bye." Sonja started the engine and drove to the freeway. Back to Salton.

CHAPTER FIFTY-THREE

Driving down the I-8, Sonja and I quietly watched a new day rise up over the Eastern horizon. She managed to return me to my cell without incident. The guards barely lifted their heads as she marched me back to my cell, once again shackled and dressed in my prison clothes. No one even bothered to look twice. For the next few days, she kept a reasonable distance, just in case.

That morning, as the sun stretched up over the hills, inexplicable peace flooded my mind. Regardless of Aaron's fate, I had joy—the kind that Lorraine always spoke of. I became aware of the fact that something was now missing. Something that had hung over my life from the day Aaron was born and followed me around like a prowling lion since he was an infant.

Fear.

Fear that had compelled me to pad over to his room in the middle of the night when I didn't hear him breathing over the baby monitor. Fear that brought my ear down to his face to check if he was still breathing. Fear that he might run off into the street and get hit by a car. All gone.

I had every intention of keeping my newfound faith to myself, but I must not have been doing such a great job of it. During breakfast, the other inmates gave me odd stares. "What's with the smile?" Possum even asked.

I couldn't wait till rec time, when I'd get on the pay phone and call Rachel about Aaron. Something told me he'd make it. I had no logical basis for this, and perhaps my faith was just a way of coping, but a huge burden had indeed been lifted.

Standing in the line to return my breakfast tray, I found myself behind Bishop, of all people. I wanted to tell him that I had taken his advice and prayed. I wanted to talk to him about my experiences. Better judgment and the desire to live prevailed.

I took a step forward. A sudden twinge in my head stopped me. In my mind, I saw an image of Bishop.

He leans over a sickly, middle-aged woman lying in bed, holding her hand. Weeping. A flash of light and now he is lying in his prison cell bunk, holding his head and in anguish.

The image clung to my mind with talons of recognition. I dropped my tray and faltered. The half full bowl of cereal and milk hit the floor and splattered on the back of Bishop's pants.

"Hey!"

Great. "Sorry, man." I bent down and gathered up the mess and set it on a table with an unintentional bang. And a splash. Several droplets of milk dotted Luther's crinkled nose.

"Mutha—!"

"Gotta go."

Though two very dangerous, very perturbed inmates had me in their crosshairs now, I was too disturbed by the vision to care. Halfway down the hall I stopped, pressed my back up against the wall. "Okay" I whispered to God. "What are you doing?"

Eventually, the anxiety ebbed. I took a deep breath and set my eyes on the pay phone. Now, more than ever, I needed to speak with Rachel, let her know about what had happened. With most of the inmates still at breakfast, the line was short.

The morning sun blared down from a blue and cloudless sky. The back of my neck and arms felt like baked pork rinds. A Mexican guy chattered incessantly on the phone, holding up the line. If there had been a couple of Riechers or Blacks behind him, he wouldn't have been taking his time like this.

Finally, the line began to move. The next calls were quick. In about five minutes, there was only one person in front of me. He slammed the receiver down when he got an answering machine.

I had Rachel's cell phone number memorized and anticipated a great report from her. I could just about hear the buoyancy in her voice telling me of Aaron's amazing recovery. But just as I lifted the handset, someone grasped my wrist, forcing me to drop it.

Bishop glared at me, his grip unrelenting. My arm was about to snap like a twig.

CHAPTER FIFTY-FOUR

Having spent the entire night at the computer forensics lab with Judy Prine, the lead cybercrime investigator, Anita saw no point in trying to sleep. Might as well put her shocking discovery to use. The implications for Sam Hudson's innocence didn't matter as much as the fact that she, herself had been violated. *How could I have been so stupid?*

"You sure about this?" Judy asked. "More than seventy screen names with some variation on Fox, *Huli* and DrHu, have crossed your ISP alone."

Anita stared down into an empty mug on the table top on which she perched. Five cups and eight trips to the ladies room in the past four hours, and they hadn't made any progress. "What about Hudson's ISP or Walker's?"

Judy pecked at the keyboard, clicked her mouse and shook her head. "Hudson used Road Runner, Walker used Comcast."

"So you can't compare them to my ISP?"

"Cox Cable turned over their records quicker than the others, but I think I can run some comparative scans. It'll just take some time."

"How long?"

She glanced up at the wall clock and clicked the mouse a few more times. "A couple of hours, unless I find a match early on."

"Okay, do what you can." Anita felt the effect of all the coffee heading south again and went the ladies room. A couple of minutes later, she returned to the lab to find Judy typing away at a breakneck speed.

"Judy, did you—?"

She held a finger up. One final bang on the enter key and Judy said, "Yes!"

"What?"

She waved Anita over. "Have a look." The detective leaned over her shoulder and examined the data. It was so neatly compiled, the conclusion was overwhelming. This MrFoXxX was in fact the same person that had contacted Hudson and Walker. Though he used different variations on the screen name, and though over the course of the past few years he had spoofed the IP addresses from sixteen different ISP's world wide, he had not anticipated the powerful detection programs available to the state's computer forensics lab.

Anita gasped. Waves of revulsion tossed like a storm in her belly as she scanned the billing information connected to this freak. She was going to be sick all over the computer. Her cyberlover was not from Omaha. He was from San Diego. The spreadsheet displayed his real name. Anita grabbed the back of Judy's chair to keep from falling.

CHAPTER FIFTY-FIVE

He'd kept so many steps ahead of the authorities that he never had to think twice about getting caught. He lived by rules and principles—his own, of course, and devised all the contingencies. Forget about Plan B, he had everything up to plan X in line.

Intellectual superiority was a lonesome burden. But it afforded him the right to go forth and take what was his. If a tree fell and nobody heard him dismember it, did it really fall? Had it ever existed? Better still, if someone else was caught with the chainsaw, then that person might as well be given the credit for the fallen oak.

But he was now experiencing something entirely alien. Anxiety. How could he have possibly misstepped like this? He'd taken every precaution: IP spoofing, cryptic screen names. And yet, they had connected the dots!

"Stupid!" He slammed his fist on the computer desk. Coffee splattered onto the morning paper. No, not stupidity. Hubris. He could have easily plugged this hole a long time ago.

Forget it. Don't question past choices. Where would the challenge be if there was no risk of getting caught? "All right, breathe." He squeezed his eyes shut and rubbed his eyebrows. Why had Anita signed off so abruptly? Wasn't like her. In the three years they'd been having cybersex, she would always say something, even if she had to sign off suddenly.

Maybe it was that little Asian lawyer, Rachel Cheng.

No. Anita could not have learned anything from her. Especially since he'd run the little upstart off the road last night at 85 miles per hour.

Unless...

Think.

THINK!

He picked up the phone and dialed Sharp Memorial.

Swore at the recorded menu.

He drummed his fingers on the desk, feeling the morning rays toast the back of his hand. Finally, he punched in the correct selection. "Yes, I'm calling about Rachel Cheng."

"Please hold." More infernal elevator Muzak.

Finally she picked up again. "Sir, may I ask who this is?"

"I'm her brother," he lied. "Just got into town when I heard. Did she survive?" A pause on the other end. "I'll speak slow-ly so you can understand," he said. "Did...she...make...it?"

"No need for sarcasm, sir. Yes, she did. She's in the ICU right now."

"Can anyone visit her?"

"Only next of kin and police authorized—"

"Hello? I said I was her brother."

"I know that."

"Okay, look. I apologize. I'm just...worried."

"Of course you are, Mister Cheng."

"When are visiting hours?"

"Between now and—"

He clicked the end button, smirked and tossed the phone onto the sofa and bounded over to his closet where he rifled through the clothes, past all his different uniforms, past his formal attire. Outfoxing the authorities would be a piece of cake.

Ah, this one was perfect. A doctor's scrubs and lab coat.

Time to pay Rachel Cheng a visit.

CHAPTER FIFTY-SIX

As far as Mack was concerned, this case was about as abundant in clues as hair on Kojak's head. That is, until Rachel's lucky break from the bowels of the Salton Sea State Penitentiary.

Lucky, right.

Poor kid. Some bozo pulls a hit and run and now she's in the ICU, hanging by a thread. He stayed by her side as long as he could, but eventually had to lie down on the sofa in the waiting room.

"Mister Mackey?" A young female doctor approached the waiting area.

"That'd be me." He stopped pacing and ran his hand over his whiskery mug. Covering morning breath with his hand, he said, "How is she?"

"She ought to be dead."

"But she's not, right?"

"And with her injuries—"

Mack took a deep breath, began silently counting to five. Doctor Janet Wells smiled and shrugged. "She's going to be okay."

"Can I see her?"

"As a matter of fact, she sent me to come get you."

Mack double-timed down the hallway.

Rachel sat slightly elevated, tubes running from her nose and arms. "You look like hell, kid," Mack said.

"Nice to see you too," she answered, with a weak smile.

"Still the prettiest face I know."

"I'm so sorry."

"For what?"

"All this trouble." Rachel tried to sit up, but grimaced and settled back. "All I wanted was to talk to you before we brought those files to the police."

"I already sent them to Pearson."

"Oh no, come on, Mack!" Her eyebrows crinkled. "I thought we'd agreed to discuss it first."

"Look, Pearson's my only real connection."

"Not exactly the first person on my list."

So naive. Mack loved her like a daughter, but this girl had a few too many stars in her eyes. He couldn't blame her though, not after the way they had gone head to head like a Mongoose and a Cobra—Pearson being the snake—during Hudson's trial. "You're getting way ahead of yourself, Ray."

"Maybe so. But I don't believe in coincidence. There's a reason we got this info. I just know it." Her eyes lit up with urgency. "Wait! What about Aaron?"

"Oh yeah. Well, Alan called me this morning."

"And?"

"Well, seems there was a little commotion last night in the hospital, some unauthorized visit—"

Rachel's mouth fell open. "Did something happen to him?"

"Nah. But a couple of police officers got some egg on their face, real good."

"What about Aaron?"

"Tell you what, this is a day for miracles. Not only did the kid make it, his fever broke and his breathing's getting stronger."

"Oh, thank God," Rachel said.

"Uh... yeah, whatever. I'm going to play the lotto today."

Just then a bear-like growl erupted from Rachel's stomach. Her cheeks turned crimson. She smiled and patted her stomach. "Excuse me."

"You gotta be starved."

"I'll live."

"Why don't I go and bring up some breakfast? We'll talk about what we're gonna say to The Ice Prin—-I mean, Detective Pearson."

"Thanks, Mack."

As he stepped out into the hallway, he nearly collided with a doctor with a stethoscope dangling from his neck and a clipboard in hand. "Sorry, bud." Mack stepped aside and allowed him to pass.

"No worries." The doc smiled and did a double take. "Hey, aren't you that personal injury attorney on TV?"

"Uh, no," Mack said. "Not me."

"Funny, you look just like him."

"Besides," Mack said, hiking a thumb towards Rachel's room, "she can represent herself just fine."

"So many ambulance chasers these days preying on accident victims."

"Nah." Mack shook his head. "I'm just a friend."

"I'm Doctor Reynolds," He said and stuck out his hand. "We're going to take a quick look at her vitals. Can you give us a few minutes?"

"Sure, I'm just going out to get her something to eat. She can eat, right?"

"Of course." If the doc's smile grew any wider, Mack could drive a Hummer through it.

"Back in ten, kiddo, " Mack called back to Rachel.

"Perfect," the doc said, patting Mack on the back. "She'll be finished by then."

CHAPTER FIFTY-SEVEN

I once read that Baboons in South Africa could be found on the roadside in the hills. Friendly looking creatures, but they have the strength to rip a man's arm right out of its socket or eviscerate him, whichever it fancied most. Far be it from me to call Bishop a primate, but I was about to learn what those unfortunate tourists in Capetown had. The hard way. Bishop twisted my arm and I fell to my knees.

"You're starting to get on my nerves, Hudson!"

"I'm sorry about the tray, okay? Just...let go!"

Luther stood a couple of yards back, his arms folded over his chest.

"Okay, I get it," I said. "You're working with Butch now, right? Finishing me off for him because he hasn't got the—"

"Shut up! I don't do anything for that little turd!" The dull pain in my wrist turned white hot as he twisted harder. He threw me to the floor and grabbed my throat, bearing down with formidable weight. All because I spilled cereal on his pants?

"It was an accident," I sputtered.

Luther huffed. "You disrespected The Bishop! And for that, you gonna have to pay. Just like everyone before you, just like everyone after you. That's just the way it works, ain't that right, Bish?"

"Damned straight." He released my neck and then struck my face with a cast iron fist. The ferrous taste of blood filled my mouth.

My first day as a believer and I was about to meet my maker. The vision replayed in my mind. Bishop as a younger man, holding a dying woman's hand. "It must have really hurt to see her die," I said.

He pulled his next punch and blinked. "What?"

"Was she your mother? Because I know how it feels to lose someone you love." He yanked me to my feet. Shoved me and backed away as if I had suddenly grown a third eye. "We need to talk," I said, wiping the blood from my busted lip. Something within me rose up, stronger than anger, stronger than self-preservation or vengeance.

Compassion.

It made no sense, he was about to beat the living daylights out of me. One sharp look from Bishop and everyone near the pay phone scattered like cockroaches. Luther lingered, but when Bishop nodded at him, he too left. We were alone.

"What do you think you're pulling?" Bishop said.

"Can we just talk? That's all I'm asking." It felt like an ice pick in my jaw when I spoke. Flecks of light danced about my eyes. I was going to pass out.

Bishop straightened up and shook his head as if by doing so he could clear it. "Chapel in ten minutes. That's all you get."

"See you there." Every beat from my heart drummed in my ears and eyes. Finally, I picked myself up and leaned on the pay phone. I still had to call Rachel to ask about Aaron.

A gruff male voice answered her cell phone. "Yeah?"

"This is Sam Hudson. I'm looking for Rachel Cheng. Who's this?"

"Sam! It's me, Mack." He was speaking with his mouth full, stopped, swallowed and continued. "I've got her cell phone. She's been in an accident."

"What? When?"

"On the freeway last night. Someone ran her off the road. CHP's don't have any suspects yet."

"How is she?"

"She pulled through." So many questions. Where she was being treated, what kind of injuries had she sustained? I almost forgot to ask about my son. "Do you know anything about Aaron?"

"Well, I spoke with Alan this morning."

"What did he say?" I was about to crawl out of my skin.

"You hear about that weirdo who snuck into Aaron's room?"

"No," my ears started to burn. "How's my son?"

"Out of the woods."

I shut my eyes and exhaled long and slow. *Thank you, God.* For a moment, nothing else mattered. *It's going to be fine.*

"You there, Sam? He's out of danger."

"Yeah, I heard you. Thanks, Mack."

"Still in a coma, but he's a helluva fighter, your boy."

"Yeah." Someone was looking out for him.

"Hey listen, I'm bringing some juice and bagels up to Rachel. I'll have her call you when I get back to her room, okay?"

"Okay, thanks." Astounding. And yet, strangely inevitable. What was happening? I had to speak with Bishop about the vision about him and the dying woman. His reaction told me it rang true with him. There had been a reason it was revealed to me. With the chapel just twenty yards away, I was about to find out.

As per Father Speedy's preference, the blinds were drawn. And since there was no service in progress, the overheads were left off. Bishop sat alone in a wooden chair that gave off a scent of expiring varnish. He didn't turn around when I arrived.

"Hey, Bishop." Not so much as a lifted eyebrow, so fixed was he on the cross in the front of the chapel. I took a seat next to him. Would I walk out alive? "I don't know what it was that I saw, or why I saw it."

"Just spit it out already," he grunted.

Trying hard to remember, I shut my eyes and. A moment later, the vision returned but with so much more detail than before. "You're kneeling at her bedside. Her hair is white, but she doesn't seem that old. A quilt— patchwork—red, brown, tan. Her eyes are shut. I think she's dying. And you. It's you, but... I don't know, maybe twenty years ago. You're by her side, holding her hands, pressing them to your lips. It's clear you love her very much. And this is the oddest thing, she's given you something. Something small. It's an ivory locket, I can't read the inscription on the inside but... somehow I know what is says. It's a verse from the Bible."

"Impossible," Bishop said shaking his head. "No one knows about that. No one could possibly know." He turned to face me. Cautiously, I backed away slightly.

"So it's true?" I said.

He didn't answer.

"Besides this vision, I've recently experienced other things I simply can't explain. So, you being a priest, I thought I'd ask."

"I'm not a priest anymore. Anything but. I'm so far from that life now, you couldn't possibly hope to get anything useful from me."

"You must still believe."

"I must?"

"So, am I going crazy? Am I going to end up in PSU, thinking God is talking and end up hanging myself? Like Walker?" Bishop pressed his face into his hands resting on the back of the pew before him. His large frame rumbled. "What's the matter?

"I thought I could escape," he said.

"What, from Salton? I don't think anyone's ever managed that."

"Not what I mean."

"Escape from what, then?"

"Not what. Who."

"All right. Who are you trying to escape from?"

"God." To my great discomfort, he pulled a shiv out of his pants and began sharpening it against a rock, which he pulled from his shirt pocket.

Bishop had begun the long process of euthanizing his faith years ago, he just didn't realize it. First with the untimely death of his mother, then with the scandal that put him on death row. "I served Him, dedicated my life! I was a good priest."

"How did it happen?"

"There's a reason I've never told anyone." He held up the business end of the shiv and examined it as if he were a jeweler. Then went back to sharpening it.

"Right. Your image: Big, ruthless killer."

"Not just that."

"Then why?"

"Because," he lifted his head and sniffed—snorted actually. "You'd never believe me if I told you."

"Would you believe me if I told you I didn't kill my wife, rape my daughter and bludgeon my son into a coma?"

"Who cares?" He squinted at me. Put the shiv in front of my face. "Whadya think?"

"Looks fairly deadly."

He nodded, and lowered it. Relieved, I leaned in closer. "Seriously though, how does a Jesuit priest get convicted of murder?"

"I was framed." He scrutinized my face in anticipation of a snort, a chuckle, anything indicative of incredulity. I knew better.

"I believe you."

"You would."

"I believe you because I was framed too."

His eyebrow cocked upwards. Glad I could amuse him.

"Anyway," he continued, pulling a cigarette out of his shirt pocket, "there was an investigation of my Parish for sexual abuse by priests. I was clean, but one of the other priests had been accused. I didn't know one way or another if he'd done it. But when they started pressuring me for a statement against him, I refused. The victim was Janice D'Amati."

"Wasn't her father—?"

"Tony D'Amati."

" Tony D'Amati, the mafia kingpin?"

Bishop picked his teeth with the point of his shiv. Spat on the floor. "Yeah. His whole damned family attended St. Ignatius regularly. I took confession from him more than once. And you should know, that I used to work for the bastard, years before I cleaned up my act and joined the Jesuits."

Wasn't this supposed to be privileged? Bishop lit his cigarette, puffed a cloud away from our conversation. He coughed, cleared his throat and went on. "D'Amati was working *with* the D.A., you believe that? He wanted to bring Father Connor to justice." Bishop took another drag. "D.A. wanted me to cook up some testimony against a fellow priest."

I rubbed my eyes which were beginning to water. I could hardly believe my ears.

"You know," he said. "If I had even an inkling that Father Phil had even touched Tony's girl, forget about taking the stand, I woulda' castrated him myself! I got no patience for scum like that." He let the thought trail off, then flicked the cigarette on the ground and stepped on it. "But I *didn't* know for sure. So I refused to bear false witness. Hell, I had someone a lot bigger to answer to."

"So that ticked D'Amati off."

"You have no idea. But Tony? He don't get mad, he gets even. Two days after I told the D.A. what he could do with himself, I come into my office and notice that Father Phil's door is open. He always kept it shut in the morning to pray. I walk down the hall to his office and smell it. He's lying there on the floor face down in a puddle. Someone shot him six times, once in the head, five times in the back."

"Oh come on, they couldn't put it on you just like that."

"Don't be naive. It happened to you, didn't it? Or so you say."

"But you were a man of God. Priests don't murder other priests."

"Most priests ain't former mobsters either," he said with a dry smirk. "Look. You got law enforcement and the D.A. hungry for a conviction, add to that Tony D'Amati working together with them.

Planted evidence, bought witnesses. They could prove Mother Teresa a chester if they wanted to."

"Chester?"

"Prison lingo for child molester. How long you been here anyway?"

My head was hurting. I rubbed my jaw. "So that's it?"

"What. Not good enough for you? I was convicted of first degree murder. I guess my past career and my very outspoken words against the sexual abuse by Priests didn't help me much when it came time for the trial."

I sat silent. The sound of inmates shouting out in the yard came through the door.

"I was already struggling with God because of how he let my mother die of AIDS, ten years back. A needle. You believe that? Frikkin' druggie's needle."

"Man, that's—"

"She was a nurse, dammit! She helped the sick, faithful to God till the end. And *this* was how He rewarded her? How could I go on serving a God like that? And when I was convicted of killing Father Phil? Forget about it! I was *done* with Him."

Still processing it all, I said, "I'm really sorry."

"I don't need your pity."

"You don't need anything, do you?"

"I need..." he paused and stared at the stained glass image of Christ kneeling at a rock and praying. "I need to get the hell out of here. No way I'm going to sit around, rotting in this hole, waiting to be executed for a crime I didn't commit."

"You got a plan?"

"I always got plans. They're just waiting to be executed."

"No pun intended, I'm sure."

"Shut up. First chance I get, I'm out of here. And anyone getting in my way is going to wish they hadn't."

"For what it's worth, I feel your pain."

"Whatever." He stood up, stretched his arms up and let out a

Moose call of a yawn.

"Look Bishop, you've had a long history with God. Me, I just started and now I have all these questions. Can't you put your anger aside and help me out a bit? I mean, there's got to be a reason he gave me that vision of your mother."

He turned and glowered for a moment, then stared at the wooden cross again. He wasn't going to talk to me. He'd already said more to me than he probably had to anyone else here at Salton. After a while, I figured he was done with me. "Thanks for your time." I got up to leave.

But Bishop grabbed my shoulder, and forced me back down into my seat.

"All right. You got questions? Ask."

CHAPTER FIFTY-EIGHT

All things considered, the amount of pain Rachel felt seemed reasonable. She thanked God quietly. The doctors and nurses hadn't yet explained the extent of her injuries. One thing they were sure of: it was a miracle that she had survived. And Rachel knew a bit about miracles. Though grateful, she was not quite as astounded as her physicians.

When she tried to sit up, a sharp pain stabbed her side. She yelped. Was that a broken rib? Whatever it was, it reminded her that she had nearly been killed. The memories flashed back. The speeding headlights, the spine-whipping collision, the Corolla spinning out of control.

It wasn't an accident. She had a good idea who might have wanted her dead, too. But how did he know? Though she and Mack hadn't yet connected an actual name with the virtual killer with the *Huli-boy* screenname, it was just a matter of time. And the killer must've been aware of it.

Rachel's stomach vociferously protested the neglect. She strained to reach the remote control that would lift her back and head up. As her torso bent, needles shot down from her spine to her toes. Out of sheer reflex, she pulled her foot up.

At least I can still move it.

"You're a very, very lucky lady," someone said, as he entered the room.

Rachel gasped.

"Sorry, I didn't mean to alarm you. I'm Doctor Reynolds." He was a good-looking—though somewhat geeky— man in his mid-thirties. His black, horn-rimmed glasses were so thick it nearly obscured his face. His mustache was equally thick, so much so that it looked like it had been stuck on with spirit gum.

"I don't believe in luck, Doctor."

"Me neither. I believe in science."

Not about to debate, she smiled and asked, "How's it looking?"

"Vitals are good." He flipped a few pages on the clipboard and nodded. "We're still waiting for some tests, but I think you're going to be just fine." Regarding her with the friendliest smile, he seemed like someone Rachel might like to get to know better. "But I can see you're in a bit of pain."

"It's not so bad," she said.

"Oh, but we're here to make you more comfortable." Taking hold of the IV drip, he said, "It's obvious this stuff isn't working. Those nurses. If you don't come in yourself and watch over their shoulders."

"Thanks, really. But I'm okay."

"Nonsense. This is the wrong stuff anyway. It's not going to kill you, but it sure isn't doing anything for your..." he smiled and gazed right into her eyes, "...your discomfort." Without giving her a chance to protest, he removed the transparent pouch and dropped it on the floor with a slap. "Oops. Don't worry, I'll get that." He proceeded to insert a large syringe into the drip line.

"What's that?"

He slowly pressed the plunger and the clear fluid began to travel through the tube. "There. You'll be feeling it in no time."

"But I—"

"Shhh."

The blood in her veins ignited with pain so intense that she opened her mouth to scream. The doctor slapped his hand over her mouth and held her down.

"It's easier if you keep quiet." Rachel couldn't tell how much time had elapsed. A sharp pain radiated from her chest out to her hands, her feet. Her chest felt as if it were being crushed in a vise. Her eyes went wide. She struggled to draw a breath. Nothing.

The entire room blurred into a bloodshot lattice.

Then it all went away.

CHAPTER FIFTY-NINE

Of the three emotions burning in Anita's heart—humiliation, anger, and sadness—one towered far above the rest. Anger.

Anger at her cyberlover, who led her to believe that he was not just another lying, cheating, sonofabitch. Anger that he made her believe he really loved her for who she was. Anger, most of all, at herself. *I should have known.* She slammed the steering wheel and let out a furious shout, as she drove down Broadway to the place where she'd fix all of this. Uniformed officers followed in black and white squad cars.

There was hell to pay. With Judy's help, and admittedly Rachel Cheng's and Mack's as well, they were hot on the trail of a person who was not only suspect in multiple counts of identity theft and credit card fraud, but also tied into the Walker and Hudson cases, and who knew how many others? How exactly he was connected had yet to be seen, but forensics traced a boat load of cybercrimes to this dirt bag. She had her search warrant and arrest warrant. Probable cause was in the bag.

Despite his gun, pointed and ready, Lieutenant O'Brien seemed nervous when they got to the door, which gave way with ease when he kicked it open. The old apartments in Hillcrest were the easiest to break down. After a minute of shouting, identifying themselves, and calling for the suspect, they found the apartment empty. Anita immediately began her search for evidence. She found it. And so much more.

Five laptop computers, all running with live internet connections. All seized. She went to a tall file cabinet. "Bingo!"

O'Brien stepped over. "What've you got?"

"Everything."

"So it's him. I can't believe it."

Anita bent down and opened the bottom file cabinet. Each folder was arranged alphabetically. Her stomach turned as she read the labeled tabs, each alphabetized with names, each one more familiar than the last.

One particular folder caught her eye. She covered her mouth. When she looked at the contents, she gasped.

"Oh my god."

CHAPTER SIXTY

I had been in prison for two years now and by all counts, should have been long dead. Rapists and chesters don't stand a chance in Gen Pop. Something was definitely going on.

"Trust me," Bishop said, "I'm not pulling any strings for you. Hell, I would have killed you myself, you were so annoying."

"So why didn't you?"

Our eyes locked. Then something remarkable happened. Bishop smiled. "Those boys who tried to shank you during the riot? I heard that Butch's got them so pumped full of meds they can hardly talk."

"Yeah, but you know, before they were put in PSU, something weird happened."

His right eyebrow arched slightly.

"Just when they were about to do me in, they looked up—behind me, I think—got this look of fear in their eyes and ran." Bishop took out his shiv again and started picking under his fingernails with it. "And it happened again last night, with Butch," I said.

"Butch too, eh?"

"You think it's related?"

"You've heard the rumor, haven't you?" Bishop said, biting off part of his index fingernail then spitting it out. "Ah, those punks were probably on crack."

"What rumor?"

"You see, it didn't make any sense. Not until today, anyway."

Had I the strength or chutzpah, I would have grabbed his collar and shook the answer out of him. But I still retained a certain fondness for breathing. Instead, I turned my palms up and looked harder at him. "Well?"

"Rumor has it they'd seen two huge figures, must have been about seven feet tall, their clothes were bright white and shone so bright that it hurt their eyes. And they also said that these figures brandished huge swords that blazed with fire."

"Really?" I chuckled. But you don't often see two hardened criminals running scared from the same hallucination.

"That's the rumor, anyway." Bishop started using the tip of his shiv as a toothpick again. "So what happened with Butch?"

I winced at the site of blood lining his gums and said, "Last night, while he was taunting me in my cell, he acted the same way. Looked like he saw death itself and ran away."

"Well, I'll be."

"You think he saw the same thing those Nazis saw?"

He shrugged. "Anything's possible. But if you ask me, and I'm not real certain, I think they were angels."

"Whoa, now hold on. I thought you didn't believe in God, much less angels."

Bishop pointed the shiv into my face, accentuating every word with a jab, half an inch from my nose. "I said I was done with Him, not that I didn't believe."

"Why the change of heart?"

"I didn't say I've changed anything. I'm just thinking."

"About?"

"It's definitely supernatural. Look, Hudson, you a believer or not?"

I thought about that for a moment. "Yeah. I guess I am."

"Well, what you've experienced was the attendance of angels, sent to protect you. And your visions? You *did* tell me things that you couldn't possibly know otherwise. That's called a word of knowledge."

I stood up, started pacing around the altar, chin in hand, holding my elbow. "All I did was say a desperate prayer for my son last night and—"

"And how is he?"

"He made it. He's going to live." Bishop took a deep breath then let a silent "wow" float out of his mouth. It was slamming me hard now. The recognition, the awareness. "I've also had some other experiences looking at verses in my wife's old Bible. Sometimes the words just leap out at me, addressing the very issues I face. Too relevant to be a coincidence."

Bishop rested his head in his hand. Then he stood up again and fixed his eyes upon the wooden cross. Didn't say a word.

"You think I'm nuts," I said.

"No. I believe you."

"Why?"

"Years ago—before I got screwed so badly by D'Amati and the D.A.—" he clenched his fist and shook it at the cross, "—the same kind of things happened to me. Turned me from a life of crime to the priesthood."

CHAPTER SIXTY-ONE

On the way back to Rachel's room, Mack ran into the nurse again and spilled coffee on her sleeve. "I'm such a klutz."

"It's okay," she said wiping her arm. "Is she resting now?"

"Doubt it. Dr. Reynolds just went to look at her charts just as I—"

"Doctor Reynolds?"

"Yeah. You know, Caucasian, 30-ish, thick glasses, slim, about 5 foot 10?"

She just blinked. Mack's pulse kicked up a couple of notches.

"You do have a Doctor Reynolds working here, don't you?

"Yeah, but he's like 5'6 and chubby. And he's black."

The white styrofoam cup fell to the ground along with the bagels and donuts. "Get security up there, now!" Mack sprinted down the corridor and cursed himself.

When they arrived on Rachel's floor, alarms were sounding, nurses and doctors scrambled.

"Rachel!" Mack shouted as he swung open the door. "Oh no." The nurse hit the intercom button and shouted, "We need a doctor, now!"

Alone, laying flat on her back, Rachel's eyes were opened wide and fixed to the ceiling. A nurse felt Rachel's neck. She swore. "No pulse."

The nurse began performing CPR and speaking a mile a minute into the intercom, something about a Code Blue. "I don't care!" she said into the intercom. "Send them down stat! She's coding!"

CHAPTER SIXTY-TWO

It took about three hours, but the doctors finally stabilized her. Rachel had gone into cardiac arrest, the result of acute Potassium toxicity. Had Mack arrived a few minutes later, it would have been too late. She was in worse shape than before.

Mack ran a gentle hand over her hair while a ventilator assisted her unconscious breathing. If there had been any doubt before, it was all gone. The crash on the freeway was no accident. Now this. "I'm sorry, Ray."

He would have gone to see Detective Pearson right away, but he was the only person who saw the man impersonating Dr. Reynolds. A statement and description was required and he was going to give it to the police in five minutes.

Three attempts to contact Pearson resulted in two urgent voicemails. Mack hadn't studied Rachel's notes extensively prior to emailing them to the detective, but he had a strong suspicion the person they'd fingered was the same one who'd been trying to kill Rachel.

Time to speak with the police. Mack kissed Rachel on the forehead and left. Upon exiting, he inspected the badge and ID of the uniformed officer posted outside of Rachel's room. Satisfied, he thanked the officer and went to give his statement.

CHAPTER SIXTY-THREE

Things were falling apart quicker than he could have imagined. He could only hope that the doctors wouldn't get to Rachel Cheng in time. Or that the Potassium Chloride he'd pumped into her blood was concentrated enough. If enough time elapsed, they'd be hard-pressed to determine the cause of death, because once the body expires, the cells would begin to rupture, releasing their own stores of potassium, making it impossible to distinguish it from that which he'd injected. If only he could have stayed around long enough to watch her die. That far-off gaze, the gasping, the final breaths. Exquisite. He licked his lips. *Would have been sumptuous!*

But the little Asian lawyer had been resourceful. Walker contributed too, that retard. He slammed his fist on the steering wheel, ignoring the CHP that just passed him. No one should have been able to connect the dots so quickly! He'd been doing this for years and his system was fool-proof, always afforded him the luxury of leaving those masterful clues with his victims' bodies. For without drawing them with clues, how would he know if his adversaries were worthy? More important, where would the authenticity be? True artists always left their signatures. Was it a subconscious desire to get caught or a dangerous way of ensuring credit where it was due? Probably both.

Traffic was clear and he was keeping with the flow. Not like that punk that just cut him off in that black Benz. He didn't realize he was doing 80 on the I-805. Until another CHP on a motorcycle flashed his lights in the rearview.

Interesting. Perhaps he could outrun this guy. Or just smash him up so bad that he'd never live to tell. Hardly anyone around to witness it.

The beige uniform closed in. *Don't hesitate.* His foot never let off the accelerator. The siren began to wail. In a way, this excited him. Never before had he killed someone that could actually arrest him, blow the cover off his entire career. Or blow his head off, for that matter.

The officer trailed just one car's distance behind him now. Best to catch him off-guard, pull over to the shoulder, lure him in, then slam the brakes. The thought of mangled flesh, splintered bones and, blood—mmm, yes, blood— it made his scalp tingle. Of course, it would make a huge mess, but it wasn't his car anyway. The owner of this hot-wired vehicle would have to answer for the damage. And the blood.

He signaled right and eased his way towards the slow lane. Lightened his foot off the accelerator. And then something he didn't expect happened. Was this a good thing?

The CHP pulled around and zoomed ahead, siren still wailing. Away. Aha! After the speeding Benz! Pity. Nailing a cop would have been a fantastic addition to his repertoire.

Didn't matter though. Things were still falling apart. Still too many loose ends. Not the least of which, one of the most dangerous challenges of all. Something he'd have to deal with by proxy again. Sure, it wasn't as fulfilling as rolling up your sleeves and getting your own hands dirty, but it was the only way. Severing this loose end would have to wait until tomorrow.

Anita Pearson's day off.

CHAPTER SIXTY-FOUR

Jim O'Brien and another uniformed deputy, whose name escaped Anita, took positions with her behind doorframes and sofas. The plain clothes had just radioed: Suspect on the way. ETA, one minute. This S.O.B. was a slimy manipulator, a master at deception and evasion. *Kitsune.*

And Anita had been playing out her sexual fantasies over the internet with him all this time. Bile oozed up in her throat. She felt the play in her trigger. *Come on you bastard. Give me justification.*

This would go down real quick. Always did. Anita thought about what she might say to him. Pushed it aside. Did the growing *thump-thump-thumps* betray the freak's approaching footfalls or her pounding heart? She jiggled the trigger again, seeing just how close she could get without actually pulling it. Bad habit. *Focus!*

The serial killer's apartment lay at the end of a hallway. Sergeant Murphy waited out of sight, around the corner and ready to intercept. Finally, the freak arrived at the door. Keys jangled. The lock clicked and the door creaked open.

His next step would determine the response. In a sudden flurry, the suspect yanked the keys and dashed back down the hallway.

"Go!" Anita shouted. A split second later, Murphy began shouting. The suspect turned around and rushed back. Anita and O'Brien stood ready to intercept him as soon as he turned the corner.

Then she saw him. The very first time she'd ever seen him in the flesh. After a split second, Anita cocked the hammer of her gun. Aiming for his head, she squinted. *Come on, slimeball, show me a weapon.* Their eyes met. A look of surprise on his countenance gave way to an expression too difficult to read. Slowly, he opened his palms and held them in the air. The corners of his mouth crept upwards. "So nice to finally meet you, darlin'."

Anita braced her back against the wall, struggling to keep her hands from shaking. "Lieutenant?" she whispered to O'Brien through gritted teeth. O'Brien nodded and stepped forward, his gun trained on the bastard's face. Murphy now stood behind the suspect with his gun aimed.

"Hands on your head!" Anita shouted, unable to conceal the slight tremor.

He complied and winked. "I've always dreamed of meeting you...in carbon space."

One at a time, Murphy grabbed his wrists and cuffed them behind his back. When they secured him, Anita flew back into the apartment and went straight to the kitchen sink. Wretching violently, her stomach clenched so hard it felt like someone had reached in and tied her innards into a knot. Between heaves, just before she collapsed, Anita heard Lieutenant O'Brien Mirandizing the perp.

"*Brent Stringer, you are under arrest for multiple counts of cyber-fraud and the murder of...*"

CHAPTER SIXTY-FIVE

Rachel seemed to have dropped off the face of the earth. Each day, out in the yard, I left urgent voicemails. It took several days for me to hear from anyone outside. It was Alan who told me of Brent Stringer's arrest.

The award-winning columnist and best-selling novelist had been charged with multiple murders. To say I found it ironic would be a gross understatement, considering the vitriol he'd published against me before my conviction.

It made for a media circus, despite the fact that the D.A.'s office and the Police Department were so tight-lipped. To think, I actually shook hands with Stringer, had him in my home for an interview.

I was shocked to learn that Rachel was recovering from a lethal injection of Potassium. Lethal injection. Wasn't that my fate? I realized that I was spending as much time thinking and praying for her recovery as I had been for Aaron.

"Look, Silk. I don't mean to be rude or nothin'," Possum said leaning against our cell door, "but you need to go out and get some fresh air. All this time in here can't be good for you."

"I was going to spend some time in prayer," I said, yawning and stretching.

"Yeah, whatever. But remember, there's a time for everything. Ain't that from the good book? Thou shalt go and smelleth the freakin' roses?"

I jumped down from my bunk, put on my blue CDC shirt, and patted his shoulder. Before I could say anything, he said, "And that's another thing that you keep doing. It's weirding me out."

"What?" I said, and removed my hand.

"Not that."

"What?"

"That." He pointed at my face.

I felt my cheeks.

"You keep smiling. What's up with that, anyway? Look like an idiot walking around like that." He put on his cap and shook his head. "Nobody smiles in Salton. Except those fruit loops down in PSU, maybe. But they're so pumped with drugs...what's your excuse?"

"Honestly? I hadn't noticed."

"You wouldn't. Probably this new religion kick."

I put my arm around Possum's shoulders again. "Come on, man. Just hear me out for once—"

"No way. I ain't gonna become a brainwashed, brain-dead smiley face on legs. Me? I like my dangerous look." He pulled away, scowled and gritted his teeth at me. Not quite the fierce look he was going for. The more I tried to hold in a laugh, the more I sputtered.

"Oh sure, yuck it up! Easy for you, mister six-foot, muscle guy. Guys like me have to make up for our size with ferocity." Baring his fangs again, he looked about as scary as a Chihuahua. I started to laugh. Couldn't help myself.

"Oh, thanks a lot!"

"Come on, Poss. Get your leash, let's go for a walk."

Because the line for the pay phone was longer than usual, I decided to wait at the concrete table while Possum did his Meerkat sentinel routine. Every now and then, he turned his head back to reported suspicious activity.

Man's got to have a hobby.

Just for kicks, I pulled out that new Brent Stringer novel that had been sitting at the bottom of my pile of junk. I couldn't believe this guy was the *Kitsune* Serial Killer, as well as *Huli-boy*, the Instant Message user who manipulated Leonard Walker. For that matter, he'd manipulated the entire state of California when he wrote his diatribes on me, and on Matt Kingsley. Thanks to Stringer, we'd been convicted in the press long before the gavel came down.

Nevertheless, I found myself curious about the kind of novels this guy wrote. How could Jenn have been such a fan of his? Turns out, Stringer's book was quite good, a page-turning thriller that you'd expect from Patterson or Koontz. His characters were completely believable and you'd lose yourself in the story if you didn't watch the clock.

I had just gotten to a chapter in which a murder was to take place. The murder of a mother and her daughter. Dread wrapped around me like a python. I had to put the book down.

"Yo, Silk!" Possum called out, craning his neck at the Fourth Reichers on the opposite side of B-Yard. "Rumor has it you're some kind of psychic."

"Yeah, rumors." I tossed the Stringer book into a puddle.

"So, you're a mind reader." Possum bent down and picked up the novel and eyed me. "What?"

"Not in the mood."

Possum shrugged and brushed some mud off the novel. He remained quiet. But not long enough. "Hey, if you are psychic, I wanna ask you something."

I let out a slow breath. The brilliance of the midday sun was starting to hurt my eyes. I put my head down on the cold concrete table and muttered through my arms.

"All right, shoot."

He walked over and sat across me and spoke *sotto voce*. "Yeah, well. I've been having this recurring dream, see? In it, I'm this bird—can't say if I'm a pigeon, a crow or an eagle—"

"How about a Dodo?"

"Cute. Anyways, I'm flying in the air. Suddenly I'm in a cage. I hit the bars and fall. Someone's rattling the cage like crazy. Feels like I'm going to die, it's so violent. Out of the blue, the door swings wide open. It's my only chance. I fly to the door. But just as I'm about to clear it, someone slams it shut on my wing. Hurts so bad, like it's going to snap my arm—I mean wing—right off. Then I wake up in a cold sweat."

"So that's why." For several days now, I had noticed him waking up with a gasp. But he never looked like he wanted to talk about it, so I never bothered to ask.

"Sounds crazy, I know. I never told you because, I don't know, you might have told someone and I would've ended up in PSU. But since you found this religion crap and got all peaceful-like, I figured I was good. I mean, they'd put you in there before me, for sure, right?"

I gave him a shove. "You had a question?"

"Yeah. Sorry. I was just kidding, you know that PSU crap."

"Right."

"Okay, well. Seeing that you got this psychic hotline stuff going on—"

"I'm not a—"

"Just let me finish, okay?"

"Fine." I said, ready to leave Possum to his own devices.

"I was just wondering." Possum twitched his nose. "Could this dream be a message from, I don't know, God?"

"What, am I an expert now? I just became a Christian last week."

"Yeah but you've been getting pretty chummy with Bishop since."

"We only had that one talk, once in the chapel." After which Bishop withdrew and barely spoke a word to me again. Whenever I'd approached him, he'd just walk away. As if the very sight of me made him uncomfortable.

"Do me a favor, Silk. Okay? Think about my dream. I dunno,

pray about it. I gotta know what it means."

I actually sat there, head throbbing, trying to see if anything would appear in my mind. What did I know? I still had trouble believing those visions I had were real. "Sorry, man. I'm not getting anything.

"Eh. Maybe it was just a dream. It don't mean nothing. Except maybe I'm going nuts."

"I know a place you can go for that," I said, with a grin.

"Oh, a psychic *and* a comedian, eh?"

The phone was available now. "Hey, catch you later, okay?" I got up and jogged over before anyone else could beat me to it.

This time, when I called Rachel's cell phone, she actually picked up. Painkillers dulled her speech, but she expressed joy at my recent conversion, which she'd learned of through Pastor Dave.

When we spoke of Brent Stringer, however, her tone became grave. "He's sicker than anyone could have imagined," she said.

"How do you mean?"

"He's the creep who ran me off the road, the one who tried to kill me in the hospital."

"I can't believe it. Are you all right?" I asked.

"I guess."

"I mean, *really*. Are you all right?"

She sighed. "I don't know. No one's ever tried to kill me before."

"Rachel, I'm so sorry. I don't know what I'd do if—"

"I'm alive."

"Thank God." I looked out to the mountains that reached up into the sky. They could all come tumbling down, for all I cared. With Aaron constantly teetering at the brink, if God had allowed Rachel to die, I might have to reconsider my faith.

"There's more, Sam."

"Why am I not surprised?"

"You sure you're up to this?"

"I'm calling collect, it's your dime."

"Okay. Now, they haven't announced this publicly yet, because the investigation is ongoing. But Stringer was responsible for much more than initially believed. Something much closer."

Wasn't the fact that he had claimed responsibility for the recent murders enough? He had somehow gotten into the heads of these businessmen to murder their wives and daughters.

"I know. Walker was just the tip of the iceberg," I said.

"No, it's worse."

"Worse?"

"He's claiming responsibility for the Matt Kingsley murders."

The receiver nearly dropped out of my trembling hand. "No way. He couldn't have gotten into Kingsley's mind like that."

"Not his mind. His bed."

"You mean—?"

"Yeah. He didn't manipulate those men, he framed them."

I couldn't speak.

"I haven't gotten to the worst part yet," she said. I knew where she was going. Should have seen this from the start. "Sam, Detective Pearson found something at Stringer's apartment. A file cabinet full of mementos. Each folder labelled with the victims' names. He kept fingernail clippings, locks of hair, jewelry. All in ziploc bags."

"No."

"They found a folder with—"

"No!"

"I'm sorry, but you have to know. He kept one labeled Hudson, Jennifer and Hudson, Elizabeth."

Gnashing my teeth, salty tears seeping through my lips, a tsumani of emotion crashed down upon me. All at once, months of anguish, frustration and rage boiled to the surface.

"Sam?"

I held onto the hood of the payphone and caught my breath. It would take me the rest of the day to fully process this.

"Sam," she said when she heard me take a breath.

"Yeah?"

"I've filed a motion to reopen your case, based on this new evidence."

"Evidence? They found my semen on Bethie, remember? How did that happen?"

"I don't have all the details, but Pearson says Stringer's cooperating."

"So, new evidence?"

"His confession, the nail clippings, hairs. They're as exculpatory for you as it gets."

"Are we talking about—?"

"Exoneration"

I don't think I smiled. But that was good news. I asked about Aaron. Nothing new. Though he'd survived, he showed no signs of improvement. No sign of ever coming out of his coma.

"He's on a ventilator now," Rachel said. "Can't breath on his own."

Despair encroached. I quickly replied, "He's going to be fine. I just know he is."

"Sam, listen."

"You were the one who got that word, remember? Trust me, I know a thing or two about that kind of thing now. You can't stop believing now."

"It's just that, well...sometimes God answers our prayers, but the answer is no."

"Rachel, stop it."

"You know, if Aaron is taken home, to heaven, he'll be in a better place."

"I can't believe this. You, of all people."

She'd always been the one to sustain my hope. Now she was giving up. I had never been angry with Rachel before. But now... "Doctors say he's in a persistent vegetative state."

"You listen to me, young lady! God didn't spare my son just to let him die this way. That's just not the way God works!"

"Your entire life you're an atheist, you become a Christian for a few weeks, and now you're a theologian?"

"I thought you were a lawyer, not a comedian." I huffed. "Maybe you'd do better—" I bit my lip and smacked my forehead.

Silence.

Come on, shout back, call me a jerk. Anything but silence. Then came a twinge. I'd told people off before, but never felt guilty about it.

"Rachel."

"I have to go."

"No, wait. I'm sor—"

Click.

I wanted to crawl back into my cell and lock myself in. Forever.

CHAPTER SIXTY-SIX

For the next few weeks, there were no visits because, for the most part, Rachel was still recovering and was stuck at home. All I'd have to do was to call her and apologize. I couldn't work up the nerve. Stupid pride.

The press remained relatively hushed about the Brent Stringer case, except that he'd been denied bail and had exercised his right to a speedy trial. Jenn's parents, who had not once ever come to visit, write or call, sent me a letter. After an entire page of beating around the bush, they wrote:

> *...As Aaron's legal guardians, we feel it is in our grandson's best interest to terminate his life-support.*

"You coming out to the yard, Silk?" Possum said.

I stumbled back and fell onto the lower bunk.

"Hey, buddy," he said. "What is it?"

In a violent fit, I started to shred the letter, threw the pieces onto the floor slammed my hand against the steel bars of my cell. Possum's eyes stretched wide. Backing out of the cell, he said. "O-kay.... catch you later."

I wanted to scream, but instead cried out to God silently. *Why? You brought us this far, only to have them go and pull the plug?* I stormed out of the cell, uncertain who I was more furious with; my in-laws, that accursed Brent Stringer, God, or myself.

At the exit to B-yard, a backlit shadow stood in the doorway. "Well, well. If it ain't my favorite pretty-boy," Butch sneered, coming half into the light.

"Out of my way!"

"Oh, you're giving me orders, are you?" His eyes darted around, looking over my shoulder and around.

The pressure within threatened to explode. I clenched my teeth, my fists, did all I could to control myself. "Butch, if you don't mind."

"I've been keeping an eye on you, Silky-boy. You don't fool me one bit, you and this..." he waved his hand, "...religion thing."

"Fine. Now, move!"

He pulled out his night stick and slid it over my face, my lips and then let it linger down my chest. "Or what?" Where were my guardian angels now? He slid his stick down and around to my rear.

Shouldn't have done that. Not in the state I was in.

With one swift move, I grabbed his arm, twisted it and threw a punch square into his nose. Butch screamed. I swung him around and shoved him back so hard that I could feel the thump when he hit the wall. But he didn't fall. He touched his face, looked at the blood. His face became demonic. Out came his gun, aimed it at my forehead.

"Nobody gonna' question self-defense, here." He grabbed my arm and pushed me out the door. "Kiss the dirt, bitch!" If not for that gun, I might have given in to rage. But I complied, laying down on my belly. He pressed the muzzle into the back of my head.

"Yeah, you were eye candy, pretty-boy. But you know what? I'm tired of you." He pressed the gun in, cocked the hammer. I felt the click. Shut my eyes. Couldn't believe my life was about to end like this.

All I heard was the heavy breathing of a maniac about to kill. He was excited, pleased with himself. The sound of footsteps on the pavement grew louder. I opened my eyes and saw Bishop standing with Luther and a couple of other cons.

"Bishop," I called out. "You're a witness. You're all witnesses here. Don't let him do this."

All silent.

My eyes locked onto Bishop's. Would he just stand idly by while Butch put a bullet in my head?

Butch pulled back slightly and addressed Bishop. "You and Silk got something going on?" Bishop scoffed. "'Cause if you and Silky-boy here are together, you know I'm going to—"

"He's nobody," Bishop said, raising his voice. "Now, you keep your word."

"Don't I always?" Bishop folded his arms over his chest and glowered. "Okay, don't matter how often I do or don't," Butch said. He stepped back but kept his foot on the small of my back. "You gotta prove to *me* that you'll keep up your end."

"Whatever."

"No, you listen to me, Bish! This here boy disrespected me."

"Like you're so respectable."

"I wanted him dead, but y'all had to go on and show up here." Butch let up and stepped away. I rolled over, kept my eye on Bishop. Behind his tough façade I sensed a man who actually feared Butch. Or something Butch could do to him, anyway. Bishop just glowered at him without a word. On his way out the door, Butch said, "Fine. Then at least make sure he never forgets his place."

Looking desperately to Bishop, I asked, "Are you actually bending to him?"

"Shut up!" He grabbed my shirt and pulled his fist back. "Always getting in the way!" Words failed. I couldn't believe he would do this. He was about to throw a punch but stopped short. Instead, he dropped me on the ground and stepped away. Then he turned to Luther and the other cons.

"Do it."

CHAPTER SIXTY-SEVEN

I regained consciousness in the infirmary, aching all over, barely able to speak. My last memory was Bishop standing by, arms folded over his chest, while Luther and company proceeded to puree me.

A sharp pain skewered my shoulder when I reached for the bedrail. I let out a terse groan and propped myself on my side. That hurt too. There wasn't a side of my body that wasn't bruised or bandaged. *Just be grateful you're alive.*

Victor, the doctor that checked in on me, was a firm believer in the thought that laughter was the best medicine. Interesting in theory, but he just wasn't funny. He'd laugh at his own jokes, snort when he laughed, then keep on laughing and snorting. Finally, after a while, I asked him if I could just go to sleep. He agreed reluctantly.

The next morning, Victor discharged me with two broken ribs, a sprained wrist, seven stitches, and one very bruised spirit. On my way back to my cell, I ran into C.O. Sonja Grace.

"Oh Sam," she said. "What happened?"

"Long time," a pained grunt cut me off.

"I got transferred to C-Block. You okay?"

"They seem to think I'll live."

"Better do more than that," she said, with a sympathetic smile.

Just as I began to answer, a guard from B-block interrupted us. "Yo, Hudson. Someone to see you!" Great. The last thing I needed was to show any one my beaten face. I said good-bye to Sonja and dragged my chained feet, scraping against the concrete and made my way to the guard.

Because my guest hadn't yet entered the visitation room, I couldn't see who it was. Maybe Dave or Alan. My head swam in an ocean of painkillers as I took a seat at a vacant table, put my head down, and tried to block out the sounds of thugs and sweethearts babbling and flirting. Two minutes. That's all I'd wait.

Images of Aaron's face kept flashing through my mind. His chestnut hair, fine features, freckles, all inherited from his mother. As my thoughts turned to Jenn, something frightening happened. For the first time since her death, the thought of her didn't tear my heart to bits. Was I forgetting her? Bethie? It had been over two years now, but I never wanted to stop feeling the pain. It reminded me of how much I loved them.

I just wanted to curl up and die. Two years in prison had numbed me. Now I was having trouble even conjuring up memories of my beloved wife and daughter. I was losing them. Before I could get up and leave, a warm hand touched the back of my neck. I lifted my eyes.

"Hey, Sam." Rachel's arm dangled in a sling, a couple of stitches crossed her left eyebrow, and her forehead was bruised. She was the most beautiful sight I'd seen in a long time.

Without thinking, I stood up and wrapped my arms around her like she was the last human being alive on the planet. "Rachel. Oh God. I'm so sorry." Our last argument was still fresh in my mind.

She reached her good arm up and around my neck. We embraced for just a bit longer than ordinary friends. She pressed her face into my chest, the warmth of her breath seeped through my shirt. "No," she said. "I'm sorry"

I gently pressed my lips into her ebony hair. Jasmine and silk. All the tension in her body dissolved as she leaned against me. Though her last visit wasn't that long ago, it felt like years. "You have no idea how glad I am to see you," I said, slowly releasing her and taking a step back to have a good look.

Her eyes glistened, naturally brown. "Pardon my appearance," she said, holding up her slinged arm. "My doctor would kill me if he knew."

"First do no harm?"

She smiled and gazed at her shoes.

"Don't we need a private room?" I asked. She gave me a tentative smile. "I mean, you know, attorney-client?"

"I'm here as your friend," Rachel said. As we spoke, the awkwardness from our little spat melted away like December frost in the corner of a window. She had come in an unofficial capacity, but there were some urgent matters.

Oscar and Maggie had been speaking to their attorney about the possibility of keeping legal guardianship over Aaron, in the event I was exonerated. They knew how I felt about keeping Aaron on life support and were concerned that I was not thinking in his best interest.

"We're definitely going to fight it," Rachel said. "But the first order of business is reopening your case." Brent Stringer was being held in San Diego Central and the D.A.'s office would offer no deals. As Rachel reported what she'd learned about Brent, the light in her countenance faded. "They've combed through all his computer records, his notebooks. The guy was as meticulous as he was arrogant."

"How'd he do it?"

"You know why he calls himself *Kitsune*, right?"

"Among other things."

"He likens himself to a messenger of *Oinari*, a Japanese deity. I think he takes the metaphor of being a shapeshifting fox beyond the metaphoric. In addition to his extraordinary ability to manipulate people, he studies his victims, their lives, their entire family. Then he devises a fool-proof method of leaving behind just the right evidence. Evidence which incriminates the husband. For all intents and purposes, he becomes the husband, the father, forensically speaking."

"Did this have something to do with that Instant Message session?" My stomach cramped at the thought.

"Well, he's also a brilliant computer programmer, or he knows someone who is. Stringer used the internet to upload spyware onto his victim's computers. He did that to mine. We found some on your laptop too." She brushed a lock of hair behind her ear, squeezed my hand with concern. "You said he contacted Bethie with the *Huliboy* screen name, right?"

I was pressing my forehead into my palm now, cursing myself. "I should have known. I should have known!"

"Known what?"

"He impersonated one of Bethie's classmates over Instant Messenger, I uploaded a game. A kid's game! That must have contained the malicious software. He used it for identity theft, didn't he?"

Biting her lip, Rachel nodded.

"So everything, the credit cards, the porn?" Back into the fiery pits of Hell, all over again. "Oh God."

"Can you think of any other way he might have gained access?" Rachel reached into her briefcase and took out a memo pad and started taking notes.

"The day we first met to set up that Superdad interview. He was waiting in my cubicle at work when I got there."

"That explains it. We found some hidden executables in the system restore volumes dated that day. They were programmed to scan the hard drive and send information such as cookies and URLs of websites you visited, shopped at. Eventually copied those kiddy porn images to a shared network drive under a directory with your name."

"A lot of personal information on my work computer too." I thought back to the day Stringer and I first met, shook hands. "He was also looking at the manual for my new alarm system, which I'd left on my desk. Jenn was complaining of a problem with the access code and I was going to research it. Stringer said he had the same model, didn't know how to program it." A stab of recognition tweaked my mind. "Oh no. I can't believe it."

"What?" Rachel pulled her chair closer, flipped to a fresh page, and continued writing down everything I said.

"He must have taken down the model number."

"And found a way to disarm it."

"I can't believe how careless—" I looked to Rachel as if she held the answer. The answer to one of the most pressing questions which festered like an open sore. "Why me? Why Matt Kingsely, why any of us?"

"I wish I knew." She put the pen down and held my hand. "One thing, though. Each of you had appeared in the media before Stringer targeted you: Kingsley for rescuing that stray dog from the freeway, and you for the superdad photo. Maybe it's part of his obsession." For a few minutes, we sat and allowed the tension to ebb.

"Is he going to make a full confession?"

"I'm not sure," she said, taking the papers back as I hadn't even glanced at them. "Stringer's killed a lot of people. And he's being really weird about what he tells and what he withholds."

"I've got to get out of here. Right away. Aaron needs me."

"I promise I'm working two hundred percent on it. We're back in discovery now, going over all the evidence, old and new. The hearing could be set sooner than you think."

"Hope so."

"In the meantime," she said, grasping my hand and brushing the bruise on my cheek with velvet fingertips, "stay out of trouble."

"You mean stay alive."

"Yeah." She consulted her watch. "Gotta go. Call me tomorrow. Same time." For the past two and a half years, whenever she left the visitation room, she never looked back. We'd said our good-byes already so there was no point. But this time, she stopped at the doorframe, looked over her shoulder and with a poignant smile, whispered, "Bye Sam." I stood by the table, watched her go down the corridor. Rachel's admonition resounded in my mind.

Stay alive.

CHAPTER SIXTY-EIGHT

For the next couple of days, I continued with the anti-inflammatories. Possum seemed relieved to see me when I returned from the infirmary. He graciously offered his lower bunk, since the very thought of climbing caused my stomach to clench. And that in itself hurt enough to make me sit down right away.

One morning, Possum sat staring out the open cell door with his elbows on his knees, his jowls resting in his palms.

"Why aren't you out in the yard?" I said, straining as I lay down.

He didn't answer.

"Poss?" Still, no answer. "Okay, well. If you don't mind, I'm going rest up." Not so much as a look or hint of acknowledgment. Finally, without averting his vacuous gaze, he said, "You been praying for me, like I asked?"

A grin tugged the corners of my mouth. "I just don't know if God honors prayers for a convict to break out of prison."

"*And* make it out alive."

"Honestly, no. That's not exactly how I've been praying for you."

"I'm just saying." He missed his wife, his son, so much it was making him crazy. When his wife started writing him about taking their son and moving back to Minneapolis with her parents, he became distraught and even less rational than usual.

"Hang in there, Poss."

"Easy for you to say. You'll be getting out soon. Me? I got ten more years, five if I'm a good boy and confess at the parole hearings."

"There you go."

"You dope! By then, Pam's gonna be screwing the postman in

Minneapolis and Jack'll be a teenager."

"Oh. Right. I hear you, man." Must've been all the Naproxin, there had to be a better reason for my density. For the next few minutes Possum didn't speak. Fine with me, my head was pounding anyway. But silence with Possum in the cell seemed about as natural as pirouetting pachyderms in pink tutus. He was sullen, withdrawn. "Hey," I said. "You all right?"

Nothing.

"Come on, Poss. What's the matter?"

"Sometimes, I just don't feel like talking, okay"

"Since when?" I said.

A smirk. "Well fine," he said. "But only 'cause you're twisting my arm."

"Whatever you say."

He shook his head, lowered his eyes and sighed. "I'm going to die."

"I've got news for you, buddy. We all are."

"Wiseguy. I mean if I don't get out of here soon, I *am* going to die."

Despite the pain, I sat up and craned my neck to see past his feet. "Poss, listen. I know how you must feel, believe me. Your wife, your kid? At least they're still alive."

He jumped down from his bunk and threw his pillow at me. "That's not it, you idiot."

"Hey!" I threw it back.

"I'm getting this really bad feeling. Did you know that dogs can sense disaster before it strikes? I heard about this dog in Thailand, see? It suddenly ran for the hills just before a huge tsunami hit them. Me? I'm that dog."

"I thought you were a possum."

"Come on, Silk."

"Do possums do that too?"

"I'm serious! Something really bad's gonna happen to me in here. I can feel it." If not for the unequivocal fear in his eyes, I would have continued to rag on him.

"Look, Artie," I said, "Lots of people think that—"

A noise like the sound of an approaching truck interrupted me. Possum grabbed the edge of open cell door and peeked outside. "What the hell?" He looked to the right, then to the left. The rumbling crescendoed like a tympani in a Shostakovich symphony. Soon the entire building began to shake.

"Oh my god!" he squealed.

"Take it easy, Poss! It's just an earthquake." I shouted, although it was the biggest one I'd ever experienced. The lockdown klaxon blared. Inmates began shouting. Plaster and concrete rained down. Possum dropped and curled up on the floor, hands covering his head, trying in vain to crawl under the bed.

On all fours, I crept to the bars, took hold and shouted for the guards, who were nowhere in sight. The tremors came in waves, each punctuated with an earth-shattering boom before starting up again.

"I'm gonna die!" Possum cried, as another wave started up. "I'm gonna frikkin' die!" The steel shelf fastened to the wall began to rattle, books and picture frames fell to the ground. Shattered glass spread across the concrete floor.

Then it stopped.

Possum let out a startled gasp. The klaxons continued to squawk as a C.O. barked orders over the PA system for us to stay in our cells. But none of the cell doors could shut or lock. Malfunction.

Scrambling about like a swarm of waterbugs, inmates shouted and swore, some in Spanish, some in English. Again, the tremors started up. Again, the guards attempted to shut the cell doors from the control room. And again, they jammed halfway.

Possum's feral eyes flashed. He grabbed the bunk frame and pulled himself to his feet. "I'm coming, Pam!" He stumbled out of our cell, looked all over the place. God only knew what he was thinking. Whatever the case, he was in no state to be out there in the middle of an earthquake.

Each time I tried to stand, my legs became jello, the prison shook side to side, sifting me like dirt in a prospector's pan, only there was no gold. Possum called back to me. He popped his head back into the cell. His expression had changed from that of panic to wild excitement. "Come on, Silk! Something's going down at the control room!"

I froze.

"I ain't passing this up," he said. "You coming or not?"

"You want to get yourself shot?"

"Suit yourself. I'm outta here." Away he went. On his own, however, he wouldn't last five minutes. If he didn't get crushed by falling concrete, he'd surely be killed by an inmate or an overzealous C.O. I had to stop him.

Just as I started for the door, something flashed so clearly in my mind that I had to stop. It was there, clear as glass. I sucked in a choking breath of dust.

That image.

It hadn't been mine, this was Possum's nightmare.

A raven, squawking in pain.

Its wing caught in a closed door.

CHAPTER SIXTY-NINE

Ironically, the first thing that came to Frank "Bishop" Morgan's mind, as the ground shook, was Saint Paul and Silas in the Phillipian prison. Bishop, however, was no saint. Not by any stretch. And he wasn't going to sit around praying or singing hymns.

If God had any sense of justice, this had to be a sign. Bishop peered across the yard and saw a pack of inmates closing in on three guards. Luther had gotten hold of one of their weapons and shot one of them.

Animals.

Because the quake was so violent, guards in the sentry towers fled their positions. Bishop held onto the chain link fence and waited for the waves under his feet to stop. Each set of tremors seemed worse than the last. He hadn't experienced anything this bad since the '79 El Centro quake. This was far worse.

But he saw an opportunity. A chance to finally get out of this hole, make a run for it, and get a new identity in Mexico. From his waistband, he pulled out his latest insurance policy. Something he'd worked on every moment when the guards weren't looking or listening. It had been honed to perfection, from the crudest materials he could extract from his bed frame—created for a moment such as this. The shank was short, but sharp enough to slit a throat or slice an artery.

It's about time, God, he thought. *You owe me.* No one had better interfere with this divine restitution. If anyone did, his insurance would cover it. Sure, the premium would be sky high, but the deductible was negligible.

A troop of *La Fraternidads* brandishing the guns they'd snatched rushed into B-block. The Blacks followed behind. The Reichers as well. Mortal enemies united by the idea of shooting their way out of prison.

Taking advantage of the pause between quakes, Bishop entered B-Block amidst the crowd. He could just imagine the C.O.'s scrambling helplessly around the control room. There were just too many revolting inmates.

He watched them overtake a pair of guards by the exit. A couple of sharp pops and one of the C.O.'s from C-block went down. The other one was taken as a hostage, a gun jammed into his skull. The tier door slid open. With a roar, they charged through, straight for the control room.

Bishop steadied his breath and anticipated the next wave of tremors. Thirty seconds. That's how long it would take for them to break into the control room. Then he'd make his move. Stealth was something he'd perfected back when he was dumping stiffs into the bay for Tony D'Amati. All he needed was the distraction of the rioting inmates.

Seconds later, every door in the block slid open. Swarms of prisoners poured out into the corridors like smoldering magma. Bishop scoffed. So predictable. Time to fly. After years of planning his escape, he knew exactly which corridor, which door, which staircase he'd take. But first, he'd find Butch Hurley. He owed the bastard for using him to control the gangs in Salton. For running all kinds of sick schemes under the Warden's radar. The warden, whose ass he routinely French kissed. But most of all, for the threats against his sister Karen. Butch threatened to have her tortured, raped and mutilated if Bishop didn't do everything he asked. And Butch certainly had the means to carry it out. There was only one way to eliminate this threat.

Reap what you sow, Butch.

CHAPTER SEVENTY

For a guy with short legs, Possum ran quickly. He turned a corner away from the dozen or so inmates that had just broken through. Careful to avoid the brawl, I trailed him. By the time I reached the corner, the wolf pack had already gone through the opposite door. Sergeant Sonja Grace, lay face down in a crimson puddle.

Oh Lord, no. I considered checking on her but knew it was already too late.

A loud boom echoed beyond the door. The inmates had just broken into the control room. Soon every cell door in B-Block that had not yet been unlocked, slid open. I raced down the corridor after Possum, who was headed for serious danger. His dream had been a premonition. Something I was meant to discern.

I tripped over a chunk of concrete. Fell onto a stitched wound on my side. The stitches barely held together. I squeezed my mouth shut, stifled a scream. As if that wasn't painful enough, when I stood up it felt as if a rusty steel rod had impaled me from the foot, up though my leg. I'd twisted my ankle.

With my hand against the wall, I hobbled towards the door at the end of the hallway. No way I'd catch up to Possum at this rate. Finally, I arrived at an exit door which opened to a staircase. To my surprise, it was unlocked. Just one flight below, on the ground level,

Possum lay crumpled and curled up by the door.

"Poss!"

"I can't... move!" he cried out. Each agonizing step down the staircase brought chilled perspiration to my brow. I started to hop on my good foot when the tremors started up again. These tremors were accompanied by a rapid bumping sound from above me.

Grunting and panting, someone came rushing down the stairs.

Only five more steps and he'd be upon us.

Head still down, Possum stretched his hand towards me.

The thumping grew louder, closer, until it reached me.

"Bishop," I said. "What are you—?"

His face contorted in rage, Bishop whipped out a shank and put right up near my face. "Get the hell out of the way!"

Then a huge shockwave hit. A nauseating sound of crumbling concrete and twisting steel filled the tiny stairwell. The staircase gave out and we both tumbled down. Possum let out a blood-chilling scream.

"Poss!" I called out.

White dust engulfed the entire staircase. Amber floodlights tried in vain to cut through. The shock wave dissipated and I struggled to get onto my hands and knees. I felt my leg. Blood. But there wasn't enough pain to indicate just how bad a laceration it was. My twisted ankle upstaged it.

Bishop cussed, shoved me out of the way and clambered through the rubble.

I reached out and found Possum's hand.

Cold. Dry. Unmoving, the rest of him trapped under layers sheet rock, concrete and shards.

CHAPTER SEVENTY-ONE

Butch Hurley thought he'd prepared for every imaginable contingency in life, especially at Salton. Gang wars, prison riots, loose-lipped cons. Everything. He'd lived in Southern California most of his life and should have expected something like this to happen eventually. Had to be the biggest damned earthquake in his life.

The radio transmission from Control-B turned to static and his stomach went sour. He was standing out in the parking lot when the first wave hit. It subsided and returned again, each time stronger than the last. With his team, Butch entered B-Block and heard the one sound that for as long as he'd worked in corrections, he'd hope never to hear: the roar of an uprising. He swallowed and motioned for his men to file in, guns ready.

A frantic Sergeant Kincaid burst out of the security door, trying to decide which way to run. Butch stopped him before he could dash outside, running like a chicken without a head. "Whoa! Steady there, son. What's the situation?"

"They've taken over the control room!" Kincaid said, breathing hard. "Grace is down, they've got Elison hostage."

"One lousy earthquake and those punks think they own the place." Butch plucked the walkie-talkie from his hip and radioed the central control room. "Yeah, this is Hurley. We got Ten-Ninety-

Eights and a Ten-Ninety-Nine in B-Block's control room."

"Warden wants your recommendations."

"Transfer controls to AUX-B, flush 'em out, then seal 'em in the corridors. Send a tac-team over to get Elison out of there."

"Ten-Four."

Within minutes, the room would be disabled, its controls rerouted. Tear gas would be released from nozzles in the baseboards and every slimy sumbitch in there would be fumigated like the vermin they were. The trick would be doing all this without getting Elison killed.

Or at least making it look like everything had been tried to prevent it.

CHAPTER SEVENTY-TWO

It took a couple tugs on Possums arm to realize that one: he was trapped, and two: he wasn't conscious. With scraped hands, split nails and all the strength afforded by the adrenaline pumping through my veins, I dug through the rubble.

Bishop rubbed his eyes then scanned the area, craned his neck upwards some fifteen feet up to the door in which we'd entered the stairwell. The stairs were gone, all access above blocked off by twisted steel and concrete.

"Are you just going to stand there and gawk?" I said, heaving a chunk of concrete over to the side. He glared at me and climbed over the wreckage.

Right past me and Possum.

"He's down here!" I said, struggling with a very large wooden beam. "Give me a hand!"

All his attention, all his concern lay beyond the tiny glass window in the steel exit door at the ground level. "Guard tower's unmanned," he said and rattled the door handle. It wouldn't yield. "Dammit!" He kicked the door and thunder filled the staircase.

Still digging as best I could, I called out to him again. "Forget it, man. You'll never make it past the perimeter." He muttered something and grabbed a pipe. Started whacking the door handle. I wasn't going to waste another breath on him.

I could finally feel the right half of Possum's torso. His legs were still under a couple of panels of sheet rock. With my ear to his chest,

I could barely make out a heartbeat, thanks to Bishop's relentless assault on the door.

"Artie!" I called out, patting his crusted face. "Come on, man. Answer me."

Bishop growled, grunted with each blow.

Possum stirred. Groaned.

"Don't move," I said.

He coughed, grimaced from the ensuing pain and said, "Does it look like I can?"

"Attaboy, Poss! Stay with me, okay?"

"What happened?"

Bishop stopped for a moment and turned to look.

"Can you feel your legs? Arms?" I said.

He lifted his exposed hand and wiggled his fingers. "Can't feel the rest." I reached under a concrete support beam that had fallen diagonally over his body. His legs and left arm and shoulder were pinned. I felt just enough space for them not to have been pulverized, but not enough to slide out from.

Grasping the beam with both hands, I stood expecting, at the very least, a slight budge. But the beam was so heavy I lost my grip and fell on top of it.

Possum screamed. His eyes rolled back.

A loud crack. Did I just break some of his bones? No. Bishop had just broken the jammed door handle.

Possum began to cough. Blood-tainted spittle dotted his face.

"Oh no," I murmured. I wasn't certain what was happening to him, but it didn't take a doctor to know. It wasn't good. Galvanized, I pulled, pushed, and even wedged a splintered two-by-four underneath the beam for leverage. But to no avail.

Using his shoulder, Bishop rammed the jammed exit door with the determination of a wolf chewing off its own leg to escape a trap. Each blow forced the door open a bit more.

Crouched and with my back against the beam, with every ounce of strength in my legs, I strained to push it off of Possum. I shouted in frustration.

One more slam and Bishop stopped. He sucked in his gut, making himself as thin as possible and proceeded to squeeze through the opening.

"Bishop, don't!"

"I'm outta here."

I kicked the beam repeatedly accomplishing nothing more than hurting my good foot. "I can't do this alone."

"No one asked you to." More than half of Bishop's right side was out the door now.

"He's going to die!" Our eyes met. I refused to look away. Bishop didn't say anything. "I don't know you that well," I said. "But something tells me you're not a killer. And I know you're not just going to walk away like that Levite."

"So what are you? Freakin' good Samaritan?"

"You know what He said. *Go and do likewise!*" He opened his mouth but stopped short of words. Pointing a finger at me, like he was going to teach me a lesson, he huffed with vexation. He swore, pummeled the door with his fists.

And then, to my astonishment, Bishop squeezed back into the stairwell and climbed over towards me and Possum. "I'd kill you if—"

"But you're not going to. We both know it."

"Two minutes. That's all you get." He reached around the beam next to me.

"Fine."

"After that, I don't care. I'm gone."

"Whenever you're done blabbing," I said. Bishop cracked a surprised smile. With his eyes, he signaled his readiness. Two minutes might spell life and death for Possum. And for Bishop, the next five would change his life irrevocably.

CHAPTER SEVENTY-THREE

Butch Hurley watched them on a monitor in the auxiliary control room. Luther, The Führer, and 'Nando, blood-enemies thrown together into the same spittoon.

Filthy opportunity whores.

No audio over the monitors, but he could see they were all coughing violently in the long corridor that connected the control room to the security checkpoint. Even Sergeant Elison covered his face and doubled over.

"Hit it," Butch said, tapping Kincaid's shoulder. Kincaid pressed a button and on one of the monitors, Butch watched a set of steel bars slide over the doors. One shut off the entrance to Control-B. The other cut off the exit down the corridor. Butch then radioed a team of marksmen. "The inmates have been contained."

"Elison?"

"They still have him. Your primary objective is to disarm the convicts, is that understood? Don't care what it takes, I want those stinkin' animals back in their cells."

"Got it."

"Hold on." Butch was about to return to the central facility when he thought about all that stinking paperwork he'd have to file. It would ruin his weekend if he had to go line by line and explain everything, no matter how much the Warden trusted him. "Who you boys got on point?" he said over the radio.

"Johnston." The Cubscout?

Butch clicked his tongue. "I'm coming down there now." Without another word, he stepped out of the auxiliary control room. No time for this crap. The situation was going to be resolved in the next five minutes.

One way or another.

CHAPTER SEVENTY-FOUR

"Push!" Bishop snarled, his arms under the cement beam.

"I am!"

"Put your back into it!"

"I'm putting...my whole *body*...into it!" Despite all our shouting and grunting, we only managed to move it about an inch or two before having to set it back down. Possum was so out, I couldn't tell if setting the beam back down hurt. "He's not looking good," I said, catching my breath.

Wiping dust-caked sweat from his brow, Bishop said, "One more minute and I'm gone."

"Don't you hold out on us!"

"If I was going to hold out, I wouldn't have come back in the first place."

"Fine. Let's go." This time, I got myself as far under the beam as possible. Bishop did the same. On the count of three, we extended our legs, backs and arms with all our might.

It moved.

"Okay when I say go," Bishop hissed through his teeth and pointed his chin towards the wall, "roll it that way!"

I gave a Neanderthal reply. For a moment, the beam actually lifted off of Possum's body. The muscles in my entire body burned like gasoline-soaked logs.

Bishop's eyelids squeezed so tight they could have wrung out blood. "Go!" he shouted. I leaned forward and pushed with him until the beam slipped out of my hands. It landed with a heavy boom that echoed up to the top of the hollowed out stairwell.

"Damn!" Bishop said.

"What?" I was afraid to open my eyes. When my vision finally cleared I looked down. Blinking in disbelief, I wanted to ask him if he saw what I was seeing. Before I could, he trudged over to the door and began squeezing through the opening. Did I expect anything else?

I looked down at Possum's motionless body again. "What the—?" His T-shirt was now stained with black soot in various spots. There were minor cuts on his arms and shoulders, but the only blood came from his chest.

I knelt.

Looked closer.

A blotch of dark red blood stretched across the center of his shirt. The shape, the pattern was so distinct that for a moment, though I was staring straight at it, I couldn't process it. The blood spread and the shape became amorphous.

Then it was just a spot of blood. Again.

But its momentary form became permanently etched into my memory.

I've never forgotten it since.

The shape of a bird's wing.

CHAPTER SEVENTY-FIVE

Muttering every step of the way down the steps, Butch checked his gun. It'd suck if it jammed at a critical moment. At ground level, he exited and went around the back of B-Block where to his annoyance, he caught a glimpse of an inmate squeezing through a tight crack in a damaged service door. Butch clicked off the safety of his Smith and Wesson .38 and waited until the con got out. "Freeze!"

It was Bishop. The big ape actually thought he'd just walk out and climb over the fence right under the abandoned sentry towers. Bold. Stupid, but bold.

Bishop didn't bother raising his hands in the air, the smug bastard. Butch stepped towards his target with caution, never letting him out of his aim. Their relationship was about to change. "Going somewhere, Morgan?"

Bishop glared.

"Get 'em up, now!" Butch hollered from a distance of only ten feet away. Bishop slid both hands into his pockets and looked down his nose at him. "I said get them up! In the air, or so help me God—"

Bishop shot him a corrosive glare. "Of all the places to turn for help."

Butch took three steps forward, both hands on his gun, trying to keep it from shaking as he pointed it up and pressed it into the ex-priest's ear.

"I got a feeling if I pull the trigger, this bullet will just come out the other ear—no damage done. Wanna test my theory?"

Without so much as a flinch, Bishop said, "You ain't got the balls."

"No?" Butch cocked the hammer, hoping the ominous click would at the very least make him blink.

Nada.

"See?" Bishop said. "Ball-less."

He just had to make this difficult, didn't he?

"All right, Bish. Tell you what. I'm going to hand you a pair of cuffs. You be a good ape and put 'em on and *if* I decide not to put a bullet in your thick skull, maybe—just maybe—I'll think about telling my guys in National City to let Kathy keep seven of her fingers when we're done here.

This time Bishop jerked back and grunted.

Much better. High time he remembered who was really in charge around here.

"That, Butch, was a mistake."

"I don't think so." He began weighing his options. Which would bring more paperwork, more hassle? Shooting an escaped inmate in self-defense or bringing him back in?

CHAPTER SEVENTY-SIX

Blood notwithstanding, I put my ear to Possum's chest and felt his wrist for a pulse. Weak, but beating. His breath was irregular, he needed medical attention immediately.

With the staircase collapsed, the only way out was the exit. If I didn't resist capture, maybe they'd listen and go back for Possum. If anyone was out there.

There was.

And that person was in some kind of shouting match with Bishop. Whoever it was, however, he had to be able to get some help. A man's life was at stake here.

With my face halfway through the opening exit, I pressed through and looked back. "Hang on, buddy," I whispered to Possum. "Back soon."

They didn't notice me standing at the door, just about ten yards behind them. But I saw them clearly. Butch had his gun pressed into Bishop's ear. I couldn't make out what they were saying. Although Possum needed help, the situation was so tense, I dared not move.

Butch reached back for the handcuffs at his belt.

If I had blinked, I might have missed what happened next.

In a flash, Bishop dropped his head, reached back and twisted Butch's arm so forcefully, I wondered if he'd just broken it. A shot rang out. He twisted Butch's wrist again. The gun dropped to the floor.

Before my next breath, he had Butch in a choke hold, a shank at his neck.

"Bishop, don't!" I called out.

He turned to me, his eyes smoldering like a brush fire. "Grab the gun!" I froze. "Dammit, Hudson! Pick it up!"

I stepped over, bent down and retrieved it. The handle was still warm and moist. I wanted to rub my hands on my pants. Better judgment dictated that I keep it pointed at... who was I supposed to point it at anyway?

Bishop leaned his face right up against Butch's. He was going to kill him.

"No, wait!" Butch cried. "We can work something out. Anything you want, just name it!"

"You throw me into Gen-Pop, threaten my sister, and now you ask what I want?" he tightened his grip. Butch groaned.

"But...I made you... you rule Gen-Pop! You're the—"

"I want you dead, is what I want!" Bishop tightened his grip around Butch's throat, cutting off his words. He pressed his shank in and Butch let out a girlish squeak.

"Come on, Frank," I said. "Do not do this."

His eyes lit like napalm, aimed straight at me. "What?"

"You've had it rough, and yeah, you're no saint," I said, getting closer. "But you are not a murderer." I curled my right index finger uncomfortably around the trigger.

"Listen to him, Frank," Butch stammered, his eyes wide.

"Shut up!" Bishop yanked the C.O.'s head back, then turned back to me. "You don't know what the hell I am, Hudson!"

"I know you didn't kill that priest— You've never killed anyone." Somehow, I just knew. He hesitated. Then his features galvanized again.

"You have no idea how many I've killed."

"No. This is cold-blooded—"

"Sonofabitch deserves it!" There was no stopping him. I knew that look of desperation, where there was nothing left to lose. No one could stand in Bishop's way and hope to live. He inhaled deeply, let out a slow but savage growl.

I was about to watch Butch's throat get slashed open.

And then, as if all time was suspended, another vision came to me, clear as day. It was Jenn, the night she was murdered, dying in my arms, struggling to speak. A warm, tingling sensation coursed through my body, my mind. I understood, finally realizing what had to happen.

Out of nowhere I shouted, "Mercy, not sacrifice!"

Bishop froze. Both he and Butch looked up at me with disbelief.

And then I knew what I must do.

I aimed the gun.

And pulled the trigger.

CHAPTER SEVENTY-SEVEN

Bishop hit on the ground and rolled to his side.

In an instant, Butch made a run for it. "Stop!" I yelled, and cocked the hammer again. With his back turned to me, he raised his hands. "You're not going anywhere."

"Oh, you're in way over your head, pretty boy!"

I walked over to Bishop. Looked down. He was holding his leg and grimacing. "I'm sorry, Frank."

"Sonofabitch," he strained. "I can't—" he gritted his teeth, "can't believe you did that." Keeping the gun aimed at Butch, I knelt down, moved Bishop's blood stained-hand away. The bullet had passed straight through his calf.

"How did you know?" he groaned.

"Whenever you girls are done gabbing," Butch said "My arms are cramping here!" I straightened up and went over to the C.O. Got up close and looked down into his face. He sneered, trying to suppress the tremor in his lip.

I held the gun up to his head. Pressed it into the spot where his bushy eyebrows were conjoined. "Bishop's right," I said in an icy tone. "You deserve to die."

Butch squeezed his eyes shut. His entire body shook. Then I did something that surprised me as much as it did him. It was unplanned, just acting on gut, the same intuition that led me to shoot Bishop.

I grabbed Butch's forearm. Turned his palm up. And slapped the gun into his hand.

He opened one eye. Then the other. Total bewilderment.

"What the hell are you doing!" Bishop said.

"Why?" Butch's mouth hung agape, his eyes bulged.

"Two things." The words just seemed to flow out of me. Only after I spoke them did I realize that I meant it. "First: As much I'd love to pull the trigger, I'm not the one who judges. That's God's job."

His eyeballs were about to pop out of his head. "What?"

"Second: I need your help."

"What makes you think I'd—?"

"Because your throat isn't slashed open, because you don't have a bullet in your head."

"Oh. Right."

"Get medical help now. For Bishop. And Possum. He's back in that stairwell, hurt really bad."

"Sam, you stupid little— Don't!" Bishop slapped the floor. Butch nodded and jogged towards the building. Every couple of steps he'd turn back and look at me. The sun's rays blazed down from a cloudless, azure firmament. Sweat rolled down my back.

"You're an idiot!" Bishop said.

"Tell me about it." I removed my t-shirt, tore strip from it and wrapped a tourniquet around his leg, keeping pressure on the wound. "He'll be back, trust me." Bishop just shook his head. I grabbed his shoulder and said, "You going to kill me now?"

"No," he said, then smiled. "Not now, anyway. How'd you know?" Bishop tilted his head and looked deeper into my eyes. "Those words. Mercy, not sacrifice. How?"

"They were my wife's last words. To this day, I still don't know why she said that."

"Well I'll be. They were my mother's last words too," he said. I shuddered. "And no one ever knew what was written in that locket."

"Locket?"

"The one you saw in your vision. No one could have known

about it. Those words, that verse. It was inscribed into my mother's locket. She gave it to me just before she died." It was too much of a coincidence to actually be one.

I checked the tourniquet and retied it. "So why did you stop when I said it?" That hardness in his demeanor, that great rampart, that fortified citadel of anger and disillusionment, it all began to crumble—like the Berlin wall—brick by brick.

"You were right about one thing," Bishop said as the infirmary staff arrived. "I may have turned my back on God, but I've never stopped believing in Him." He tried to stand but grimaced and stopped. With my arm behind his back, I helped him settle back.

"Last night," he said. "I came to a decision. I was going to give God one more chance." He scoffed. "Yeah, I got some nerve. I told God that I wanted a sign. Anything. I mean, I figured, *you'd* been getting all these visions."

"I didn't think you gave them any credence."

"Well, I didn't at first. Anyway, I figured, no harm asking. Then this earthquake hits. Stupid cons riot and take over the control room. There was my sign."

An armed guard walked out of the staircase door with Butch. They exchanged a few words and the guard approached. From a distance he said to us, "Stay there. We've got a situation inside."

"How's Possum?" I called out.

"They're looking at him now." The guard gestured sharply at Bishop's shank, still in his grip. Bishop tossed it to him.

"Anyway," Bishop continued. "I'm ready to slash Butch's throat, I'm at a point of decision. You know, if I decided there really is no God, then what's to stop me? You know firsthand the things Butch has done."

"Don't remind me."

"When you showed up, screwing up all my plans, I figure it wasn't a sign, this earthquake. Just stupid luck. And there was no God. As I'd suspected all these years, I was on my own. No way out unless I killed Butch."

"But you stopped."

"Don't you get it?" He cleared his throat and annunciated. "But if ye had known what this meaneth, *I will have mercy, and not sacrifice*, ye would not have condemned the guiltless. For the Son of man is Lord even of the sabbath day."

"Sounds familiar."

"Matthew Chapter 12. Point is, it can't be a coincidence. When you said, 'Mercy, not sacrifice,' *that* was my sign." He let out a bitter chuckle. "Not sure it would have been enough to stop me from cutting Butch's throat, though."

"But it did, long enough for me to... Sorry about your leg."

He grasped my arm firmly. "Something happened. I haven't felt it for years. But when you spoke those words, it was like a door opened. Something came through, came back to me. Something I haven't had for years."

"What's that?"

"Peace."

That day, Bishop walked away with much more than peace. The riot had been quelled when a Special Response Team smoked the inmates out of the control room. They nearly lost the hostage in the process but ultimately restored order.

Three inmates made it outside the Prison walls during the riot. The heads of La Fraternidad, the Blacks, and The Fourth Reich. Had I not stopped Bishop, he might very well have joined their exodus.

But they didn't make it very far. All three of them had been shot and killed.

On a day that so many had lost their lives, Frank "Bishop" Morgan rediscovered his and re-dedicated it to God. Because *'Mercy, not sacrifice,'* the very words uttered by his mother and by my wife at their deaths, had saved his life.

CHAPTER SEVENTY-EIGHT

It was a day that would forever be engraved into my memory. Not only had the worst earthquake in over two decades struck, but it had brought about a transformation at Salton.

Six weeks after the quake, Butch resigned. A week later, the warden took an extended leave which later became permanent. Artie the Possum, my cellmate had survived his injuries. He would never let me forget that he owed me his life. Each day, I exercised with him and assisted him during rehab until he could walk again.

"If you hadn't come after me," he would say, "I would have died."

Frank had a different way of expressing gratitude. Not like Artie, gushing all over the place. It was much simpler, but every bit as sincere. He now greeted me with something he gave no one else at Salton. Respect.

With tears, I mourned the loss of Sonja Grace—how aptly named she had been. Forever in my mind, will she remain that angel, who risked everything so that I might see Aaron.

As for Butch, I don't know how much he appreciated that I'd spared his life. All I know is that before he left, he met with Bishop alone and had sworn that he would not allow any harm to come to his sister.

"You put the fear of God in him," Bishop told me.

CHAPTER SEVENTY-NINE

Three months passed and my case had been reopened, based on the evidence found at Brent Stringer's apartment. I began to anticipate each conference with Rachel, making sure to time my showers as close as possible to our meetings. Neither of us would, however, admit to the feelings we'd fought so long to repress. My appeal dominated our attention, anyway. That, and the mounting legal battle with the State over Aaron's life support.

Whatever it took, I *had* to be exonerated. I needed to get out of prison and reclaim legal guardianship of my son. But in this fight, time was no ally.

There was, however, one positive development. The exoneration hearings were about to begin. So that I could appear in court with expediency, I'd be transferred back to San Diego Central.

"So this is it, Silk," Possum said, shaking my hand as I stood by our open cell door, two armed guards and a C.O. standing outside and waiting. "Man, this place is gonna be a whole lot quieter without you."

"You were the talker," I said.

"Only around great listeners."

"Right."

"Well, okay, but my point is—" he choked up. "I'm...oh hell, I'm going to miss you!" He wrapped his arms around me and pressed his head into my chest.

Taken by surprise, I patted his back with my fingers and hugged him back. "I'll be praying for you, for Pam and little Jack," I said.

"Don't give up. I know a great attorney."

He just nodded, still in my chest. I was starting to feel awkward and lifted my hands, my arms. But he just stayed there, not letting go.

"Artie?"

"Hmm?"

"Not in front of the cons, okay?"

He pushed away, wiped his eyes and sniffed. "You be good, hear?" He stuck out his hand again. I gave it a firm shake.

"You too." With a smile, I took one final look into my cell—the pale walls, stainless steel sink and commode, the bunks. Dreadful as it was, this had been my home for the past two and a half years.

"Good-bye, Poss."

"Yeah." He sniffed and turned his face back into the cell. Who'd have thought he'd be so emotional? I turned my back to the cell. The door slid and slammed shut, sending a jolt though my body. As I walked down the tier, fellow inmates who had once looked at me with disdain, cheered me on.

"You go, Silk!"

"Knock 'em dead, Hudson. You're gonna beat this rap!"

"There goes my homie!"

"Nice ass!"

I smiled and waved, passing each one of them with high fives, fist grabs, and hope—the culmination of faith and determination over the past couple of years. At the end of the corridor, I found Bishop putting up some new drywall in the corridor that led to B-block's exit. He had been promoted to a managerial position in P.I. (Prison Industry). Never mind that the point of P.I. was to prepare for a transition back into society—Bishop was still on death row—the new warden thought highly of him and afforded him a long leash.

"Frank," I said, stopping for a moment. "I'm off to San Diego Central."

He wiped his hands on a rag and stepped over. "All right, man," he said, grabbing my hand and shaking it in a tight grip. "Remember what we talked about, okay?"

"I will."

"If you're ever in doubt, remember, confirmation of the scriptures." He'd taught me to recognize the promptings, the quiet voice of God, as I'd experienced so early in my faith. But I also learned that His voice would never contradict the Scriptures.

"You've got a gift, Sam. A real gift. But like all spiritual giants, it's going to be tested, refined."

"Never ends, does it?"

With a warm smile, Bishop pulled me into a manly, one-armed embrace. "Ends once, and then begins eternity."

"Thank you, Frank."

A heavy thump on the back and he released me. "No. Thank *you.*"

"For what?"

"Your faith, your obedience to God. For letting him work through you to help me find my way back."

"Just doing what I knew I must."

"You go out there and keep doing that. No matter what anyone tells you."

Presently, I became aware of an odd contradiction in my heart. I'd been caged like an animal, brutalized, abused, all the while innocent of the crimes of which I'd been charged. Justice had not been served, it had been violated. Shouldn't I have been elated to leave this legal and moral cesspool? But now, realizing that my time at Salton was over, that I might be a free man in a matter of weeks, I found myself looking with nostalgia at this, my spiritual birthplace. The home of unexpected brethren.

Frank lifted his hand, pressed his thumb against my forehead and drew a tiny cross. "*Dominus vobiscum.*"

"And with you also," I answered. I had been concerned for him, daring to hope that he might one day be exonerated. After all, like Jenn always said, "Miracles are happening every day, if you know how to spot them."

I turned, nodded good-bye and then began to worry for his safety. True, he didn't fear for his own life, he'd entrusted it to God. But he was no longer the dreaded Tiger of Salton. Heading up P.I., helping the chaplain with religious services, Bishop was now a model inmate with a reputation as the kindest, most gentle soul in the prison. But kindness and gentleness didn't lend itself to survival here.

I said a silent prayer for him and started to walk. Just before exiting, I turned back and saw something which I recognized right away. I wasn't seeing this with physical sight. Two bright lights shaped like formidable warriors flanked him. No reflective glow, no shadow cast. No one else seemed to notice.

It's going to be fine.

CHAPTER EIGHTY

Otherwise known as "America's Finest City," San Diego had never seen such tumultuous times. The judges had not issued gag orders for the many hot cases on their dockets.

As multiple high-profile criminal cases ran concurrently, the media enjoyed its wildest three-ring ever. Brent Stringer, a.k.a. *Kitsune*, faced multiple murder charges, while my own appeal got fast-tracked.

The court entered its final stages in the deliberations over Aaron's fate. This too had garnered national attention. True to form, politicians and all manner of organizations, religious and non, gathered on both sides of the moral divide, mounting their soapboxes, ostensibly in the name of what was best for "the Hudson boy." A politician's playground. Not one of them had ever known him.

The Stringer case was now in discovery. In an ironic twist, D.A. Thomas Walden, the man who prosecuted me got me convicted, now called me as a witness against Stringer. For that reason, and because he knew it was inevitable, he did not plan to contest my exoneration. It wouldn't take Barry Scheck and the Innocence Project. Frankly, it would reflect better on the D.A.'s office if they laid low and focused on convicting the real killer, a heftier flounder for their legal skillet.

My hearing was to take place tomorrow morning, but that didn't stop Walden from sending in his Deputy D.A., Kenny Dodd to prep me for my deposition as a witness for the Stringer case.

Alone in a secure meeting room within the skyscraper-like building of San Diego Central Jail, I sat on a steel folding chair behind a steel framed table, waiting for Kenny Dodd to arrive. Just a day before my exoneration hearing and my feet were still shackled. I was beyond it, though. A couple of years at Salton made commonplace these chains, which once stripped me of dignity, lowering me to the status of a wild beast.

The wall clock read 10:15 AM. Half an hour late. I found the quiet within the soundproof room soothing. Nothing but the steady hum of the fluorescent overheads. The square window in the door was barely wide enough to see the guard outside stand, exchange words with another guard, yawn, and sit back down.

Ten minutes later, I was ready to crawl out of my skin. This journey had been long and painful. Aaron was alive. His quality of life, however, had fallen under question. Rachel and I had been fighting the court with every reasonable argument for the reinstatement of my guardianship, not the least of which being that I was, in fact, his father. By some inane technicality, the judge maintained that I was still not eligible to take on legal guardianship. Something pertaining to my current inability to provide financial support.

My head bowed and fists clenched, words of wisdom came to me.

One step at a time. In His time.

I shut my eyes, held fast to that thought, tethered to all my hopes of seeing that promise fulfilled. *It's going to be fine.*

"You okay there?" I opened my eyes and she was standing there. I had forgotten that she was coming along with the D.D.A.

I took a slow, deep breath. Tried to smile. "Hello, Rachel."

Dodd stepped in front of her and shook my hand. I wanted to go to Rachel, but my chains were fastened to a heavy steel screw eye, imbedded into the concrete floor. I sank back into my chair.

"Mister Hudson, Kenny Dodd. Remember me?" His hair was cut short, but still golden. Though it had only been a few years, he seemed to have aged and put on a few pounds since the last time I saw him. In court at the prosecution table next to Walden. Gone were the tan, the sheepdog bangs, and the sleepy surfer eyes. Working for the D.A.'s office probably left him little time for surfing. Or exercising. He should try prison.

"You're late, dude."

"Technical difficulties." Dodd pointed to his laptop bag.

"I haven't forgotten."

"Yeah, well. That was like, three years ago." He tugged at his collar.

Rachel took a seat across the table. I kept trying to make eye contact but she managed to avoid it. I had at least expected a smile.

"Let's get started, shall we?" Dodd said.

"Rachel?" I wanted to at least ask her a question or two. She glanced my way, then back down to a stack of papers within a manila legal folder. "I'm only here to ensure that everything's done legitimately," she said with cool professionalism.

"We're off the record, Ms. Cheng," said the D.D.A.

"I know." Back to her stack of papers.

Dodd opened his laptop, unzipped a square case full of disks, popped a shiny silver one into the DVD drive, and turned the LCD towards me. As soon as the image appeared, he hit a button, pausing it. "We need to know if Brent Stringer's statement is consistent with what you recall the night you found your family attacked."

On the screen, Stringer's face was calm, his eyes benign. That he was a murderer, you'd never know it to look at him. Until now, I'd only seen his post-arrest pictures in the newspaper. Now, an acrid brew of anger and disgust boiled within me. In vain, I struggled to wring words from my lips. Instead, a hissing sound emerged as I took a breath.

Dodd crinkled his brow. "I know this must be difficult for you, Mister Hudson. But we're calling you as a witness for the prosecution. Do you think you'll be able to handle this?" I could only stare at those eyes on the screen. So innocuous, so matter of fact. It made him all the more monstrous. "Mister Hudson?"

"Yes. Yes, of course. Let's get this over with."

He reached over and tapped the laptop's charcoal touchpad and resumed the playback. A chill ran through my body as the off-camera voice of District Attorney Thomas Walden started the interview. "Mister Stringer, you've been read your Miranda rights but have waived your right to legal counsel at this time. Is that correct?"

I watched for a hint, anything that might indicate that Stringer was being coerced or mentally incompetent. But he smiled, smoothed a wrinkle on his orange prison shirt, leaned forward and rested his chin on his cuffed hands. "That is correct."

"Do you understand the charges?" said Walden.

"Don't patronize me."

"Murder, rape, aggravated assault, rape of a minor—"

Stringer flicked his fingers, sweeping away the D.A.'s words as if they were stale crumbs. "And you ask if *I* understand? One might actually infer that you were calling me a criminal."

"And just what would you call yourself?"

"To put it simply, such that even someone as simple as you can understand, you can think of me as..." Once again, he gave an endearing smile, as if explaining something to a child. "... a deity." I wanted to smash the screen.

The interview went on for another ten minutes, during which time Walden got only a little more cooperation, despite his harsh tone and threats. Stringer confessed to the Matt Kingsley murders. When pressed for why or how, he simply dismissed the questions. "Child-minds cannot possibly appreciate such matters."

The more Walden squeezed, the more condescending Stringer became. "Just how many deaths are you responsible for?" The D.A. asked.

"Oh, let me think." Stringer looked up as if the answer was

written on the ceiling. "I would say, roughly—and, mind you, this is over the course of eleven years... twenty-four."

"Twenty-Four!"

"Oh please. Don't overreact. There are billions of people on this planet. Nobody's going to miss twenty-four of them. Really, it's not a big deal." Given all a district attorney routinely faces, Walden's pause surprised me. But not as much as when Stringer redirected the discussion. "I was up to fifteen when one particular subject caught my attention."

"Sam Hudson?"

"You've done your homework. Very good." If his hands were free, he would undoubtedly have reached over and patted Walden on the head. "Now, Tommy-boy, what do Matt Kingsley, Kevin Scherer, John Bauman and Samuel Hudson have in common?"

"They've all been charged with multiple counts of first degree murder and rape. All domestic."

"Very good, Tommy-boy." He took a deep breath and let out a self-satisfied sigh. "Now, every divinity has his favored subjects. Each of them—Matt, Kevin, John and Sam—were granted the honor of my incarnation, my taking on their likeness, if you will."

"But why them?"

"Because they were worthy. They had each distinguished themselves. Each of them had gained a certain degree of notoriety. I hand-picked them."

"For what? Going to prison in your place?"

"Prison?" Stringer chuckled. "An unfortunate inconvenience. No, I have chosen them as the subjects of my creation."

"You don't mean—"

"Only if you're bright enough to imagine."

"Research for your books?"

"How better to identify with the visceral reactions to such heady matters? Watching a spouse die in your arms, seeing your child battered, atoning for the sins of the father? Don't you see? I am the creator, my word, inspired."

"Last time I looked in Border's, your novels were listed under fiction."

"Ah, but the verisimilitude, the authority. It all lies in the genuine responses of the characters I create. My chosen subjects have been transfigured by a sacrificial atonement. They are immortalized in my word."

"Wait," Walden said. "What was that book, *The Shadow of Death?* The protagonist, James Colson. He's based on Matt Kingsley, isn't he?"

Stringer lifted his bound hands into the air. "He's seen the light!"

"And Kevin Scherer," Walden said, his voice rising in pitch. "Timothy Edwards in *Prowl.*"

"My glory is manifest."

"And Sam Hudson," he said with a finality that twisted my entrails. "How did I miss that?"

"How? I'll tell you how." Stringer lowered his gaze at the camera. The smile was gone. "You got your conviction. Hudson was history. You moved on, moved up. You weren't interested in the truth."

Kenny Dodd leaned over and whispered to me, "We'll move to strike on that one."

Walden continued to ask questions, laying the foundation for the case he would present against Stringer, who seemed all too happy to volunteer information. "You're obviously proud of your work."

"In the book of Genesis," said Stringer, "at the end of each creation day I proclaimed all my work as good."

"With one exception."

Stringer tilted his head to one side. "Really? I'm intrigued."

"I'm intrigued that you're intrigued."

"Please, you must tell me."

"There was one thing, one situation that God had created which he said was not good."

"No." Stringer leaned forward, his countenance glowing. "Pray tell me."

"It was in His final act of creation."

"I would have remembered."

"He said, it is not good for the man to be alone."

Stringer's eyes grew wide. He blinked. "Well there's got to be a mistake in the translation."

"Not likely. It says God created woman in reaction to the man being alone. And you basically made sure that those innocent men would be alone till the day they die."

Stringer shrugged. "Divine prerogative."

"Now, if your highness would so kindly indulge us. How did you do it?"

Stringer leaned back into his chair. A disturbing grin stretched across his mouth. "Are you offering anything?"

"Get real. I've got your life in my hands."

Stringer shook his head. His chest heaved and the patronizing smile returned. He rested his cuffed hands in his lap and said, "I work in mysterious ways. But I suppose my subjects *could* benefit from knowing."

I almost asked the D.D.A. to turn it off. But I had to know how he'd accomplished taking away all that was dear to me and pinning it on me.

CHAPTER EIGHTY-ONE

Anita had managed to avoid Brent Stringer since the arrest. Let the stupid pencil pushers handle the administrative crap from his incarceration. She took a few days personal leave, with the excuse of a family matter. In truth, she spent two of those days in a bathrobe, in bed with a box of Godivas.

She'd never actually had any physical contact with her cyber-lover, but when she learned who he really was, what he'd done? Three or four hot showers a day weren't enough. The filth was so deep, she feared it would never wash off. After a few sessions with a useless therapist, she'd just have to return to work feeling dirty.

Anita drummed her fingertips on the splintery arm of a wooden bench. Waiting outside the doctor's office at San Diego Central's Auxiliary Psych Unit made her anxious. Perhaps she belonged on the other side of the door. But when she considered who was in there, more than likely shooting the breeze, charming the psychologists, manipulating them as he'd done to so many others, a chill ran up her neck to the very top of her scalp. So much so that she had to scratch her head and grunt in frustration.

"You okay there, Detective?" Lieutenant O'Brien said, he and another uniformed Sheriff flanking her.

"Yeah. Fine." She wasn't. Her shrink had encouraged her to confront Stringer. But she'd never been a victim. Damned if she was going to start being one now. The thought made her sick. And yet, this was her pain. It was real. Too real.

"You don't have to be here," O'Brien said, crouching down to meet her eyes. "Davis and I can take him back."

"It's okay, Jim," Anita replied, twirling her hair in her fingers. "I have to question him once more before—" She pictured herself sitting alone in a room with him and became aware of her pulse increasing, her palms sticking to the varnish-worn bench arm.

"Doesn't the D.A. handle that now?" Corporal Davis said.

"In general, yes. But I haven't finished filing my report. I just need five minutes with the suspect. Paperwork."

"We'll stay during the questioning, if that'll make you feel safer." Jim patted her arm and gave it a gentle squeeze.

She recoiled and let out an embarrassing gasp. "No!" She put a hand to her chest and exhaled slowly. "I mean... that won't be necessary. He'll be completely restrained and I'm armed. You're not allowed to be present for these questions."

"What?"

"Some kind of new State law, I think." Truth was, she didn't want anyone to know about the cyber affair. "You understand, don't you?"

"I suppose." He stood up and waited by the door. Maybe this wasn't such a good idea after all. Closure might not be all it was cracked up to be. Anita stood up and got ready to tell Jim never mind.

But just then, the locks clicked and turned. Anita tensed up. The door squeaked open and the sound of footfalls blended with the counterpoint of chains scraping on the hard tiled floor. Getting louder, closer. Anita stood and fast-walked towards the elevator.

Closer.

She stopped.

"Detective?" Jim said.

Closer.

She kept her back to the entire group. Stay or go? This would be her only chance before Stringer became completely inaccessible behind a legal wall.

The chains stopped. The relentless hammering of her heart filled her mind.

"Anita! How nice to see you."

Plastering on the toughest, coldest mien she could conjure up, Anita made up her mind. She could handle this. She needed to face him. She was ready. Before she even turned around, she said, "Mister Stringer, I'm going to need to ask you a few—"

"Not without me present," said a petite, but bitchy-looking woman whose eyes were reminiscent of the Tasmanian Devil Anita saw last month in the San Diego Zoo.

The detective approached but kept a healthy distance. Brent smiled at her with boyish innocence. She quickly averted her eyes back to the beady-eyed woman at his side.

"And just who are you?" Anita said.

She whipped out a business card and stuck it under Anita's nose. "Bauer. Jodi Bauer." Minimalist business card, polar white, the name typed in a 3-point font under the firm's name: Chatham, Young & Bauer.

"Jodi the Piranha?"

The attorney smirked. "One in the same. You are not going to so much as wink at my client without me present."

Stringer shrugged. "Helen of Troy never felt so desired." Neither woman responded.

"You watch yourself, Detective," the Piranha said. "I've got a list of constitutional rights violations as long as my client's novels. And you, being the arresting officer, are cited repeatedly."

"That supposed to scare me?

"You're either scared or stupid."

Anita rushed forward and got right into the Piranha's face. Close enough to see the whites of her razor teeth. Jim grabbed the detective's elbow and restrained her. Though it didn't stop her from jabbing a finger at the attorney's face. "You're defending a bottom-feeding scum-bag. I can think of a few choice words for people like you."

"Legal watchdog, protector of human rights—"

"I was thinking more of the four letter variety."

"Officer O'Brien, may we go now?" Jodi said.

He released Anita's arm. "Detective?"

She glowered at Stringer and his lawyer. They both wore stupid smiles. Now more than ever, she wanted to have it out with the creep. Let him know what she thought of him. Hell, she'd even pistol whip him, bitch-slap him, and dig her stilettos into his privates!

But this would never happen with Jodi Bauer present.

"Fine. Take him."

CHAPTER EIGHTY-TWO

"Can we take a break, counsel?" Rachel said as Kenny Dodd popped the first DVD out of his laptop.

"We're just about to get to the part that we need Sam to verify," Dodd replied.

I looked to Rachel and nodded. I was okay to continue.

"I need a few minutes to confer with my client," Rachel said.

"That's fine," Dodd got up. "Back in ten." When he left, Rachel came over. She slid a chair and sat beside me. "How are you Sam?"

"Fine, you?"

She didn't answer right away. Instead she set a stack of legal papers on the table in front of me. "These are for your hearing tomorrow. It's going to be one of the quickest exonerations ever because Walden knows that—"

"What's the matter?"

"Nothing." She adjusted her glasses, her eyes never leaving the ever spreading pile of documents. "What are you talking about?"

"Why are you being so, I don't know, professional?"

"Because that's exactly what you need me to be right now." Making little x's on the pages where my signature was required, she continued flipping the pages.

"We're still friends, aren't we?"

"Sign these, please." She pushed over the first stack, pointed to the signature line and handed me a pen. I did as she asked, but kept waiting to see if she'd make eye contact. She didn't.

After ten pages and zero words exchanged, I finally said, "What's going on? Why are you being this way?"

"What way?"

"So distant, impersonal."

She turned and faced me. Finally. Behind her glasses, her eyes were red and shimmering. "Do we have to talk about it now?"

"I just want to understand. Did something happen?"

"No. It's just that..." she bit her lip and frowned. Then turned her back to me and wiped her face. "It's no good."

The serial killer who called himself *Kitsune* had been caught, I was about to get exonerated, what wasn't good? I reached out but I hesitated for a moment. She took a deep breath but didn't turn around. Then I touched her shoulder. She seemed to deflate before my eyes. With conflicted urgency, she put a warm hand on mine and held onto it.

"Help me out here," I said, rubbing her soft knuckles with my thumb.

"Sam, don't." She sniffed, exhaling a trembling breath.

"A clue, anything."

"Here's the thing," still holding my hand, she turned around to face me. For the first time that day, she looked me in the eye. Then held both of my hands. "You've been in prison almost three years."

"This much I know."

"You know how hard I've been fighting for you."

"Yes."

"Part of me never thought you'd get out. That was my safety net."

"Safety net? For what?"

"Just let me finish, okay?" She removed her glasses, wiped the corner of her eyes. "I figured it would be okay. I mean, nothing could possibly happen, right? Stupid, I know, but I just allowed myself. And over time, before I realized it—"

The door clicked open.

"Oh, I'm sorry," said Dodd. My ears were burning, my face

flushed. But I didn't let go of Rachel's hands.

"Give us another five," Rachel said.

"You got it." He stepped out and shut the door.

Rachel gripped my hands, got even closer. "All right, I'm just going to say it."

"Good...I think."

"I don't know how it happened exactly. But Sam, I've developed feelings for you." I sat there looking into her eyes not knowing what to say. Strange, but I wasn't surprised. It wasn't arrogance. It was mutuality.

"Rachel."

"Wait. Before you say anything. It won't work. Truth is, as much as I worked for it, as much as I hoped for it, I've never prepared myself emotionally for the day that you'd become a free man. But last night, while in bed, I was thinking about it. And I just... I just couldn't." Rachel's words accelerated. "I'm your attorney, for heaven's sake! And there's Aaron, I know it's been a few years, but you lost your wife, I mean, what was I thinking falling in love—?"

I put a finger to her lips. Before I could think, much less utter a word, I ran my hands through her silken hair and drew her towards me. I pressed my lips to hers and we began kissing, desperately yielding to the inevitability of it all. Between breaths, she kept trying to say my name.

Finally, she stepped back and said, "This isn't what I planned."

I pulled her back and kissed her again. This time we held each other until it ebbed on its own. Her eyes were still shut, lips still parted. I brushed the hair from her face. "It's never about our plans."

CHAPTER EIGHTY-THREE

You idiot, Anita couldn't help but thinking. Despite her training, she very well could have ended up like one of Brent Stringer's victims. All because he had made her feel... what—desirable? Feminine? That freak was going to get a piece of her mind, lawyer or not. Jodi the Piranha had returned to her office, anyway.

Anita trailed O'Brien's squad car as he drove Brent Stringer back to San Diego Central. The hot midday sun should have caused the grey leather upholstery of her Six, a BMW 650i, to waft that new leather smell she'd always loved so much. It now seemed stupidly bland. She'd traded in her previous Beamer for a newer black one. On a Detective's salary, she couldn't quite afford it. But this was San Diego and she had decided long ago that she was, in fact, too sexy for her car—a vintage VW Bug.

O'Brien pulled into a parking space on Front Street. Heat waves visibly rose from mirages, pooled in the asphalt. The tower of the damned arched up, glaring at all who approached.

Jim and his partner led Stringer out and to the receiving entrance. Even from a distance, the sound of the chains scraping against the pavement irritated Anita like sandpaper on a chalkboard.

The alarm on her Six chirped twice, its headlights winked. Anita strode briskly to the officers. "A word," she said.

"Listen Pearson," Jim said, reseating his black sunglasses and holding one of Stringer's arms. "You heard what his attorney said."

"Just a couple of minutes."

Stringer winked at O'Brien whose shoulders heaved. "You pull anything and I'm going to get named because it happened on my watch."

"Trust me," Anita said. I'm not looking for any legal trouble. This is personal."

"That's the part I'm not comfortable with."

"Come on, Jim."

"No way."

"Five feet."

Jim removed his shades. "What?"

"I just have a few things to say to this guy. You and your partner can stand five feet away, right here in plain view."

He turned his head to the side and stared at the entrance. "I'm sorry, Anita. No."

"All right, look." She reached behind her back and pulled out her gun, held it by the muzzle, walked towards the squad car. The officers yanked Stringer back. She set her weapon down on the roof of the vehicle and then returned. "You can keep your guns aimed," she said.

Jim pulled his lips into a taut line. "The department's already under scrutiny, all the wrongful conviction suits since we pulled this slimeball out from under his rock." He shook Stringer. Rattled his chains. "Pearson, you gotta promise—"

"I swear. Just talk, is all."

"Two minutes." Jim nodded to Anita's gun and Davis went to retrieve it. With his own weapon, he pushed Stringer into the shadow of the building.

"One wrong move...," Jim said.

"Better keep an eye on her," said Stringer, turning to show his hands cuffed behind his back. Anita took him by the arm and gripped it such that her nails dug into his flesh. He didn't say a word, didn't so much as flinch.

Finally, she stopped and confronted him. His demeanor seemed so genuine, so sincere, Anita had to keep reminding herself what he really was. But she missed him. The way he'd made her feel, how he could draw her tears with the beauty of his letters, his thoughtfulness, and at the next moment make her sides ache from laughing. And laughing was not something that came easily.

"A question," she said.

"Anita," he said. "I know how all this looks, but you have to—"

"I haven't asked it yet."

His eyes still trained on her, pleading, he said, "Are we off the record?"

"Yes."

"Okay, go ahead and ask," he said.

She took a deep breath. "How could you?"

"I'm innocent."

"You've been boasting about the murders!" A couple of uniformed SDPD officers passed by and entered the building. Anita looked away until they were out of sight.

"That was just legal strategy," Stringer said.

"Strategy my sweet—!"

"No, really. I'm going to instruct my attorney to switch to an insanity plea later. I had to act that way during the confession. Don't you see? I'm not some psycho serial killer, not *Kitsune*. I'm one of his victims. I've been—"

"Stop it! Just stop!"

He took a cautious step forward, reached out to her with his eyes. "Anita, please. If you believe nothing else, believe this: I love you." His words ripped through her like a jagged knife. A single tear fell from her eye. God, she wanted to believe him. There was no other man for her, even if that man had only been an illusion.

"Why?" she needed to know.

"After all we've been through. Won't you help me, Annie? "

Don't call me Annie. Never call me Annie again! "Please, just tell me."

"I just need you to testify that—"

"WHY!"

"Why what, you irksome little girl!" Stinger shouted, his chains jangling. O'Brien and his partner lifted their weapons and took a couple of steps forward.

Anita waved them off. Sniffed. "Why me?"

In that instant, Stringer's expression morphed, like one of those billboards with rotating louvers. Then, the earnest lover, wrongfully accused, pleading with the one person who might still believe in him, now a hideous creature, with his smile a canine snarl. And though she was already at a safe distance, Anita took a step back.

"I chose you, Anita Pearson," he said, pausing as if withholding just a tiny bit longer would cause her even more pain, "because you were *easy.*"

The ice walls refrosted, refortified, her jaw trembling from the fierce clamping, Anita flew at him. Threw her entire body weight into a right hook to his nose. Stringer fell back, landed on his back. As his back hit the pavement, he laughed.

"Get this scumbag out of my sight!" Anita shouted to O'Brien.

"I chose everyone else because they were remarkable, noteworthy," Brent said, his countenance a maniacally glazed sheet of ice. "But you. You were simply for my amusement. Poor misunderstood Annie. Poor little orphan Annie. Did you like my poetry?

One shade the more, one ray the less, had half impair'd the nameless grace... Illiterate slut! That was Lord-frickin'-Byron!"

"Shut up! Shut the hell up!" she was covering her ears now, internally cussing her inability to cope. Jim and his partner heaved Stringer to his feet.

"One more word and I'll tazer your sorry ass," Jim warned.

Anita turned her back.

Stringer's chains scraped the concrete. Stopped abruptly.

Just long enough for him to offer one final parting shot.

"You're pathetic!"

Anita spent the rest of the day at the Pistol Range. She named every target she shredded, Brent.

CHAPTER EIGHTY-FOUR

Kenny Dodd's grin betrayed that he was on to us. Thankfully, he made neither mention nor allusion. Just pretended he hadn't seen me lip-locked with my attorney. Everything was back to normal in the room except for the fact that Rachel now sat next to me.

On the next video, Brent Stringer proceeded to explain how he pulled everything off. I verified each familiar step and grew more and more queasy. Somehow Jenn had ended up on Stringer's database because of an email she sent him through his official fan website. That was the initial point of contact. He'd sent bogus and anonymous e-card email links that appeared to be dead. When Jenn clicked them, they silently downloaded hidden surveillance software.

He also uploaded keystroke trackers through Instant Message sessions with Bethie. Invisibly, they installed themselves onto our home computer shortly after my name and picture appeared in the news over the Coyote Creek school shootings.

"From that point on," Stringer said. "I studied Hudson's life, his credit card spending habits, his daily and nightly schedule. He was the perfect subject. Consistent, predictable."

Walden stared at the ceiling. "And Hudson's work computer?"

"Oh, the kiddy porn? Brilliant. And I do say so myself."

"Right."

"Child's play, if you'll pardon the expression." A demented grin. "USB flash drive. Plugged it into his computer before he returned to his desk. It takes a mere ten seconds for an autorun executable to install itself and run as a background service."

"About the night you murdered Jennifer and—"

"Murdered? No, no, no. Wrong word. They were beatified!"

The D.A. cleared his throat. "No sign of forced entry, no physical trace of you, no hairs, no DNA." *Nice ass-armor, Walden.*

"As I said, Hudson was the perfect subject and entirely too easy. Before he returned to his cubicle to meet with me for that Superdad interview, I got the model number of his security alarm panel from the manual he left on his desk. Later, I got the override codes from manufacturer's technical support line. I stole into his garage as soon as he drove off that night for his client meeting. As for traces? Come now. What can I say? Clever as a fox."

"So you'd devised a method of leaving zero evidence."

Stringer yawned. "Yes, yes. Latex gloves, hair nets, shoe covers—blah, blah, blah. Don't you watch CSI?"

"But what about the DNA? They matched the semen found on Hudson's daughter to his own."

"Ah, now that was beautiful, wasn't it?"

"What did you do, bribe someone down at the crime lab?"

"That'd be without class, Tommy-boy. And besides, bribery's so...unimaginative."

"Well?"

"Let's be clear about one thing, before you launch a witch hunt over the chain of custody of evidence. The semen *was* in fact Samuel Hudson's." There came an uncomfortable pause. Under the table, Rachel grasped my hand. Dodd pulled on his collar and cleared his throat. I wanted to disappear.

Stringer smiled. "But Sam never raped his daughter. No. He was a model father—another reason he was chosen."

"Then how?"

"For an officer of the court, you're pretty thick, aren't you? Hudson's life ran like clockwork. Every Thursday night, while his wife and kids went to Bible study meetings, Sam went to meet clients at dinner meetings.

"Every *Wednesday* night, he and his wife had a date night. And that didn't mean going out to dinner or the movies. They had sex every Wednesday night. You can learn a lot from those webcams and microphones in people's bedrooms if you have the right spyware running."

Some three years after the crime, the mystery finally started to unravel—stitches tearing off a festering wound that time could not heal. I was reliving the violation all over again.

"Thursday is trash day in Rancho Carmelita," Stringer continued. "Based on his online orders from condoms-express.com, I knew Sam's mode of birth control and hence where to find samples of his DNA. A bit messy, but easily dealt with."

"So you're a dumpster-diving deity? You planted Hudson's own semen on his daughter's body." Walden said.

"You may bow before my brilliance."

The revulsion was exceeded only by the urge to grab Stringer by the throat and snuff out the smugness on his face. Rachel must have sensed my tension because she put her hand on my back and rubbed it. "Turn it off," I said, my fist trembling.

"Are you sure?" Dodd said. "We still—"

"TURN IT OFF!" I bolted up from my chair. It slid back, scraped the concrete floor and slammed into the wall. For nearly three years, I imagined what I'd do to the sick bastard, if ever I got my hands on him. Now, with a face to put on these violent thoughts, I felt so much closer to it. I stopped, trying to remind myself, *Do not repay evil with evil.*

"Shut it off, please," Rachel said.

Dodd hit a button and flipped down the LCD. "Well. I think there's enough to go on there."

"Counsel," Rachel said. "I think my client needs some time to—"

"No," I said and pulled my chair back into place. "It's all right. Let's finish this."

We went over every detail of Stringer's statement, verifying credit card accounts, email accounts, ISPs, and yes, even the scheduled date nights. These questions would come up in the upcoming depos, and when I took the stand.

By the time the interview was over, I felt as if I'd just finished a marathon. I asked Rachel if we could meet later that afternoon instead of right after this meeting. I needed time to settle down. She completely understood. We started for the exit.

Walking through the door, I saw something that turned my legs into putty. I grabbed the doorframe. Dodd noticed and caught me by the arm. Shocking as the confession had been, nothing could prepare me for what awaited outside the meeting room.

CHAPTER EIGHTY-FIVE

Directly outside, a steel gate enclosed a corridor connecting the main entrance to the bowels of San Diego Central. A metal grid divided this corridor. Though you couldn't fit more than a finger or two in the grid, you could see clearly through it. I stepped out and heard not one, but two buzzers sounding.

Over at the entrance gate, a pair of guards brought a prisoner in. An everyday occurrence you get used to. But something about *this* inmate alerted me. He turned his face to the ground as he approached in the opposite corridor. Without taking my eyes off of him, I walked to the grid. Just steps before our paths brought us directly across from each other, the inmate looked up. It must not have been more than a second or so, but our eyes locked for an eternity.

"Oh no," Rachel whispered.

Fire and ice blasted through my veins. I slammed my hands against the grate, stabbing fingers through, clutching, clawing.

"Well, well, well. What have we here?" said Brent Stringer, a malevolent smirk slashing through his features. He pulled free from the guards and put his face just outside my fingers' grasp.

"What is this!" Rachel demanded.

Dodd sputtered. "I didn't work his schedule."

"Sick sonofabitch!" I said, snarling at Stringer. "You killed my wife—"

"Don't forget, I did your little girl and beat the crap out of your son!"

I let out a savage cry that echoed through the corridor. Grabbed the grate, rattled it as hard as I could, slammed it, and shouted.

"Move it!" The guard grabbed Stringer's arms and shoved him down the corridor. He kept his face turned to me, mocking me with his eyes. Kenny Dodd gently took hold of my arm. I spun around and shoved him back so hard he fell onto the ground.

"Sam, no!" Rachel cried. I leapt back to the grate, threats and vituperation on the tip of my tongue. I squeezed the metal grate as if it were Stringer's throat and didn't let up until it began to hurt. He was so close I felt as if I could will him to death. No one would blame me. He'd shown no mercy, not even to a child. It would be the justice he deserved.

A distant echo, Rachel was calling my name. She touched my arm. By sheer reflex I coiled back a fist. She winced, shouted my name one last time and I realized it was her. "I'm sorry," she said. "You weren't supposed to see him."

"I...He was just..."

She took my hands in hers and held them firmly. Dodd got up, straightened his tie, and blew air through his lips. I couldn't speak. All manner of emotion raged within.

"Is he going to be all right?" Dodd said.

I held up a hand and nodded yes. "Give me a moment." I went back to a corner in the corridor and began slamming the grate again. Over and over and over again. After a minute, my hand became numb. I kept slamming it, shouting, until finally Rachel stepped over, her eyes beseeching. "Sam."

I shouted and slammed the grate one last time. She reached out, the velvet pads of her fingertips touched my face.

Then the dam burst.

CHAPTER EIGHTY-SIX

It must have been the quickest hearing in the history of the San Diego Superior Court. Judge Matthew Schermerhorn had been wrestling a docket bloated with exonerations, of which mine was merely the first.

It was reported that upwards of three hundred and fifty people attended in the audience, many overflowing into extra courtrooms and watching via closed-circuit television.

As I approached the tall mahogany doors of the courtroom, I remembered the first time I had been brought before the court—shackled like an animal. Immediately I remembered Dave Pendelton's words, as he sat directly behind me in the gallery. "*Keep your head up.*"

Cameras flashed, whispers hovered. Excitement infused the air like an open field during a lightning storm. But I dared not appear overconfident. Anything could happen. Rachel said that this judge was a straight-shooter. But one never knew, temperaments and all.

Decked out in a charcoal suit Rachel had brought me, I shifted in my chair, tugged at a sleeve here, fixed a wayward collar there. All while she presented Brent Stringer's recorded confession. The entire courtroom bristled as they viewed the video. Stringer claimed responsibility for everything I had been accused of. He explained just how easy it was to hack into a computer and implant surveillance software. Identity theft was merely the prelude to his fugue of malice.

Walden sat at his table, made no arguments, never looked in my direction. He spent the entire hearing scribbling on a legal pad. Probably playing tic-tac-toe with himself.

The entire hearing wrapped up in about an hour. Judge Schermerhorn turned my way and spoke.

"Will the defendant please rise."

I stood, fastening the top button of my jacket. I'd heard of exonerations going afoul at the last moment, kicking the case back into an endless appellate loop. Three years at Salton flashed before me—Bishop, Possum, Butch. I wasn't afraid of that place. It wasn't prison that caused my heart to thunder like a herd of mustangs. It was the thought of not being able to fight for Aaron. Time was running out.

I didn't move, didn't breathe.

Schermerhorn scowled and read from a paper in his hand. "Having heard the new evidence which is clearly exculpatory in nature, it is the court's decision to vacate Samuel Hudson's convictions on all counts." The entire room rumbled with a crescendo of murmurs. "This case is hereby dismissed with prejudice."

He struck the sound block with his gavel and I started breathing again. The noise in the courtroom grew so loud I could barely hear myself think—a juxtaposition of cheers, jeers, sighs of relief, and murmurs of indignation.

Rachel turned to me, a look of overwhelming relief on her face. I tried to speak but ended up like a goldfish flipping about the kitchen floor. She rushed over and embraced me. My arms floated up, wrapped around her. "Thank God," she said quietly. "Thank God."

For the past three years the thought of dying in prison—or surviving long enough to be executed—dangled over my head. And though I saw this exoneration coming from the moment I learned of Stringer's confessions, I couldn't believe it was finally happening.

"I'm free."

PART III

"He is no fool that gives what he cannot keep
to gain that which he cannot lose."

— Jim Elliot

CHAPTER EIGHTY-SEVEN

It's not until you have them taken away that you realize just how precious the simple things in life are. Walking on the sidewalk without a guard, without chains. Rachel and I pushed past a multitude of reporters offering them a brief statement. I was too numb for bitterness, just filled with gratitude.

I would have gone straight to Aaron, but the restraining order—the most difficult part of my newfound freedom, would not be lifted until next week. So my first act as a free man was to visit Jenn and Bethie's graves. Rachel and I exchanged scarcely a word on the trip up to the cemetery. Riding at freeway speeds on the 805 was surreal. Completely alien and at the same time, completely familiar.

Grey clouds obscured the afternoon sun. A brisk gust carried the sweetness from a wall of jasmines that lined the cemetery's boundaries. Their graves had been lovingly maintained. Fresh flowers stood in urns attached to the sides of their headstones. Rachel stayed back, affording me privacy.

I laid bouquets of red and white carnations and stargazers wrapped in greens with baby's breath on each of their graves. "How are my favorite ladies?" I said, trying to smile through my tears. I knelt between both graves and rested my hands on their headstones, then lowered my head. What started as words constricted my throat and soon turned into sobs. I wiped my face and I tried to regain some semblance of composure. "I've missed you both so much," I said with my head hung. *I failed to protect you. Please forgive me.*

Heavy teardrops rapped against the cellophane bouquet wrapping. A white dove cooed in a branch above me. The sun had nuzzled its way through a small fissure in the clouds, its beams shone down and warmed my face. Rachel came to my side and knelt silently. She reached out, hesitated, and then pulled her hand back. "It's okay." I took hold of it.

Once again, the dove cooed in the pale branches of the camphor tree. She tilted her white head to one side. We remained motionless. Then a sense of peace beyond understanding filled me. The air had warmed and a gentle breeze caressed my face, ran through my hair lovingly, like Jenn's fingers once had.

Rachel's head was bowed, solemnity enshrouding her. With a deep breath, I looked back at the dove, who hadn't taken her eyes off of me. Then she cooed one last time and in an elegant flurry of white, she flew off.

"I'm ready," I said and wiped a tear from my eye. Rachel took my hand and squeezed it. I knelt and kissed Jenn's headstone. "I will live to honor you. Whatever it takes."

CHAPTER EIGHTY-EIGHT

In all the rush to prepare for my hearing, and not wanting to count my proverbial eggs prematurely, I had neglected several details pertaining to my reintegration into society. Not the least of which was where I would spend my first night as a free man. No job, no home. Nothing. Rachel had plans, though. I spent the ride from the cemetery blindfolded, in compliance with her, "Trust me."

I didn't dare imagine where she was taking me. Being deprived of sight only enhanced my other senses. I became acutely aware of the honey timbre of Rachel's voice, the delicate distance from one digit to the next on her soft fingers.

"Almost there."

"The suspense—come on, just one hint."

"Nope."

"Please?" I felt her shove my shoulder. We laughed. Sighed. Stayed quiet for a few minutes.

"I didn't know Jenn or Bethie well," she said.

"It's a big congregation." My blindfold started slipping. I pulled it back up.

"I wish I had. I can tell they were really special."

"Yeah."

"Especially Jenn," she added and slipped her hand behind my neck and began to massage it. "Never mind. I'm sorry..."

"No, it's okay. What's on your mind?"

"It's nothing." The silence grew less comfortable. Something was troubling her.

"If you want to talk about Jenn, I'm okay with it," I said. Really."

"She was, I don't know, so..." Her voice faded.

"What?" The roar of a truck went past my right ear.

"She was perfect, Sam."

"Nobody is."

"Still, I wonder—" she huffed. "This is crazy. One kiss and—I'm way ahead of myself."

"Rachel, relax. And for the record, I'm the one who kissed you."

"But what about Jenn?"

"I'll always love her. But she and I talked about this many times. You know, if one of us should ever go first, what we'd want for the other."

"I don't know."

"I've had almost three years to come to grips with this. I know she'd bless this. If it were the other way around, I'd want her to find love again."

"So have you?" Rachel said.

"Have I what?"

"Found it?"

I took a moment to weigh all the implications, lest I toss out a careless answer. "With you, I have." The next thing I knew, Rachel's warm lips were upon mine, her arms wrapped around me. I returned the kiss with equal fervor. But the realization hit me like a sledgehammer. I pushed back. "The car!"

Anticipating a seventy mile an hour collision into the back of a semi, I ripped the blindfold off. Rachel grabbed my face and kissed me again.

"Welcome home, Sam."

She had parked up on the driveway of my former house in Rancho Carmelita.

CHAPTER EIGHTY-NINE

"It's not exactly the way I'd planned your homecoming," said Rachel, taking me by the hand to the door. "But when you freaked out behind the blindfold, I just couldn't resist."

My heart continued to pummel my rib cage.

"I had no idea you could be so—"

"Impish?" She handed me a key.

"Among other things. What's going on?" I held the key up and examined it.

"Sam, I really meant it, back there in the car."

"This prank kind of killed the mood."

"I'm sorry."

"No you're not."

"Yeah, you're right. But the look on your face? Priceless. Are you going to open the door or not?"

Strange. Prior to selling, I was able do this with my eyes closed. Now, I could barely get the key in. I just couldn't steady my hands.

"Here," she said and took my hand. I could just guess what awaited inside: a welcoming party, people from church, old acquaintances as well as people I'd never met, but had been praying for me. I'd have to act surprised.

The door creaked open.

Dark.

I braced myself. The surprise came when I flipped on the light.

Empty. Quiet.

Good.

The house had minimal furniture, none of which I recognized. Just about everything I'd kept in storage seemed to be here. All six cardboard boxes, a couple of them open. Photos, paintings, and other memorabilia festooned the walls in a close approximation to where they'd originally hung.

"Rachel," I said, gazing in wonder. "How?"

She snaked her arm around mine and led me to the dining room. "Monsieur." She pulled out a padded folding chair—the kind you can buy at Costco. I sat at a card table adorned with a white table cloth. A yellow rose in an alabaster vase stood in the center of two settings of fine paper flatware and plastic utensils.

"This is really nice," I said. "But how'd you manage to—?"

"Be right back," she said, patting my back and vanishing into the butler's pantry. She hummed a tune to the accompaniment of a microwave's beeps and droning. Despite her best efforts to recreate my home, the walls were still devoid of the beauty of Jenn's touch. But they did seem to echo the laughter of my children, Bethie's violin playing, the late night keyboard clicks of Jenn's writing. I shut my eyes, recalled memories that would live on in perpetuity whenever I set foot in this house.

"Dinner is served." Rachel returned with a tray full of steaming take out containers. "Hope you like Chinese."

"I like you, don't I?"

"I mean Jumbo Shrimp in Black Bean Sauce, Kung Pao Chicken, Szechuan Beef. How's that sound?"

"Ever try prison food?" Tendrils of aromatic steam rose from the containers and tempted my appetite. So many questions, but they could wait. Rachel had been so thoughtful, why spoil things with an interrogation? We gave thanks and dug in.

My greatest challenge was not making a complete swine of myself. Reheated take-out from Golden Wok struck me as the finest cuisine I'd had for a very long time. We exchanged few words, too busy eating. Prioritization was paramount. Finally, I pushed back from the table, wiped my chin and asked, "What are we doing here?"

"Pigging out?" Rachel said, wiping the corner of her mouth.

"You know what I mean."

"Do you have an objection?"

"No, I just want to know how I can be sitting here in this house. How'd you get the key?"

Rachel put her chopsticks down and slid her chair closer. "The buyers backed out while the house was still in escrow."

"Why?"

"California Real Estate laws require that the seller's agent disclose just about everything, including deaths on the property. Guess it was too much for them."

"So who finally bought it?"

"City on a Hill."

"Your church owns this house now?"

"They hold the title, yes. A bunch of members anonymously pitched in and paid for it in cash. Some of the proceeds helped pay for a good part of Aaron's hospital bills."

"I can't believe it."

"We haven't stopped praying for you since. Oh, and the deacons board felt led to keep your house off the market."

"Why?"

"Because they had faith you'd come home one day."

I stood up and walked over to the dining room window and gazed at the darkened window of Dave's house. I recalled how during the months leading up to and during my trial, I would stare out at my house like one banished from his homeland. Sometimes, living next door to the house I was forced to sell seemed more difficult than If I had left town altogether.

"I can't afford to buy it back." I slid open the window and wished the lights were on next door. It would have been nice to see Dave right now. But he was away again with a team in Mexico on a short term mission trip.

"In time, you'll be back up on your feet," said Rachel. "They're not looking to make a profit."

"I will buy it back. Just as soon as I can."

"Until then, consider yourself home," she said, coming to join me. She wrapped her arms around my waist and pressed her face into my back.

I turned around and held her close. "I've been to hell and back. And now I'm home. I'm actually home."

We stayed up until about 11:00, talking about everything from legal strategy in Aaron's case to the Padres' recent losing streak. The thermostat hadn't yet been set so it was getting chilly, as it often did on March nights in North County inland. Rather than turn on the forced air heat, I found a zippo in the kitchen and lit up the fire place.

Rachel snuggled up with me at the hearth. She removed her glasses and looked at me with her deep brown eyes. Amber flames reflected in those glimmering pools, her moistened lips, parted in anticipation. We began to kiss with such intesity that we could only stop long enough to breathe. It had been so long.

Her fingers raked through my hair, pulling me closer, deeper into the kiss. Our passion swelled with the inevitability of a runaway train. She pulled the shirttails out of my pants and she began exploring my chest with her fingers. I sensed she would welcome my reciprocation. But just as I reached for her buttons, we both stopped.

Simultaneously, we pushed back, released each other with reluctance.

Took a deep breath. Smiled.

Spoke at the same time.

"I'm sorry."

"I shouldn't have—"

Half-turned, I put my arm around her. "I don't know what I was...well, I wasn't really thinking."

"No, it was mutual," she said.

"I was married, the last time I did this."

"That makes one of us." I pulled back and gave her an

incredulous look. She thumped me in the chest and giggled. "Meaning, I've never."

"Been married or made love?"

"Neither."

"No way. Someone as smart and sexy as you?"

"Believe it or not, there still are adult virgins in this world." It hadn't occurred to me that my newfound faith considered premarital sex wrong. The issue had honestly never crossed my mind while in prison.

Leaning into my shoulder and nuzzling me with feline affection, she said, "I'm every bit as guilty. If we kept going..."

"We should wait, shouldn't we?"

"For a number of reasons."

I couldn't help but apologize again.

"It's okay, Sam. I've waited three years for you—actually, much longer if you think about it—there's no rush." We both exhaled. She checked her watch. "I'd better get going. I've got an 8AM depo tomorrow."

I walked her to the door, gave her a hug and kiss on the forehead.

"You're disappointed," she said.

"I'd be lying if I said I wasn't." Another kiss on the lips. "But yeah, I think we'd better take it really slow. Besides, with the Stringer case, and Aaron—we've got a lot to deal with."

"We'll win this, Sam. I promise, I'm going to do everything I can."

"I know you will."

Rachel pulled out of the driveway, waved, and blew me a kiss. I waved back and shut the door. With my exoneration, one huge battle had been won. But even as I prepared to retire for the night, another war, more profound than could be imagined, was mounting.

CHAPTER NINETY

The fireplace continued to burn. I sat on the sofa staring at the flames refracting crimson beams through the glass of brandy I had poured myself. My eyelids grew heavy.

I should get some sleep.

But I wasn't ready to go up to the bedroom. That could wait. Besides, the sofa which the good folks at City on a Hill probably bought from Ikea, actually felt quite comfortable. I grabbed one of the throw pillows and pulled the blanket that had been draped over the sofa over me and drifted off.

Her cries for help fade. I fly up the stairs, nearly stumbling on the way.

Oh God, it's happening.

Why didn't I come home earlier? Should never have left.

A long blade of light slashes the darkness though the crack in the door. I swing it open. The sheets are in disarray, filled with blood.

"Jenn!"

She gasps for breath in my arms, her very life bleeding out of her.

"The children..."

"I'm sorry, honey," I cry. "I should never have—"

Her eyes turn blood red. Her pupils become pointed diamonds.

"It's your fault!" she hisses.

"No, Jenn. Please!"

She bares her teeth, serpent-like fangs. "*You've* killed us. *You're* responsible!"

"No..."

"And now, you're going to hop in bed with that Asian whore! You lecherous pig!" She lifts her hands. The long, curved fingernails, rotted black-talons of an infernal dragon. She sinks them into my neck and squeezes with inhuman strength.

"You faithless, worthless excuse for a human being!" she gurgles. Maggots squirm from the open wounds in her arms, her neck. "What did Jenn ever see in you!"

I try to scream but nothing comes out. I try to move but I'm utterly paralyzed. The creature clutching my throat decomposes before my very eyes. The foul smell of death makes me queasy.

"You deserve to die!" it shouts. Its mouth is open so wide its jaw dislodges, its breath like rotting meat. My life drains out. "It should have been you, Sam!"

In my heart I call out to God, "Help me!"

The creature's maniacal laugh echoes.

"Your God!" it scoffs. "He's dead!"

"Lord!"

"I killed him two millennia ago!"

And then I understand. Nothing has changed. Not for two thousand years. "In the name of Jesus!" The creature convulses. Its claws tremble in my bleeding neck. "In the name of Jesus and His blood!"

Its entire body quakes. The demon won't let go of my neck but isn't able to prevent it. It releases me. I can speak.

"In the name of Jesus, I command you to leave!"

With a blood-coagulating shriek, the creature explodes into shards of decaying flesh, which dissolve into crawling maggots.

Then evaporates.

I woke up gasping, my face numb, my back wet and cold.

A dream.

Had to be the most horrible thing I'd ever experienced. Its foreboding effects lingered like the stench in my nightmare. The sense that I was not alone in the house caused me to shudder. Despite the fireplace which still burned, the room felt cold.

I pulled the blanket around my shoulders and went to my duffle bag in the hallway. Back on the sofa with my Bible, I sat and read by the light of the fire. A few minutes later I sunk deep into meditation, more at ease and secure as I prayed for Aaron, for guidance regarding Rachel.

My eyes were still shut when I heard it emanating from the fire. A sizzling sound, a familiar hiss that reminded me of moisture evaporating from burning wood. Only this was a gas burning fireplace and the simulated logs were made of concrete.

SSSSSSSSSSSS...

I peered into the fire expecting to find a crumpled newspaper or piece of wood burning. Nothing. Just the concrete logs.

SSSSSSSSSSS....

Neither loud nor abrupt, it seemed to respond to my movement.

Sssssssssssss....

The hissing grew fainter but not a bit less distinct. A tingling sensation ran through my body. Considering the nightmare, which was a bit too real, I should have been freaked out of my mind. But instead, my heart pounded with anticipation.

Sssssssamuel.

I knew this voice. It had called me before.

"I'm here, Lord."

I clutched the Bible to my chest and rubbed my eyes. Began perceiving images in the fire. Images, impressions of things, wondrous and strange:

I see myself as a teenager, a college student, even as a married man—many of the sins I'd committed and had long forgotten. The lies, petty theft, cheating on exams, lust, hatred. That homeless panhandler back in New York that I walked straight past on Christmas Eve. Never thought twice about these things before. Now they grieve me, fill me with shame.

Jesus hangs on the cross, streaks of blood drips line his face. He lifts his swollen eyes to heaven. "*Father, forgive...*" He looks down and down by his feet, I see myself in my cell back at Salton Sea, kneeling in prayer on the night I accepted Christ as my lord and savior. But I am naked, my body covered in festering sores.

A pair of radiant angels drape a dirty sackcloth over my head. From above, a drop of the savior's blood falls on my back. The sores evanesce and the sackcloth begins to glow—brilliant and white, like the angels attending me.

My shame is replaced by indescribable joy.

"Thank you, Lord."

Once again I hear the voice. "*Samuel.*"

"Yes."

"*Behold.*" I see Him forgiving the very people who have driven a spear into his side, who have scourged him, beaten him, mocked him. And then...

Another image appears.

Words. Whose meaning I already understand, yet refuse to acknowledge.

"*Forgive, as you have been forgiven.*"

Brent Stringer sits at a table, his hands chained. I am there on the other side of the table. Our heads are bowed, my Bible rests between us. He is weeping, nodding. Repentant.

"*Go to him, Samuel.*"

"Lord?" I had never had such a clear vision before, but this could not be. I was appalled.

"*Befriend him.*"

"I can't do that, Lord."

"*Forgive.*"

I stepped back from the fireplace, wishing this had been another nightmare. I shook my head, trying to clear it. There was absolutely no way I would ever forgive Stringer, much less befriend him.

"No." My jaws ached from clenching. My hands shook violently. I gripped the Bible as if I could choke the life from it. How could anyone ask this of me? Brent Stringer deserved to burn in Hell, to have his eyes eternally plucked out by ravens, his entrails torn from his belly and gnawed by rats.

In an urgent whisper, the voice from the fire spoke again—gentle, yet firm. "*Forgive us our trespasses...*"

"NO!" With a tempestuous grunt I hurled the Bible at the voice at the fireplace, shattering the wine glass. Crimson brandy bled darkly onto the hearth, onto the wood floor. I stormed out of the living room without even looking back. What kind of insane dreams and visions were these anyway?

I leaned back against the wall, sank to the floor and buried my face in my knees. "Why, God? Why!"

No voice this time.

Only the sound of crackling flames.

And a growing rumble.

Before my eyes, shadows danced on the wall. Then came the acrid fumes. I leapt to my feet and stuck my head back into the living room. The top of the hearth, the rug beneath it, ablaze. I ran over and tried to stamp it out. But the glowing embers flew up and the fire ran down the rug and under the curtains. Within seconds, everything that seemed it could catch fire did.

The entire house would go up in flames.

CHAPTER NINETY-ONE

A long, hot shower, herbal tea and vegging with truTV while lying down on the sofa would ordinarily have done the trick. But tonight Rachel just couldn't rest her mind. Her feelings for Sam had simmered for almost three years. Now everything moved at frightening pace. At least it was mutual.

Sam had been a widower for as long as she'd known him. Still, it felt like she was in love with a married man. Could he ever love her the way he'd loved Jenn?

Don't be pathetic, Ray.

She took a sip of tea and despised her insecurity. The television announcer's voice droned on about an unsolved homicide. Rachel yawned and clicked it off with the remote. She'd had enough of murder cases. Time for bed.

Running her fingers through her long, ebony hair, Rachel stood in front of her dresser mirror and noticed that her blouse had been open a button lower than usual, revealing a subtle glimpse of cleavage. Not exactly buxom, but what she had was actually quite pretty.

Cute, even.

She blinked in surprise. Plenty of women dressed this way. But she never went out of the house like this. Had it become undone when she and Sam started pawing each other? Had she subconsciously left it that way?

What must he think of me? And at the same time, she almost hoped he'd noticed. *You're crazy, Ray.* Staying chaste for some thirty years could make a person that way. She meant to be a pure woman. But she was a woman nonetheless. Best guard against temptation and focus on Aaron's case. And helping Sam readjust to society.

Rachel shed her clothes, sat at her dresser in a white satin robe and brushed her hair. That look on Sam's face when he thought they were going to die in a car accident—all for a fleeting moment of passion. It made her smile, nearly made her laugh out loud. A few tiny lines gathered at the outset of her eyes. Laugh lines? No. She hadn't truly laughed for most of her adult life. Though she certainly had it in her.

Just ask Joey.

The smile withered. Lord, how she missed her big brother, the pranks they used to pull, like hiding *Poh-Poh's* dentures, dropping water balloons on that crabby, old Russian lady from their fourth floor apartment in Chicago.

All those years, Joey had always been there for her, always helped her. If only she'd been able to do that for him before he got his throat slashed while doing life at Cook County. For a crime he did not commit.

When she finally got herself under the covers, she realized just how exhausted she'd been. Sam's exoneration wasn't just a relief, but a victory, both personal and professional. His reciprocation of affection was both comforting and validating.

For the first time in years she could now breathe easily. God had not forgotten the suffering of the falsely accused. Finally, she could afford herself the luxury of a relationship.

Don't mess this up.

She turned over on her side and slipped her hands under her pillow. The clock radio read 2:30. It took long enough, but she might finally be able to sleep now. She didn't even realize that her eyelids had fallen shut until she was jolted by the cell phone buzzing on her nightstand.

Not bothering to look at the caller ID she answered. "Sam?"

CHAPTER NINETY-TWO

After three extra hours at the station, Lieutenant Jim O'Brien was finally heading home. One of the advantages he enjoyed over his married buddies was putting in all the overtime he wanted without worrying about an irate spouse or clamoring kids. He came and went as he liked. Almost made being single and forty-five bearable.

Still, it would've been nice to come home to loving arms, a hot meal, and stories about his incredibly smart and talented kids—the way his married buddies did every night. Jim came home to Millie, a fat orange tabby who barely opened one eye when he stepped into his condo. Unless, of course, she was hungry.

Driving down Camino del Gato in the wee hours of the morning, any sound out of the ordinary, an occasional car or truck passing, crickets chirping in the crisp breeze, felt like a disturbance in the force.

So when a Rancho Carmelita fire engine raced ahead of him on the single lane road, honked so loud it nearly scared the crap out of him, Jim pulled over to the shoulder, slapped the magnetic flashing beacon on his roof and tailed them.

The curtains caught fire as if they'd been doused in high octane gasoline. Out of sheer instinct, I ran to the kitchen and opened the cabinets beneath the sink, where we used to keep a fire extinguisher.

Used to.

For a moment, I considered filling a bucket with water, but I realized that I would probably run into the same problem: *used to* have a bucket. I ran back only to find that the fire had now spread to the adjacent curtain. Gradual, but not slow enough.

The curtain on the left fell to the ground and sent glowing ashes into the air. I grabbed my duffle bag and bolted out the front door. Out in the middle of the cul de sac, I called 911 on my cell. After that, I gave Rachel a quick call. She'd be right over. I'd have gone to Dave's next door, but he was out of town.

Flames leaped into the night air. Smoke spewed out of my front door. The alarm mounted to the outside of my house began to ring. I stood outside in the middle of the street and watched my living room burn. Lights came on in the surrounding houses. Faces peeked out from behind curtains and vertical blinds.

Within minutes, the fire department arrived. If you've never seen these guys get their gear setup and attack a burning house fire, you don't know the meaning of efficient. To my surprise, Jim O'Brien showed up and came to my side. "First night back and already you're causing trouble?"

I couldn't speak, just shook my head.

He began to ask me questions which, not surprising, were meant to determine if any foul play was involved. Finally, I said, "To the best of my knowledge, my own stupidity caused it."

The fire fighters worked quickly, yet remained calm and methodical. Some initial motion within but not a lot of noise. Fifteen minutes and they were wrapping things up. It was over. One of them came over, removed his mask and said, "Damnedest thing I've ever seen."

"How bad?" I asked.

"Well, the room had no doors, you know? Opens to the hallway and the dining room, which opens to the butler's pantry, which opens to the kitchen. Should've spread all over the house. But it acted like a compartment fire. Amazing."

The fire engine pulled out of the cul de sac and flashed its beacon without sounding its siren. The entire neighborhood was awake anyway, gawking at the scene. Some from their open doors and some from their windows. Welcome back, Sam.

"The rest of the house is fine," Jim said. "Don't do any cooking tonight, okay?" I nodded my appreciation. He got back in his car and drove off just as Rachel pulled into the driveway.

"Oh, Sam," she said, pulling her jacket tighter around her shoulders. "You all right?" Rachel shivered.

"Been better." I put my arm around her and held her close.

The tattered remains of the living room curtains hung like dead leaves in the windows. I would not mention the dreams or the voices. She'd think I was insane. And cliché. Who was I anyway, Moses? Instead of a burning bush, God spoke to me in a burning fireplace? Right. Was it even God? What about that devilish nightmare?

"Rachel, could I spend the night at your place?"

"My place?"

"I'll stay on the sofa."

She looked back at the house. "What happened in there?"

"I was careless, threw something in the fireplace."

"You look like you've seen a—"

"So, can I?" She hesitated for a moment. I understood her pause. But hormones be damned, I was so shaken, they wouldn't be a problem tonight. "Please, Rachel. I can't spend my first night here."

"Of course." She put her hand behind my neck and pulled my face down to her lips. I thanked her and went back to lock the door.

"Don't worry," I said as I climbed into her car. "I'll be a perfect gentleman."

She inserted the key, started the engine and grinned.

"It's not you I'm worried about."

CHAPTER NINETY-THREE

Except for my rude snoring that kept Rachel awake most of the night, I had indeed been a perfect gentleman. So she said. She was going to a deposition downtown and dropped me off at my house on the way. As she left, she blew me a kiss.

The first thing I noticed when I stepped into the foyer was the absence of that musty, smoky, post-fire odor. You'd never know anything had happened. One look in the living room corrected that perception.

Slats of golden sunlight sliced through the air and illuminated the charred remains of the sofa, the rug and curtains. Ash-tainted puddles gathered around the hearth. I brushed a couple of glass shards away with my shoe and crouched down. I thought of the fire from which City on a Hill had just recently recovered. The hate crimes committed against City on a Hill because of their support for me. And I remembered Lorraine, who in effect paid for her belief in me with her life.

I continued in, scanning the damage. All these years, I had managed not to be angry with God by pretty much ignoring His existence. But last night was too much. Yet, I felt a twinge for reacting so rashly. It was Jenn's Bible, after all, one of her most beloved possessions. And I pitched it into the fire. *I'm going to hell.*

Fixed on the ashes within, I wondered if the voice would return if I relit the fireplace. Then I noticed something under the black debris.

No. It couldn't be.

I reached in, brushed away the soot and felt its texture under my fingertips.

Impossible.

I grasped it firmly and stood. Blew a layer of ashes off and wiped away the rest.

It was Jenn's Bible. And it had not burned. Practically untouched. I leafed through the pages from Genesis to Revelation. Not one page singed. I had experienced miracles first hand. But this truly astounded me. So much so that in the absence of my mind, the Bible fell from my hands and landed with a heavy thump on the floor. I could still remember that voice calling my name.

Sssamuel. If it had really been His voice.

How could I possibly do what He asked?

The nightmares hadn't returned. Which was helpful in my getting reacclimated. Nor had I heard any more from that voice which urged me to forgive and befriend Brent Stringer. And this was helpful because in my second week back, I had to testify against him a deposition. Speaking the truth never felt so good.

Despite that progress, two things plagued me in the days of my custody battle with the State. One: No matter how early I went to bed, no matter how tired I felt, I simply couldn't sleep well. I'd toss and turn all night, fall asleep for a bit, then awaken with my heart racing for no apparent reason. At best, I'd get about three hours total.

And two: I could not find a job. Been there, done that. During my trial, no one would hire a murder/rape defendant. But now more than ever, I needed to find gainful employment, as it was the one technicality that the judge used against me. Without financial stability, I had no means of supporting my son, paying his medical expenses.

The termination of his life support pressed forward as scheduled. Less than seven weeks left. Despite my hope in God's promise, I wondered if my refusing to listen to His voice hindered my prayers for Aaron. Accusatory voices kept whispering, *Faithless hypocrite!*

On a Tuesday morning in early November, I opened my eyes and beheld what looked like a dark stain on the wall, up in the corner under the crown molding. Odd. It hadn't rained last night. And even if it had, water stains would take longer to become that dark. A shadow, perhaps.

I sat up, rubbed my eyes and looked up at the wall again. The sun wasn't coming through that side of the house. It wasn't a shadow. On closer examination, I noticed that this form on the wall had turned deep red. Like blood. Like those three dimensional Magic Eye posters that were so popular in the 90's. But those images didn't move or change shape. This form began to morph with an oozing fluidity. I stumbled back and braced myself on the door frame.

Samuel.

That voice. Profound, resonant. The stain took on an unmistakable form. The face of a man, blood dripping from his brow. A crown of thorns. Looking right into my eyes. My soul.

"Samuel."

The reply became ensnared within my throat. "I'm...here, Lord." Instead of judgment, I found something unexpected in His eyes. Compassion. For me. If I were anything less than certain, I might have believed that insanity had set in.

"Samuel, do you believe in me?"

My legs became gelatinous. "Yes, Lord." I lowered my head. Shut my eyes. I was not afraid.

"Forgive, even as you have been forgiven."

"Samuel," He said, again. "Do you love me?"

Yes.

And before I could say another word, He said, "Samuel Ian Hudson, do you trust me?" There was so much I wanted to ask, so much I needed to know. But in the time it took to blink, He was gone.

I found myself lying on my pillow, having just then opened my eyes. This was entirely too real to be a dream. The stain was gone. Had it ever been there? But to this day, I still remember the voice.

And what it compelled me to do.

CHAPTER NINETY-FOUR

I kept my experience with the apparition of Christ to myself for the next couple of days. Who would believe it anyway? I hardly believed it myself. Still, it nagged me. Could it really have been a divine message?

A week later I attended a service at City on a Hill with Rachel for the first time. She was glad that I had been the one to bring up going to church. Hiding behind an uneasy smile, I stepped into the church where several members came up to greet me. Alan and Samantha from the Bible study group waved from across the sanctuary as the worship band did a sound check. We took a seat and Rachel held my hand. "You okay?"

"Yeah. Great," I said, almost truthfully.

"You seem a little tense."

"I was thinking about Lorraine." The arsonists were never caught, but they had made it clear why they hated this church so. I wondered how they felt about what they'd done—especially that Lorraine had died in the fire—when news of my exoneration came out.

Rachel lowered her eyes. "It's hard to come into this new building every Sunday and not think about her."

"And too, I haven't been in a church since I was a six."

She patted my arm and leaned on my shoulder. The bandleader

said a brief prayer and for the next half hour led us in a set of contemporary Christian praise and worship songs. There's nothing quite so uncomfortable as being clueless amidst a crowd of people singing their hearts out, clapping and dancing for joy to songs they all know by heart. Despite the lyrics projected onto a huge screen, the only song I could sing was their jazzed up version of *Amazing Grace.* I joined in the applause at the end of the singing as the leader pointed a finger heavenward. This wasn't half bad. In fact, it was kind of fun.

It was the first time I'd seen Pastor Dave in his role as a preacher. He never stood behind the pulpit on the stage. Instead he preached in front of the pews, up and down the aisles, between them. He shared some amazing stories of how he and the mission team helped rebuild houses lost to flash floods down in Cabo San Lucas. After the sermon, he made some announcements—a deacons' luncheon at 1:00, Food and Clothes for the Homeless at 3:00 downtown. Then came the welcoming of visitors.

I slid down into my seat. Rachel elbowed me. There were three people visiting. After they were introduced, a pair of ushers handed them welcome brochures and bestowed them with Hawaiian leis. "If there are no other visitors..." Pastor Dave said, scanning the sanctuary. He stopped right at me and his face lit up. "Well! Everyone, we have a very special guest with us today."

The stigma of my criminal conviction warmed my cheeks. I sank lower, still. Rachel raised her hand, stood and pointed down to me.

"Rachel," the Pastor said, "would you like to introduce our honored guest?"

Ears ablaze, I stood and whispered, "Oh, you're so going to get it."

She just winked and turned to address the congregation. "I'm sure some of you already know." She nudged me and I turned around. I might as well have been looking into a mirror, for just about every face bore the very uncertainty I felt.

At that moment, Pastor Dave came to my side and patted me on the back. "Folks, this is the man you've spent the past three years praying for. Sam Hudson!"

Instantly, eyes brightened with recognition. Smiles emerged. A wave of applause swept the hall. Dave shook my hand and welcomed me. All around, congregants filed in to meet me, squeeze my arm, shake my hand.

"Welcome home, Sam," said an oddly familiar man. Then he took my hand and gave me a little brown paper bag.

"Jerry!" The quiet man from the Bible study group who always carried a bag of pistachios with him wherever he went. He lowered his eyes to the bag and nodded. I wrapped my arms around him and gave him a massive bear hug. Timid as a church mouse, Jerry had been a quiet prayer warrior in all the time I knew him. In my darkest hours, he'd been there for me, along with the rest of the Bible study group. He smiled, picked a pistachio out of the bag and walked away. Rachel shrugged and giggled.

And finally, Samantha and Alan. Their daughter was still in Sunday school but they promised to introduce her again, later.

"Sam!" I said.

"Sam!" she also said, and we laughed. I kissed her cheek, shook Alan's hand. They were welcoming me into the fold. For the first time in years, I experienced something that was missing since it had been torn from my life.

Family.

Lunch was at Pat and Oscar's in Mira Mesa, Dave insisted on buying. He invited Rachel and me along with Jerry and Samantha. Alan had to take their daughter to a play date. We ate *al fresco* and basked in the warmth of the sun, of new and renewed friendship.

Samantha asked me about life in prison. While I described it, she covered her open mouth, trying not to appear overly incredulous. "Must've been just awful for you." She reached out and touched my hand. "You never told us it was that bad."

"I didn't want to depress you guys. Would have spoiled your

visits. But God's been with me," I said and took a bite out of a breadstick slathered in butter. "I just... Aaron's got to come through."

"Rachel's doing her best," Dave said, picking a proffered pistachio out of Jerry's paper bag. "But you know, this battle isn't going to be won in the courts."

"How do you mean?" I said.

"For our struggle is not against flesh and blood, but against the rulers, against the authorities, against the powers of this dark world and against the spiritual forces of evil in the heavenly realms."

"Ephesians 6, right?"

"You've been reading your Bible," he said with an impressed grin.

"I've had some time on my hands."

Rachel reached over and filled our cups with lemon water. She groaned an apology to Jerry, whose cup she'd knocked over. I got up to help her blot the spill.

"Sam," Dave said, "I was wondering, do you believe that God can do anything?"

"Well, if He's God, He can do anything."

"Is there anything you think he can't do?"

I sat and thanked Rachel for the water. "It's not a matter of if He can as much as if He will. Why?"

Dave leaned in closer. "I sense that you're facing an impossible situation. There's something you think you can't do, yet must." Had *he* received a word of knowledge? Ought I to mention my dream—or was it a vision—of Christ speaking to me? "You know, come to think of it—"

"Turkey Club for you sir?" The waitress said, placing my plate down in front of me and taking my number card from its stand.

"Thanks."

Our dishes came out at the same time and the conversation was diverted. Dave said a blessing and we spent the next half hour enjoying our food and discussing lighter subjects. Sometimes a continuance is just what's needed.

When the meal came to an end, I decided that I needed to ask someone about this dilemma that afflicted my sleep. Sooner or later, Rachel was going to ask why I looked so tired every day.

"All right," I said, "You've all been Christians a lot longer than me." Rachel put her fork down and wiped the corner of her mouth with a yellow napkin. Curiosity filled her eyes. "We all believe that God can do anything, right?" I said.

Nods.

"And there's nothing that He can't do, even if it contradicts the laws of nature, of science."

Yes.

"We call those Miracles, right?"

"Is there a point in there somewhere?" Rachel asked, squeezing my hand gently.

"Okay, maybe I'd better just go ahead and ask," I said, my cheeks warm, and not from the sun. "Here's the deal." I went on and described in detail everything from the demonic nightmare, to the voice in the flames, to the face of Christ. When I finished, I anticipated a huge wave of laughter. Or uncomfortable smirks. "Couldn't have been real, could it?"

Not a word.

"I don't know," Rachel said, her face static.

I held my breath for a while and then exhaled. "I knew it."

Samantha however, tapped my hand. "I think you're crazy to doubt it."

"What?"

"For one thing," Dave said, "the visions. Nothing you heard contradicts what scriptures teach. Forgiving ones enemies, while revolutionary in concept, is one of the pillars of Christ's teachings."

"Maybe it was all my imagination."

"I don't think so," said Samantha, looking around.

Jerry crunched some more nuts. "Nope."

"If it was," said Dave, "I'm sure you'd have imagined something more palatable. I mean, why would you conjure up something so distasteful?"

Jerry said, "I'd imagine pistachios." More shells, more crunching.

"Think about it," said Dave. "Have you a deep seated desire to forgive Brent Stringer?" I didn't answer. Of course not. "Is it unlike God to ask his people to do something that seems impossible, but to have faith in Him?"

Moses led the Israelites out of captivity, parted the Red Sea. Jesus walked on the water and told Peter to walk out to join him. God asked Abraham to sacrifice his son, Isaac. A chill went through me. "No. I guess not. It seems just like Him."

"And finally," the pastor said, "the word of knowledge *I've* been given. From the moment I touched your shoulder back at church. I sensed you were facing an impossible challenge. You just confirmed it."

"You're right. It is impossible." Moments like these, when you realize something awful, or awesome is going to happen, you expect to hear the low-pitched droning of an ominous orchestral movie score to underline the scene. Instead, I heard birds chirping in the trees above, a large UPS truck rumbling by Mira Mesa Boulevard. I realized then that it had been real.

"God wants me to forgive Brent Stringer."

CHAPTER NINETY-FIVE

They all seemed intrigued by this epiphany, excited that I'd experienced God's supernatural manifestation. But not Rachel. Her features darkened.

"I'm not sure I agree," she said. All eyes but Jerry's turned to her. "I mean, sure, God speaks to us. Once in a while, I get words of knowledge myself. But this?" She turned to me with apologetic eyes. "You want my honest opinion, right?"

I nodded.

"I'm not convinced that God would ask this of you," Rachel said.

"Why not?" Samantha said, passing me a piece of devil's food cake.

"Look, Brent Stringer is evil. I mean, he's got to be demon-possessed. I know Jesus preached forgiveness, but the Bible doesn't forbid capital punishment for those who deserve it." Rachel's agitation increased with her volume. The trial lawyer in her emerged. "And trust me, if you'd seen the evidence, seen the collection of fingernails, hair, photos and keychains, you'd be the first to pull the switch!"

"It's okay. Take it easy." I pressed down on Rachel's shoulder, guiding her back down into her chair. She shrugged my hand away, turned away from the table and muttered something indistinct. "What was that?" I said.

"I said, he needs to be punished!"

Samantha reached a comforting hand to her, but I shook my head. Don't worry, she'll be okay. "I'm sorry everyone," I said.

"Think nothing of it." Dave put down a gratuity for the servers.

Rachel simmered with her back still turned to me. It was quite a shock to see her react this way, but I understood how she felt. Finally, she turned around. Her expression softened once again, she said, "Sorry. I'm not usually this—"

"Oh please, sister," Samantha said. She reached out and took her hand.

"I just can't...I just don't think you should jump to conclusions," Rachel said to me. "Unless you know for sure it's from God."

I put my hand on her shoulder and caressed. "But what if it is?"

CHAPTER NINETY-SIX

Life was returning to normal, if you could call it normal. The fight to regain custody of Aaron continued daily, as did the search for a job with sufficient income to overcome the legal technicality.

From a superficial glance, you'd never know I was unemployed. I kept myself well-groomed, my clothes, though three years out of fashion were clean, and I lived in a nice house. My résumé, however, was probably collecting dust in the offices of several law firms for whose positions I'd applied. A 'no thank you' letter or phone call, at least, would have been nice. Fine establishments such as McDonald's, Blockbuster Video, Ralph's and Walmart were much better about this. They rejected me on the spot.

One victory, though: the restraining order was finally lifted. Though it wrung my heart to see him so fragile, so pale, I went to see Aaron daily. Hours breezed by just sitting with him, reading *The Chronicles of Narnia* to him and most importantly, praying for him. My hopes rose and fell like the Powell/Hyde line in San Francisco. And there was still the issue of Brent Stringer.

From the moment I'd given myself to God, my entire life would be an act of faith. So, after a couple of weeks of struggling, against all human wisdom, against all the rage, I decided to put my faith into action and try to forgive the man who murdered my wife and little girl. *Try.*

The discovery stage of the *Kitsune* serial killer case was over. *Voire dire* had proven difficult and Jodi Bauer's motion for a change of venue was denied. The preliminaries were over in two days and the trial date set for next Monday. This meant that Stringer would be kept at San Diego Central until and during the trial. Much more convenient than visiting him at Salton Sea if and when he got convicted. Though I'd agreed to testify against him, I was torn. How could I do this and at the same time befriend him?

I drove downtown in a faded blue Nissan Sentra that someone from church had donated. Not one person at the jail failed to show surprise when I asked to visit Brent Stringer. I had to answer a million screening questions.

Yes, I'd consent to police monitoring.

Yes, I'd consent to a weapons search, contraband, etc., I knew the drill.

I was turned away.

The inmate was not willing to see me.

Fine. I'd done my part. Couldn't force Stringer, could I? My relief was short lived. I knew better than to wimp out like that.

The next day, I sent Stringer a letter requesting a meeting. I meant him no harm, but I would really like to speak with him before the trial. I returned to the jail with hopes that my letter had helped. This time I got a hand written response: "Drop Dead." *Is this some kind of joke, Lord?*

Over dinner at Rachel's place, she began to wonder if I should consider letting it go. "Why can't you just forgive him in your heart?" she reasoned. "Do you have to become his friend?"

"I've got to do this."

"If God really told you to, why doesn't he change Stringer's mind?"

"I just have to keep trying."

"Well," she scoffed. "If it makes you feel better."

"Oh, thanks for all your support!" My neck tensed.

She threw her napkin down, went to the kitchen and began to wash the pots and pans. We'd just started eating.

Steamed, I said, "You know, if you're wrong—"

"If *you're* wrong you'll be the biggest joke since *where's the beef!*"

I slammed my cup down so hard on the table that the dishes and utensils rattled. Noir, her little ebony cat, bolted out from under the table and disappeared into the bedroom. I got up and walked over to the kitchen. "So, that's it. You're afraid I'll embarrass you!"

"You're embarrassing yourself!" As soon as she said it, a twinge of regret appeared on her face. I didn't wait for her to say another word.

I slammed the door behind me.

What's the game plan? I wanted to know. Would I lose Rachel over this obsession to obey God? How was I supposed to befriend that freak, Brent Stringer, if he wouldn't see me?

That freak.

The very thought caused my blood pressure to spike. I finished praying and my fists were clenched so tight they'd gone cold. Given the opportunity, there was no doubt I could kill Stringer with my bare hands.

Ironic, since I'd just prayed for the opportunity to speak with him.

Forgive us our trespasses as we forgive those...

I didn't truly know what that meant. So, despite the late hour, I called Pastor Dave.

"It's not as simple as forgive and forget," he said.

"Good, because I can't forget."

"God can't either. Not in that sense. You don't forget chronologically, you forget practically. You no longer hold it against the offender, nor do you seek vengeance."

"Always thought I understood this. But it's entirely different when..." How could I possibly apply this to someone who'd murdered my wife and daughter?

"It is different," Dave said. "And yet, it's not."

"Do you think God can forgive someone like Brent Stringer?"

"A really smart man I know once said, 'If He really is God, He can do anything.'"

"Wise guy." The old family Bible sat open on the coffee table. Jenn's Bible, a pillar of her faith. Though all the answers seemed to be right there, in those pages, I still had to ask. "But *would* He forgive him?"

"What do *you* think, Sam?"

Parked outside San Diego Central, I sat in my car and wrestled with the toughest problem I'd ever faced. *God allows that bastard to kill my wife and daughter, and now He wants me to forgive him?* I'd tried and what did I get for my efforts?

But the question kept revisiting. *Do you trust me?*

Yes. I did trust God. But my faith was weak.

An anguished tear streams down my face as I imagine myself the judge, Brent's fate resting in my hands. Will I exonerate him, though he is in fact guilty beyond a reasonable doubt? Though he's shown not a trace of remorse?

Jenn, Bethie, and Aaron are standing in the gallery as I raise my gavel, about to pronounce my verdict. They smile and reassure me. To my own surprise, I pronounce him not guilty. He will be released from all culpability and punishment.

Instead of a tidal wave of resentment, I experienced peace. *It's going to be fine.* The hatred for Stringer, which had been hollowing me out, was now gone. No longer did it haunt me, grip me. The same relief and anticipation I experienced, that day I left Salton and the gate slammed behind me, filled my spirit.

I was free.

Once again at visitor check-in, I anticipated the rolling of eyes, the shaking of heads. "Please," I said to the guard at the desk, a petite African-American officer who you'd best not mess with. "Just ask him again."

"And what makes you think today will be any different?" she said, without bothering to meet my eyes. More typing at the keyboard.

"I don't know for sure that it will."

"Mmm-hmmm."

I took a step back and turned to the wall. There had to be some way. I steepled my fingers and pressed them to my forehead. *God, I could use a little help here.* The answer came in another vision, like water flowing down a brook, without the drama of previous visions. Then a word, or a name, rather:

Sally.

Had no idea what that meant, but I knew it was for this very moment. I turned back to the guard and rushed over. "Tell him I want to talk to him about...Sally."

The keyboard pecking stopped. "Sally."

"Just tell him, please."

"You're as crazy as he is," she said, getting up and reaching for her handset.

"Perhaps."

She phoned the instructions over to the guard at Brent's cellblock and gave me a dirty look when she said the name "Sally." When she hung up, she looked at me as if I'd grown an extra nose. "What's with you anyway? How can you even stand breathing the same air as him, after what he's done?"

"I'm on a mission of sorts."

Her fists went to her hips. "Don't you try none of that vigilante stuff. Save it for the court and let the legal system do its work. You hear?"

"Of course." Did she have any idea what the legal system had done to me? Anyway, I wasn't about to tell her I was on a mission from God.

"So you here with R.J.M.P. or something?" she said.

"R.J...?"

"Restorative Justice Mediation Program. You know, confront the offender, make him write you a check every month. Where's your mediator?" She looked over my shoulder.

"I'm not with R.J...whatever."

"Then what do you want?"

"You wouldn't believe me."

"Trust me, I heard it all."

No. She'll think I'm crazy. Even Rachel thinks so. Her phone rang.

"Really?" she said. "Well, all right. I'll let him know." She met my gaze, blinking and trying to speak with several false starts.

"What?"

"I don't believe it," she said.

"What did he say?"

"He said he'll see you."

CHAPTER NINETY-SEVEN

"You think you're pretty clever, don't you," Stringer said to me, his tone frigid. Seated and bound, the sleeves of his orange jumpsuit were rolled up to reveal a pentagram tattooed on his arm. In the middle was a goat's head and a triune epigraph which read Leviathan, Samael, and Lilith. The Sigil of Baphomet, a Satanist symbol I remembered from my college roommate's creepy friend who called himself 'Leege'—short for Legion.

"Apparently not as clever as you," I said. "Up till your arrest, at least." I took a seat and two armed guards stood at the ready, one behind me, the other behind Stringer.

"How do you know about Sally?" he asked.

"Hard to explain. It'd take some time."

"I've got nothing but."

"She was special to you, I know that much." The room was spacious enough, but his unblinking stare made me uneasy.

"What exactly do you want?" he said.

"I..." What would I say, that I forgive him and wanted to be his friend? The words just wouldn't form.

He scoffed and turned to the guards. "Think we're done here." He got up and they took him to the door.

"Wait," I said. He stopped, regarded me with glacial contempt as I rose and turned to face him. "I came here to tell you something."

"What? You hope I get the death penalty, that I get gang raped in prison, that I rot in Hell? How cliché. You're just like the—"

"I came to tell you that..." I swallowed a dry lump, "...that I forgive you."

As if for the first time in his life he was at a loss for words, he stood silent for a moment until the guard said, "You ready?"

Stringer didn't answer. Finally, a crooked smile twisted his mouth.

"Nearly had me there, buddy."

Questions floated around my head while I cruised the slow lane of the 163. How had Stringer taken it? Would he permit further visits? And if I had really forgiven him, why did I still feel such bitterness?

It was Aaron's birthday today, of all days. Hard to believe that he was now seven years old. He'd lived nearly half of his life in a coma. Now, in just another couple of weeks, if nothing changed, the State of California would take him from me.

Was I being selfish, as so many had accused? I found myself questioning my motives, wondering if indeed I was merely prolonging this because of my inability to face "reality." Didn't have to figure it out today. I was going to see my boy. Perhaps for his last birthday.

I arrived to find another visitor there with him. Someone I wasn't prepared to see just yet. "Rachel?" She was sitting at his bedside, her head bowed and holding his hands.

"I thought you were downtown," she said and got up. "I'll leave."

"No, wait." I took her hand. She kept her eyes from me. It was then that I noticed the balloons, a birthday card on his nightstand and a new teddy-bear, sporting a San Diego Padres uniform and cap.

"I should be leaving," she said.

I released her hand and said, "It's not so much that you disagree with me. I just... I can't stand that you're embarrassed by me."

"Really, I should go."

"Please. Just... hold on, okay?" I picked up the card and read what she'd written.

Happy Birthday, Aaron. May you awaken soon and learn what an awesome father in heaven you have. And what an awesome father you have on earth.

Suddenly, the gifts I'd bought him seemed insignificant. I put the card back. "Thank you," I said and I bent down to kiss her.

But she moved away and started for the door.

"Rachel, come on, would you just—?" her hand slipped down my arm and I caught it by the fingertips. Held gently. She held on for a moment too.

But then let go.

"You still don't get it," she said, sniffing and wiping the corner of her eye.

"Most of life, I don't get."

"You think I'm upset with you over a theological matter—should you forgive someone like Brent Stringer or not—but you just-don't-get it." She glared at me, her fingers trembling as she wiped her eyes again. It was hopeless. If I didn't know, she wasn't going to tell me, right?

She then looked to Aaron, stepped over and kissed him on the forehead and walked out the door.

"Rachel, please. What is it?"

She turned around and said, "I understand how hard it is to

overcome all your rage over what he did to Jenn, to Bethie, I really do. But not once— You haven't given it much thought have you? You're so ready to let him off the hook—" She stopped her rising pitch and accelerating words abruptly. "I know this'll sound self-serving, and I'm sorry. But... he tried to kill me too. Where's your anger over that?"

For the next two days she didn't answer my calls.

CHAPTER NINETY-EIGHT

Stringer finally agreed to see me again. Every now and then, I found myself checking my emotions. If this wasn't the hardest thing I'd ever had to do, I couldn't imagine what was. He seemed different today. That cockiness, that condescension I'd come to expect, strangely absent. Was it merely the act of a psychopath?

"Will we ever know why you did it?" I asked.

With eyes far off, he scraped his cuffed hands across the table, plopped them into his lap and slumped his shoulders. "I don't know what to say."

"How about starting with an apology?" He sighed and lowered his head. "All right," I said, "tell me about Sally, then."

Studying his thumbs, he smiled and chuckled. "Your pretty lawyer friend and that P.I. of hers, they're thorough."

"They don't know anything about Sally."

"Can't see why you'd want to deny it."

I pushed back in my chair. It scraped the floor so abruptly that Brent winced. "Take it easy," I said repositioning the chair.

"Sally was..." his eyes lit up. "She was my best friend."

"Rough childhood?"

"Think what you want. She was a puppy. How do you know about her?"

"You won't accept my answer."

Clicking his tongue, he said, "Probably not. Anyway, Sally was my first."

"You're first?"

"Oh, don't be sick. I just meant that Sally's was the first death I'd ever witnessed."

"And that's how it all started?"

"I don't know. You asked me about her, I'm telling you."

I held my hands up. "Fair enough."

"I wasn't like other kids—soccer, little league, video games. I kept to myself, read a lot. No siblings, no friends. Mom worked nights and days. Dad..." his jaw muscles rippled. "Dad was a drunk. Just hung around the house watching porno tapes and getting wasted. Couldn't hold a job if he tried. I was careful never to let him see me playing with Sally because he hated when I was happy."

"Why'd he get her for you then?"

"He didn't. She was a stray who just followed me home from school one day. I suppose Mom let me keep her because she felt guilty leaving me home alone with Dad all the time."

"So you killed the dog because you were angry?"

"No, you imbecile!" His eyes and nostrils flared. "My father killed her. Kicked her over and over. I was too scared to do anything, too scared to cry, even. When he was done, he went back into the house and had another beer. I watched Sally die a slow and painful death." The anguish in his eyes gave way to the look of intoxicated sensuality. "But that was when I realized just how exquisite it is... those last moments of life when life slips away. It's hard to explain. But man, what a rush! The final gasps, the fading consciousness." Thousands of miles away, he licked his lips and sighed. "I was hooked." He started whispering to himself a long list of names, with each, his eyes closed and he smiled.

This was Brent Stringer, award winning journalist, a best-selling writer? An army of red fire ants nibbling on my back would have felt less creepy. I stood and quietly lifted the chair legs off the floor.

"Here." I reached into my jacket pocket and handed him a new leather bound Bible that I'd picked up from that Christian bookstore in Clairemont. "This is for you." With his eyes still closed he sat there savoring something I didn't want to know about. I set the

Bible on the table before him and padded to the door. "See you."

Nothing.

The urge to go home and soak in a tub of hydrogen peroxide threatened to overtake me.

When I pulled into the driveway, I noticed Rachel waiting inside her car. She came out as soon as she saw me and met me at the front door with a stack of documents. "You got my voicemails, didn't you?" she said.

"Forgot to turn my cell on. Come in?"

We sat at the breakfast nook and I offered her a drink, which she declined as she leafed through the pages. "Need your signatures," she said. "State legislature's denied the governor any right to intervene. We're filing for a motion to take Aaron's case up to Federal Court."

I looked over the documents and signed them.

The reinforced concrete in her voice began to crumble. "I've got to be honest with you. It's not looking good."

"I'm going to see Aaron, right now." I handed her the papers.

"I'll come with you." She added, "If it's okay."

"Why are we doing this, Rachel?"

"Doing what?"

"We get into one stupid fight and we're reduced to attorney-client?"

"You walked out," she said, her eyes fixed on mine.

"If I'd stayed I would have said something I'd regret."

"So you don't regret anything you said?"

"I do, but—!"

Stop.

Deep breath.

"All right, this is crazy. We're chasing our tails." I reached out for her. She pulled back initially, but then responded by putting her hand in mine.

"You're right," she said. "This is petty."

"Isn't it?"

She touched her forehead to mine. "I'm sorry."

"Me too." I kissed the tip of her nose. "Move to retry?"

Her soft fingers caressed my face. "Granted."

Our lips brushed. My spine tingled. We were all right again.

Thank God. We got into my car and drove to Children's Hospital. Directly into the eye of the storm.

CHAPTER NINETY-NINE

The sound of chanting and singing and shouting and swearing, rose up into a putty-colored sky as we climbed the concrete steps out of the parking lot to the entrance of Children's Hospital. The first thing I saw was not the heads of protesters, but their picket signs and posters, bobbing irately.

LET AARON LIVE!
SET AARON FREE!
FIRST DO NO HARM!
TORTURE FOR RELIGIOUS GAIN!

Police barricades separated the factions on both sides and news reporters spoke into video cameras. I stopped midstride, grabbed Rachel's arm and turned around.

"Did you know about this?"

"They weren't here yesterday."

"Any chance we get in without being recognized?"

"Don't you want to say anything to the press?"

"Like what?"

"Let's leave," she said, glancing over to the mob. "We'll take our chances later tonight."

I considered it but became angry. "No, wait. It won't be any better later. And there's no way I'm going to let them keep me from my son."

"You sure?"

I took her hand and led her to the top of the steps. She started to jog ahead of me and would have broken into a sprint if I didn't hold her back and say, "Hold on. We walk. Keep your head high." Facing the entrance, hardly anyone in the crowd looked elsewhere. But then a woman with the SET AARON FREE sign turned, met my eyes and pointed.

"It's him!"

The crowd let out a roar of antiphonal strife. On one side, tearful men and women reached out trying to touch my hand. But at the same time, on the other side, snarling protesters gritted their teeth and hurled insults along with wadded up papers at their opponents.

We hadn't even gotten a quarter of the way to the entrance when a half-emptied Pepsi can flew at us from the LET AARON GO side. Rachel shrieked as it hit her in the ear and splashed all over her face and shirt.

"Legal whore!" shouted the man who threw it.

My hands and forearms became rigid. With all the ferocity of an ex-con, I marched over to him with my fist balled up.

"Sam, don't!" Rachel said.

Just as I got to the barricade, the man sneered and faded back into the shouting crowd. Lucky for him. But just then, a boy, about Aaron's age who sat on his father's shoulders shouted, "Yo!" I'd never seen a child's face so twisted with hatred. "You bastard!" he shouted, then leaned over and spat in my face.

"Tommy!" his father said and brought the boy down from his shoulders. He regarded me apologetically, but couldn't seem to utter the words. He just took the boy by the hand and led him away.

A hand bearing a white handkerchief stretched over to me. It was Dan DeMarco of Channel Seven News. His camera man stood next to him. "Mister Hudson," DeMarco said. "How're you holding up?"

Rachel pushed in front of me and shouted, "No comment."

My thoughts lingered upon little Tommy. So young, so angry. No child should know hatred like this. "Come on, Sam." Rachel tugged on my arm. "Let's go."

I took a couple of steps forward to return the handkerchief.

The reporter said, "Mister Hudson, a statement please."

Three or four more reporters pushed though on both sides closing on our position. I said nothing and started for the hospital entrance.

The crowd started up again.

Just as we reached the glass doors, I turned and looked at the crowd. Both sides angered me. None of them knew Aaron. And while I'm certain the purest among them believed they were picketing in his best interest, most of them were everything their opponents thought they were.

"What are you doing?" Rachel asked, realizing that I'd let go of her hand.

"I'm going to say something." Two steps forward and the clamoring died down. News cameras were aimed, microphones telescoped. I didn't speak until the drumming of my heart settled. Finally, with a deep breath, I looked up and into the crowd.

"You all seem to know what's best for my son." Though some in the distance probably couldn't hear me, I didn't shout. They leaned forward. "Truth is, I don't think any one of us really knows. Only God does." A whoop emerged from the Pro-Lifer's side. I shot them a glare. "And far be it from any of us to define or to limit divine wisdom. I appreciate all your prayers, but I don't believe what you're doing here is particularly godly."

"Yeah!" cried a woman on the Let Aaron Go side.

"That said, I'll be damned if I let politicians or special interest groups play God with my son's life! He is *my* son and to deny me legal guardianship because of a policy-serving technicality—!" The words caught. "It's not just an offense against me, it's against all of us."

Unsatisfied, the crowd started to grumble. I held a hand up sharply and shouted so loud my voice echoed down to the parking lot. "HEY!"

All eyes came forward.

"I have just two more things to say." I scanned the pavilion, made contact with as many of them as possible. "Go home and leave us alone!"

CHAPTER ONE HUNDRED

Each visit grew more difficult than the last. Aaron showed no signs of improving. His legislative death sentence didn't make things any easier. Rachel and I spent the entire visit pleading with God to work a miracle or two. Was I deceiving myself? Two hours later, we left through the back entrance to avoid the crowd. Neither of us said a word on the way back.

Rachel begged off dinner. She still had tons of work for my case and a new civil suit. Wouldn't be the best company with all that on her mind, anyway, she said. Dinner was once again a solitary affair.

The evening news featured my statement on the steps of Children's. I came across as self-righteous and pompous. Nice. Dan DeMarco faced the camera and said, "That was Sam Hudson, recently exonerated for the murders of his wife and daughter. No stranger to the media and the court, Hudson is reported to have been visiting confessed serial killer, Brent Stringer. Also referring to himself as *Kitsune*, Stringer will appear at his murder trial as it begins next Monday. Hudson is scheduled to testify against him as a witness for the State."

Later that night, Rachel arrived at my doorstep. She stepped in as soon as I opened the door and spread out her office across the living room table, the sofa and floor. "Sorry, I really need to finish this brief."

"Where were you?"

"I was in my office when you called."

"You didn't have to come."

She went back to organizing her papers. "I'm going to be pulling an all-nighter. Don't worry, I'll be a proper lady. Promise."

"It's not you I'm worried about. Need a blanket and pillow?"

"There it is!" She pulled out a sheet of paper and held it triumphantly. I've been looking all over for this lousy affidavit..." She stopped herself, realized I had no idea what she was talking about. She dropped it back into the organized stack and came over to put her arms around me. "I've been so caught up with this civil case."

"MacClellan vs. Donnell?"

"Wrongful death. I work on Aaron's case at night." She pointed to the paper. "That one's from a doctor at Johns Hopkins. Says that Aaron might not qualify as being in a persistent vegetative state. Something about neurological frequency response."

"Will he testify?"

"I'm working on him. As long as they're denying your guardianship, I'm going to try every angle." She shrugged. "I'm going for Constitutional rights tomorrow."

"Give it to me straight. Not like I'm his father, attorney to attorney. What are the chances?"

There was no smile on her face to start with. She managed to look even more severe. "I'm still praying."

That wasn't the answer I wanted to hear, but did ask for the truth. "All right, then," I said, rubbing the knot in my neck. "Make yourself at home. Not much in the fridge, but help yourself. Sure you don't need a blanket or anything?"

"Maybe coffee. Like I said, all-nighter."

At 4:06 AM I came downstairs to find Rachel curled up on the sofa, an empty coffee mug in her hand. I set it on the table, tucked her in with a comforter from the guest room and dimmed the lights.

"Just try to stay awake in court," I whispered and kissed her on the head.

CHAPTER ONE HUNDRED AND ONE

The news wasn't good. Rachel was still working on legal briefs and when she texted me: *Motion Denied.* Despite vocal opposition from various interest groups, the State's mandate to terminate Aaron's life support had prevailed. The *Union Tribune* quoted them saying, "We are loathe to incite another Terri Schiavo incident."

Incident? Since when were matters of life and death mere incidents?

The faith needed to sustain hope for Aaron and to befriend Brent Stringer was beyond my capacity. Still, after all I'd seen, after all I'd been through, I was determined to hold fast. Two more days passed and Brent was refusing visitation again. But on the third day something truly remarkable happened.

He asked to see me.

"What I don't understand is this guy hanging on the cross next to Jesus," Brent said, his tone calmer and more down to earth than ever before. "I mean, he's about to die and he's got the nerve to ask the Son of God to forgive him?"

A good question, but I still wasn't all that comfortable with this manipulative psychopath acting like he was letting his guard down. "So you've been reading the Bible I gave you."

"Not much else to do in a jail cell. You ought to know that."

Where was that smug air of superiority? That wise-cracking attitude? Was he just luring me into something only his mind could conceive? These visits were becoming quite a chore. Still, I made God a promise and I intended to keep it.

"What do you think, Sam? Do you think Jesus really meant it when he told that criminal he would—"

"What are you going on about?"

He shut his eyes, concentrating on God only knew what. Then he began to recite:

> *"We are punished justly, for we are getting what our deeds deserve. But this man has done nothing wrong." Then he said, "Jesus, remember me when you come into your kingdom."*
>
> *Jesus answered him, "I tell you the truth, today you will be with me in paradise."*

"That's from the gospel of Luke, Chapter Twenty-three. Just before Jesus died on the cross."

That passage came back to me as soon as he quoted it. "Yes, I do recall that."

"Do you think then, that it could mean that it's never too late?"

"I'm not God," I said, skeptical at Brent's sudden interest in salvation. Part of me wanted for him to continue rejecting it, so that he'd burn in hell. But to be honest, that was the part of me which wanted to rebel against what God had asked of me.

"Sam." A cold shiver crept up my neck when he said my name. "Help me out here. How can I be saved?"

"Don't ask me. I'm not a priest."

"Then what are you doing here? Why do you keep coming to see me?"

'*Because God told me to*' seemed too trivial to articulate. I just shook my head and stood up. "I'm not really sure anymore." I turned to the guards and they opened the door.

"Wait," he said. "Just tell me, what must I do to be saved?"

"You're pretty good at finding your own answers in the Bible," I said. "Look it up yourself."

This had to be another one of his acts. To what end, I would probably never know, but I wasn't buying it.

I was out of there.

CHAPTER ONE HUNDRED AND TWO

It disturbed me that my initial reaction to Brent's query about salvation was cynicism. Might not this have been God's purpose all along? That was what angered me. And at the same time, troubled me. He had supposedly received my forgiveness, why not God's? For the next few days I pondered this before returning to see Brent again.

The familiar aroma of Friday cafeteria fish wafting through San Diego Central as I made my way to the visitation room. Brent had shaved his whiskery mug, his hair now trimmed and combed. The only thing missing now was a suit and tie. What was I doing here? Had I truly forgiven him? Or was I just like every religious hypocrite I'd condemned throughout my life.

He stood to greet me. "Hey, bro!"

"Brent?"

"I'm so glad to see you," he said, his smile beaming.

"You are?"

Sitting in the meeting room, he seemed even more different than before. So much so that I became instantly suspicious. He regarded me as though reuniting with an old friend.

"Please, have a seat."

My brow tightened. I sat and scrutinized his face. "Okay, I give.

What's going on?"

"I have you to thank."

I turned to the guards, but as usual, they didn't return my gaze. "The trial begins in two days," I said. "You don't have time for games."

"My attorney's not going to be happy."

I shifted in my chair, leaned forward. "Help me out here."

"I'm thinking about changing my plea to guilty."

"You're—? Hold on. You're changing your plea?"

"Guilty as charged."

"Walden offered you a deal?"

The corners of his mouth pulled down and he shook his head. "No, I'd already agreed to tell him where the Samberg girls are buried. There's no deal on the table."

"You realize that you'll get the Death Penalty."

"Counting on it."

"I don't understand." My eyes fixed on his chained wrists resting on top of his Bible.

"A lot's happened since—Well, I've got so much to thank you for."

"What are you talking about?"

He took a deep breath, a story bubbling to the surface. "When you came that day, talked to me about my past, I was still—I don't know—on the verge."

I narrowed my eyes, trying to comprehend.

"You gave this to me," he said pointing to the Bible. "Man, I hadn't read the good book since my mom—since Sunday school."

"Where is she now?"

"Oh man, Sunday school," Brent said, nostalgia drawing his eyes towards oblivion. "That was a lifetime ago."

"Brent, your mother?"

"She and Dad both died when I was eleven." His smile fled. "And before you jump to conclusions, it wasn't me. You can check the Boston police records, June 25, 1975. Murder-suicide. Nice family, huh?"

"He killed her?"

"She killed him."

"I'm sorry." Wasn't sure I believed him, but why would he bother lying now? "Anyway. I didn't mean to snuff out whatever it was that was making you smile."

"It's all right, I'm cool."

"So tell me. What is it?"

"You're still testifying against me, right?"

I nodded.

"Good."

"I'm just not getting it."

"All right," he said, leaning forward. "You want the long version or the Reader's Digest?"

"Whichever."

"Long story short: I'm forgiven."

I shrugged. "I told you I forgave you, it's just sinking in now?"

"Took me a while, but when I finally started to believe that you meant it, it made me think, if you could forgive me, then maybe God could too. For everything."

It seemed too easy, too convenient. I had to admit, part of me felt disappointed.

Brent's eyes sparkled with sincerity. Disturbingly so. "So I asked to see Reverend Wilson, the chaplain."

"Don't tell me."

"I've accepted Christ, Sam. Don't you see? I'm saved." The guards stood in their usual position. As if they weren't listening. One of them clicked his tongue and shook his head.

Straightening up, I said, "Pardon me, but I'm finding this hard to believe."

"I don't blame you. Really. But it's true." He flashed a smile. "What's the matter, you don't think God can forgive me?"

"It's not a matter of if he can." I stood up and scratched the back of my head.

"I thought you'd be happy."

"Look, I don't know what to say, all right?"

"Why did you come to me in the first place? And you never explained how you knew about Sally."

"I told you, you'd never believe me."

"You never believed I could change."

"All right!" I said, gripping the back of the chair so hard my nails dug into the upholstery. "I came because I thought God wanted me to forgive you, to befriend you! You wanna laugh, go ahead! It's all a big game for you anyway, isn't it?"

In a freakish reversal of roles, Brent sat calm while I lost it. I had never anticipated this. I thought for sure he'd be defiant to the end, burn in Hell for what he'd done. And I was supposed to be set free from all my bitterness.

"It's not a game," he said with a deep sigh.

"Then it's an act! You're a psychopath and you're faking it." Deep down I hated myself for saying it, because there was always a possibility, no matter how small, that he might be sincere.

"You'll never know how great God's love is, how great His forgiveness is, until you've been as guilty as me."

"If that's what it takes, then I never want to know."

"Sam, listen. All my life, I was convinced that I was going straight to hell. So you know, what difference did it make if I—?"

"Guard!" My thoughts turned dark, like drops of blood infusing a once clear glass of water. Condemnation boiled to the surface and nearly made it past my lips.

"Sam, wait. Hear me out."

I lifted my hands to deflect his words and went to the door. "If you think they're going to reduce the sentence just because—"

"No," he said. "I still have to pay."

"Got that right!" I stormed out.

For the next half hour , I sat in the parking lot yelling at God and cursing myself.

CHAPTER ONE HUNDRED AND THREE

The weekend was miserable. Having tossed and turned until dawn both Friday and Saturday nights, I could barely function during the day. The only person I spoke to was Rachel, and that was only for a few minutes. We were so involved with Aaron's case that I hadn't gotten to telling her about Brent.

Both Rachel and I were sleep deprived. I had just gotten my first solid hour of sleep when the doorbell rang. Must have been ringing for a while, because an urgent pounding accompanied it. My head still in a fog and my butt still in my shorts, I got out of bed and noticed the voicemail indicator flashing on my cell phone.

More pounding.

"I'm coming!" I opened the door and found Rachel just at the end of a call on her cell phone.

"Are you all right, Sam?"

"Yeah, I just dozed off."

Rachel stepped forward and entered the house. "I've been calling you for an hour." As she entered the house, she seemed distracted.

"Everything okay, Rachel?"

"Yeah, I just..." She sat down in the sofa and from the look on her face, I could tell she needed me to say something to get the conversation started.

"Oh, I need to tell you," I said, suddenly remembering. "Have you heard?"

Rachel opened her eyes and blinked at me.

"Brent Stringer."

Her brow knitted. "I've been a bit involved."

"I think he's going to change his plea."

"What?"

"Any idea why he'd do that?" I asked, more curious than embarrassed at my toddler-like grasp on criminal legal strategy.

"Besides the fact that he *is* guilty?"

"He'll get death."

She started putting the documents back in the manila folder. "I don't know, maybe he just wants to get it over with without drawing the trial out. Saves on taxpayer dollars, anyway. Didn't you ask him why?"

"I was so thrown by it, I just left."

"So how have your visits been going?" she asked.

"I don't know. When I told him I forgave him, he just laughed it off. But a couple of days ago, he opened up about his childhood, how he became fascinated with death while watching his dog die."

"Okay, now that's just creepy." Rachel grimaced, shuddering at the thought.

"I'm pretty sure that was the beginning of it all because—"

"Sam?" Rachel whispered through gritted teeth. Her face began to crumple and the hinges of the floodgates came apart, one screw at a time. "They've denied our motion."

"What?"

She began to sob. I went over to hold her but she was inconsolable. Finally, she lifted her face and said, "I keep asking myself if I'd missed something, a precedent, a loophole, but it's just no good!"

"What about challenging the guardianship issue? I'm still waiting to hear from a firm or two."

"Even if you were to start a new job today, they'd require at least six months of steady and sufficient income, along with continuous health benefits. Never mind that our church is holding half a million in escrow, with affidavits of financial support. They don't care."

"I can't believe it." My mind raced with any possible idea or alternative. All but prayer had been exhausted. Then it struck me like a semi. In just two days, by court order, my son would die.

Pastor Dave and the church group visited that night. They'd missed me and Rachel at church and brought us dinner. Afterwards, we adjourned to the family room and carefully navigated the emotional minefield.

"What's God been telling you recently?" Dave asked me.

"Actually, he's been pretty quiet."

"You've had enough burning-bush experiences for a lifetime," Rachel said.

"To be honest," I said, "I haven't taken the time to really pray recently. Not sure He'd want to hear from me now, anyway."

"Why's that?" Alan said.

I explained what had happened with Brent, how I couldn't believe that he'd just accept Christ after a lifetime of murderous cruelty. How I doubted his sincerity. "Guess I'm disappointed with God," I said. "If someone like Brent could just get off scott-free, after all he's done."

"But he's still getting the death penalty," Dave said.

"My forgiving him was hard enough. But I'm just not sure he deserves to be saved," I replied.

"He's yanking everyone's chain," Rachel said. She grabbed a throw pillow and hugged it to her chest. "Think about it. He's cunning, manipulative, displays a grandiose sense of self-worth, criminally versatile, a pathological liar. Classic psychopath."

Dave leaned forward, his brow furrowed. "If I recall my psychology classes correctly, he should also fail to accept responsibility for his own actions. According to Sam, he's not even going to contest the death penalty."

"Has his attorney dropped him yet?" Rachel asked, and took a sip of tea. "I mean, has she even heard about his change of heart, much less his change of plea?"

I shrugged.

Samantha spoke up. "I've been giving it some thought and I have to say, I'm with Rachel. It's all too convenient. He's just saying whatever he thinks the jury or the judge will want to hear. I'm sure he's got a big surprise up his sleeve."

"All right, everybody," I said as the discussion heated up. "I'm the one who has to testify tomorrow." Rachel turned around and leaned apologetically against my shoulder. "This is a compelling topic," I conceded. "But I still have to get up on the stand and testify against him. When Jodi—"

"—The Piranha," Rachel added.

"When she cross-examines me, I'm sure she'll bring up my visits and even use them against me. I'll be impeached in a second."

"In case you've forgotten," Rachel said. "Walden's pretty sharp, himself. He'll recover you on the redirect."

"Problem is, I can't just take Brent at his word," I said. "Dave, can we know if someone is really saved?"

"Forget it," Rachel said. "Psychopaths don't change. Ever. Stringer's lying."

"I agree," said Samantha.

"But is it impossible for God to change him?" I said. "How can we know?"

Dave rested his chin on his fist, hemmed and hawed a bit then said, "A tree is known by the fruit it bears." I seemed to be the only person who didn't get it. Everyone else was ready to drop it now. An awkward silence fell. Soon all eyes were on me.

Dave said, "Guys, the reason we're here tonight is to support

Sam. We've been avoiding it, but we ought not leave this house until we've addressed it." He regarded me with a poignant smile. "It's why you asked us over, right?"

I nodded.

At that moment, everyone put their arguments aside and encircled me. Dave said, "Let's pray for Sam, for Aaron." They each laid a hand upon me—my head, my shoulders—and began to pray for me, for Aaron.

Thy will be done, on earth as it is in Heaven.

CHAPTER ONE HUNDRED AND FOUR

Apparently, the media hadn't gotten wind of Brent's plea change. It would have been all over the Monday morning news, otherwise. Nevertheless, reporters swarmed the courthouse from the gray steps outside to the hallway that led to the courtroom.

Instead, the recent headlines announcing the beginning of the trial were accompanied by reports of Detective Anita Pearson's inadvertent and sordid cyber-affair with the person she later discovered to be the *Kitsune* serial killer. I would later learn that the detective had not shown for work that day, nor for the past two days. She was not returning her voicemails either.

I spent a good forty minutes with Thomas Walden going over my testimony. By the time we were done, I felt like the rung of a ladder. My story was important in establishing Brent's guilt, the horror of what he'd done, but as far as the D.A. was concerned, I was just a means to an end.

The morning sun hadn't yet burned through the thick marine layer. Pale fog and clouds blanketed the entire city. Rachel had come for moral support, but was consumed with paperwork in hopes of ever finding an eleventh hour miracle for Aaron.

While Walden and Bauer gave their opening arguments, I sat in the witness room reading the Bible for what seemed like an eternity. There had to be a verse or passage with pertinent wisdom. I prayed, sought a word of knowledge, a vision.

Nothing.

My thoughts were divided three ways between that soul-hollowing angst over Aaron, bewilderment at the big picture that was God's plan, and wondering what in all creation Brent was up to.

As for Brent, I was starting to incline towards Rachel and Samantha's belief that his ostensible salvation was nothing but a ploy. Or perhaps, despite his apparent joy, he had simply become suicidal and wanted to convey a more favorable public image, before taking his own life.

A knock came at the door.

I stood and a female deputy entered. The first thing I noticed was not her blue eyes, nor her fair hair. It was the radio transmitter clipped to the lapel of her beige uniform. And the gun holstered in her belt. I felt a slight pang as I remember Sonja Grace.

"You're on," she said.

Rachel shut her briefcase and came to my side. "Ready?"

"As I'll ever be."

"Good," she said and took my hand.

"The State calls Samuel Hudson," Walden announced.

The bailiff swore me in and I took my place on the witness stand. How odd to be here once again. As Walden asked his first question, my eyes were drawn to Brent. He was dressed in a dark suit with a red tie. Nothing on his face suggested a man who'd committed multiple counts of murder and rape, of one looking at a death sentence.

Nearly four years ago, I had sat in that very seat behind the defense table. Puzzling, how close the back of that chair sat to that wooden partition, the only thing separating the defendant from the public.

The honorable Janice Cunningham had permitted him to appear without handcuffs—something his attorney had insisted upon so as not to bias the jury. Seemed insane, but there he was, unrestrained. There must have been more than a few people in the jury box and gallery glad to see the gun strapped at the bailiffs' waist.

"Please state your name for the record," Walden said.

We went through establishing my identity, address and background. I then gave an account of the night Jenn and Bethie were murdered. Though I'd rehearsed it many times in my mind, made an allowance for the pain it might conjure up, I had no idea just how difficult it would be to relive that night in full detail. I started to choke on my words, quickly wiped the tears from the corner of my eye.

With not so much as a sympathetic word, Walden stared at me, his hands in his pockets, rocking on his heels. Get a grip, Hudson. Rachel kept watching me with concern. A couple of jurors dabbed their eyes.

Before we could continue, a small commotion erupted at the defense table. Jodi Bauer gesticulated violently, hissing at her client. The argument grew more intense.

"You can't do that! Not now!" Bauer said.

"Do it, or you're fired!" shouted her client.

Judge Cunningham glared down. "Counselor, is there a problem?" Bauer didn't answer. She continued waving her hands, arguing with Brent. "Ms. Bauer!"

"Tell her!" Brent shouted at his attorney.

The Piranha stood, her lips drawn tight. You could almost see the steam billow out of her ears. Many of the people in the gallery were leaning forward, gripping the backs of the chairs, not missing a word.

"Your honor, my client and I are—"

"Disrupting this trial," the Judge said. "Now what's the problem?"

Bauer huffed and said, "My client is contemplating a change of plea at this time. But I'm advising him against it. Clearly, in his current state of mind it would not serve his best interests to—"

"I am completely competent!" Brent shouted.

"Given the gravity of the charges, it would be malpractice for me to agree or advise a guilty plea without even a chance to defend him."

"I would like to hear opening arguments before I rule on that. Mister Stringer, would that be all right?" the judge said. "Take the time to seriously consider this."

"Yes, your honor."

"Also be aware that if you change your plea to guilty and the court accepts the plea, the court is to discharge the jury from giving a verdict in the matter and will find you guilty."

"Yes, your honor."

"The finding has effect as if it were the verdict of the jury, and then you shall be liable to sentencing accordingly." Cunningham paused and stared straight at Brent. "The State *has* recommended the death penalty."

He nodded and looked down.

"Please speak up for the record."

"Yes, your honor."

"Very well then. And Ms. Bauer?"

Just about to sit, Bauer stood up again. "Your honor?"

"Keep the histrionics to a minimum."

The Piranha nodded and took a seat again.

Walden continued, his questions going towards quantifying the losses I'd suffered, as a result of Brent's crimes. As if you could put a dollar amount on them. By the time Walden finished, I felt like I'd just sold my family to the state.

The Piranha stood to cross-examine me. She flashed a mouthful of flesh-stripping teeth. Her moniker had been well-earned. "First, Mister Hudson, let me say how sorry I am for your loss."

I dipped my head in acknowledgment.

She then turned so that as she questioned me, she was also facing the jury. "I'd also like to express my sympathies for the egregious errors of the District Attorney's office, which resulted in your spending almost four years in a maximum security—"

"Objection," Walden said. "Beyond scope."

Undaunted, Bauer continued the charge. "It was Mr. Walden who erroneously tried and convicted you—"

"Objection, irrelevant!"

"Sustained." Cunningham said.

Jodi snapped back, "I haven't asked a question yet."

"Then ask one, counsel," Cunningham said.

Satisfied that her first bite into Walden had drawn blood, Bauer turned back to me and said, "You've been visiting my client in jail, haven't you?"

"I have."

"What was the nature of these visits?" Walden had coached me to avoid looking in his direction when I wasn't sure about a question. But piranhas can smell blood. "That information isn't privileged, Mister Hudson."

I turned to the judge. She nodded. Answer the question.

"For one thing, I wanted closure."

"And did you find it?"

"I don't know." Brent was looking at me with concern. I averted my eyes as soon as I realized.

"Isn't it true, Mister Hudson, that after all my client has been accused of, after all your loss, that you told him you've forgiven him?" Walden stood up to object, but Cunningham shooed him back into his seat with two fingers.

"Yes," I replied.

"Thank you. And you brought him a gift too, didn't you?"

"Yes."

A wave of shuffling and murmuring snaked through the courtroom.

"Please tell the court what that gift was."

"A Bible."

"A Bible." The Piranha paced around before me with hungry eyes. "Are you aware that my client has since converted to Christianity? That you are to thank for—"

"Objection," said Walden. "The defendant's religious convictions have no—"

"Mister Hudson," Bauer didn't even wait for the judge. "Do you believe the teachings of the Bible?"

"Objection. The witness' religious beliefs are irrelevant."

"Overruled, the witness will answer the question."

"Yes," I said.

"You believe in the Bible, the Holy Scriptures of Christianity."

"Asked and answered," Walden said.

"Specifically," Bauer continued. "Do you believe in the Bible's message of forgiveness."

"Yes, but I don't see how—"

"Is it your testimony then that you believe that my client would be forgiven by God if he repented and accepted Jesus as his savior?"

"Your honor!" Walden exclaimed. "There's no foundation for this. The witness is neither a theologian nor a member of the clergy. Furthermore, *his* beliefs are not relevant to this case."

"This is a capital murder case," Bauer said. "It's my ethical duty to make every possible argument in my client's best interest."

"I'll admit, this is somewhat irregular." Cunningham said. "But I'll allow it.

I wasn't sure how to answer Bauer's question and was glad for this pause. But I was under oath. My innards began to knot up.

"Mister Hudson," Bauer said. "The question was, and I repeat: Would Brent Stringer be forgiven by God if he repented and accepted Jesus as his savior?"

CHAPTER ONE HUNDRED AND FIVE

"I'll rephrase the question," Bauer said after I took perhaps too long to respond. "As a Christian, do you believe that my client should be shown mercy, grace, and forgiveness?"

I caught myself staring at the worn chestnut rail. I pulled my head up, looked Brent in the eye. If he was putting on an act, it was almost believable. Finally, I answered. "If he sincerely repented and—"

"Yes or no, please."

Brent's eyes sought mine as if for approval. Desperate defendants and their attorneys would do anything. I started to wonder if the whole argument they'd had over the change of plea had been staged. Then Dave's words echoed in my mind.

A tree is known by the fruit it bears.

"I repeat," said Bauer. "Would he be shown mercy, grace, forgiveness?"

"If he is sincere, then yes. God would forgive him."

"Do *you* forgive him?"

"Objection!" said Walden.

"Withdrawn. During one of your visits, did you or did you not say to my client—and I quote, 'I forgive you.'"

"Yes. I did."

"Nothing further."

Already on his feet, Walden buttoned his jacket and approached the stand for his redirect. He strode right past Jodi, brushing shoulders.

"Religious convictions aside, do you actually believe that the defendant should, if found guilty, be allowed any reduction of his sentence? In light of all the women and young girls he's raped and murdered, all the innocent men like yourself, who he's framed and whose lives are forever marred?" Walden said, stabbing his index finger in Brent's direction.

It was dawning upon me that as a witness, I was no more than a marionette, both attorneys fighting for control of the strings. "Reduce his sentence?" I said. "I'm not even sure if *Brent* himself believes that."

"The question is, do *you*?"

"Objection," Bauer droned. "The witness' opinion on verdict or sentencing is irrelevant."

Walden smirked at her. "This is your line of questioning."

"Overruled," said the judge.

"Again, do you, Samuel Hudson, one of the many victims of this psychopathic killer and rapist, believe that he, the defendant, should receive any reduction in his sentence?"

I could admit that God would forgive Brent. But for him not pay with his life? I hadn't ever thought that through. If it were based solely on emotion, I'd answer negatively, without hesitation. "I'm not sure."

"Yes or no," Walden said, growing impatient.

"Give me a minute." I didn't know the Bible well enough. Never discussed Christian perspectives on capital punishment with Pastor Dave. "I think he should pay for his crimes. But I'm not sure the solution to murder is necessarily killing the killer."

Before I had a chance to consider what I had just said, a cold, yet familiar voice arose from the gallery and said, "*I* object." The crowd stirred.

"Order," said Judge Cunningham.

"You of all people, Hudson," the voice said. "You're trying to get him off the death penalty? You've been conspiring with him from the beginning! You, Kingsley, all of you!" Gasps and murmurs rose up as everyone now recognized that it was Detective Anita Pearson. Dark circles rimmed her bloodshot eyes.

"Order!" Cunningham shouted and rapped her gavel. "Detective, take a seat!"

Her gaze vacant, the Detective stood from her chair and approached the front of the courtroom. "You deserve to die every bit as much as he does," she said to me, and opened the wooden gate to cross the bar and enter the well of the courtroom. The court clerk lifted his head and turned back, regarding the judge with confusion. Was she about to make a speech?

"Detective, you are in contempt of court," Cunningham said. "Bailiff, escort her out!" The bailiff began to approach Pearson, who was now standing in front of the clerk's desk. An armed deputy also came forward from the back of the courtroom.

Just then, Pearson reached behind her back and pulled out her gun, aimed it straight at me. With an ominous click, the hammer cocked.

Rachel cried out to me with deathly inevitability.

I was going to die.

"No!" Brent shouted, and leaped up from his chair.

I squeezed my eyes shut.

Chairs hit the ground.

Sleeves and pant legs shuffled.

Then, a thunderous gunshot.

I tensed up, anticipating a bullet entering my forehead.

Another shot.

More screams.

The sickening thud of bodies hitting the ground.

I opened my eyes. The bailiff and another deputy had wrestled Anita to the floor. Her gun fell to the ground as the deputy twisted her wrist back. "It's justice!" Pearson cried through clenched teeth, her eyes feral, hair flailing as her head thrashed about. "Justice, God Dammit!"

Before her, Brent Stringer lay on his side, a crimson pool expanding on the floor by his chest. Two scarlet stains on his white shirt revealed that he'd put himself between me and Anita's gun. I went over to him.

He looked up with a faint smile. I knelt, unable to comprehend how I could possibly be feeling sorrow for him. "Do you really think..." he coughed and grimaced. "... God will forgive me?"

I reached out, grabbed his hand. Cold, trembling. "Remember that criminal, crucified next to Christ? Jesus told him, *Verily I say unto thee, Today shalt thou be with me in paradise.*"

He smiled. Coughed and winced. "Mercy." A tranquil smile came over his face, like that of a child, asleep and secure in the arms of a loving father.

CHAPTER ONE HUNDRED AND SIX

Local authorities took Anita Pearson into custody. She would later face murder charges. Her attorney, a partner from Jodi Bauer's firm, planned to argue temporary insanity, pending a psychiatric evaluation for trial competency. In the meantime she had been committed to Patton State Psychiatric Hospital, where Diana Napolis was sent for stalking and threatening Jennifer Love Hewitt, after a judge declared her incompetent to stand trial.

Brent's death troubled me more than I could have imagined. Had I answered in haste when I assured him that God would forgive him? Had he truly changed and found redemption? Or was this more of his psychopath games? I'd never know for sure. But one thing I did know and have held onto since:

A tree is known by the fruit it bears.

The fruit we bear from our hearts is not our words and attitudes, so much as they are our actions. And Christ said, *Greater love hath no man than this, that a man lay down his life for his friends.* Brent never meant to escape punishment for his crimes.

And his final act can only be judged by God.

CHAPTER ONE HUNDRED AND SEVEN

The Stringer case ground to an abrupt halt. Rachel and I spent the next day in civil court arguing an eleventh hour appeal with a judge who was apparently deaf.

And dumb perhaps, but not mute.

His vociferous condemnation of my cruelty towards my son caused the hairs on my neck to prickle. It fueled more than a few juicy headlines. But I'd grown accustomed to such nonsense. Any thought for my own reputation had long since been eclipsed by my concern for Aaron.

Hudson vs. California was dismissed with prejudice. My legal rights had been determined and lost, and the case could not be brought to action again. An appeal was possible, but that process would take a couple of weeks just to schedule on the already distended dockets of every potential judge. Aaron's court ordered termination date was slated for tomorrow.

I consider myself a strong man. Certainly toughened by three and a half years in a Supermax Prison. But that night, I clutched a photo album with all Aaron's pictures from birth until the last one we took of him, to my chest and cried myself to sleep at his bedside.

CHAPTER ONE HUNDRED AND EIGHT

It's like running a marathon, blisters bursting, skin peeling, only to arrive at the end and learn that you've been on the wrong track altogether. I'm sitting by Aaron's bed holding his hand, the warmth of which makes this even more difficult to accept. My tears moisten his frail hand.

I don't want to let go.

But I must. Jim O'Brien and another deputy are posted outside with the unenviable task of making sure that the law is upheld.

"I'll be right outside," Rachel says, bending down to kiss me.

They're doing it by the clock mounted on the wall. When the minute hand reaches the twelve, it will be over. My son will stop breathing.

"My precious boy," I whisper, a lump lodges in my throat. "Daddy did everything he could to fight for you." *You've got a purpose, don't You, God?* I suck in an anguished breath through my teeth. Don't You*?*

Aaron's chest rises and falls. He hears me, I know he does, and it twists like a jagged blade in my heart. Sinking my face in his hands, I am haunted by the images of my child, his first single-toothed smile, learning to walk, the way his big, green eyes transform into tiny slits whenever he laughs. The first time he looked at me and with purpose, said, "Da-da." Flying in my arms like an airplane down the hallway.

"You know I love you, Aaron." I am overcome with grief and anger and desperation and too many indescribable feelings. A natural death would be difficult enough. But to willingly and knowingly deprive my son of breath? It's like standing by and watching someone kill him, and not doing a thing about it. Goes against everything that makes me a father, a human being.

I want to curl up into a corner and disappear. I want to smash something—destroy it and myself in the process. I want to run out into the middle of the freeway, dragging the whole accursed court and state legislature with me.

God! You said it was going to be fine! What kind of sick, cruel joke is this?

I'm cursing myself.

Did Abraham feel this way when he was commanded to take his beloved son Isaac up the mountain and sacrifice him? And is this how Mary felt when Jesus breathed his last breath on the cross? *I am the resurrection, and the life. He who believes in me, though he may die, he shall live.* Hold on to that. Claim it.

Taking long, deep breaths, I calm myself. I don't want to say good-bye in this condition. I've got to be strong for him, reassuring. *You've held on so long, Aaron.*

Why, God? After all those miracles? Why this? I fall to my knees by his bed and wring the tears from my eyes. A hand alights upon my shoulder.

"Sam." Rachel touches my shoulder. I reach back and put my hand over hers and rise. "It's almost time."

"I know." I turn around and through the blur of my tears I see the backlit outline of the nurse standing by the door. Lieutenant O'Brien is standing in the doorway as well, holding his hat in both of his hands.

I nod.

Jim looks at me and nods back. Steps outside.

Pastor Dave comes in, says a quick prayer, committing Aaron into the bosom of the Almighty. Rachel is weeping. "Good-bye, sweetie."

She kisses him on the head, touches his face tenderly and then turns to me burying her sobs into my chest.

The minute hand has reached twelve. The nurse looks to me with sympathy. She's done this before. So many times I suppose, she doesn't allow it to affect her professional demeanor.

Releasing Rachel, I move closer to my boy. Rachel's fingers hang on then reluctant to let go. I kneel by Aaron's side and run my hand over his forehead, through his cornsilk hair. Never have I been so aware of the steady hissing emanating from the ventilator. Breathing for him. Giving him life. Albeit artificial. Isn't that Your job, Lord?

"Aaron." My voice breaks. "It's time to go now."

His chest rises and falls.

I take his hand, squeeze it twice. *Love-you.*

His fingers twitch.

All those nights he fought not to go to bed. *Just one more story, Daddy. Just one more, please?* What I wouldn't give now. "It's time to go, buddy. It's okay."

Rachel sobs softly.

"Go ahead, son. You go on and fly, now. All the way into the sky, past the moon and into the heavens. To infinity—" my words are arrested by a sharp sob. "They're waiting for you." Not even trying to hold back the tears, I regard the nurse. We're ready. "Aaron, Daddy loves you so much."

The nurse reaches behind the ventilator.

She clicks the machine off. I gasp.

I won't let go of Aaron's hand until the very end. Maybe not even then. His chest rises and falls. A deep and final breath.

Then a long and peaceful sigh.

"Good-bye," I whisper, pressing my lips to his hand.

The room has become a vacuum. In tears, Rachel leaves the room with Pastor Dave and the nurse. And though the silence is deafening, my soul reverberates with Aaron's laughter, Jenn's voice calling us to dinner, Bethie humming passages from a Mozart concerto. It doesn't seem possible that I could miss them any more than I have, heretofore. But now, I realize just how utterly profound and dark this pit is.

I kiss Aaron's head one last time, reluctant to go.

Sounds of the past fade.

His hand begins to slip.

All the miraculous things I've experienced are insignificant now, even as I now hear that divine voice which I haven't heard for so long. One last time, He says, *It's going to be fine.* For the first time in months, an undeniable vision appears before me.

Golden light spilled across a wide meadow more lush, more verdant than anything this side of existence. *Where is this place?*

I'd never before beheld such breathtaking landscapes, taken in such sweet air, my bare feet never alighted upon so silken a floor. No terrestrial bird ever sang so gloriously. And yet, it all felt as familiar as a song from my youth.

In the distance, I saw them. *Dear Lord, it's them!*

Jenn and Bethie waded across a placid river and onto the shore. Their faces shone. Their eyes, those beautiful green eyes, brightened. They need not speak, I heard their souls.

Daddy, Bethie said. I can't wait till we're together again. Her hand extended out over the water's edge. I reached out, and though we could not touch, I sensed her warmth.

I love you so much, Babygirl.

Jenn's warm presence enveloped me. Sam, she said, Don't grieve. You are loved with an eternal love. Time will pass like the blink of an eye, when you finally come home.

I'll always love you, Jenn.

Go on, then. Live, love, and serve. When you cross the river, in just a little while, meet us at the gate.

I will, Love. I will.

Suddenly, there came a tug on my hand. Aaron! He was looking up and smiling at me, completely whole. His face shone with heavenly brilliance. I bent down and wrapped my arms around him.

My boy! My sweet boy!

Daddy.

Oh, that angelic voice. How I'd longed to hear him say, *Daddy*. I held on to him, wanting never to let go.

He let me stay, Daddy. For as long as you needed me to.

I know, Aaron. I know. At last, I understood. My sorrow was replaced with pure joy.

You're going to be fine, Daddy.

His tiny form became pure light and glided across the river, over to his mother and sister and once again, he appeared as a little boy. Jenn picked him up, kissed him. The three of them began to glow with unearthly splendor.

One last time, Jenn said, "At the gate, Love. We'll be waiting."

And they were gone.

Or perhaps it is I that have left.

Lying there, he looks as if he's fallen asleep. Peace beyond all understanding fills my soul. All along, I wanted to be there for my son, when instead, God let Aaron stay for me, instilling within me a reason to fight, a reason to live.

For the rest of my years, be they thirty, forty, or even fifty more, I will be free. And then, I will see Aaron again, and Jenn and Bethie. And a lifetime will be as the distant memory of a dream, when we are reunited.

For all eternity.

Acknowledgements

This book would not be possible without the help of countless people whose support, insight and encouragement brought the characters and story to life:

Drs. Stephen and Vivien Tseng, David DeLee, Chris Hagan, Michael Hiebert, Adrian Phoenix, Pastor Luke Chen, Dr. Glen Scorgie, Lori Moss, Anthony Davis, William and Ckristina Sutjiadi, Chris and Carol Essex, Christy and Tom Giangreco, Pastors Jerry and Tami McKinney, Steve Fitzpatrick, and all the wonderful people in The City Church San Diego, and many others who helped me and cheered me on.

For this second edition, I would like to thank the countless fans who helped me spot typos in the first edition. Some in particular made and extended effort and I would like to thank them by name: Susan Goble and Nanci Rogers, thank you for the time you took.

A special thanks to Dean W. Smith who believed in my writing enough to buy my first professional fiction works and invite me into the august gathering of minds with Kristine Kathryn Rusch and the entire Oregon Writers Network. I would not be a writer if it were not for you all.

I would also like to honor my father Rev. Paul F. Tseng, who taught by example to dream beyond what you can see, and to live by faith. Also, my late mother Anna, whose life was a testimony of grace and unconditional love.

Thanks also to my awesome children for putting up with a busy dad, and for showing me just how much I can love another person. You will never know how much that helped me write this book from the bottom of my heart.

Finally, I wish to thank my beautiful wife Katie, for being my friend, my lover, and my constant source of emotional support as well as the inspiration for all my work. You've put up with endless hours of my talking about writing books, so I dedicate this and all my coming books to you, my love.

A NOTE FROM THE AUTHOR

Thank you for taking the time to read BEYOND JUSTICE, a very personal work for me. If you were in any way touched by the story, challenged by the themes, or even changed by the message, I would love to hear from you. Please connect with me via the links at the end of this note.

The themes of grace and forgiveness are very important in this book, and while you or I will likely never have to face what Sam Hudson did, we can still benefit from being released from a prison of resentment or bitterness.

Someone once said, unforgiveness is like drinking poison and hoping the other guy dies. I believe that when we don't forgive, we are shackled and put in an emotional, even spiritual prison of solitary confinement. So I want to challenge you today, if there is anyone whom you have not forgiven yet (it could even be yourself), purpose in your heart to do so.

If you need help with it, please talk to someone who can help, like a pastor, a counselor, even a trusted friend. The old adage says, *"To err is human, to forgive is divine."*

Sometimes we need help from that higher power to heal us, to release us from years of holding onto pain.

I also want to encourage you to share this book with anyone who might be interested in a story like this one, or who might benefit from the message. If BEYOND JUSTICE has been a meaningful reading experience, won't you please share that with your friends or family?

Since the initial release of BEYOND JUSTICE, readers have been contacting me with testimonies of what the book has meant to them, or how it has helped their friends or relatives. As you've taken all this time to read my story, I'd love to hear yours!

Please connect with me on facebook or my blog and leave a wall post.

You can reach me at:
http://joshua-graham.com
http://facebook.com/J0shuaGraham
http://twitter.com/J0shuaGraham

Thank you!
Joshua Graham

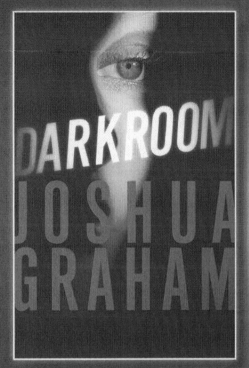

32968788R00269

Made in the USA
Lexington, KY
08 June 2014